Sylvia

VIKING

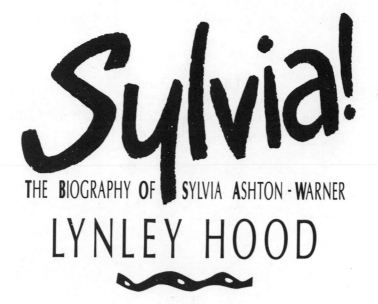

Sylvia!

THE BIOGRAPHY OF SYLVIA ASHTON-WARNER

LYNLEY HOOD

VIKING

To
Elliot Henderson,
who said,
'I'm looking forward to reading your book about my mother,
I'm hoping it'll tell me who I am.'

VIKING

Penguin Books (NZ) Ltd, 182–190 Wairau Road, Auckland 10, New Zealand
Penguin Books Ltd, 27 Wrights Lane, London W8 5TZ, England
Viking Penguin Inc., 40 West 23rd Street, New York, New York, 10010, USA
Penguin Books Australia Ltd, 487 Maroondah Highway, Ringwood, Australia 3134
Penguin Books Canada Ltd, 2801 John Street, Markham, Ontario, Canada L3R 1B4

Penguin Books Ltd, Registered Offices: Harmondsworth, Middlesex, England

First published 1988
Copyright © Lynley Hood, 1988

ISBN 0 670 819379

Designed by Richard King
Typeset in Bembo by Typocrafters Ltd, Auckland
Printed in Hong Kong

CONTENTS

*I am a child of five. I was an adult once
but that time is bracketed in dream.*

Sylvia Ashton-Warner

AUTHOR'S NOTE

This story is true. All the characters are real, even Sylvia Ashton-Warner. Her life is as strange a mix of truth and fantasy as you will find anywhere, but the important point is that it is her fantasy, not mine.

The book may read like a novel: I felt that a colourful character like Sylvia Ashton-Warner deserved a lively biography, and I wanted to engage the reader emotionally as well as in the mind. But every detail in this biography was established by painstaking research. The conversations used were reported to me in direct speech. Sylvia Aston-Warner's thoughts, feelings and fantasies were either written down by her or told to friends, who in turn told me. I have made up nothing.

I am indebted to the late Sylvia Ashton-Warner and her family for their co-operation with this project, and to the people and institutions with whom she was associated for their willingness to share their memories and memorabilia. In particular I would like to acknowledge the generous assistance given by Elliot Henderson, Joy Alley, Barbara Dent, Bob Gottlieb, Jeannette Veatch, Selma Wasserman and the late Lionel Warner.

Financial support was provided by a New Zealand Literary Fund Non-Fiction Writer's Bursary, a Winston Churchill Memorial Trust Fellowship, a grant-in-aid from the New Zealand-United States Educational Foundation, a Harriet Jenkins Award from the New Zealand Federation of University Women and a Tressa Thomas Award from the Auckland branch of the New Zealand Federation of University Women.

More than thirty institutions assisted with my research. Special thanks for outstanding helpfulness must go to the Alexander Turnbull Library, the Hocken Library, the Dunedin Public Library, the New Zealand Department of Education and the New Zealand National Archives.

At a personal level I am grateful to Anna Marsich, Julia Faed, Jules Older, Jack Shallcrass and Charles Croot. They listened to my interminable musings on the meaning of Sylvia Ashton-Warner's life, they read my rough drafts and they gave freely of their expertise. They all deserve medals. For their steady support and encouragement, I would also like to thank my agent Ray Richards, and Geoff Walker of Penguin (NZ).

Finally, for their cheerful acceptance of the domestic re-organisation made necessary by my work on this book, I wish to thank my husband Jim and my children David, Christina and Lyndon.

Lynley Hood
Dunedin
1988

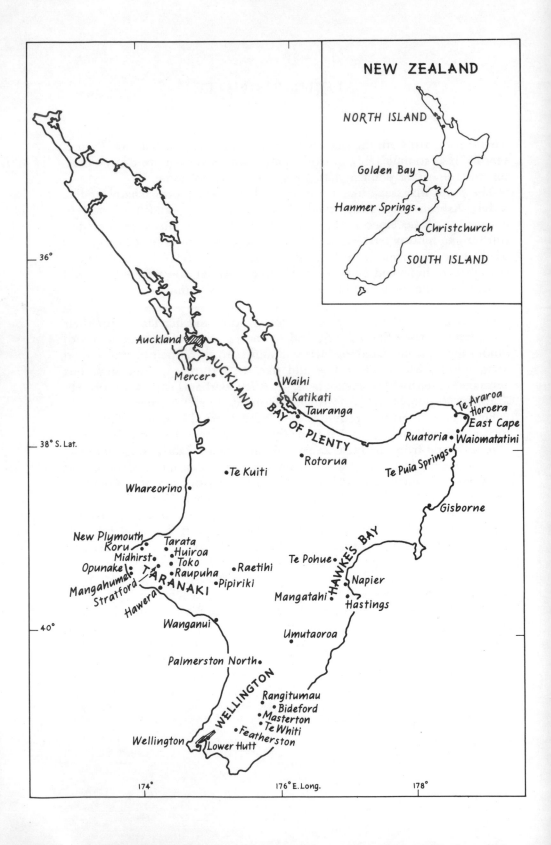

NEW ZEALAND

NORTH ISLAND

Golden Bay

Hanmer Springs

Christchurch

SOUTH ISLAND

36°

Auckland

Mercer

AUCKLAND

Waihi

Katikati

Tauranga

BAY OF PLENTY

Te Araroa

Horoera

East Cape

Ruatoria

Waiomatatini

38° S. Lat.

Te Kuiti

Rotorua

Te Puia Springs

Whareorino

Gisborne

New Plymouth

Koru

Midhirst

Opunake

Mangahume

Stratford

Tarata

Huiroa

Toko

Raupuha

TARANAKI

Pipiriki

Raetihi

Te Pohue

HAWKE'S BAY

Napier

Mangatahi

Hastings

Hawera

Wanganui

Umutaoroa

40°

Palmerston North

WELLINGTON

Rangitumau

Bideford

Masterton

Te Whiti

Featherston

Wellington

Lower Hutt

174°

176° E. Long.

178°

PROLOGUE

It is the contradictions in Sylvia Ashton-Warner's nature that puzzle and fascinate. How could such a self-absorbed woman develop a teaching method that so radiates understanding for children? For that matter, how could anyone who claimed she never wanted to be a teacher, that she hated teaching and was never any good at it, make any worthwhile contribution to education at all? Let alone write a book hailed as one of the great educational works of the century.

Then there's the puzzle of her literary work. How could a woman who lived much of her life in a tortured fantasy-world write a novel that so illuminated the common human experience that it became an international bestseller? And what was the cause and nature of the rejection she wrote of experiencing in her native New Zealand? When pressed for details she would reply archly, 'You have approached me on a subject on which I must remain forever unapproachable.'

Because she never explained herself, the public formed its own conclusions. To her admirers she was a saint and a martyr, to her critics she was a fraud and a poseur. She was loathed by some as passionately as she was loved by others. To everyone who knew her, in person or through her writing, she was an enigma.

But contradictions are in the mind of the beholder. Her audience measured Sylvia Ashton-Warner by its own standards and was bewildered; Sylvia Ashton-Warner conducted her life on her own unique terms and it is only on those terms that her life begins to make sense.

ONE

Beginnings

TO UNDERSTAND SYLVIA YOU NEED TO REWIND YOUR LIFE, LIKE falling backwards through a dream. You can feel the years, the confidence, the understanding all peeling away. . . . Stop! This is your raw childhood self, wide-eyed and vulnerable and only five years old.

Now stand here where Sylvia's standing, in front of this mirror. Reflected back is a barefoot, unsmiling, blue-eyed waif of a girl. Her tawny plaits are roughly tied with string, her dress is a loose and faded hand-me-down. Around her jostle three brothers and six sisters. Muriel, the eldest, is followed in birth order by Grace, Ashton and Lionel. Next comes a ghost — the first Sylvia, who died in infancy — followed by Daphne, the second Sylvia, Norma, Marmaduke and Evadne. Mama, fierce and stout, and pale crippled Papa* complete the picture. A lonely, isolated group in a deserted backblocks landscape. Only when you look closely can you see far in the distance the bustle of life in the outside world.

To Sylvia, Muriel is a shadowy figure rarely at home, but each of the others is truly remarkable. Grace and Norma (and the dead baby Sylvia), with their black curls, deep blue eyes and snowy complexions, are great beauties. The auburn-haired, green-eyed Daphne is not only beautiful but talented and witty too; Papa calls her 'the flower o' the flock'. As for the boys, they're worshipped by both Mama and Papa — just for being boys. The last born, Evadne, is special for that reason alone. And how does Sylvia see herself? As a freckled non-entity, shy, ugly and untouchable.

Six girls, three boys, and a ghost; that adds up to ten. And if you include, as Sylvia did, Mama's miscarriage at Mangitahi, that would be eleven. But Sylvia said the miscarriage would have made twelve. . . . Perhaps the twelfth child is one that only Sylvia sees: her wonderful dream-self. She's a princess, beautiful and talented and rich. Everybody adores her. Her dress is velvet, her eyes are brown, and her black tresses gleam in the sun. We don't know her name. It's probably a breathless secret, for Sylvia has learnt from her dead sister of the powerful magic contained in a person's name.

Have you noticed something strange about this mirror? It distorts. Like a trick mirror in a fairground it's good for a laugh if you're big, but when you're only five it can be terrifying. If you cower, your reflection shrinks

---

*The spellings 'Mama' and 'Papa' were always used by Sylvia and her siblings in family letters. SA-W used 'Mumma' and 'Puppa' only in her writing.

and everything around becomes menacing. . . . But Sylvia has discovered
a marvellous trick. If she stands tall and glares and says a few sharp words
her reflection grows giant-sized.

'Instead of cringing you call their bluff,' she wrote in her autobiography.
'Don't look hangdog, keep your face up and don't let them guess what's
happening inside you.'

The mirror is Sylvia's looking-glass view of her world; a world where
fantasy and reality overlap and merge, a world cursed, blessed and dominated by imagination, creativity, pride and guilt. Sylvia inherited this mirror
from her parents.

Her father was Francis Ashton Warner: eldest son of an eldest son of an
eldest son and so on, with a branch or two through the other sons, back to
the fourteenth century. In the court of Edward III there was a nobleman
named John le Warner, so called because his task was to warn the king when
visitors were coming. A six-hundred-year-old portrait of proud, fierce John
shows his costume smothered in the red roses of the House of Lancaster and
his scarlet banner streaming in the wind. The War of the Roses brought
defeat to the king but the Warners flourished down the centuries as
explorers, scientists, pirates, knights. To be a Warner is a noble thing indeed.

Francis Warner was heir to all this; the name, the romantic history and
a large black box of heirlooms. (Inside were twenty-one handwritten
volumes of family history, several family Bibles and a faded piece of carefully folded silk — the ancestral banner of John le Warner.) That was all.
There was no title, no political power, no fortune, no property. Francis
Warner's father was secretary to the East London Hospital for Children, his
mother was the daughter of an officer in the Indian Army. There was no
family business, no profession, no trade.

Francis grew up among ghosts. Of his thirteen siblings one was still-
born, five died in infancy and another died in early adulthood. Two of his
four surviving sisters became actresses and another went insane. His
brother George became a 'flogging magistrate' in South Africa, his brother
Ashton became a sailor.

In 1877, when he was only sixteen years old, Francis joined the great
nineteenth century exodus of Britons seeking a new life in the colonies.
Armed with the box of heirlooms, his cultured English accent, a few
clothes, a little money and a letter of introduction to a man in far-flung
New Zealand, he set sail from London. In part he was a frightened child,
escaping his father's harsh discipline; in part he was a romantic adventurer,
seeking his fortune. After five harrowing months around Cape Horn he
arrived in Christchurch to find that the man who was to introduce him to
New Zealand had died.

Seeking his fortune was one thing, actually having to work for a living
was something else again. Francis Ashton Warner was not suited to work.

During the boom years of the 1870s, when the interior of New Zealand was opened up with road, rail and telegraph links, through the bust of the 1880s when wool export prices fell, and on into the 1890s, when the nation began to recover from a long depression, Francis travelled the country, and reluctantly turned his hand to manual labour. He chopped wood, he panned for gold, he joined the Armed Constabulary and fought the Maori. Eventually he found work using one of his few practical skills, the ability to add and subtract. He was thirty-five years old and working as a bookkeeper in Auckland when he met his future wife, an attractive school teacher fourteen years his junior. Her name was Margaret Maxwell.

The Maxwells were a poor Scottish family but they too were the stuff of legends. Not legends of grandeur and nobility, but legends of courage, determination and driving ambition.

One story, endlessly retold throughout the ninety-one years of Margaret's life, is of her father, David Maxwell — an unschooled child trapped into a lifetime of industrial work in Edinburgh — and how he became fired with a dream. One day in a sudden fit of anger and despair he shook his clenched fist at the high factory windows and vowed to escape — from that place, from the country.

And escape he did. He sought physical freedom in emigration to New Zealand, where he worked as a blacksmith. Liberation of his mind came through self-education: legends tells of David Maxwell riding to his black-smith shop each day with a book of Latin grammar in his lap.

Despite his dreams, David Maxwell was a coarse, violent man. In 1872 he married a small and feisty sixteen-year-old, New Zealand-born Annie Shepherd; they are said to have fought consistently and bitterly the entire length of their two long lives. In 1876 their eldest daughter, Margaret, the third of their nine children, was born in a ponga whare at a redoubt near Mercer. One of Margaret's earliest memories was of lying in bed on a clear night and gazing up at the stars through holes in the roof.

Margaret was everything the Maxwells could have wished for in a daughter; musically talented and academically able, she had inherited her father's determination and ambition, his deep reverence for education, and a measure of his violence as well. From her mother came a defensive pride and an unquenchable resistance to adversity, known to her descendants as 'the Maxwell spirit'. Her brothers and sisters became manual workers and housewives, but Margaret wanted more from life.

At the age of fifteen, when she was in standard seven at school, she passed the Probationary Teachers Examination. The headmaster, a fearsome man by the name of Mr Iremonger, brought the news.

'Stand up, Margaret Maxwell!'

She stood, trembling.

'Come out here!'

She obeyed.

'You don't have to sit down as a pupil any more. You are now, officially, a teacher.'

The examination had been a knowledge test in English, arithmetic, geography and history. Margaret had proved she knew what to teach and Mr Iremonger taught her how; how to maintain an iron discipline, how to intimidate the children, how to keep them chanting and how to keep them quiet.

The following year Margaret was appointed to the staff of Katikati School. During her five years there she passed another knowledge test, the Teachers D Examination, and thus became a fully qualified teacher.

One weekend in February 1897 she attended a dance at Waihi. It was there that she met Francis Ashton Warner.

'Papa was lying down on the sofa in Flett's Hotel, Waihi, when I first met him,' she wrote in her old age. That was in the raw colonial days when real men lived and died on their feet, but Margaret was far too impressed by his charm to worry about his languor. 'He was most fascinating,' she added, 'so refined and sophisticated.'

One month later Margaret was appointed sole-charge teacher to Huiroa School in Taranaki, but she kept in touch with Francis by letter. After a fourteen-month separation she took the initiative and travelled to Auckland by boat to see him. There they fell passionately in love, and the very next morning they were wed. They were supposed to live happily ever after, but the real world intervened. Francis Warner's occupation on the marriage certificate reads 'gentleman', which may be a euphemism for 'unemployed', for on the day of their marriage Margaret returned alone to Huiroa School and three months passed before the marriage was consummated.

Back in Taranaki the resourceful Margaret found clerical work for her husband with the Egmont Farmers' Union, and after the twelve weeks apart the Warners set up a home in Hawera.

At first they lived as a conventional married couple: Francis provided the family income, Margaret bore the children; they even had something of a social life and often sang together in concerts. But in 1904, after six years at a steady job, Francis Warner's health collapsed. His upbringing had pre-pared him for only one role in life, that of a privileged English gentleman. So it was not surprising that the loyal Margaret attributed his collapse to overwork, while her unimpressed Maxwell relatives told each other, 'The trouble with that man is he just doesn't *want* to work.' Nobody knew then that Francis Warner's tiredness, and his vague aches and pains, marked the insidious onset of an affliction that was to cripple him for the rest of his life.*

Early in 1905 he was sent to the Rotorua health spa for four months' treatment. While he was away the couple's fifth child, the first Sylvia, was born. She was a pale, weak baby with a heart defect that made each breath a struggle. For three days Margaret cuddled the baby in bed beside her,

---

*Francis never worked again, but so powerful was the Warner family mythmaking that when he died twenty years later, his death certificate stated 'occupation: accountant'; and when Sylvia married seven years after his death, his status on the marriage certificate had risen to 'bank manager'.

warming the tiny blue feet in her hands. On the fourth day the baby died.

Margaret had a brother living in Taranaki at that time; it was he who made the little coffin and carried it under his arm to the Hawera cemetery where the dead Sylvia was buried in an unmarked grave.

There was no time to grieve. With her husband a helpless invalid and four young children to care for, Margaret became the family breadwinner. In that same crisis year of 1905 she was appointed sole-charge teacher to the twenty children of farmers and sawmillers at Raupuha, a village nestled in the low rolling hills of inland Taranaki.

Another four months in hospital, this time at the Hanmer spa, brought no improvement for Francis. When he rejoined his family at Raupuha he was just able to walk with the aid of a walking stick. He took up the role of house-husband, and when the premature Daphne was born in 1907 Margaret continued to teach and Francis cared for the baby. That experience became to the children one of Papa's wonderful stories; a piece of rough reality fossicked from the stony riverbed of his life and lovingly polished over decades of retelling until it shone like a gem: 'Do you know, children, that when Daphne was born her little bottom was so tiny it would fit into the palm of my hand!'

The following year another baby, the second Sylvia, was born. That name, together with the probability that she was conceived very close to the anniversary of the first Sylvia's death (normally a time of heightened parental longing for a dead child) strongly suggests that she was intended as a replacement for her dead sister.*

Sylvia Constance Ashton Warner was born in Stratford at seven o'clock in the morning on 17 December 1908, at the beginning of the summer school vacation.

Those first six weeks of her life were filled with children's voices; children talking, shouting, crying, laughing, singing. And then there was the piano. No matter where they lived, no matter what crises beset the family, Mama had to have a piano. On a salary of around £120 a year she couldn't actually afford a piano, but she always acquired the best piano available. Token instalments were paid, but usually only when repossession was imminent. There were one or two black occasions when the running battle with the debt collector was lost and the piano was taken away: indomitable Mama went straight out and acquired another one.

All through the school holidays the old house overflowed with piano music. Mama taught each of the children to play, and in between lessons — usually in response to a maternal decree that any child at the keyboard

---

*The first Sylvia was born on 18 March 1905, and died four days later. Childbirth normally takes place thirty-eight to forty-two weeks after conception. The second Sylvia, a full-term baby, was born on 17 December 1908, exactly forty weeks after the anniversary of the birth and death of the first Sylvia.

was exempt from household chores — they practised enthusiastically.

Late in the evening, when all the cooking and cleaning and milking and woodchopping and ironing was done for the day, when the children were tucked up two or three to a bed, when the inevitable flea between the sheets had been stalked by flickering candle and crushed between the thumbnails with a satisfying click, then it was Mama's turn to play. With grim reality hidden in the shadows she would escape for hours to the wonderful candle-lit world of music.

Sylvia drank in all this music with her mother's milk. Quite possibly, like Germaine in her novel *Incense to Idols*, she spent some of those early weeks in a basket on top of the piano — that would be the only place in that sparsely furnished home where a baby would be safely out of the reach of the toddler Daphne. And like Germaine, Sylvia grew up with a love of music and a violent aversion to loud discordant noise.

By the time school reopened in February, Papa's health had deteriorated again. Overwhelmed by the pain in his swollen joints he could do nothing but lie in bed. So Mama secured the baby basket onto the horse in front of her and galloped off to school. What an astonishing experience for a baby! The unearthly swooshing through the air as the horse cantered down the mile of dusty road, the bump bump bump as it slowed to a trot at the school gate, and the peaceful rocking as it ambled into the horse paddock. No wonder Sylvia loved horses.

Each day Mama took a different child behind her on the horse. The others, whatever their ages, had to walk. At first Sylvia spent her days in the classroom, but later, when she became more wakeful, Mama moved her into a makeshift pen on the school porch.

At about fourteen months of age she became too active for Mama to cope with at school, so for the next four months, until bedridden Papa was hospitalised again, she was left at home.

We know that during those months whenever Sylvia was hungry or thirsty she would toddle to Papa to be fed with the bread and milk Mama left each morning on a box by his bed, but the rest of her life at home is a mystery. Mama wrote in her memoirs, 'I don't know what Sylvia did all day. I do not know.'

Let's guess. . . .

The barefoot Sylvia is padding about the empty house; searching. In one of the bedrooms, with its peeling wallpaper and exposed scrim, she finds only unmade beds. In the wood-panelled living room there's the silent piano, an old wooden table with forms on either side, a sideboard, and the hot coal range. In the other bedroom there's Papa — lying in bed moaning with pain and shouting to God.

Sylvia is desperately lonely and aching for love. She is also often wet and soiled, for accidents would be inevitable during so long a time alone. So there's another sound in this house more harrowing than Papa's distress, the sound of Sylvia crying, wailing, sobbing for Mama.

'I was the greatest bawler not ever choked,' she wrote in her autobiography — and she always believed it was because she was a naughty child.

In the world of Sylvia's infancy one of the central images of her looking-glass view of reality is starting to take shape. At an age when most children are learning that crimes are followed by guilt and punishment, Sylvia is discovering the sequence in reverse. These sad and lonely months feel like punishment, but the punishment is coming first. Before long she will begin to experience a pervasive sense of guilt — a feeling that to be so severely punished, to be left all day in what seems like solitary confinement, one must surely be guilty of *something*. Later, there will be a secret and often frantic quest to define, conceal, reveal, deny and accept the crimes of which she feels herself to be guilty . . . but for now she has only an oppressive sense of being punished.

It has something to do with Mama, who keeps leaving her; it has something to do with Papa and his crippling affliction; and it has something to do with a cruel God to whom Papa cries in anguish, 'O God, why must I endure this infirmity? O God, release me from this hell.'

Mama stayed five years at Raupuha School. It was the longest teaching appointment of her married life. For the next eighteen years the family would trek like nomads from one sole-charge school to the next across the lower North Island, staying only a year or two in each place. The usual cause of the moves was 'inspector trouble'.

In Mrs Warner's classroom lessons were learnt by rote. You weren't expected to understand, you just had to learn. And mistakes in school work, like disciplinary transgressions, were freely and vigorously punished with the strap. The more traditional inspectors, and there were many, would have accepted that; it was the proper way to teach. They may even have been impressed by Mrs Warner's encouragement of poetry chanting and choral singing. But they would not have liked her neglect of lesson preparation, her regular absences for childbearing and her isolation from new educational ideas.

There were often problems with the school committee. Though the Warners' stay usually began smoothly — a farmer would lend them a cow and a few hens, sometimes also a horse — before long the rent would be unpaid and there would be complaints of harsh discipline.

When the problems were aired it was Mama's fierce pride and quick temper that triggered the final explosion. To Mama, any criticism was an outrage. She would lash out verbally — and sometimes physically — when angered; at one school she attacked the landlord with a lump of wood, at another she whacked the school committee chairman across the face with her handbag. In circumstances like these compromise was impossible. There was only one thing to do; pack up and move on.

Mama's next school was at Koru on the northern coast of Taranaki, where the streams that fan out from Mount Egmont cut deep gullies through a sloping fertile plain. When the Warners arrived in 1910 the Land Wars of the 1860s were still a bitter memory, though most Maori had moved away. Timber milling was the primary industry, and wherever the tree stumps and bracken had been cleared away dairy farms were being established.

There were two other family crises that year: Papa went away again to hospital at Rotorua, and another baby, Norma, was born. The indomitable Mama soldiered on, sometimes taking Sylvia to school with her and sometimes leaving her with a baby sitter who was never paid.

Papa's return after weeks in hospital was a milestone in Sylvia's life, for by then she was old enough to share in his wonderful stories.

There he is sitting up in bed, his blue eyes sparkling, his elegant moustache curling proudly. The pain has eased, but his joints are stiff and gnarled with what the doctors have told him is incurable rheumatoid arthritis. He has one thin arm around his favourite child, Daphne, the other around Sylvia. The rest of the children crowd around the bed or clamber onto it, wherever they can find room.

Hush, the stories begin . . . beautiful princesses in shining towers . . . brave knights riding Arab steeds . . . brutal floggings . . . savage pirates with dazzling treasures . . . enchanted lands just beyond reach where Papa can walk and everyone lives happily ever after. . . .

And all this spun from a golden thread of words. Plot upon breathless plot woven together into an entrancing rope ladder. Papa climbs, grandly leading the way, and the children rush to follow.

Exciting new worlds were opened to Sylvia through Papa's stories. There was the powerful and treacherous world of the imagination:

> All I wanted in the real world and didn't have I simply supplied in the unreal world of the imagination. No trouble. It was a well-exercised faculty.

There was the intoxicating magic of language:

> . . . we flung to the wind shouting great words to the sky: 'The Gulf of Carpentaria! The Gulf of Carpentaria!' . . . we crouched and muttered occult words: 'Nizhni Novgorod, Nizhni Novgorod.'

And there was the eternal joy of story-telling:

> We played in the wilds, three little girls telling endless stories.[1]

But most important of all was the love Sylvia found in the comfort and reassurance of Papa's closeness; for despite the deprivation of her early years, Sylvia grew up with the capacity to love: as a training college student she fell in love with, and later married, a stable and loving man; and despite the unhappiness and instability of her later years she stayed anchored to her marriage and family. That is quite an achievement after so rough a beginning. Somewhere in her childhood, Sylvia must have learnt how to love.

She probably didn't learn it from Mama; Sylvia always believed that her mother didn't love her, and at the age of six embarked on a compulsive, lifelong 'search for a mother'.

'Mama never made a gesture of affection,' she recalled sadly in her old age. 'She never put her arm around me, or kissed me.'

Mama may have loved Sylvia, but she was the product of the undemonstrative puritan ethnic of the times, and in her single-handed struggle to keep her family fed, clothed and sheltered she would have had little time or energy for displays of affection. So it was probably from Papa and his wonderful story-telling sessions that Sylvia learnt how to love.

At Koru Sylvia's brothers and sisters became part of her life.

Norma must have made quite an impact, for it was she who replaced Sylvia as the baby of the family. It was 14 October 1910, and there was a flurry of activity in the household.

'Muriel, you take the children down to play in the gully, Gracie, go and tell the Maori lady I'm ready.'

And when the children returned — there was the baby. Sylvia was very jealous.

Nor could Daphne go unnoticed, for although Sylvia had replaced her as the baby, Daphne was a born performer and had retained centre stage. And then there was the dead Sylvia who lived on in the family consciousness, and in Daphne's teasing: 'Sylvie, you're named after a ghost.'

The grief process is better understood now than it was when the first Sylvia lived and died in 1905. We know now that a period of mourning, however painful and disabling, is essential to the acceptance of the loss of a loved one, and that if an infant death is not fully mourned the parents may never cease longing for the dead child and the other children may suffer from survivor guilt. The risk is greatest for the 'replacement child' whose identity is confused with a different and dead baby. So it was with Sylvia — the guilt:

> None of which, however, prevents me from wondering whether, had it been the first Sylvia who'd lived rather than I the second Sylvia, things might have gone better with Daphne. Daphne called Auckland Unlucky City and I call myself Unlucky Sister.[2]

And the confusion:

> 'You say you are only five but how old are you really?' 'I'm either 62 or 64,' she said. 'My mother . . . named two of her daughters Sylvia Ashton-Warner. One of them died and I don't know which one I am.'[3]

At the top of the family were the two big girls, eleven-year-old Muriel and ten-year-old Grace, who to Sylvia were probably little more than babysitters. But the boys, eight-year-old Ashton and six-year-old Lionel, were definitely worth noticing; they played the violin.

Mama was never one to let hindrances like work, childbirth, or Papa's illness get in the way of her educational ambitions for her children. She had long ago resolved to teach her sons to play the violin. (It had something to do with an old boyfriend who was a violinist.) Lack of money and the fact that Mama knew nothing about the instrument were no obstacles. She acquired two half-sized violins and a couple of tutor books and at first she did the teaching herself, devoting up to two hours each evening to the task. Protests from the tired boys were met with a swift clout to the ear. 'PLAY!' Through their tears they played on.

When the boys became more proficient they played duets, Ashton taking the part of the first violin and Lionel taking the second. But long before that all the Warner children were playing second fiddle to the adored Ashton.

Ashton bore his father's name and was the hero of the family. As Francis Ashton Warner, glorious eldest son and heir to Francis Ashton Warner, he was the focus of all the family's unresolved conflicts between fantasy and reality. Eventually Ashton rebelled. When he passed Standard Six at the age of thirteen he refused to go to high school and began running away from home. Such disrespect for that holiest of holies, education, broke his mother's heart.

But all that is in the future. Right now it is 1912 and the whole family is together at Koru. Dinner is over and someone shouts, 'Last one out to the shelter shed is "He"!' While Papa struggles on crutches to collect the dishes and wash them in a tin basin the children charge around outside, shouting and laughing, until it's too dark to play any more. Except for Sylvia. She's more likely to be playing alone under the pines, savouring the aroma of the soft pine needle carpet and telling herself stories. For Sylvia has found in the outdoor world, as yet confined to the school playground and the nearby wooded gully, a peace and freedom she hasn't known before.

But there would be no peace or freedom inside the schoolroom door, as Sylvia discovered later that year when Papa went away again to hospital and her formal education began.

TWO

Primary School

SYLVIA IS STARTING SCHOOL. SHE'S JOINING ALL THE BIG KIDS. SHE'S about to come face to face with that much-honoured mystery, education. She sits down at one of the wooden desks and studies the slate in front of her. Then she reaches out to pick up the slate pencil. . . . And by that innocent act she triggers one of the most profoundly disturbing experiences of her life. She's known Mama's wrath before, she's often felt the sting of Mama's hand on her bare bottom, but never before has she been singled out like this, and never before has she been so relentlessly punished. The humiliation burns deep.

This is her crime: in this black and white colonial world of left and right, and right and wrong, Sylvia was born wrong. In picking up the slate pencil . . . *she picked it up with her left hand.* From this day on Mama's first task at the beginning of each school day will be to pin Sylvia's left hand firmly behind her back.

To Mama, and indeed to every right-minded person of her generation, left-handedness had connotations which 'gauche' and 'sinister' only partly convey today. Her belief was drawn from a millennium of religious, mystical, philosophical and medical prejudice: on the one hand there was the traditional association of the left with witchcraft and evil and on the other there was the Bible, full of righteousness:

> Then shall the King say unto them on his right hand, 'Come, ye blessed of my Father, inherit the kingdom prepared for you from the foundation of the world. . . .' Then shall He say unto them on the left hand, 'Depart from me, ye cursed, into everlasting fire, prepared for the devil and his angels. . . .'

Think about this: Mama's merciless suppression of her daughter's left-handedness would have brought the diffuse sense of punishment and guilt which shadowed Sylvia's months alone with Papa to a sharp personal focus. Now she has something specific to feel guilty about; this sudden painful binding of her natural left-handedness to sin and the devil would make her feel like a lightning conductor for evil. In the depths of Sylvia's undermind it would make sense. It would explain why Mama never cuddled her, it would explain why she, the ugly unlovable second Sylvia, had lived, while the angelic first Sylvia had died; it would explain why God had crippled Papa. . . . To that guilt-ridden child it could explain every last bit of unhappiness that had been visited on the family.

When Sylvia reads the Bible later in her primary school years, and indeed all through her life, she will find much to confirm this early impression that she has been personally singled out by a vengeful and unloving God.

Now consider the biological explanation: the hand a person prefers to use is determined by the side of his or her brain that is dominant. If the left hemisphere is dominant the person will be right-handed, while left-handedness is the result of a dominant right brain. Apart from the difference in dominance, the two hemispheres control their opposite limbs in much the same way. But in most other aspects of brain function the two sides are very different. Popular myth ascribes different personality traits to left- and right-handed people, and these are to some extent supported by scientific evidence: the left brain is the scat of logic and reason, the right brain is the home of feeling, intuition, and imagination. Right-handed people generally read better and pay more attention to detail; left-handedness occurs with surprising frequency among story-tellers, actors, musicians and artists.

There is actually quite a bit of cross-wiring in the brain, so that no matter which side is dominant both hemispheres normally work smoothly together. But interference with the natural pattern can, and often does, cause problems. Something very strange happened to the wiring of Sylvia's brain when Mama forcibly suppressed her natural left-handedness. It was as if the delicate circuitry between her right and left hemispheres overheated and burnt out, and she was left with two half-brains, each functioning independently. The practical effect was an astonishing ambidexterity: Sylvia's artwork never failed to impress but her technique was even more stunning; as an adult she was known to take a piece of purple chalk in her left hand, a piece of white chalk in her right, and proceed to draw, simultaneously, bunches of grapes with the one and kittens with the other. When she printed on the blackboard she would start at opposite ends of a sentence and simultaneously write forwards with her left hand and backwards with her right to complete the sentence neatly in the middle.

Sylvia was split emotionally, too. The left-handed dreamer, the loving imaginative child, was suppressed; she never died, but neither did she grow up. She played in the wilds when Sylvia was young, and she played in Sylvia's psyche as her body grew older. All through her life, the spontaneous five-year-old was there, ready to appear unexpectedly when conditions were right, to the delight of children and the bewilderment of grown-ups.

I have a very vivid memory of one occasion when Bruce and I and the three children visited Sylvia in the 1960s. She started to tell a story to the assembled children, Jasmine's and ours, about a mouse with a very long tail. She drew the mouse on a blackboard that was fixed to the living room wall. Then she went right on drawing the mouse's tail, with chalk, around all four walls of that elegant room. My children's mouths dropped wide open, I could see their minds going, 'My God!!! This is an adult defacing a wall!!!' Sylvia had a marvellous time; she had something she wanted the children to share and she made it so vivid for them. There was no suggestion that drawing on the walls was a silly thing to have done. It was all good fun and was certainly greeted as such by the children.[1]

That Sylvia was the same five-year-old who in 1913 was faced with a double burden; she had to find some way of dealing with her massive load of guilt, and she had to find some way of surviving six years in Mama's classroom. She coped by suppressing her spontaneous left-handed self, and by developing a protective persona for her now painfully dislocated inner being. This right-handed self, apparently based on her looking-glass view of Mama, was a proud, ambitious, short-tempered loner. 'I had this thing from Mama about being, first, best, most and frontest.'

When Sylvia moved out into the world she continued to use the right-handed persona to mask her vulnerable inner self. There was always a tension and an affectation about that mask; few adults saw the authentic Sylvia beneath it, but despite her best efforts most people sensed that it was just pretend.

Sylvia's formal schooling began in 1913, which was also the year that her brother Marmaduke was born, and the year that Mama lost her job at Koru.

For the months that Mama was out of work the family lived at Toko in a house owned by Mama's father. Their only income was the £2 a week she was allowed to withdraw from her superannuation. Day by day meals became more meagre and clothing more worn as the debts piled up. Mama applied for help from the only assistance available at that time, Charitable Aid.

The local policeman, who administered Charitable Aid in Toko, surveyed the family: eight children ranging in age from a few months to fourteen years, Papa so crippled that his knees and hips were locked at right angles, strong fierce Mama. He proposed that since Mama couldn't find teaching work she should seek domestic employment.

'What about the children?'

'The police will arrange for them to go to homes.'

Lose the children? Lower herself to domestic work? Unthinkable.

Apart from the income from a few weeks' temporary work at Tarata School the family struggled on unaided until, in October 1914, Mama obtained a teaching appointment at the Hawke's Bay school of Te Pohue.

Te Pohue, hidden high in the bush-clad ranges, was a lonely coach stop on the winding, precipitous Napier–Taupo road. The forest, the lake, the swamp, the orchard, the clearing bright with foxgloves — for Sylvia this richness was much more than a setting for real life, it was a place where the verdant world of the imagination could burst from its nurturing hot-house around Papa's iron bed and grow rampant and luxuriant across the landscape. 'Te Pohue, for some reason, in the pristine beauty of the ranges, enriched my store of imagery with more drama and colour than any other spot we alighted upon.'

See the three little girls, Daphne, Sylvia, and Norma, padding along dusty sheep tracks or squishing through the swamp, listening to the rattle of the raupo leaves and the broom pods snapping in the sun, sniffing the warm-scented flax, chewing on rosehips, and telling each other wide-eyed stories. . . .

> Whenever we went on walks we'd sit in the long grass on the side of the hills and Sylvia would start off on these beautiful stories. One day she found a lovely stone shining in the sun — 'Norma, suppose we picked up one of these stones and there was a beautiful shiny door — and we'd open the door and go in — and on the shelves inside we'd find lots and lots of money — piles of half-crowns and florins and shillings and six-pences and threepences and pennies and halfpennies — and every time we picked up a half-crown another one would take its place. . . .' These stories would go on and one. I was enthralled.[2]

Money, lovely shiny money; there was never quite enough for the rent or the grocery bill or the payments on the piano. The donated cow, and the potatoes dug from the school garden helped the family to survive.

> For many years our menu each day consisted of porridge and milk for breakfast, bread and butter for lunch, and potatoes and milk for tea. Now and again a farmer would give us some meat and sometimes we had eggs, but we didn't have any fruit; we didn't have any vegetables.[3]

By 1916 the four older children had left home; Muriel was nursing, Grace was training to become a teacher, Ashton was roaming and Lionel was attending high school in Napier.

The family continued to rock from crisis to crisis: Norma almost set fire to the house when Mama was away giving birth to Evadne; the big children kept stumbling home from bruising encounters with the outside world (to the impressionable seven-year-old Sylvia love seemed to be the cause of all their troubles); one dark night there was a terrifying earth-quake; and Papa went away again to hospital.

> 'When I come back,' he proclaimed from the parapet of his castle in the air, 'I'll be able to walk! I'll make millions of money. I'll buy a lorryload of books and a boatload of oranges. The dolls I will buy will be the size of yourselves and each one will walk and talk. I'll buy you each an Arab steed and you'll all be dressed in velvet. I'll buy your mother an enormous house, the grandest in the country, with wrought iron gates, balustrades and romantic balconies. I'll provide an army of servants bowing and scraping all day long and springing at her slightest wish. You'll see her dressed in silk and satin and with buckles on her shoes. . . .'[4]

Mama carried the flame in his absence. 'When Papa comes home,' she told the children, 'he'll be able to walk. We'll throw his crutches away.' And she made velvet dresses with big satin bows for the three little girls: green for Daphne, blue for Sylvia, red for Norma. Then Papa came back from hospital in a wheelchair. . . .

In times of crisis the cry would go up, 'Come on, Daph, make us laugh!'

With green eyes flashing and auburn curls swinging, Daphne would re-enact the drama as melodrama; suffering participants were transformed into amused onlookers. This magical transmutation of unbearable reality into bearable fiction was a technique of coping that shaped Sylvia's auto-biographical writing throughout her life.

At school Sylvia learnt to read. First came the alphabet, then mysterious two-letter words strung into even more mysterious sentences: *It is an ox. I am on it. Go up to my ox. Go on, do go on, ox.* After mastering those, imagine the heady excitement of moving on to three-letter words — *the, was, not, and* !

For mathematics the class chanted multiplication tables and worked out written arithmetic on their slates. Geography lessons focused on a map of the world patchworked with the proud red of the British Empire. Mrs Warner pointed and the children chanted: countries and their capitals, the oceans, definitions of capes, bays and islands.

History too was chanted: sovereigns and their dates, battles and their dates.

At poetry time the chanting told of romance and bravery — 'The Arab's Farewell To His Steed', 'The Charge of the Light Brigade' — then the chanting was replaced by rousing singing for 'Rule Britannia' and 'Soldiers of the Queen'.

All that work! The strap-enforced teaching, the backbreaking family chores, the clashes with landlords and inspectors, meant that to her children Mama was a distant, busy, unpredictable and ill-tempered woman. Yet even her outbursts of unrestrained anger were not without dramatic value; as an adult Sylvia recalled that Mama's violence and abandonment used to appall her audience into unintentional appreciation.

As a child Sylvia withdrew from this harshness. She felt herself ugly and unlovable and became increasingly a loner as, in the boundless world of her imagination, she embarked on a lifelong search for a loving mother and a lovable self.

Writing stories became part of that search, and the ambition to become a writer gradually took root. Mama herself talked of wanting to be a writer and when Papa wasn't reading his Bible or telling stories he was likely to be found working on the family memoirs. So whenever Mama demanded, 'Where's Sylvie?' Daphne's standard reply was, 'She's out in the pines writing sentimental piffle.'

Within the privacy and comfort of her imagination Sylvia's inner world grew richer and her dream-self more wonderful:

She was an astonishingly beautiful princess; her hair was as black as a tui's back with the same iridescent sheen, her face was as white as the thousand-jacket and easily as soft, if not softer, her lips were as red as that puriri blossom growing outside on the tree, and her eyes like deep forest pools. They were liquid and dark, they were deep and still and

reflected the mystery about them. As for her royal body it put to shame
the rain wraiths that drift the length of the river.

Yet she was unhappy. She had run away from the palace, she confided to
a fantail, because she had not been able to see eye to eye with her stepmother,
who as is usual with stepmothers, had committed the unforgivable sin: she
was not exactly like the real mother. . . .[5]

The dream-mother she sought was bewitching and beautiful, her eyes were
'as blue as a roadside daisy', she had 'a cloud of golden hair', and her voice
had 'a low-running quality like a hidden stream at night'.

Fantasy spilled over into reality in the form of a schoolgirl crush on the
landlord's daughter:

> . . . who wore patent leather shoes to Sunday School and ribbons on her
> hair every day of the week whereas Puppa tied ours with string. Also her
> father could walk whereas our father couldn't. But sometimes Bella Axel
> asked us in the hotel to see her walking doll or her big sister's brand-new
> baby. Dream stuff indeed.[6]

There was also a dream-horse, a shining Arab steed 'with proudly arched
and glossy neck, with dark and fiery eye'. But Mama's horse at Te Pohue
was a bad-tempered old nag. Real horses, like real people, were a terrible
disappointment. Sylvia kept her ideal girl on a distant pedestal to ensure
the survival of that particular dream.

For Mama life was far from easy at Te Pohue. The inspector who visited
in February 1915 noted that the school was cold; the pot-belly stove barely
worked and the chimney flue was in need of repair. But he approved of
Mama's teaching and recorded in his report: 'The Mistress is capable and
hard-working . . .' and 'Instruction is intelligent'.

But the next inspection, in March 1916, came when Mama, in her
eleventh year as sole breadwinner, was growing heavy with her tenth
pregnancy. Mr W. W. Bird, Senior Inspector of the Hawke's Bay Education
Board, found little to his liking:

> The teaching . . . is not satisfactory unless pupils are taught to think for
> themselves and draw their own conclusions: the mere copying of notes
> is not sufficient, nor is it effective.[7]

There were also problems with the landlord. He first began trying to evict
the family towards the end of 1915; when verbal threats didn't work he
pushed over the water tank, and when that didn't work he took out the
windows. But it wasn't until Mama obtained a teaching post at Umutaoroa
School that the family actually packed up and left.

For the children the insecurity of homelessness was drowned in a surge
of excitement and hope: 'We loved moving!' Again there's a little school
in the pines against a backdrop of wild mountain ranges, but Umutaoroa
lacks the magic of Te Pohue. Perhaps it's because unwelcome reality keeps
tramping in across the castle drawbridge; unspeakable unhappiness from

the older children's lost battles with the outside world, frightening tension between Mama and Papa.

So tortured was Sylvia by the discord between her parents that at her father's death, when she was seventeen, she buried the experience deep in her undermind. Even during her treatment for a nervous breakdown at the age of thirty, despite lengthy discussions of her childhood, the terrible memories did not surface. A few months later she wrote to the doctor who treated her:

> . . . from babyhood until I was seventeen there was 'something in my life'. . . . Its concealment had become part of my spiritual body, to sepa-rate which however gently would have provoked mental bleeding, with which during that illness I would have been powerless to deal. . . . The 'something in my life' until I was seventeen, baldly put, doctor, was our mother's persecution, spiritual and material, of our crippled father.[8]

She then began to write about her childhood, and of her fear as Mama abused, ridiculed and physically attacked Papa. The saga eventually became the novel *Greenstone*, and when a reviewer found the book unduly fanciful Sylvia responded:

> That family was the family I belonged to, and that's how the family was. . . . Most of the incidents were fact . . . and much of the conversation was verbatim. . . . Mama did knock out Papa's eye — I saw it.[9]

But Mama and Papa were two lonely people and they had only each other. There were often companionable times when Mama played the piano and Papa sat close by, singing in a beautiful tenor. Then the children would all gather round and everyone would sing, and sing and sing.

The school premises at Umutaoroa were no better than those at Te Pohue.

> Inspector's Report. March 1918: The buildings present the appearance of a haunted house rather than a school in active operation. There are in all 10 panes broken among the windows, which are festooned with cobwebs. The spouting is broken in several places: the tap on the tank defective. . . .

Mama also had problems with unruly children and hostile parents. She wrote in the school log; ' F . . . C . . . has been grossly impertinent & when I punished her they tried to have me up for assault.'

But worst of all the inspector was the man who had disapproved of her teaching at Te Pohue, Mr W. W. Bird. In March 1918 he complained that Mrs Warner's workbook was not up to date, that she had no scheme of work and that the general standard of teaching and school work was poor. In July Mama retaliated to a threat of dismissal by summarily demoting every child in the school, except her own, by two classes. The outraged parents recalled Mr Bird to investigate. He reported:

> This is the most extraordinary procedure that has ever come within my

knowledge. . . . In my opinion the state of things ascertained during my
visit shows that the teacher is not capable of conducting the school.[10]

As the drama surged around her, inspectors must have seemed to nine-
year-old Sylvia nothing less than human manifestations of the cruel God
of Papa's Bible.

Three months later, when schools throughout the country reopened
after a major influenza epidemic, Mama found work at another sole-charge
country school, Mangatahi. The Hawke's Bay Education Board may have
had some misgivings about the appointment, but Mangatahi had a history
of difficulties in attracting and retaining a teacher; there was probably no
one else for the job.

Family tensions multiplied on the flat, empty Hawke's Bay plain. The
children misbehaved, the local people were unfriendly, Papa tried to run
away from home, and Mama had a miscarriage. Twenty years later, in a
never-ending, never-posted letter to the doctor who treated her for a
nervous breakdown, Sylvia recalled this phase of her life. Here's her
account of the family's response when Papa calls for his crutches:

'Go on, Lionel,' we'd urge, always most fertile in our ideas for others,
'Papa wants his crutches.' He would turn over abstractedly another page
of music, setting the violin beneath his chin. The matter would sag
momentarily. I would hope ardently from my back room where I was
sitting on my half-made bed drawing a horse that someone would find
Papa his crutches. No, the neck wasn't curved enough to make the horse
look Arab. . . .

'Is someone there,' rose the cultivated voice. 'I want my crutches.'

'Go on, Sylvie, you lazy thing,' came Norma's voice from the kitchen,
'You're not doing anything. Find Papa's crutches.'

'I'm making my bed,' I retorted angrily. 'You're nearest.' . . . I lovingly
curved the arched neck with my pencil. . . .

'Lionel,' came a throated roar from the side room. 'Daphne, Sylvia,
Goddammit, Norma, Maggie,' he calls my mother. 'Would you pass my
crutches.'

. . . Mama comes storming in from the wash house, 'What's all this terrible shouting Frankie! What does he want! What's that lazy little devil
Sylvie doing?' glimpsing me through the open door sketching. . . . Her
voice rose to a sharp shriek, 'Why don't you give the man his crutches!'

. . . I made sure the window was open before I answered back. 'You
always make me do everything,' I whined. 'Norma's closest. I'm making
my bed.'

'She's not doing a thing,' accused Norma. 'She hasn't done any dishes
or anything.'

'She's just drawing,' added Daphne.

'I'm not drawing I'm making my bed,' I fumbled with the blankets.

'You lazy creature,' fumed Mama, searching for the crutches. . . . As I
muttered — Oh shut up — she lowered her head and charged up the
narrow passage . . . having a delicacy about having my eyes boxed, my
bottom smacked, and my body punched I sprang through the window. . . .

I heard the familiar climax, '. . . I'll tell your father. The world'll take it out on you. I'll jist tell your father.'

'Don't say jist, say just,' I corrected, as I made sure of a safe distance. Mama had been known to throw stones. . . .[11]

With the possible exception of Muriel, all the children had a reputation of some sort, a claim to fame within the family. Gracie was beautiful and had unfortunate love affairs, Ashton was tough and told whopping lies, Lionel was musical, Daphne was an actress, Norma was Mama's helper, Marmie was always crying, Evadne was the baby, and Sylvie was a spitfire: 'I was a wretched girl at Mangatahi, let's face it, selfish, disobedient, gazing inward on my imagery.'

That imagery focused on a mysterious girl who lived in a white house behind trees.

> She was rich and had a governess and was too glorious to appear at all. The more we didn't see her the more we talked of her. In mind I garmented her in all the characteristics desirable to me; she adored me, admired me and followed me round. She thought I was simply wonderful, especially my steed.[12]

Sylvia's description of that mysterious girl in *I Passed This Way* evoked much discussion in Mangatahi. Who was she? None of the older residents could identify her. Perhaps she was too glorious even to exist?

In October 1919, when the Warners had been in Mangatahi only ten months, there was another round of inspector trouble and again Mama was out of work. As always, she turned to poetry for sustenance: 'For men may come and men may go but I go on forever.'

Papa was put in an old people's home near Napier while Mama took the children to Palmerston North on a fruitless search for work. They returned to Hawke's Bay so poor that Mama had to accept Charitable Aid.

Daphne, Sylvia and Norma were boarded in Hastings with a kind lady of incomprehensible values:

> Mrs York gave us healthy food at regular times like lettuce and hard-boiled eggs . . . and expected us to come to the table when called. And we were not allowed to run outside when it rained in case we got wet. . . .[13]

The three girls ran away from Mrs York and moved in with Mama, Marmie and Evadne, who were boarding across town with the Lawson family.

The housekeeping job to which Mama had been sent by the Charitable Aid Board came to an abrupt end over the issue of menial work.

> I've never cleaned a stove in my life, I told him. Me, a certificated teacher, cleaning the stove of a sour old wretch, ignorant too, when I'm married to an English gentleman.[14]

For both Mama and Papa reality was not to be found in the grim poverty surrounding them, but in the grand dream of nobility and wealth. At election time they always voted for the right-wing party: 'It's better to have everything distributed by the rich than the grasping of the poor,' they told their children, though in 1919 there were none poorer than the Warner family. They had no money, their health was weakened (Sylvia had been laid low with rheumatic fever), and when their short, crowded stay with the Lawsons ended they were without even the basics of food and shelter.

Mama set up home in the derelict ground floor of a condemned house. Ten-year-old Sylvia drowned the hardship in a tidal wave of dreams. Dreams of dolls — big dolls, beautiful dolls, walking dolls, talking dolls, black-haired dolls with eyes like emeralds, blonde dolls with eyes like sapphires, dolls in satin, dolls in velvet. . . .

See the three little noses pressed to the toy shop window:
'That's mine. And that one — the one with the black curls and blue eyes.'
'That's mine.'
'And that one's mine.'
Listen to them telling each other wonderful doll stories . . . dozens and dozens of breathlessly beautiful dolls. A whole sea of reality-drowning dolls.

On one day — or many days — they stole two dolls, or many dolls. Daphne whispered, 'Come and see the beautiful dolls, Norma.' And there they were — two brand-new dolls under the thistles in the long grass by the railway station. Sylvia happily submerged herself in doll-dreams. When she recalled the episode in her old age she saw in her inner vision no less than 144 purloined dolls sitting unblinking around the walls of a disused upstairs room. But Norma, who was part of the adventure, remembers only two, and Lionel, who was supposed to have discovered the cache, remembers none at all.

There were also railway station dreams:

> I'd lurk, loiter, linger in that place looking up widely about me, intensely agog; absorbing the flashing exposed emotions, compulsively living them through, catching them myself contagiously.[15]

These dreams swirled around a sentimental song Mama had taught the children at school:

> 'Upon a railways station stood a little child that night. The last train was just leaving and the bustle at its height.' This song continued through several verses, every word of which I know, describing how the stationmaster asks her what she's doing there on her own, to which she replies that her mother died when she was born, Sir, and her father has just left for heaven. She's concerned that he might be lonely travelling all that way on his own so, 'Give me a ticket to heaven please before the last train has gone.'[16]

The drama and the glamour of the railway station brought a new dimension to Sylvia's fantasy life — that enchanted kingdom where dreams come true drifted down from beyond the rainbow and settled enticingly on earth, somewhere far away along the railway track. It was simply a matter of obtaining a ticket. . . . These dreams were Sylvia's survival rations in an outer life of overwhelming destitution.

By the end of the summer Mama, Daphne, Sylvia, Norma, Marmaduke and Evadne were living at the back of a boarding house in what, from Sylvia's description, sounded like a dilapidated shed, '. . . very small, unlined, unpainted, broken panes, they kept their tools and sacks and things there. . . .' But it wasn't a shed. It was a cottage — kitchen, living room, two bedrooms — built in 1905 for the parents of the owner of Dean Court, the boarding house. People were still living in the cottage in 1985 — surely it can't have been that terrible in 1919?

The problem probably wasn't the cottage, but the boarding house:

> Dean Court was a two-storeyed Victorian boarding house, pretentious with decorative woodwork at the front, fine windows and balconies on which graceful people languished. Lawns, trees and flowers facing the street; in the idiom of the period, elegant.[17]

So grand, so wonderful: Dean Court had stepped straight out of Papa's stories — a perfect home for aristocratic little girls who dressed in velvet and rode Arab steeds. But here they were skulking round the back to a life of poverty. And when the stove didn't work their misery was compounded:

> . . . Mumma used to go the rounds at night covering us with anything that might keep us warm, even sacks. In the morning she would light a fire on the frost-white grass with scraps of boxes or any piece of wood she could scavenge from somewhere, and cook our porridge on it. . . . It seemed we lived on porridge alone. . . .[18]

Mama's iron constitution buckled under the strain and she developed a terrible fever — groaning and screaming all day long and all night too, pulling old coats and sacks over herself in a desperate effort to keep warm. After a few miserable weeks she recovered, and through it all she made sure that the four older children attended school.

Mama believed her offspring to be much superior to the average. At Hastings Central School she enrolled Sylvia, who after five years at primary school should have been in standard four, in standard five. Daphne, Norma and Marmie were similarly elevated, but after one week all four children were dropped back a class. Outraged, Mama blamed the school. 'The common creatures,' she sniffed, 'Calling themselves teachers.'

Sylvia blamed the stigma of poverty: 'It was because of my sandals, Mumma. I saw them looking at the hole in the toe of this one and the sole flapping loose on the other.'

It was a grim year for Sylvia. At home she was cold and malnourished, at school she had to cope with a teacher who was not her mother — and that teacher was a man: '. . . I did learn the strange excitement of being pressed close to a man's body . . . he was picked up years later for this very sort of thing.'

That, or some similar encounter, was probably the basis for the experience Sylvia wrote about twenty years later. Driven to raw self-examination by the probing questions of the doctor who treated her for a nervous breakdown, during her convalescence she wrote an allegorical account of a youthful encounter with sex.

> The attractive fellow Sex made early advances and the attraction being mutual we began talking together at once.
>   Nature said: 'It is wise to become well acquainted with Sex as he will ultimately help you to keep the other part of your pact with Life: to preserve your race.'
>   Convention screamed: 'Ignore Sex completely! He's indecent!'
>   Habit, who was concerned only with what I had done in the first place persuaded me to do it again. My parents missed the whole episode. Experience wrote it all down and told me to learn it.
>   But the mutual attraction proved too great and with a gentle prod from exasperated Nature we began to talk again. Convention was furious and set the dog of Guilt barking at my heels. My parents turning hastily threw a musty cloak of secrecy over Sex, enveloping and almost suffocating him. Experience continued her writing and, as I had failed to learn what she had written in the first place concerning Sex, gave me a lash with the birch of Consequences. I learnt it at once. We ceased talking and I retreated more into Fantasy, pulling Sex with me.[19]

Echoes of a sexual experience with an older man occur in two of Sylvia Ashton-Warner's novels. In *Spinster* Anna Vorontosov weeps over her unconsummated affair with Eugene, who used to take her on his knee, tuck her head under his chin, and say, 'There . . . there . . . look at my pretty girl', and in *Incense to Idols* the wayward Germaine and one of her lovers compare their relationship to that between a father and daughter.

Ten-year-old Sylvia did badly in the end-of-year exams, coming near the bottom of the class in writing, composition and arithmetic. The only subjects she was good at were reading and comprehension. The next year she was kept back in standard four.

The following year, 1920, brought another male teacher with qualities and values that to Sylvia were a revelation:

> I trusted him, not only because I'd encountered for once in my life a man who was operative . . . but also because with this one we knew where we were. . . . My year with Mr Burns was a turning point in my education. He was so thorough and detailed and consistent and, in the context of the times, implacably fair.[20]

Under Mr Burns Sylvia discovered the stimulation and satisfaction that comes from intensive study.

There was another ideal girl that year:

> She was almost a replica of those in the past: a very pretty sweet girl, clever too, a Mummy's darling and only child, patent leather shoes, hair ribbons, the lot . . . an ideal on which to model myself.[21]

And there was a handsome boy. 'In my mind he could have doubled for the story-prince, given a prancing white steed, a flowing velvet cloak bordered with ermine, a crown and a gleaming sword.'

Sylvia never spoke to either of them, to do so would risk breaking the spell.

Meanwhile, out in the wide world, Grace had discovered the existence of other families of Warners and some of them were quite frankly common. But Grace was of noble blood, a descendant of the Ashton branch of the Warner family. She began to call herself Grace Ashton-Warner, and it was under that name that in April 1919 she became sole-charge teacher at Te Whiti School, near Masterton, in the Wellington Education Board District. During the 1920s Mama and Sylvia also adopted Ashton-Warner as a surname, and Sylvia used the name again when she became a published author.

After a futile trip to Christchurch in search of work in September 1920, Mama eased herself in as relieving teacher at Te Whiti while Grace was away sitting university exams. Then, when Grace was appointed to Lyall Bay School in Wellington from the beginning of 1921, Mama became Te Whiti's sole-charge teacher.

The family lived three miles from the school. The verandah boards of their house were rotted and broken, the wallpaper was stained and peeling, and their only floor rugs were sacks. But Papa was home, they had a piano, and at last the children could wander again in the wilds.

Behind the sheep paddock was a swamp with towering kahikatea trees:

> . . . spires of castles in fairyland that Puppa told about. In mind you could see the rippling locks of some princess languishing, waiting for a knight on a prancing steed to steal her for his own. . . . Deeper within it was dark and mysterious like hidden recesses of a mind where we didn't presume to intrude.[22]

And the azure pukeko that stalked the swamp served as inspiration for a story and drawing that Sylvia sent to the *School Journal*.

Half a mile away was the Taueru River, a place for swimming and exploring. A place where Mama boiled the dirty clothes in a kerosene tin over an open fire and hung them on a fence to dry. A place where Mama affirmed Sylvia's image of a merciless deity every time she went for a swim: 'Oh this cold is cruel. Oh God is cruel to me. God is cruel!' A place where Sylvie and Norma played among the foxgloves:

> We'd tear the end off the foxglove bell to make a skirt and leave two legs hanging down — they had dear little shoes on — they made lovely little girls. Where the river came into a backwater through the stones we'd put our little girls on boats made from foxglove leaves and play for hours. . . .[23]

The Maori presence at Te Whiti could not be ignored: several Maori children attended the school, there was a Maori cemetery in front of the family home, a Maori orchard close by, and the Warner children found many deserted whare in the course of their explorations. Papa worried that his untamed brood might think that they too were Maori.

'Remember that you are English children,' he would lecture them. 'You have English blood in your veins and you're from the aristocracy of England. Don't ever think you're Maoris or try to be Maoris. You are English and don't forget you've got the English blood. . . .'[24]

He used to go on and on about it — when he was at home. But at Te Whiti Papa developed cardiac problems. 'Oh these cursed heart attacks, these cursed heart attacks,' he'd say, striking his chest. And once again he was away in hospital almost as much as he was at home.

During the six-week summer vacation at the end of 1920, partly under Mama's coaching, but mostly at her own initiative, Sylvia studied and passed the entire standard five syllabus and joined her peers in standard six at the beginning of 1921. There were three children in standard six at Te Whiti School: Sylvia Warner, Rita Pike and James Garrett. Sylvia bestowed ideal-girl status on Rita Pike and set about earnestly modelling herself on her. She dressed and talked like Rita, she adopted her hair-style and posture. In retrospect Sylvia acknowledged that this ideal girl was far from a glamorous figure: 'God, the people I've garmented in glory unrelated to what they were.'

It was a life-long problem for Sylvia, this inclination to project her ideal self onto another and to attribute all sorts of wonderful but totally unrealistic qualities to the admired person.

In Jim Garrett, Sylvia found a less distant, and therefore less perfect, male hero. 'He wasn't the dark prince I knew so well in mind on a fiery white Arab steed — his pony was sleek, placid and fat — but he was the handsomest boy any of us had ever seen.'

He shared his pony with Sylvia for the journey home after school until, as Sylvia tells it, he suggested they go together to '. . . that green-shade glade down by the white pine swamp' and she ran away, '. . . setting a basic pattern for future encounters with men: coquetry'.

A couple of days later, Jim again offered her a ride but Sylvia had seen him the day before riding home with Helma Wilder. The fact that Helma was only seven and was riding her own horse didn't matter. Sylvia could not forgive:

> I give him no second chance, confirming an earlier pattern. Second place is not for me, in school or with men. I'm not Mumma's daughter for nothing. I'm prepared to lose everything. I think now it was Puppa's lineage, the pioneers and knights honoured by royalty. Blood pride.[25]

Coquetry, jealousy, and pride: note these three facets of the essential Sylvia spinning around the vortex of her need for unconditional love — a need that continued unabated and unfulfilled all her life.

That winter Sylvia spent a few weeks staying with Muriel in Taranaki. Mrs Warner wrote in the Te Whiti school log:

She attended Midhirst School and I was surprised to hear that they used the out of date Dominion Arithmetic and the drawing was of a simple and unambitious order. She had no homework to do and learnt no Latin roots and prefixes and I consider she lost ground in attending that school.

Muriel's parting gift for Sylvia was no doubt well intentioned: '. . . she'd given me a waist–high walkie-talkie doll . . .', but 'To me it was no more than a transient status symbol'. Reality was an unacceptable substitute for dreams.

At Te Whiti Sylvia and Jim competed energetically while Rita stayed in the background.

'12 August. Rita Pike 15 years old refused to do mental arithmetic as she could not do it,' Mrs Warner wrote disapprovingly.

Sylvia recalled that after a year of intense rivalry she finished one mark ahead of Jim in the proficiency examination and thus became dux of the school. In fact the official marks were Sylvia Warner 318, Rita Pike 260, and James Garrett 249 — but Sylvia was never one to let facts cloud the drama of a good story.

At home Sylvia was developing her other talents. She began to see in music a vibrant language of feeling and intuition: 'I'd learn this language and be able to say to others the real things inside me and then people would love me.'

Her art, which had begun with drawings of horses and only horses, now included water-colour paintings and covered a whole range of subjects. She won a prize at the Carterton Show for her drawing of a boy's boot: 'Such easily won, joyfully won money confirmed to me I'd be an artist the moment I got out into the world.'

Her first real taste of the outside world came the following year, when she entered form three at Wellington Girls' College.

THREE

Secondary School

INSIDE THEIR MAGIC KINGDOM THE WARNERS WERE AT THE TOP OF the status ladder, out in the world they were at the bottom. In 1922, after thirteen years of social isolation, Sylvia Warner crossed the castle draw-bridge and entered the outside world alone. She had learnt to see the world through her mother's eyes; it was a hostile place when all you had for protection were your talents, your pride and your dreams.

Sylvia was supposed to attend Masterton District High School, but that changed when Grace decided to take Daphne to live with her in the capital city, Wellington. The family had always found Sylvie's formidable temper difficult to combat; over the years she had used tantrums and sulks to totally exempt herself from household chores and from anything else she didn't want to do. It was with impassioned use of these same techniques that Sylvia persuaded Grace to take her to Wellington, too.

Daphne and Sylvia enrolled at Wellington Girls' College. Perhaps it was the knowledge that her home background was safe from discovery that made Sylvia a more relaxed pupil in Wellington, but there was still an element of performance; she had learnt from Daphne that one must perform in order to be liked. Her classmates in 3C remember Sylvia as a thin, rather untidy girl who fitted in easily. In class she was alert and receptive, and she was always making the other girls laugh.

Sylvia made two close friends, '. . . who chose the role of followers and audience while I played leader and performer'.

She sometimes spent weekends with them, but she was never at ease in their homes. Making friends outside the family and visiting them at home was a new experience for her. She had been raised so far beyond the main-stream of New Zealand life that she had only the dimmest perception of the norms and values of the wider society, and no idea of what she should do or how she should behave. Throughout her life Sylvia's divided self coped with this problem in two different ways: while the wondering inner Sylvia searched for a set of values uniquely her own, the outer self played the grand lady, fumbling her lines and overacting in a frantic attempt to conceal her vulnerable core.

Sylvia did not look on her new friends as ideal girls:

> Was it because these two were accessible to me, whereas it's the unattain-
> able that lures? . . . Quite irrelevantly it turned out to be a teacher who

supplied this inspiration, a botany lady regally out of reach. This was the
first crush that I'd had on a teacher and I must say I did go under. . . .
She was a tall fair circumspect holy spinster with piled high hair in golden
plaits and eyes as blue as wonder. . . .[1]

Of course the fact that Miss Pope was a teacher was far from irrelevant. In
Sylvia's search for a mother, a teacher was the obvious choice. Here was one
with blonde hair and blue eyes like the loving mother of her dreams; Sylvia
was speechless in her presence.

Note too that Miss Pope was a holy, and indeed wholly admirable, spinster. In her attitude to spinsters Sylvia was fifty years ahead of her time; until
the women's movement of the 1970s, spinsters were widely regarded as
sour and frustrated objects of pity. Sylvia's attitude probably derived from
her childhood experience of a strong breadwinning mother, and from the
gradual realisation that in the wider society married women were second-
class citizens. No feminist consciousness developed from this awareness; like
Mama, Sylvia distanced herself from women in general and made her
struggle for status a strictly personal one. Her ambition was to be first class,
and when she looked for role models beyond her family she found — spinsters. With their independence, their dedication to their work, and their
freedom from the love-pain of family entanglements, spinsters were a source
of inspiration, awe and romantic attraction.

After supporting her sisters for a term, Grace's money and patience were
exhausted. She sent both Daphne and Sylvia home to Te Whiti. The
transfer to Masterton District High School brought a painful loss of status,
a dusty seven-mile bike ride to and from school each day, and another
spinster, Miss Sutherland, to whom Sylvia transferred her passion.

Sylvia withdrew into Daphne's shadow and nursed a smouldering
resentment for Daphne's new bike and her outgoing personality. Former
students of that time agree that Daphne was popular, but only in Sylvia's
inner vision was she so dazzlingly and eternally centre stage.

At the end of the winter term Grace took Daphne back to Wellington
and Sylvia inherited the new bike. And at the end of the year Masterton
District High School was upgraded, moved to new premises and renamed
Wairarapa High.

Even without Daphne's shadow across her Sylvia was quiet and withdrawn. The sheer size of the school was intimidating enough; two hundred
and fifty pupils and a headmaster with so much power and authority that
he seemed to Sylvia like God on earth. The headmaster's name was Mr G.
H. Uttley, though Sylvia referred to him as Caesar. But what really troubled
her was the terrible dissonance between the grand Warner dream of
nobility and wealth and the aching poverty of their lives.

Compared to the destitution they had known in earlier years, the
Warner's life at Te Whiti was actually relatively comfortable. The Education Department was now providing vegetable seeds for the school garden;

the family enjoyed the addition of peas, cabbages, beans, parsnips and rad-
ishes in their potato-based diet. Their meat came from sheep heads, which
Mr Pike, a local farmer, regularly left in a bucket on the gatepost and
which Mama boiled in a big iron pot. A disembodied sheep head in a
bucket is not a pretty sight and the same object staring up at you through
a cauldron of boiling water is even worse. Sylvia hated the sheep heads.

Life was easier for Mama on the school front. Papa had been installed
as secretary of the school committee and Mr Pike was proving to be an
unusually cooperative chairman. But when Sylvia confronted the contrast
between her own home background and that of her school friends, she felt
nothing but shame. She compensated by making up stories about her
family; to explain her father's lack of visible occupation she claimed to her
classmates that he was an artist. Before long her stories of Warner grandeur
began to grow out of control, and the reality of her family life at Te Whiti
became for Sylvia a 'smouldering explosive secret'.

The sad truth was that anonymity in a small town like Masterton was
too much to hope for; the Warners were undoubtedly different and their
ways did not go unnoticed by the local gossips. *You see there was this tough
old battle-axe with a tribe of scruffy kids who owed money all round town and you'll
find this hard to believe but she had the damned cheek to put on airs and what's more
she even gave herself a hyphenated name and while everyone else sent their kids to
proper music teachers she used to teach them herself and to cap it off she used to enter
them in competitions but do you know what those kids played the piano so terrible
that people in the audience used to giggle out loud.*

At school Sylvia was aloof and distant. She didn't know about the
gossip; she thought her home life was a secret and she was anxious to keep
it that way. She is remembered as an untidy, sulky girl who always seemed
to be away in a corner on her own. Whenever she was called on to read
aloud she would stand up and gaze theatrically out the window before
beginning; at lunchtimes she would stalk around the playground with her
head in the air. The boys called her the Queen of Sheba.

Sylvia felt increasingly an outsider as she saw close friendships forming
around her. She could not take part in after-school activities, the seven-
mile bike ride home saw to that, but it also spared her the shame of admit-
ting that she had no tennis racquet or gym shoes. Although some girls were
friendly, she suspected it was not herself but her art and music that they
liked. Sylvia particularly remembered Penelope, who sat beside her in
class.

Her schoolmates saw her as a boastful loner, while Sylvia saw herself
increasingly as an ugly pariah. In retrospect, she concluded that her perceived ostracism was the brutal consequence of the discovery of her home
background at Te Whiti. The fateful episode took place during her first six
months at Wairarapa High; Sylvia became ill at school and was driven
home by the headmaster, accompanied by two other girls. She described
this event as 'my first downfall', bringing upon her the status of school
scapegoat and leading to a long series of injustices perpetrated against her.

One of these arose when she and several others had carved their names on the new desks. Sylvia was dramatically singled out by Caesar for punishment:

> I'm expelled. In which case so will Penelope be and some of the others, but no. . . . Besides Penelope's father is on the board of governors whereas who am I? Just a scrap of litter swept up from the roads which he had seen for himself last term when he drove me home. Moreover all the best people need scapegoats; how could you run a good school without them, or without favourites for that matter?[2]

The identity of the favoured Penelope, who features in the final version of *I Passed This Way* but does not appear in an earlier draft, is a mystery. Fellow pupils can recall no Penelope, and no board member's daughter, in Sylvia's class. The Penelope that Sylvia described was popular, pretty, brainy and sporty, and the best brought-up girl in the world; in essence she was everything that Sylvia was not. Such a dazzling mirror-image of the withdrawn, unhappy Sylvia may have lived exclusively in the reality of Sylvia's retrospective vision. On her return after being expelled Penelope still sat next to her, but they no longer spoke.

One of the boys in the class remembered the desk carving episode this way:

> The headmaster was waging war on the defacing of school property. He sent home all those — and there were many, including me — whose names were found carved on desks. It was his way of making a point, and of making parents aware. It was all over in a day or so.[3]

Shortly after Sylvia suffered the embarrassment of having her Te Whiti home background revealed, Mr Pike was replaced as school committee chairman and the Warner family moved abruptly to Rangitumau School.

She now had to tackle an eleven-mile journey to and from school, but once she had climbed the last steep mile there was a glorious setting of hills and bush begging to be explored and a respectable house to come home to. For the first time the family had a real bathroom; no more need they bathe in the river, or take their turn in a tin bath in the kitchen. It was luxury indeed.

In winter Sylvia left at first light and arrived home tired and dirty after dark. Usually she rode a horse and travelled alone, but sometimes, when she reverted to biking, she was joined for part of the journey by two sisters. In her autobiography Sylvia called them Marie and Pru, and described them as motherless outcasts. They were neither, but to Sylvia motherlessness and pariahdom were such compelling labels she tended to apply them indiscriminately.

Marie and Pru worked on their father's farm before the long ride to school each day. Sylvia disdained their dusty appearance and dissociated herself from them at school:

> . . . I wouldn't be seen conversing with them, not at school . . . I did no

more than brush with them on the road occasionally for, in the community
of pariahs, they were lesser than I. . . .[4]

Marie reacted to that statement in Sylvia's autobiography with good-
humoured astonishment:

Sylvia was always rather aloof at school, a bit of a loner, but no one
disliked her. If she wouldn't be seen talking to me at school [laughs] I never
noticed![5]

Marie became a nurse and as Sylvia recorded in her autobiography:

Fate gave me no warning that the day would come when Marie would
nurse me through an illness efficiently and generously when there was
no one else there to save me.[6]

This is something of a dramatisation. The illness that Marie nursed her
through seventeen years later was no life-threatening crisis. It was a two-
week bout of mumps.

When Sylvia rode to and from school alone, the long journey was a time
of daydreaming; she composed poems and stories, she planned pictures to
paint and music to play. The inspiration for her creative work was a third-
former by the name of Nita Ingley, the girl she wrote about in her autobiography as 'Veronica Dundonald':

She was rich, cultivated and authentically exclusive. . . . Automatically
she took her place in the succession of my ideal girls . . . she was airily
in another circle, another form, another wing and above all, in another
world, being largely a figment of my own imagination.

Dreams flooded in to bathe away Sylvia's loneliness; wish-fulfilment
dreams of a central role in the end-of-year school concert:

I wasn't included in anything though I was probably the most musically
competent on the school roll. They said I lived too far to stay after school
for practices but it was they who said it. I would have settled for getting
home at midnight had they wanted me.[7]

Then there was a last-minute hitch and Sylvia's astonishing ability was
belatedly recognised. One of her ideal girls, not Penelope or Veronica but
another one that nobody can identify, implored Sylvia to stand in for the
worshipped Miss Sutherland as accompanist. 'I was terribly happy that
night and the concert was a stunning success.'

In the report of the concert that appeared in the newspaper next day,
four well-known Masterton musicians were listed as accompanists — but
Sylvia's name was not among them.

Her schoolwork deteriorated under the combined onslaught of the long
tiring daily journey and an overwhelming surfeit of dreams:

Maybe I could have paced Penelope and Lila given all things equal, but
whereas their uncluttered minds could think a thing through my own
mechanism was so overcharged with imagery that figment blurred fact.
To find a fact that looked like a fact in what I called my mind was like

rummaging through a jumble stall in some exotic Eastern bazaar, complete with Arab steeds at hand with brass bells on their bridles, extravagantly camparisoned.[8]

At the end of the year, instead of being promoted from 4A to 5A along with Penelope and her other classmates, Sylvia was moved into 5B. In retrospect the demotion came as no surprise: '. . . my third downfall, the first two being the uncovering of my background and the expulsion from school.' As school scapegoat Sylvia fully expected to be picked on.

Her response was to work hard. Dreaming temporarily took second place to study on the long ride home; under lamplight at the kitchen table, where Mama endlessly ironed the evenings away, Sylvia settled down to more school work. After a single term her marks improved dramatically and she was promoted to 5A.

Ironically it was during that unwelcome term in 5B that Sylvia received a hint of the recognition she longed for, when the English teacher ticked a phrase in one of her essays. She was overwhelmed with gratitude and fifty years later remembered him as 'Mr Thompson who had cultivated my prose'.

It was also during that term that Sylvia took piano lessons. The teacher was never paid, but the experience affirmed the profound importance of music to Sylvia's inner life:

> . . . music became my most desired medium once I found it to be communication, a language by which to say the unsayable which pressed increasingly from me, a way of translating the powerful drives of the undermind which determine our actions.[9]

Sylvia-the-dreamer, the gifted, unappreciated pianist, was once again approached at the eleventh hour to play the accompaniment in the end–of–year concert. Perhaps it didn't happen quite as she remembered it, but it really did occur; in the newspaper report she is listed among the accompanists for the 1924 Wairarapa High School concert.

The really big event at the end of that year was the national examination: matriculation. Sylvia believed that Caesar, intent on singling her out as a scapegoat, had decided not to recommend her to sit the exam. Yet — at the eleventh hour again — her name appeared among those recommended. Someone must have prevailed against Caesar, Sylvia thought; perhaps it was the adored Miss Sutherland, or the appreciative Mr Thompson. . . .

She passed matriculation with a comfortable twenty-five mark margin, while Daphne, who had sat the exam in Wellington, failed. Most of the Warner children were home when the results arrived. That was the terrible part; Daphne had let down her audience, she'd failed in front of her family. Sylvia blamed herself for disrupting Daphne's schooling by going to Wellington with her in the third form, and thus to the load of guilt that Sylvia dragged through life was added yet another burden.

★

Despite the respectable home, Mama's Rangitumau stay was not a happy
one. Running battles between the teacher and the school committee culminated in a parents' deputation to the Education Board. Early in 1925 the
Warners moved to yet another sole-charge school, Bideford.

That was Sylvia's sixth-form year, and Caesar neglected to make her a
prefect: 'People don't give responsibility to artists if they can help it, to
wayfarers, wanderers and rejects.'

That blow, coupled with the extra tiredness of the fifteen-mile journey
from Bideford to Masterton, destroyed Sylvia's earlier wistful inclination
to become one of the crowd:

> At interval and lunch when nice people linked up with other nice people
> downstairs I stayed upstairs rather than go down since crowds got you
> nowhere. I found a little haven in this library to read in and, it must be
> owned, to rest.[10]

The library not only sheltered Sylvia from the rejection she felt around her;
it opened to her the boundless and exciting world of books.

There had been only five books in Sylvia's early childhood and by far
the most important was Papa's Bible:

> . . .a mind picture of him is not complete without a Bible in his hands
> or resting before him on his knees . . . the black Bible that seemed to me
> must contain something alive between its covers, something that only
> Papa could see as no one, I reflected, could stare all day and most of the
> night at pages like those — tiny printing and no pictures. . . .[11]

There was also a sentimental work called *The Wide Wide World*, and:

> . . . a mysterious book called *Stepping Heavenward*, which no one read at
> all and a non-existent book, *Yo Ho for the Spanish Main*, which Puppa nar-
> rated in serial form since the volume itself was lost.[12]

The fifth book, the first that Sylvia had ever owned, was *The Legends of
Greece and Rome*, which she had won at the Te Whiti School prizegiving.

So in the solitude of the Wairarapa High School library Sylvia set about:

> . . . addressing myself to the unbelievable vacuum in my reading and
> unearthed in myself a great taste for French culture until one day I took
> down from the shelves *Jane Eyre* to find for the first time in my life the
> story of a woman written by a woman and understood by a woman. The
> shock was like the crack of a branch splitting. . . . The Brontë prose I
> thought was the kind I could write myself given the mind to.[13]

During the winter term the cold and misery of the long ride to school
drove Sylvia to look for board in Masterton; at the first place she stayed
for a week, at another she left after only one night. Then came an uncomfortable few weeks boarding with one of her classmates. Sylvia hated the
loss of freedom, but more than that in her state of ugly unworthiness she
hated herself: 'I felt it was a shame that Jessica could not avoid being seen
actually walking to school with me, I didn't like it myself . . . looking back
I marvel at the charity of that girl.'

Before long Sylvia was back on the road again, this time riding a motor-bike supplied by Ashton, until Marmie smashed it up and she had to go back to boarding.

The school ball fell during her stay with Jessica. It was a glamorous occasion; the lovely Penelope didn't miss a dance but the shunned Sylvia had only one — with the understanding Mr Thompson of 5B English.

The boys hardly noticed Sylvia at this time but from her observation post on the outside looking in, she certainly noticed them. She noted their attentiveness to the art master's beautiful stepdaughter, she noted the electricity that arced across between Miss Sutherland and one of the senior boys (a phenomenon that had not gone unnoticed, or unremarked upon, by the gossips of Masterton), she read in Shakespeare of physical desire, and she fell in love with the aloof botany master, who '. . . kept himself to himself as though we were not there with him and spoke only technicalities'.

The end of the year brought a final blow from Caesar; Sylvia was not awarded Higher Leaving Certificate. That perceived injustice drove Mama, who was capable of total self-forgetfulness in the defence of her brood, to loudly and publicly remonstrate with Mr Uttley in the middle of Masterton's main street.

Then came the last event on the school calendar, the annual prizegiving. Sylvia remembered sitting near the front of the Masterton Town Hall with an empty seat on either side; no one sat next to her, not even Penelope. But she did collect an armful of prizes; some won in the outer world, and some in the inner world of dreams. When she was awarded Mrs Scholefield's Girls' Essay Prize, the guest speaker thrilled her with the words 'Keep on writing'.

As an introduction to the world, Sylvia's three years at Wairarapa High had been rough. At the end of it she looked on the school, and on the headmaster, with the same accusing gaze that Papa looked on God. She came out of that place — she said — crippled for life.

Her last year at high school was career-decision time:

> Perhaps it was time to run away. Stake out my territory in some far-fabled city and start on my real work. It would have to begin with commercial art which paid since the real stuff didn't. And what was to stop me continuing lessons with Horace Hunt to become a concert pianist? Think of it. A studio of my own and sweet new friends.[14]

In the unkind world of reality there were a great many obstacles to Sylvia becoming a concert pianist, or an artist or writer for that matter, though she did make an urgent start on a book modelled on *Jane Eyre*. The most obvious obstacle was money. Then there was the matter of Mama's expectations; teaching and nursing were the only occupations acceptable to Mama's daughters. Of office workers or shop assistants she would say disdainfully, 'Don't have anything to do with them. They're common.'

Commercial art wouldn't do, and nursing was for girls who had no

brains. For Sylvia it had to be teaching. 'The last thing in God's heaven or
earth I wanted to be was a teacher. If I had one hate it was the inside of
a classroom.'

But she had to do something. To Mama it meant making a career decision,
to Sylvia it meant finding a way to support herself until she found a
commercial art apprenticeship.

One could argue that if Sylvia really hated teaching she could have used
her formidable histrionic skills to insist that she follow Muriel and Daphne
into nursing. But it was probably obvious, even to Sylvia, that she was
temperamentally unsuited to nursing.

She blamed Fate for her teaching career; Fate was a euphemism for God,
but when you are dealing with a being as powerful and vindictive as
Sylvia's God it would be reckless to point the finger directly. In time, she
found blaming Fate so convenient that it became a lifelong pattern; the
alternative, which involved taking responsibility for her own decisions,
was too painful to face when those made in the interests of one side of her
divided self were often in conflict with what were, logically and objec-
tively, her 'own' best interests. Sylvia's teaching career was actually less the
result of Fate, and more the result of what she called '. . . the powerful
drives of the undermind that determine our actions'.

She was propelled into teaching by her feelings towards her mother, and
the process that took place is called by psychologists 'identification with
the aggressor'.[15] She had grown up in fear of her mother's power and
becoming a teacher was her way of controlling that power, for by
becoming a teacher she could step into her mother's shoes and take that
fearful power for herself. Sylvia lived the rest of her life with Mama's
power trapped inside her like a caged animal and, despite her best efforts,
it was a very difficult animal to control. Though she hated violence, there
were many distressing times in her years of teaching when Mama's reactions
took over and she lashed out in anger.

There were also positive reasons for Sylvia to choose teaching. The
classroom was a familiar place in an unknown world, teaching would call
on her talents in art and music, and she could spend her time relating to
children, which was so much easier than relating to adults. It was a
wonderful dream — the other kids would let her be boss, she'd be the star
of the show, and they could all sing and dance and paint and make up
stories and act in plays and have fun all day long.

At this first great crossroads in her life Sylvia Ashton-Warner was faced
with a choice, ultimately the decision was hers: she chose to be a teacher.

It is the last day of January, 1926. In a day or two Sylvia will depart for
her first job, as a pupil teacher at Wellington South School, but tonight
there's a dance at Bideford and all the girls are ready to leave. Papa, as
usual, is shouting from his room, calling each name down the scale of the
entire family:

Muriel, Gracie, Ashton, God-damn-it; can no one hear me? Lionel, Daphne, Sylvia, God-curse-it; someone come to me. Norma, Marmaduke, Evadne, confound you; who am I? Only the father.[16]

Then for Papa, that night there occurred one unusual and brutally final event: he died.

Papa die? But he's the only person on this earth who has ever loved Sylvia, and he's the only one that she has ever truly loved. It was unthinkable. As Sylvia recorded fifty years later:

> . . . it was like too tall a story he himself was telling: 'Once upon a time when I was a man with all my family round me, guess what I did?'
> 'What?'
> 'I unexpectedly died.'
> 'Oh you did not, Puppa.'[17]

Sylvia refused to accept it. For the rest of her life she sought through writing to cope with the pain of that night. It was like Daphne and her wildly exaggerated melodramas; the idea was to turn unbearable reality into bearable fiction, the idea was to make your audience laugh. So in *Spinster* we have the remains of the unfortunate suicide victim being scrubbed from the ceiling:

> 'We've been the whole morning,' cries Parent Number One sensationally at my back door, the next afternoon, Sunday afternoon, 'cleaning the ceiling! Been through buckets of water! And we've burnt the scrubbing brushes! Really Oi never knew a man had so much blood in him! Look, without a world of a loi, Miss Vorontosov, there were bits of heart on that ceiling! You can ask the others!'

In *Incense to Idols* the conductor husband of the beautiful concert pianist comes to a sensational end when he staggers from the rostrum and pitches dead among the first violins while his wife is playing a piano concerto; she misses only two and a half bars. Sylvia even treated Papa's death flippantly in her autobiography, but when she wrote about her childhood under the camouflage of fiction she dropped her guard and let some of the pain show through.

The constant worry of the Considine children in *Greenstone* — Is Puppa alright? — is overlaid with guilt whenever they stay too long away from home. Then one black night a terrible thunderstorm breaks. The shy, ugly Susanna runs through the house shrieking hysterically and waking her mirror image, the beautiful Maori princess, Huia:

> Unerringly the tumult stabs to the very heart of feeling . . . for an unmeasured moment a death of fear till realisation follows: plainly the taniwha comes. He is outside, he is near. The taniwha is certainly on the roof and whom has he come to get? He's come to consume the spirit of Puppa so that he'll haunt the clearing forever. The din, the taniwha, the agony. . . .
> A sound begins in her throat, the close-lipped moan of a Maori. To her it comes from beyond herself as though Puppa were already mourned.

She hears the quick thud of steps as Mrs Considine takes over, the hysterics of Susanna. The taniwha has indeed come inside and her moans grow to shrieks: 'Puppa . . . what's happened to Puppa?'

But in fiction as in life Papa's death was unacceptable. Despite this strange crisis, Mr Considine goes on as before, the whimsical centrepoint of his family, sitting on his chair by the stove with one sharp knee crossed across the other, tying the children's hair, browning potatoes in a frypan, reading the Bible and telling wonderful stories.

Sylvia fiercely suppressed her grief, and her welling fear of death and the grave. When she left for Wellington she took with her a numbness and a disbelief, and a gnawing suspicion that since he had abandoned her so completely, perhaps Papa had never really loved her at all.

FOUR

Pupil Teacher

I N THE ANONYMITY OF WELLINGTON, THE CAPITAL CITY, SYLVIA made a new beginning.

> . . . I cut off my hair in a buster cut. Surprisingly, once cut, my hair took to curling and I all but changed character. I shed the hangdog feel of the road and my spirit lifted.[1]

The buster cut actually dated from her high school years, but Sylvia's personality changed so dramatically on leaving home that for her to place the new haircut retrospectively in this period is entirely understandable.

Her dreams of grandeur, so closely entwined with her love for Papa, were suppressed along with her grief:

> When I was a child I was as full of vision as any child can be. There had been no limit to what I believed I could do and what I would be in the world, but I seemed to have gone blind since I came to Wellington. . . . No more than just another human organism floating with the current on the surface of the wrong stream.[2]

With Papa's sudden exit Sylvia began to see Mama in a positive light: wonderful indestructible Mama, struggling single-handed to raise her family. She was even far enough away to be idolised, for Sylvia's crushes on teachers and ideal girls have now suddenly waned: '. . . my ideal girl, a concept I'd grown out of, and it was plain I was finished with crushes on teachers'. And friends from these years recall, 'She adored her mother.'

These sweeping emotional changes demanded the creation of a new persona, and so began the first of Sylvia's many attempts to live her dreams, to actually become the person she really wanted to be. In Wellington in 1926 Sylvia really wanted to be a normal, seventeen-year-old girl.

In many ways she was already just that; she was breaking away from home for the first time, she had developed an interest in boys and a sensitivity to their interest in her. At the YWCA, where she boarded with sixty other girls — shop girls, office workers, factory hands and trainee dental nurses — she soon learnt the social intricacies of her new role.

On her first pay-day Sylvia bought powder and lipstick, and applied them in a thick camouflage. The aim was to attract boys and to disguise her blotchy, freckled complexion. It was a startling move at a time when only shop girls wore make-up, discreetly applied, and proper young ladies wore none at all. The effect on Sylvia's self-image was sensational; she was no longer ugly, she was beautiful.

A much-desired glamorous wardrobe was sadly beyond her means, but prior to leaving home she'd made a dusk-rose dress to supplement her collection of hand-me-downs. 'Sylvie's Paris fashion' the family had called it. Later she made a blue crêpe-de-chine dress, fitted at the waist and with folds of lace at the throat. The blue was to match her eyes: Sylvia considered, with some justification, that her eyes were her best feature. For Saturday night Town Hall dances she added an exotic touch, like a diamanté bracelet around the ankle — a laddered stocking was a small price to pay for glamour.

All the powerful feelings that had surged through Sylvia's childhood — her sense of being an unwanted outsider, her dreams of nobility and wealth, her deep ambivalence towards her mother and her need for unconditional love — did not vanish in a puff of face-powder. They went underground, deep into Sylvia's volcanic undermind. Sometimes the volcano rumbled and shook, and cracks appeared in the new persona. Sylvia quickly powdered them over.

At the YWCA she became a compulsive performer because that was the only way she knew to make friends. Comic imitations of the hostel matron were her specialty. The other girls accepted her; she was included in their shared intimacies, she joined them in attending dances and films, she paraded the crowded city streets on Friday nights, and she joined in a Confirmation class and made her vows to the Anglican Church.

The communal life of the hostel swept Sylvia into the carefully circumscribed mainstream of New Zealand society: she became part of 'the system'.

> The system could lead us girls anywhere and meant to make of us anything it wanted. Whether in the hostel or at school or out in the city, whichever way we walked, we moved in the shelter of discipline and protection from one senior after another.[3]

Sylvia's dreams flowed with her down the mainstream. The old career dream of life as a vagabond artist and concert pianist persisted:

> Yet, prospering side by side with this, was another the very opposite, a new one I hadn't worn before in which I've . . . become arrestingly beautiful and wear exotic clothes, I'd meet the man of all men, tall as usual, dark handsome and rich, who'd fallen madly in love with me. In a soul-shaking scene he'd propose to me, I'd become engaged with a diamond ring sparkling for all to see and be married in yards of white satin and a veil. . . . The wedding dream flared when I was at the hostel talking love-affairs with the girls but when I was marooned at school I favoured the recluse one.[4]

The marriage dream grew from Sylvia's discovery that in the city a young woman's social standing was not determined by her ancestry:

> . . . the real status symbol was 'Has she got a boy?' You don't know what

glory is till you've been summoned from the tea-tables of sixty girls at night to answer the telephone. The way the chosen stood up nonchalantly and pushed back their chairs in affected boredom to edge through the multitude to the hall. If a girl were called often you knew she had a Steady, though how anyone could work up to a Steady on two 9 p.m. leaves a week, one 11 p.m. on Saturday and special midnight leave once a term . . . well, apparently it could be done.[5]

Then one day a handsome stranger offered her a ride. After joining her for a swim at the beach he dropped her at the gate for all the girls to see, and Sylvia fell head over heels in love:

. . . I walked up the lane to the hostel seeing the shapes of things more sharply and in some kind of glow; the cracked paving underfoot, the slats of the fence and the tall white virgin hostel itself, the steps scooped by many feet. A white light flashing like moonlight. I knew it was love at first sight and for the first time. I was learning love itself for the first time in seventeen untouched years.[6]

For Sylvia this euphoria was more than a wonderful heightening of reality, it was a welcome antidote to the numbness that had been pressing in on her since Papa had vanished from her life. Thereafter she was rung up at mealtimes and taken out at evenings and weekends. She had become one of the chosen.

Her boyfriend was actually a man, a commercial traveller twelve years her senior named John Barron. To her friends, Sylvia referred to him as 'Moneybags', and his pet name for her, 'Bambino', was redolent with images of exotic, romantic and parental love. Sylvia adored him. 'The scent of a man so close, the touch of a man's mouth.' Her account of this relationship in *I Passed This Way* is actually a blend of her experiences with several young men, but it makes a good story.

Though in reality John Barron often took Sylvia and her friends to the theatre, she wrote of him:

. . . why didn't he take me to the pictures on Saturday night . . . or to the theatre to see the plays, visiting pianists like Paderewski and light opera companies, and it would be wonderful to walk with him through the crowded city streets in the Friday night parade. . . . Wasn't it time to meet his friends and people and for him to meet mine? I was disappointed he didn't walk up to the hostel . . . so the girls could see my man; he'd wait in the street at the bottom of the lane by prearrangement and blow his loud horn. . . . His one idea seemed to be to find a corner at a dark bay and give me free lessons in kissing, gratis.[7]

She recalled one memorable night when instead of the usual kissing session by the moonlit harbour, or on a hill overlooking the city lights, he took her to a country hotel. There Sylvia received her first lesson in drinking:

. . . I turned out a reluctant learner not only because of the shame of it and of what the family would think if they knew but because of the horrible taste of the stuff. How on earth could people drink for pleasure! Until

I felt the horrible thing change into an exciting thing as it ran through
my simple blood. . . .
   However when he pulled up in a stretch of dark road on the way home
drink lost hands down so that he no longer addressed me as a cute
Bambino but said I was a stiff little schoolmarm.[8]

As the weeks turned to months the relationship reached an impasse: '. . . he
continued to fail to mention marriage and I continued to fail to give one
inch'. When he seemed to lose interest Sylvia was shattered:

   . . . the sting of a broken heart and the worse catastrophe of a broken
   dream. A dream lost. The pain. . . . It was like falling in love at first sight
   but in reverse. . . . Pulling up abruptly in the street when I saw a car like
   his, panicking in case it was his indeed, flushing and whitening within
   a short doorway; listening for the phone at dinner time and for the
   whisper of tyres pulling up outside and maybe the squeal of a brake. So
   much feeling for him swelling my mind, bloating it, that I didn't know
   how to deal with. An enormous area of imagery was fouled, the part
   about the wedding, the lovely home, the status of marriage and the
   round-the-clock lovemaking. I couldn't tell one day from the next and
   failed even to wash my hair. . . .[9]

This crushing of a dream may have been only a temporary break with John
Barron, or it may have occurred in relation to some other man, for
according to her friends Sylvia continued to date John intermittently for
years after she had left the YWCA. Whatever the circumstances the effect
was a devastating emptiness.
   Her career dreams bubbled up to fill the vacuum. She applied for an
apprenticeship in commercial art, but was told she was too old; she practised for hours in the late afternoon on the school piano and went to the
most-mentioned piano teacher in town for lessons, but he pulled her onto
his lap. She didn't go back.

Teaching at this stage was no more than a background to the real adventures of life. 'Get through the five hours somehow, put the week behind
me and collect my cheque at the end of the month.'
   The pupil teacher system provided practical training in marshalling large
classes and instilling basic skills in the young. The pupil teacher was
required to imitate the master teacher; there was no room for innovation
or the questioning of old ideas. Sylvia did not like it. But she did find in
schools two fascinating categories of people, spinsters and children; and the
way they interacted made quite an impression.
   Spinsters had already featured in her schoolgirl crushes on Miss Pope
and Miss Sutherland, and the protective YWCA hostel matron was also a
spinster. Then in the infant department of Wellington South School, Sylvia
found Miss Little, and the following year at Wadestown School there was
another spinster, Miss Battersby. Despite her many reservations about each
of these women, Sylvia put them all on pedestals:

> . . . these saintly maiden ladies that detective story writers make up in
> books . . . these unmarried free untrammelled people whose lives belong
> to no man and who dedicate themselves to their work.[10]

She admired Miss Little's control and efficiency and was dismayed at her
own inability to emulate her, but she deplored her assembly-line
processing of the children.

> Her regimentation allowed no mind to develop as a personally operating
> organ in its own right, as an entity, but eliminated it as such. What you
> came up with was sixty small imprints of Miss Little. . . .[11]

She felt a misfit in such a setting. When she was transferred near the end
of the year to Wadestown School, though the official reason — that there
were three pupil teachers at Wellington South but none at Wadestown —
seemed both benign and credible, Sylvia was convinced that she was not
wanted.

The following year, 1927, Norma joined Sylvia in Wellington to attend
the technical college. At first they both stayed at the YWCA, but within
weeks Sylvia was out on her own. At the hostel, as at high school. Sylvia
saw herself unfairly singled out for expulsion. The injustice of it. Consider
Deodonné, the best brought-up girl in the world since Penelope: Deodonné's
mother kept sending her new dresses all the time with kid shoes to match,
and when Deodonné went out on Saturday nights she wore a fur coat and
diamonds in her ears, and when Deodonné fell in love at first sight she was
hurled flat on her back, ill for a week. And what happened when Deodonné
was late returning from eleven o'clock leave? Absolutely nothing. Nothing
at all. The matron didn't even threaten to write to her mother. But do you
know what happened to Sylvia? Do you know what happened when
Sylvia was just a little bit late? That's right, she was expelled.

Sylvia found a room at a boarding house where Grace had once stayed.
Shortly after that Norma also moved into private board. Then at the end
of the term Norma went home to Mama.

Sylvia, now at Wadestown School, was confronted with an infant mistress
who '. . . saw strapping to be indispensable to productive teaching'.

That experience magnified her ambivalence to teaching in general, and
to spinsters in particular:

> She emanated a saintly patience. The clock and the strap did much of the
> teaching, successful teaching too, for their handwriting was copybook
> standard and no one talked. . . . I did try to fit to her style and would
> have done better but for the strapping, which continually turned me
> over. I thought, if only we could teach young children without having
> to hit them, without the need to punish them all day.[12]

During the year Sylvia was moved from the infant to the primary department of Wadestown School. Again the reason seemed benign, but she was
suspicious: '. . . I was moved . . . on the grounds that I needed wider
experience. I wonder.'

At the boarding house Sylvia was befriended by two other boarders, Mrs Beyers and her daughter Jean. Jean and Sylvia called themselves Pip and Squeak. According to Sylvia, they sang together at the Royal Choral Union, they joined a club that performed plays for charity, they attended Town Hall dances, and they painted their faces on Friday nights and joined the evening parade:

> . . . assessing young men on the spot by the look of them and by the way they spoke, even by the smell of them. My word we covered a lot of boys, these accidental people in trousers; sampled all kinds, dozens. The year of the mouth we called it. The touch of a man was the true test, that elusive condition of biological rapport. Seeking the thrill of the magic of a touch and lips was the quickest way.[13]

Touch was all-important to Sylvia. In childhood she had yearned for a loving mother's touch and found only unpredictable violence. She grew up shunning human touch, even as she continued to long for it, her confusion compounded by the childhood episode of sexual touching that had left her wracked with guilt. For the rest of her life the highly charged issue of touch, whether with men, women, or children, took on for Sylvia profound sexual overtones.

After some apparently hurtful experiences with young men she resolved to take the opposite sex more lightly. Learning to play the coquette became almost as important as searching for love and marriage. But later that year she fell in love again: 'Waiting to kiss. Breathless, dizzy, almost sick and the light of magic flashing.'

As with John Barron, however, it was all kisses. There was no mention of marriage, and before long another impasse was reached: 'In his male way Aden also made it plain that kissing alone was not enough but I made it plain where the frontiers were. . . .'

Then the time came when: 'He didn't come again. Once more I was left with my two hands full of falling fragments.'

Sylvia turned to coquetry in earnest. Though she seemed to be playing games, she was probably fighting for her emotional survival. She'd been so vulnerable, aching so desperately for love; with all her heart she'd loved those three men, Papa, John, and Aden, and each in some way had let her down. Her broken heart could take no more. From now on she'd make men, and women too, love her, worship her, adore her, and before they could hurt her, she'd hurt them. Hard.

After two years of pupil teaching Sylvia passed the Teachers D examination, which qualified her to continue her studies at a teachers' training college. In blackboard drawing she was marked 95 per cent, but she was convinced she wasn't given her due:

> I was told soon after that it had really been 100 per cent but 'we've never given that before so we called it 95 per cent which looks better in the

records.' . . . That was the first time in my life that Precedent raised its head. I'd achieved something that had not been achieved before, therefore it could not be accepted for what it was. . . .[14]

At the end of the year Sylvia went home to Mama for the summer holidays. Mama's teaching career had recently come to a dramatic end when all the Bideford parents withdrew their children from school in protest; she was now living in Featherston, supported by Lionel. Sylvia scrubbed out an old building at the back of the Featherston home and claimed it as a study:

> There was already an old table so I put a chair beside it, a pad and a pencil upon it and said I was going to write a book. I didn't consider writing to be my line but since art and music had fallen through, temporarily, I'd have to try something else and if I failed all the way I'd end up at the Wellington Training College to be a dreary teacher, sufficient reason to make anyone write anything. So I sat there and stared out the window on the range.
>
> I wrote not one word of any book but in time the conditions of silence evoked an idea which all but felled me: instead of writing a book I wrote a letter to the education department in Wellington applying to be zoned at the Auckland Training College. I quoted the 95 per cent for blackboard drawing and said I wished to attend the Elam School of Art up there, and I told them I had an elder sister in Auckland. What I avoided telling them was that in this way I might extricate myself from the bloody profesh and move into commercial art. I had an approving letter back zoning me to Auckland.[15]

FIVE

Auckland Teachers' Training College

NINETEEN-YEAR-OLD SYLVIA ENTERED AUCKLAND TEACHERS' Training College in February 1928 as a vivacious, outgoing and sociable young woman. Of course she was play-acting, all her friends could see that, but it was a likeable role and Sylvia believed in it passionately.

Her flamboyance astonished her fellow students:

'She wore lipstick — and none of us did that. We were terribly prim and proper.'

'And all that powder — there was always such a contrast between her heavily powdered face and her unpowdered neck.'

'Her hair was a yellowish colour. I'm pretty sure it was peroxide gold.'

'She smoked — not many girls smoked in those days.'

'She had very beautiful blue eyes, but there were always black dots of mascara all over her eyelashes!'

At college her clothes were unremarkable — she usually wore plain frocks pulled in tightly at the waist with a wide belt. But for social occasions she dressed with individuality and style:

'She dyed her underclothes black!'

'She wore a see-through dress one night. You didn't do that in those days!'

'Sometimes she wore a big bow of rainbow tulle. And then there was a pink chiffon hanky dress, and another one with a big Elizabethan collar that framed her face. She certainly had flair — though half the time her dresses were just held together with pins!'

Sylvia's art and music also made a big impression, and her generosity with her talents enhanced her popularity:

'She could certainly draw. Even her simplest drawings were beautiful to look at.'

'She did brilliant complicated blackboard drawings with leaves and flowers and pixies — wonderfully decorative.'

'She was very generous and very helpful, and we were totally unscrupulous — Sylvia often did our art assignments.'

'She played the piano beautifully. She always played the music for our folk-dancing classes.'

Above all she was different:

> 'We were all so conventional in thought and manner and appearance —
> and there was Sylvie doing all the things we wouldn't dream of doing our-
> selves.'
>   'We used to giggle like mad about Sylvie — though she was never nasty
> or catty or anything like that.'
>   'She had magnetism.'
>   'She had style.'
>   'She was an original. She used to strike poses and dramatise herself all
> the time but it wasn't objectionable. She was just refreshingly different. I
> liked her very much.'[1]

Sylvia was no less popular at the home of the Kyle family, where she
boarded for two full years: 'From the moment she came we all adored her.
She had the most wonderful sense of humour and the most marvellous
personality. She was always very very warm and outgoing.'

She never did any cooking or housework, but her thoughtfulness was
remembered nearly fifty years later by the Kyle's eldest daughter, Marjorie:

> Once when my mother was recovering from an operation I came down
> with urticaria. I was all swollen and covered with dreadful itchy red spots.
> If it got too bad in the middle of the night Sylvie used to come in and get
> me and put me in a hot soda bath. Many and many a night she did that.
> She was never selfish.[2]

Sylvia's new self — this warm, friendly, outgoing young woman — was
sustained by a dream. She never spoke or wrote about it in later life, but
when she lived with the Kyles it was her reality — the dream of a loving
mother:

> She adored her mother. All the time she was with us Mama was upper-
> most in her mind; she never missed writing to Mama and she talked about
> Mama all the time. I don't remember her talking about her father at all.[3]

Behind the role-playing lurked the withdrawn misfit. Though Sylvia was
careful to conceal her secret self, her friends observed, 'She did live in
another world half the time.'

In that other world doors were slamming on her plans to escape from
teaching. She attended evening classes at the Elam School of Art, but '. . .
there was no kind of thrill in it; no stir in the deep places where inspiration
comes from'.

Sylvia's main legacy from Elam came from the weekend she spent at the
home of a lecturer; there she learnt The Correct Way to Iron a Man's Shirt.
This seemingly mundane exercise had a ritual glow about it that captured
Sylvia's imagination:

> My word I thought, fancy that. As it happens when I myself ran into
> men's shirts by the dozen I did them no other way and taught my
> daughter, who taught her daughter, who no doubt will teach her
> daughter in time. . . .[4]

During the 1940s Sylvia passed on the technique to scores of senior Maori girls in remote primary schools. There must have been magic in the way she did it; listen to Rosina Ropata, a pupil of the Hendersons at Pipiriki School in 1943: 'The thing she taught me that I really hold dear is the way to iron a man's shirt. I've never forgotten from that day; I always do it the way she showed us.'

The concert pianist dream seemed to have no future; it was show tunes played by ear that delighted the Kyles, and at college '. . . the masters were not called for in the common room but light stuff to dance to. . . .'

Even her dream of becoming a champion swimmer, which had taken root at high school, was swept away when two other college girls beat her effortlessly.

The acceptance and popularity she enjoyed must have brought satisfaction to Sylvia, but a superficial life of dancing and fun wasn't really what she wanted:

> Where was tne purpose I'd grown up with, the blazing confidence in some important work to do in the world waiting for me alone when I finally got there; had I lost it. . . . In the meantime three incidents did manage to penetrate to the undermind to influence the course of my thinking. . . .[5]

The first incident was concerned with teaching. Most of the time college seemed like an escape from teaching rather than a preparation for it: 'The words "education", "child" or "school" didn't occur in our vocabulary: to overhear us you'd never dream we were training to be teachers.'

So when she had to face an essay on teaching method, Sylvia was unprepared; she could remember the views of only one educational philosopher: Rousseau.

> . . . the European master who favoured learning in its natural state, his way being the only way I myself could learn anyway, freely from life itself. . . . For once I was relating this sinful teaching to the imagery within myself, abundant material spanning right back to Te Pohue when three little girls wandered barefoot. . . .[6]

Rousseau's ideal was the noble savage: the NOBLE savage! the noble SAVAGE! The spontaneous five-year-old deep in Sylvia's undermind whooped with delight. But Sylvia knew that child was unworthy — shy, ugly and untouchable — and she was clutched by guilt; 'this sinful teaching', she called it, even though her essay on Rousseau was marked 95 per cent.

In retrospect Sylvia was suspicious rather than pleased. 'I realise the 95 per cent could have been another case of the deadly Precedent rearing its head where you don't mark anything 100 per cent. . . .'

And in retrospect too she saw the Rousseau incident as an encouragement to escape from, rather than an enticement towards, teaching.

> . . . as the other escape hatches edged shut about me — art, music, swimming and marriage — leaving only the bloody profesh, here was the same

skylight inching open again as it had in the dark past: writing.[7]

The second major influence was the whole complicated business of love and marriage. By now Sylvia had flirting down to a fine art and she lost no opportunity to practise her skills. She had a reputation for attracting men and her many boyfriends were an endless source of entertainment to the Kyles.

One of her more faithful suitors was Cyril Walls, a man not unlike John Barron in that he owned a car and was much older than Sylvia. He took her to musical comedies and plays and bought her chocolates. As Marjorie Kyle recalled, with this boyfriend it was Sylvia who did the hurting, and the man who was hurt: 'She was cruel to him, she really was! Playing the coquette all the time — and she got away with it because he always kept coming back for more.'

The one relationship Sylvia took seriously was with fellow student Keith Henderson. According to friends, Keith adored Sylvia because she was exciting and different. And Sylvia made it clear to the Kyles, and to her classmates, that of all the boys in her life Keith was the one she wanted to marry. She couldn't have made a better choice.

Keith Dawson Henderson was the second son of a Methodist minister. His contemporaries describe him as a wonderful man; handsome, sporty, hardworking and dependable.

During their first year at college Sylvia and Keith dated regularly, but not exclusively. Their relationship encountered difficulties because of '. . . my absurd coquetry, playing off other men against him in the most disgraceful absence of trust in him. . . .'

Long after Keith had proved he could be trusted, when it was blindingly obvious to all their friends that they were meant for each other, she continued to test his loyalty.

'Can I really be sure of him?' she worried constantly to the Kyles, 'Can I be sure of Keith Henderson?'

After Papa, John Barron and Aden, Sylvia was reluctant to trust any man. She found it safer not to think of them as people at all, but as pawns in a game, passing objects with which one may or may not fall in love. And anyway, the coquetry was bringing its own rewards; provoking responses that fed, but never satisfied, her childhood need to be adored, to be special, to be thought absolutely wonderful.

In matters of love, or indeed of life, Sylvia could bear no competition. When on one occasion Keith dated her classmate Lucy, Sylvia was beside herself with jealousy. Months later, when Lucy developed appendicitis, Sylvia made bitter note of the attention showered on her rival. Within days she too developed appendicitis, but in her case the surgeon removed a perfectly healthy appendix.

The third experience that deeply influenced Sylvia came at the year's end when she spent the ten-week summer vacation at her sister Muriel's home in Golden Bay and took a temporary job at the local mental hospital. Here she was confronted with disturbed and broken people:

> I'd shut my eyes and brain when I'd come on staff but terror opened them
> both. In one fortnight I learnt more about the human mind than I've
> learnt in my entire lifetime since, but when my name went up for night
> duty I ran off in panic and spent the rest of the ten weeks getting over
> it. . . .[8]

Instead of working she lay on the beach and dreamed of Keith Henderson:
'He wrote me one sweet letter which I did not answer in case he thought
I was chasing him. Trust, I had none.'

The tempestuous courtship continued through 1929. Sylvia's recollec-
tion was that she played hard to get, but according to Keith's brother
Elliot, who made occasional visits to Auckland, it was Sylvia who pursued
Keith, and having caught him she twisted him mercilessly around her little
finger.

Sylvia's reluctance to trust Keith was tempered that year by the personal
strife being suffered by Daphne, who was then living in Auckland:

> It was I who secretly cared for Daphne with none of the others knowing,
> who rescued her and helped her off safely down to Muriel in Golden
> Bay, and if you want to know the source of her sorrow then spell out
> the fateful word 'love'. . . . Love was not being presented to me as an
> ideal goal for a girl after all, as it seemed inseparable from tears.[9]

In competition with thoughts of love and marriage Sylvia's old career
escape dreams surfaced intermittently. Although she'd reached the city at
the end of the railway line, none of her dreams had come true. Now she
looked overseas:

> 'Listen, Molly. I'm going to get on a ship and take off for good.' I'll pack
> a frying pan and a mug and swag it through foreign lands. Canada for
> a start, being Empire, and get a job in a factory painting china, or
> designing patterns in a textile firm. Oh for a studio in Italy where they
> sit round the wine bowl and talk till dawn.[10]

But teacher training continued inexorably, and in the final art assignment
Sylvia felt herself to be again the victim of precedent:

> You mightn't believe this but Miss Copeland marked me 99 per cent,
> which was worse than the other two 95 per cents. She'd withheld the one
> mark from excellence because, she said with some pride, although it was
> obviously worth 100 per cent there was no precedent for 100.[11]

But Sylvia saw in the art mark, if not an escape, at least a way of delaying her
entry into the teaching profession: she applied for a third year at college,
specialising in art. The principal told her, 'Far from granting you a third
year, Miss Warner, we've considered dismissing you for irresponsibility.'

And his reservations about her work were confirmed when she failed
Education II in the final exams.

With her first publication at the end of that year — a poem that won
second prize in the annual student magazine competition — Sylvia may have

felt again that her future lay in writing. The poem reveals a deeper Sylvia than she ever betrayed at college, and reflects her love of music and dance and her considerable language skills. The dedication 'To ——— ' illustrates her inclination to make her every creative act a gift to a particular person. Years later she wrote: 'I can quite truthfully say that I never . . . took up a brush or a pen, a sheet of music or a spade, never pursued a thought without the motivation of trying to make someone love me.'

DANCING SONG
(To ———)

Life in me singing!
Voice clear and ringing!
Take me to dance 'mid storm branches
swinging!
Wind soughing, sighing —
Birds fleeing, flying —
Take me to dance mid storm branches
swinging!

Moonbeams descending!
Colours soft blending;
Take me to dance o'er waves neverending!
Sea rolling, rocking —
Round moon is mocking —
Take me to dance o'er waves neverending!
Bright the lights glancing!
Love-lit eyes dancing!

Take me to dance to music entrancing!
Sighing and swaying —
Passion obeying —
Take me to dance to music entrancing![12]

Examples of Sylvia's artwork from this period also survive. They include a prizewinning sketch in the student magazine, and a drawing she did for Marjorie Kyle. The drawing dates from the day Sylvia invited Keith, and Marjorie invited her friend Doreen, to join the Kyle family for Sunday tea. Two guests, two charming visitors to entertain the Kyles, but to Sylvia the prospect of competition was unbearable. She made a deal with Marjorie — put Doreen off until another night and I'll draw you a picture of Peter Pan. And more than half a lifetime later that water-colour of the boy who never grew up still hangs in Marjorie's home.

Although she had to resit Education II at the end of 1930, Sylvia progressed along with her classmates to a teaching placement as a proba-tionary assistant and went to the Auckland school of Cornwall Park. Keith

Henderson was one of only two students that year who went straight to permanent jobs. As the sole-charge teacher at Whareorino School, on the north Taranaki coast, he would be separated from Sylvia by more than a hundred miles. His impending departure was a time of reckoning for them both.

> During the last six months or more Keith and I had gone together to the college picnics and peripatetics on the ferry up the Waitemata Harbour to Waiheke and Onetahi, to the pictures in town and the socials and were partners at the end-of-year ball. . . . It was accepted that we belonged romantically but there had been no talk of marriage.[13]

The night before Keith left they had a meal together in town, took a tram to the dormant volcano, Mt Eden, walked to the top, and lay together in a shallow grassy crater.

> Though the grass was our bed and the clouds our blanket we had not yet even begun to explore that territory of the senses known to lovers alone. In this darkest night all we knew was an abundance of stars because of being together and that we'd rather be kissing than not.[14]

And that was where Keith proposed and Sylvia accepted.

> In his orderly way he maps out the journey ahead: in two years' time we'll become engaged, two years after that and we'll marry. Four whole years . . . when I'd have married him tomorrow.[15]

To ask Sylvia to wait so long, and then leave town, was to risk losing her. During 1930 Sylvia began dating several other men. There was one who owned a fast car, another who flew aeroplanes, and many more. In her autobiography Sylvia referred to them by one composite name: Floyd Duckmanton.

The Floyds appealed enormously to Sylvia's flamboyant persona, but despite the time she spent with them — dancing, driving, attending the theatre — she never found it in her heart to love any of them, or indeed even to like them. Towards the end of the previous year she had gone to keep Grace company at her board with the Smith family. Grace was then in a love crisis of her own, a passionate, doomed affair with one of Auckland's prominent citizens. After almost two years of caring and security with the Kyles, Sylvia found only instability and unhappiness:

> For reasons traumatic, dramatic and sad I left the Smith home in Epsom and in a sequence of soap opera action with Floyd in a trail that led to the YMCA hostel in town first, a bleak stage indeed, then to Floyd's own big house in Mt Albert he'd inherited from his parents where he made me a star guest: bath, meals and school in the morning, ducking down in the car beneath a rug so the neighbours wouldn't see me, and finally to a room of my own *at last* in Manukau Road — a large room at the end of a long cornered verandah with a cubby-hole kitchen in one corner sporting a sink and a bench and shelves. And a gas stove.[16]

With a room of her own, a withdrawn dreamer could paint all day, or just withdraw and dream; the setting throbbed with possibilities. The vagrant artist fantasy had already been brightened by an unexpected £33 from the Education Board which Sylvia had banked for an overseas ticket, but for the moment she could think only of Keith:

> So much joy I knew in that room of my own, reading and reading his letters with tea in the pot, dreaming and dreaming when the pot was empty. This thing about belonging to one particular person, exclusively, to be wonderful to someone; to plan ahead with someone else, to share the future whatever it was.[17]

Keith wrote long impassioned letters and Sylvia replied with letters and paintings:

> . . . romantic pictures of long-stemmed glasses of bubbling red wine which I'd never tasted, fantastic flowers and ladies and several impressions of city streets crowded with bustling people, encounters in Queen Street on Friday night, eyes of starry intent. Glances in passing. Vivid colours. And a picture of the wheels of a train grinding out from the station.[18]

But letters were a poor substitute for being together. Sometimes on long weekends Sylvia caught the train south and she and Keith stayed with his farming friends at Whareorino. As always Sylvia made a big impact:

> We met Squeak off the bus and then rode the nine miles up to the homestead. She was beautifully done up when we started out but by the time we reached Tweedie's Slip the drizzle had become a downpour. And by the time we got home the dye in her hair and the stuff on her eyes had run down in streaks through the powder on her face. She looked like an Indian in war paint![19]

Keith's devotion to Sylvia, and the way he kept a pact to gaze at the setting sun and think of her every day they were apart, caused the locals to shake their heads in wonder. They were also puzzled by the close friendship that developed between Keith and a local misfit who shunned both people and responsibility. It seemed that popular, upstanding, reliable Keith Henderson was attracted to very unconventional people.

When the two-week end-of-term holidays came round, Keith, now the owner of a small car, drove to Auckland to see his love.

> In the room of my own at 589 [actually it was 361] I had a home of my own in which to receive my sweetheart for once, though he still boarded at Mt Eden when he came. Most of our friends had vanished from Auckland and we were mainly alone. Tentatively and shyly we began exploring together those exclusive regions of passion known to lovers alone, learning together and from each other the tumescent truths of love. At times during the year when the term was too long we'd meet down the main trunk somewhere like Te Kuiti, I coming by train and he by car. . . .[20]

Sylvia claimed that they stayed together at country hotels, or under a blanket in the car. 'Oh yes it was professionally unprofessional, deliciously risky, but no price was too high to be together. . . .'

Back in Auckland there were the Floyds, useful and unloved, occupying her time if not her thoughts whenever she was apart from Keith. On Keith's birthday she persuaded one of the Floyds to drive her to Whareorino, where she left a birthday present with flowers and a note, and disappeared before Keith knew she had been. On another occasion, when Keith delivered her to the railway station at Te Kuiti, he was devastated to find a Floyd waiting on the platform to accompany her to Auckland.

Meanwhile Grace had reached a decision. She borrowed the precious £33 Sylvia had banked for her overseas trip, and, in a dramatic enactment of Sylvia's escape dream, set sail for South Africa. Capetown was her destination, where Papa's brother George was a judge.

Back in Auckland Sylvia faced her own crisis:

> To wait and marry the love of my own life would be to return to the obloquy of the country schools circuit in the foothills of New Zealand's ranges whereas I'd already trodden that track. Nor did the resolution lie in marrying a rich city-bred airman against whom every organ in my body turned its back and who had not even asked me anyway, but in a repeat of the harbour water widening between a ship and the shore; in some far land where I could finally extricate myself from the bloody profesh and become the great artist I'd meant to be. . . . On these little islands in the South Pacific, no matter which way I wriggled and dodged, I couldn't get clear of teaching. All of which narrowed the crisis down to a clear-cut choice: love or freedom.[21]

Sylvia never did make the choice. Instead, she sought the best of both worlds; she married Keith Henderson and, though she never gave up longing and planning to escape, she carved out a freedom that was probably greater than any other lifestyle could ever have provided.

After a year at Cornwall Park School, from which she carried away memories of another 'serene saintly spinster' and a child who wept over learning to read, Sylvia passed Education II and became a fully qualified teacher. But in 1931 the nation was crushed by the Great Depression; thousands of teachers were unemployed. There was no work for Sylvia. She was delighted.

She set up her little room as a studio and, sustained by her meagre savings, began to live her artist dream. Apart from the distraction of a visit from Keith during the Christmas holidays, and two months' relieving teaching at Henderson School in the new year, Sylvia painted all through the summer and autumn of 1931 and on into the winter, exhilarated and exhausted. 'I painted all day. Could any life be more dazzling, radiant or rapturous?'

Her volcanic undermind, effectively plugged and ignored since Papa had left her, shook, rumbled and erupted; out burst the old dreams of apartness and superiority, of nobility and grandeur.

> Confidence poured over me once more like a stream in flood: of course
> I could do anything at all that I set my mind to. I felt again I had some
> work to do awaiting me in the world as I had when a barefoot vagabond.
> Nothing was beyond me. My role was to be the first, the best and in the
> front in comet-tail formation. . . . .[22]

Her eating pattern became disturbed:

> I can't say I ate well and when I did it was far too much, packing myself
> to the chin, which sometimes gave me colic and I was forced to sit quite
> still for an hour or two before it abated.[23]

She approached a commercial art studio for work but in 1931 jobs were
scarce and apprenticeships were almost unheard of. When her money ran
out she began to starve:

> But the momentum carried me on regardless so that I worked more
> madly than ever. I couldn't pull up for the life of me until vague elusive
> pains came licking round, sensations you couldn't catch. . . . Toothache
> next. The extraction of a mighty molar. I had to take a taxi home with
> my last two shillings but I still caught a chill in the face. . . .[24]

Using borrowed money, Sylvia telegrammed Mama for a train fare, and
went home.

After such an exhilarating outpouring of creativity there was a price to
be paid — a crushing depression:

> There are months and months or more around here I cannot account for;
> such a blank on the walls of the gallery of memory there must have been
> a blank on the walls of life there too. . . . All of which maybe is the way
> the soul heals itself: a black night of surcease.[25]

For months Sylvia lay on a camp stretcher in the kitchen of Mama's Lower
Hutt home; drained of will, drained of energy, drained of dreams. Then,
as her strength began to return, she went in search of work in the
Depression-ravaged job market:

> . . . I took a live-in housekeeping job in Karori which I'd rather not talk
> about. . . . Mama could stand the humiliation of my menial work even
> less than I could. 'The common creatures,' she spat. 'Let them do their
> own dirty work.' I would have too but I was sacked for inefficiency
> first.[26]

Her financial situation was eased when the Wellington Education Board,
in a move to find work for all the teachers laid off in the Depression,
appointed Sylvia to Eastern Hutt School. She began to look again to the
future, but this time her choice was a strictly conventional one: whether
to marry one of the Floyds, or whether to marry Keith.

None of the Floyds had mentioned marriage; but two years had passed
since Keith's proposal on Mt Eden, yet they still weren't engaged. Then,
early in 1932, Keith invited Sylvia to Christchurch in the May school
holidays to meet his parents.

According to Sylvia, Keith called on Mama on his way to Christchurch to ask for Sylvia's hand in marriage. Mama was impressed. Keith's parents probably weren't so impressed with Sylvia. Being rather straight-laced in their ways, the arrival of this unconventional and undomesticated young woman would have sent a few shock waves rippling through the parsonage. After a week in Christchurch Sylvia returned to teaching at Eastern Hutt School:

> . . . where I ran into even another of these excellent senior women made of patience and wisdom of whom New Zealand seemed to have endless supplies, a serene spinster. . . . I can be excused for a certain hero-worship for the senior spinster teacher, and to catch myself out wishing to model my own life on them. . . . I wouldn't mind putting it to you that senior women teachers should be required to be celibate, like priests and that's quite a good analogy.[27]

Although Sylvia made new friends on the staff, she found teaching difficult and uninspiring, and at home with Mama the stress level rose when the pregnant Daphne came home to await the birth of her baby.

The only good thing that happened to Sylvia that winter was the July arrival by mail of an engagement ring from Keith. In her autobiography Sylvia said that she and Keith had chosen the ring together in Christchurch, and Keith had paid it off in instalments. After that Sylvia had but one dream:

> . . . a man called Keith Henderson, a wedding ring on my finger to show the girls and a white wedding dress with a veil. I couldn't see through this picture of a wedding, not a yard beyond it or an inch either side. All powerful goals which had thrust me since I'd been born, all apprehension of being buried alive in the country once more, vaporised before this white picture which screened off the future like the sun in your eyes.[28]

Although it was the middle of the New Zealand winter when Keith became impatient to marry, Sylvia attributed the impulse to the onset of spring.

> And this is where spring took a hand. A letter came from my love, not the usual overweight one but something short and urgent. He asked me to marry him not in eighteen months' time but in one month's time in the coming August holidays, *next month.*[29]

Keith's father, the Reverend Samuel Henderson, officiated at the wedding. Keith's brother Elliot was the best man, and the bridesmaids were Sylvia's sisters Daphne and Evadne, Keith's sister Dorothy, and Sylvia's Wellington friend from her pupil teacher years, Jean Beyers. 'We married, Keith and I, in the Methodist church in Taranaki Street, Wellington, at seven p.m. on the Tuesday evening of August 23, 1931.'

And that is all. In one paragraph of her autobiography Sylvia dismisses the wedding she had been dreaming about for years. Where are the telling details? Where are the snatches of conversation that enliven her descriptions of other major life events? Above all, where is the all-important description of the wedding gown?

Stranger still, although formal wedding photographs were taken, the photograph in *I Passed This Way* captioned 'The Henderson man at the wedding breakfast' was taken not at Keith and Sylvia's wedding, but at the wedding of Keith's brother Elliot! Sylvia seems to be concealing something about her wedding, but what?

If this book were a novel the writer would unpick the embroidery from Sylvia's account, snip off the flawed strands and rework the original threads into an alternative version of the marriage. The plot would go something like this:

> *The story so far*: When handsome steady Keith Henderson first proposed to vivacious Sylvia Warner at the end of 1929 he spoke of engagement in two years and marriage two years after that, then they went their separate ways. During 1930 they crossed the miles for lovers' trysts and discovered together 'the tumescent truths of love'. As the months rolled by passions cooled and the miles seemed longer. In 1931 they rarely met and when 1932 came along they still weren't engaged. Was Keith going off the idea of marriage? Was he worried that Sylvia was the sort of girl his mother had warned him about? *Now read on. . . .*
> It's May 1932 and Keith is taking Sylvia to Christchurch to meet his parents. Is the meeting Sylvia's idea, because she wants to get married? Is it Keith's parents' idea, because they're alarmed by reports they've heard about her? Or is Keith thinking of marrying Sylvia after all?
> The visit is a disaster. As a possible wife for the son of a Methodist minister Sylvia is totally unsuitable; she smokes, she drinks, she wears make-up, she bosses Keith around, and she never lifts a finger to help around the house.
> But Sylvia wants to marry, and Keith certainly finds her attractive. He's not sure about marriage, but when she encourages him to resume the sexual relationship they had begun two years earlier he responds.
> For all that, when Sylvia leaves Christchurch her wedding to Keith is by no means certain. They still aren't even engaged.
> Sylvia goes home to Mama and the pregnant Daphne in Lower Hutt. In the same way that she used Lucy as her model for a phantom appendicitis four years earlier, Sylvia now studies Daphne's symptoms, and promptly succumbs to a phantom pregnancy. She tells Keith the alarming news — there's a sudden engagement by mail (two months after the Christchurch visit) — and when the planned two-year engagement is replaced by an even more sudden wedding, one month later, Jean Beyers hastily makes a wedding gown from the inexpensive curtain fabric, Nottingham lace.

But this isn't a novel. So we just have to note that Sylvia is concealing something about her wedding. And we don't know what it is.

SIX

Wife and Mother

RUGGED HILLS PATCHED WITH WIND-FLATTENED MANUKA, A shack for a home and a man who loved her. For Sylvia the transition to Whareorino at the age of at twenty-four was like a return to childhood.

Keith had already applied for a transfer on the grounds that the school residence was unsuitable for a married couple, but for four months this was their home:

> A single man's bach was all, one very small room, with a low iron roof you could reach up and touch and, apart from a stove inside and a rainwater tank outside fed from the corrugated iron roof, there were no facilities whatever: no bench, no sink, no bathroom, no bedroom, no washhouse and you shared the school lavatory.[1]

Sylvia embraced the isolation happy in the belief that though she had left behind family and friends she had gained the ultimate audience, a loving man who would care for her alone.

But Sylvia and Keith had been apart for more than two and a half years and the reality of his life did not exactly coincide with her dreams:

> The man I've married is a stranger . . . he is interested in other people and he appears to have motives in life other than pleasing me. How can this be? He doesn't play audience to me yet doesn't take the stage himself and what other relationship is there between people?[2]

After knowing only Mama's experience of country teaching Sylvia was mystified by Keith's enjoyment of his work, by the support he received from parents and by the warm friendships he formed in the district. Among the people he took Sylvia to meet was the district nurse, and in her enthusiasm for spinsters Sylvia chose to overlook the fact that the dedicated Nurse Crawford was also a wife and mother:

> A cultivated woman, English, and here we have another priesthood of women in district nurses, people with purity of intention and action only possible without domestic tumult.[3]

Keith's full and happy life was not only a revelation, it was a personal affront:

> . . . it confounds me that Keith has a large life of his own beyond the confines of his life with me and I try out a sulk about it. One afternoon when he is at school and the west wind from the sea calls aloud to me I

run away over the hills, not out of sight, but he chases after me and I hear his voice brief and stern and commanding, 'Come home.'[4]

He was the boss and she was the wife, that was Keith's understanding of marriage. But the housewife role had too little glamour and too much responsibility for Sylvia's taste. With Mama as her unconventional role model, Sylvia was probably the only new bride in the entire country in 1932 who had no interest in the domestic arts. When Sylvia's sister Norma went to stay she found Keith doing all the cooking while Sylvia painted and wrote. And when a local farming couple came for dinner:

> We got there after a fourteen-mile horseback ride and all Sylvia had for us was an apple pie in a little pie dish. She said, 'I didn't get around to cooking meat, I'm not sure how to do that . . . but we'll have dessert afterwards.' So we had this tiny apple pie, and then she produced a little piece of chocolate fudge, just one little square! That was our Sunday dinner![5]

Sylvia told Whareorino people that she was a university-educated city girl, and she gave the impression that country folk were beneath her. They recalled that she sometimes took the younger school children for nature walks, but her behaviour towards them caused resentment:

> The Pakeha parents didn't like the way she was impatient with their children but had a lot of time for Maori children. She seemed to think Maori children were more worthwhile. Then when she tried to get the Maori families to spruce themselves up that caused resentment among Maori parents. Sylvia became very frustrated over it all.[6]

Keith was tolerant of his unconventional wife. His solicitous care may have been rooted in a pastoral streak inherited from his father, and his use of diminutives like 'Midget' and 'Lamb' suggests that he enjoyed mothering Sylvia right from the start.

After a term at Whareorino the Hendersons moved on to Mangahume: 'Mangahume is his second school frolicking in the skirts of Mt Egmont, whose white cone prays to the sky.'

Then her autobiography continues, 'Five years and two babies later. . . .'

Five whole years and she writes not a word about them. Five puzzling, unexplained years. When questioned about the gap, Sylvia replied, 'Some things are too deep for tears, too close, too untouchable.'

On the surface they were conventional years, but perhaps all the role-playing made them seem unreal. The only clue to her experience of child-bearing comes in a diary entry ten years later on the subject of pain. 'You want to try having a baby without anaesthetic. You need to scream at the top of your voice for nine hours to get your bearings about pain.'

★

When the Hendersons arrived at Mangahume early in 1933, Keith joined the Methodist church choir at the nearby farming town of Opunake, and Sylvia joined the ladies guild. They quickly became accepted members of the local community and they did their best to fit in.

Keith set out to ease Sylvia into a more conventional housewifely role. His first priority was to teach her to cook, and the ladies guild took a sympathetic interest in his efforts. They particularly enjoyed the story of the rice pudding:

> Keith said, well he wasn't complaining — but could she make him a rice pudding? He loved rice pudding. 'It's just so easy to make — milk, rice, sugar, and don't forget the nutmeg.' He gave her the details and went off to school. When he came home he could smell this pudding and he was so hungry he sat straight down to eat it. Sylvia said he took two or three spoonfuls and his eyes went glassy, 'What's the matter Keith?' He'd just bitten down on a whole nutmeg. After that they rescued six whole nutmegs out of the pudding; he hadn't told her to grate the nutmeg![7]

And here's a picture of Keith trying to steer Sylvia into the considerate hostess role: the Hendersons are enjoying an evening at home with friends. A lively card game is interrupted by a knock at the door, and the unexpected arrival of a carload of Warners. Sylvia cries, 'My family! My family!' and turns all her attention to them. Keith is shocked. 'Sylvia! Your guests!'

This is the only time anyone can remember Keith publicly reprimanding his wife, for he has yet to learn that in taming Sylvia he's fighting a losing battle. There are probably occasions at Mangahume when he thinks he's winning.

He would undoubtedly have been heartened by the success of Sylvia's afternoon tea for the ladies guild. Certainly the guests were enchanted:

> She was a little actress. She looked a picture when we got there. She had a beautiful big shady hat on and a pretty frock, and she was standing posed in the garden holding a long-handled rake.[8]

For afternoon tea they enjoyed a plate of fresh pikelets that Keith had made during his lunch-hour.

After church on Sundays, Sylvia and Keith often joined another young couple, Janet and Bob Hughson, for a midday meal at their home. It was here around the family table that the irrepressible five-year-old occasionally made an appearance:

> It was so surprising — sometimes she'd act like a little child. She'd say, 'Oh that lunch was lovely, can I have some more please?' So I'd dish some more and she'd take one mouthful and say, 'Oh . . . I'm sorry', and push the plate away. Keith would blush and look ashamed.[9]

This public embarrassment of Keith by Sylvia was a recurring feature of their life together. In the early years Keith may have reprimanded Sylvia in private, his brother certainly urged him to do so, but Sylvia would not be controlled. Keith's long-term response was simply to insulate himself from hurt; in time his emotional defences became so thickened that for most of their thirty-seven years of married life Keith showed no reaction at all when his wife embarrassed him in public.

Although Sylvia threw herself into the roles of vivacious young woman and well-intentioned housewife, the creative artist and musician refused to be stifled. She found an outlet for her talents at Keith's school, where as a voluntary helper she taught art and music. Her sister Norma was staying at Mangahume when Sylvia produced *The Toy Maker's Dream* for an end-of-year school concert:

> Every child was dressed up as a different toy. Sylvia played the piano and the children sang and acted the parts of the toys waking up one by one. It was all done by candlelight. It was magnificent.[10]

With the birth of Jasmine in 1935, when she was twenty-six years old, Sylvia added the role of mother to her repertoire. She and Keith divided up the tasks of caring for the new baby thus: Keith did the practical baby care, and Sylvia played the loving madonna. It wasn't entirely an act; everyone who knew the Hendersons when their children were young says this of Sylvia: she loved her kids. She declared Jasmine to be a real Warner, so intelligent, so talented, so beautiful, and used to leave love notes for Keith tucked in the folds of her daughter's chubby little arms.

Within a year Sylvia was pregnant again. On the advice of her doctor, who was concerned about the effect of another baby so soon after the first on Sylvia's mental stability, she had an abortion.* The foetus died, but the lost baby grew in her mind like the ghost of the first Sylvia of her childhood, to become the phantom longed-for son that haunted the rest of her life and work.

Then in 1937 Sylvia gave birth to a living baby boy. They named him Elliot, after Keith's brother, and Sylvia declared him to be a Henderson. The Hendersons, as she would explain to her children later, were a boring lot.

Elliot was only a few months old when Sylvia became pregnant again. And when she faced the bleak prospect of another demanding baby she had to admit that the role of madonna was beginning to wear thin. It was at this point that she resumed her autobiography: 'Five years and two babies later I'm saying, "I'm prepared to go teaching again".'

As she explained to Keith, 'What I used to call my soul has dissolved like soap in hot water and gurgled down the plug in the wash-house.'

---

*SA-W told Janet Hughson, and one of her training college friends, that she had had a miscarriage, but years later she told the abortion story recounted here to her teenage son Elliot. The latter version seems more likely — she would have had every reason to disguise an abortion from her friends, and no reason to pretend to her son that a long ago miscarriage was an abortion. Whatever the nature of the original event, because of the lasting guilt it caused, SA-W seems to have always thought of it as an abortion.

She suggested they go to one of the 140 Maori schools scattered through remote rural areas of the country, for at that time these were the only schools where husbands and wives were allowed to teach together. Keith was appalled. Having a working wife would reflect badly on his worth as a husband, and with three little children to care for, he doubted that Sylvia could cope. And surely the idea ran counter to everything she had ever wanted? Didn't she yearn to mix with artists, writers and musicians in the glamour and sophistication of the city? Wouldn't the city be the place to develop her longed-for career in art and music? And anyway, hadn't she always hated teaching? He offered to move to a city school; it seemed an ideal solution, but Sylvia wouldn't hear of it.

Crying babies and a loving man at home, the wild countryside beyond; it was all so stunningly evocative of a distant, dream-filled childhood that Sylvia's undermind had again begun to rumble.

As the volcano trembled, the image of a wonderful mother than had sustained Sylvia throughout her teacher-training years began to crumble; now her only role model was that of the proud, unloving mother of her childhood. Once again Sylvia sought to control her fear of Mama by stepping into her shoes and taking that fearful power for herself. As Mama had always shunned and denigrated domestic work, so now did Sylvia; teaching was what mattered.

Also, she was jealous. The school was a rival in her marriage, seducing away Keith's attention and his physical presence for hours every day. 'K, we could get a Maori school. . . . We'd both be at school together. Then you wouldn't be walking out in the morning and leaving us behind all the time.'

The prospect of living beyond the frontiers of civilisation was not really daunting; Sylvia's isolated childhood had prepared her for such a fate. And think of the status she'd gain! How much brighter her talents would shine as a teacher among Maori, than as a housewife among housewifes.

In the five years Sylvia had been away from teaching, the New Zealand education system had undergone dramatic changes. There was a new flexible primary school curriculum; the recently founded New Zealand Council for Education Research (NZCER) was producing a steady stream of facts and innovative ideas; the proficiency examination had been abolished; the 1937 New Zealand conference of the world-wide movement for educational reform, the New Education Fellowship, had aroused unprecedented public interest in education; and in 1938 one of the brightest stars on the New Zealand educational horizon, a young man by the name of Dr C. E. Beeby, had been appointed Assistant Director of the Department of Education. On the way to his doctorate, C. E. Beeby had collected a First Class M.A. in philosophy, together with college prizes in jurisprudence, constitutional history, philosophy and education. He had been a university lecturer, and director of the NZCER, prior to joining the

Education Department. His dream was to change the focus of New Zealand education from rote learning and mass instruction to a concern for the full development of the individual child. With a man like that high in the Department, perhaps teaching would be tolerable for Sylvia.

True, the return to teaching would take her further from the dream of a glamorous cosmopolitan life, but that dream was fading anyway; now at least she'd have someone to blame. She blamed not Fate this time, but Keith. Twenty years later she wrote to the publishers of *Spinster*: 'I always wanted to travel and to end up in New York or Paris to live, but instead followed my husband in his work beyond the frontiers of civilisation among the Maori.'

In her own home the thwarted artist was less restrained. 'You dragged me off,' she would accuse Keith in recurring explosions of outrage, 'and locked me up in a Maori pa.'

Respectable teachers regarded the isolated schools of the Maori service as retreats for misfits. In 1931, only 64 per cent of Maori School teachers were certificated, and prior to 1934 they were excluded from membership of the teachers' professional organisation, the New Zealand Educational Institute, because they were not considered to be real teachers.

> . . . to hear it whispered of someone we knew, 'They've gone Maori teaching,' was to hear of their doom and to register the professional stigma on us all.[11]

The Native Schools Service was a separately administered branch of the Education Department, begun with the aim of assimilating the Maori race into the dominant white culture. Since the 1870s generations of Native School teachers had struggled to turn Maori children into brown-skinned Pakeha, and failed. But during the 1930s a tide of innovation had reached into the Maori service. Although the old negative reputation still lingered, Sylvia, as a reader of the *Education Gazette*, would have noted the forward-looking tone of the 'Native Schools' column in the department's monthly publication.

The column was one of the innovations introduced by a young Native School inspector, Mr D. G. Ball. When he was appointed in 1929 he found, in the words of fellow inspector, Mr T. Fletcher:

> . . . there was practically nothing Maori in the schools except the Maori children. No Maori song was ever sung, there was no sign of Maori crafts nor any interest in Maori history as part of the curriculum. The values in their own culture were ignored.[12]

After a review of the role of the schools Mr Ball issued a statement of principles for teachers. The first principle read: 'That all instruction be practical and related to the actual needs and interest of the Maori.' And he asked teachers to devise schemes that would provide every opportunity for creative activity by the children.

This recognition of the need for Maori education to draw sustenance from Maori culture and language was a major about-turn in an education system devoted to the Europeanisation of the Maori, and the wisdom of the change was frequently and vigorously questioned. Many inspectors, teachers and Maori parents remained convinced that the important business of school was the teaching of English and any indulgence in things Maori would seriously interfere with that aim.

Mr Ball also launched a programme of providing showers, woodwork and cooking rooms and laundries. By the late 1930s equipment in Maori primary schools was becoming the envy of many state school teachers. And by the time Mr Ball left the Maori service in 1940, morale among teachers had been raised to the point where they regarded themselves as a specialised service.

But the Maori, how would Sylvia cope with the Maori? In the popular stereotype of the day, Maori were uncultured savages, lazy, dirty, and dumb. . . . Perhaps Sylvia's Warner pride was outflanked by her gut-level identification with the despised underdog, for at heart she was a savage herself. Beneath the brittle mask, the churning ambitions and the dark shadow of guilt, she felt herself to be a child of nature; Rousseau's noble savage. Sylvia often wrote of an insatiable yearning to seek her own kind, those rare and sensitive people with whom she could enjoy spiritual union: she talked and wrote of finding them in the city, but her paradoxical determination to head for the backblocks suggests that it was really among the unsophisticated Maori that she hoped to discover her spiritual kin.

Then, on 14 April 1938, the following vacancy was advertised in the *Education Gazette*:

HOROERA NATIVE SCHOOL — Grade IIB. East Cape. Situated on coast, 8 miles distant from Te Araroa by unmetalled road. Head Teacher and Assistant; married couple. Salaries: Head Teacher, £210–270, with grading additions; Assistant, £85–105, with grading additions. Fares paid and a reasonable scale allowance made towards the cost of freight on furniture and effects of head teacher. Residence and glebe provided.

. . . so where was Te Araroa? At the very top of the East Coast, the atlas said, hundreds of miles north of Gisborne, which itself was hundreds of miles north of anywhere.[13]

Miles away from family, friends, and civilisation. The only other Pakeha in the district were the lighthouse keeper four miles away at East Cape and the teaching couples at Te Araroa, East Cape and Tokata. After lengthy debate Sylvia's wishes prevailed; one month later the Hendersons were appointed to Horoera School.

The new baby, due in May, still hadn't arrived by the time Keith left for Horoera at the end of June, so Jasmine and Elliot were cared for by Keith's relatives in New Plymouth while Sylvia stayed with the Hughsons in Opunake to await the birth.

Janet Hughson recalled that Sylvia settled in quietly for the two months she was with them; she was good company and spent much of her time painting and playing the piano. Her gift to Janet was a water-colour painting of a boy's head. Sylvia claimed, then and for the rest of her life, that she was an artist and artists never repeat themselves, but the truth is that she often did so. The painting she gave Janet was almost identical to the sketch of Peter Pan she had drawn for Marjorie Kyle some ten years earlier.

Janet's warm memories of Sylvia's stay are reminiscent of those of the Kyle family. But if Sylvia's acceptability as guest is any indication, something profoundly disturbing happened to her in the months that followed. All her acquaintances from 1939 onward are emphatic on one point: Sylvia was a terrible guest. The Kyles and the Hughsons may have loved having her for two years or two months, but after Horoera two weeks, two days, sometimes even two hours was too long.

The warning signals of an impending eruption proliferated with the arrival of the new baby. Sylvia recognised him as a true Warner and before she set off with the children to rejoin her husband, the infant was christened by Keith's father: Ashton Warner Henderson. But the reverberations of the name were overshadowed by the excitement of a great adventure — the move to Horoera.

SEVEN

Horoera

Horoera
Te Araroa
East Cape
Sept 4th [1938]

Janet —

Herewith the 'one little letter from Horoera' to quote carefully your
instructions — just touch me on the shoulder if you see me going over the
first page. I was just delighted to hear from you yesterday & lapped up
all the news. I was just rampant to hear how you Hughsons were faring.
And the epic news of James Hugh H sitting on his own. Applause. Has
he produced a peg yet? Ashton-Warner is just about the sweetest thing I
have done in the baby line — yet. He lost 6oz in transit but gained the
usual Henderson lb. last week. Elliot is eating beads just now — it's a
patent for peace to write a letter. He loves coloured chalk too and his
motions are such unexpected and gaudy hues. Also planes are not fast
enough for travelling with him. The next time I am required to cross the
island with him I hope to be shot across in a bullet. When we boarded the
plane he went the rounds & tore up all the passengers little paper cups to
be sick in & altho they all had looked healthy enough when they got on
they began to look *so* ill. Then he tore up all their maps & no one knew
where we were heading. I stared at the view from the window with such
a red face & pretended I didn't know him & that he wasn't one of my party
at all — but even so I felt the passengers' looks boring deep holes in my
back. And as for Daphne's place — the carpets were dreadfully expensive
& it was such a muddy day — a ghastly combination. I thought so fondly
of that Sunday afternoon at your place when Jean and the chn came. *No one*
said 'carpets' & no one said 'mud'. Oh it was 'just luffly' at Daphne's . . .

Then at the Palmerston Airport there was a highly dramatic meeting
with my old 'has-been' John — the pilot — & then when Mr Spiers put
me on the plane he gave me a box of chocolates & a smacking kiss — so
I reflected later that it was just as well I was heading for seclusion again
after a brief taste of the outside world.

Then terrible Elliot made all the passengers ill again by tearing up their
cups & maps & towards Gisborne for some occult reason they all began
weeping — Ashton in a high staccato — Jasmine dismally & Elliot in a
solid bass. The din on arrival in Gisborne was awful. Keith's expression
was mixed. I sighed — 'I feel all my troubles are over dear' — & Keith
sighed — 'I feel all mine have just begun.'

2. I hope to be shot across in a bullet. When we boarded the plane he went the round & tore up all the passengers little paper cups to be sick in - & altho' they all had looked healthy enough when they got on - they began to look _so_ ill. Then he tore up all their maps - & no one knew where we were heading. I stared at the view from the window with such a red face & pretended _I_ didn't know him & that he wasn't one of my party - at all - but even so I felt the passengers looks boring deep holes in my back. And as for Rapstein's place - the carpets were dreadfully expensive - & it was such a muddy day - a ghastly combination. I thought so fondly of that Sunday afternoon at your place when Jean & the chn. came. _No one_ said "carpets" - & no one said "mud". Oh it was just "luffly" at Rapstein's.

Letter from Sylvia to Janet Hughson, 1938.
J. HUGHSON

    We left for Te Araroa on Tuesday & as we neared East Cape the popula-
tion thickened & darkened till when we got there it was a solid black mass
of Maoris.

    We stayed with Mrs Black & came home on Thursday. It's all just
delightful & thrilling out here. I can see & hear every wave that breaks
from where I sit at the table — through the front door — & thru the
kitchen window there is an immense hill covered with virgin bush & after
a shower of rain the bell-birds always strike up a tune. The whole thing
satisfies even me.

    I hope to have a full time girl as soon as the Maoris stop dying in Te
Araroa — 10 deaths there in 3 weeks — & all the Maoris are away
attending the tangis. Mrs Black says the wailing is continuous & most
depressing. They go to all the tangis and she's just making one wreath after
another. There may be a tangi out here soon & I'll let no one say that I
can't wail with the noisiest of them. There's a huge cupboard of medical
supplies here — so it really seems that Keith is the Doctor & I the Plunket
Nurse — I devoutly hope that I'm not the maternity nurse. Allah! Here's
page 5 — why didn't you touch me on the shoulder. Which brings me to
my 5 darling chookies — they lay like mad. Marbles are the social game
here & it's no mean sight to see young Mrs Ruwhiu & I — after a dignified
cup of afternoon tea — tuck up our skirts & knuckle down to a deadly
game of marbles — I'm qualifying as a real social light. . . . Did you touch
my shoulder?

Thine — always

S————

S YLVIA MISSED JANET TERRIBLY. 'I LOVE YOU, JANET,' SHE'D TOLD
  her, 'One day you can roam the world with me.'

    But Janet was not one of Sylvia's own kind; she was calm and warm and
motherly, and her feet were firmly on the ground. 'I'll write you one
letter,' she had promised Sylvia, 'and from then on I want you to
remember that I'm always the same to my friends.'

    Janet kept her word. Since the unmetalled road of the *Gazette* advertise-
ment had turned out to be no road at all, every Saturday at low tide Keith
took a horse and cart eight miles along the beach and through two tidal
rivers to Te Araroa to collect mail and groceries. He usually stayed overnight with the Blacks and returned at low water the next day. Every
Sunday Sylvia emptied the mailbag onto the floor and searched for a letter
from Janet. There was just one, a day or two after she arrived in Horoera,
and after that, nothing.

    Perhaps she could find more love and loyalty in a spinster, but the only
unmarried white woman Sylvia ever saw was the indomitable Nurse
Banks, who rode the hills and beaches delivering babies, curing the sick,
mending the injured and preaching good hygiene and loyalty to the
Empire. She was a dedicated and competent no-nonsense woman, whose
basic task, as she saw it, was 'to turn the Maoris into proper New
Zealanders'.

On her first Monday at Horoera Sylvia had to put aside thoughts of Janet and Nurse Banks to tackle again that old bogey, teaching. That morning Keith followed his usual routine; he made the breakfast, did the family wash and hung it out to dry, and set off early for school to prepare his lessons. At nine Sylvia followed with the children.

While Keith taught most of the twenty-five pupils in the main school-room, Sylvia faced a handful of wide-eyed primers on the porch, where Keith had tacked up a sheet of cardboard between the coat-pegs and painted it for a blackboard. The children knew little English and Sylvia knew no Maori; worse still, in that cramped passageway there was no space for the communication to be found in art, music and dance. Sylvia was not enthusiastic:

> I knew very little about children, they usually bored me. Five years of training hadn't scratched the surface. Children, except for my own, were unnecessary beings with no function other than to make me go to school, who kept on needing to be taught all the time and who cut into the tex-ture of my hidden passions with the scissors of insistence, hacking at my privacy so that I couldn't dream in school.[1]

Some days she left school before lunch with a headache; on other days she didn't go at all. Sylvia was really happy only when Keith took the primers for arithmetic or writing on the porch, leaving her free to break loose on the piano and blackboard in the big schoolroom. The lessons she took there were as alien to Maori culture as the dull Pakeha reading books supplied by the Education Department, but to the pupils they were magic. Koro Dewes recalled:

> I can vividly remember her telling us the story of the Pied Piper of Hamelin; she illustrated it on the blackboard as she went. When she had finished everything was there; the Pied Piper, the rats, the crippled boy. The colours were fabulous.
>
> For music she taught us 'Little Mr Baggy Britches'. She dressed Sonny Potae up like a little Dutch boy with bright-coloured patches all over his baggy pants, and he danced around while we all sang.[2]

Teaching reading was a struggle. All those smug little words like 'train', 'bed' and 'can' spread confidently over the pages of the *Tiny Tots' Primer*, but the Maori kids just weren't interested. The only word they wanted to read was 'horse'. So like most infant teachers, within the Native Service and outside it, Sylvia introduced local words: beach, sand, fish, sea, cart. But unlike her contemporaries, who were doing their best to discourage the native language, Sylvia also added a few Maori words: kai, hoiho.

Even the additional English words worried Sylvia ('They didn't say any-thing about that in training college, K.'), though her Education Depart-ment handbook stated, 'There is no need to keep to the words contained in the *Tiny Tots' Primer* for the preliminary work,' and went on to give instructions on the preparation and use of flash-cards to present interest words to young children. But it was the Maori words that triggered the

greatest anxiety. Images of omnipotent, vindictive inspectors hovered at
the edge of Sylvia's consciousness: what would the inspectors say?

Many inspectors of that period were rigid, petty and unimaginative, but
the one who visited Sylvia at Horoera was not. When Mr Ball, senior
inspector of Native Schools, visited the East Coast late in 1938 he noticed
Sylvia's surreptitiously produced reading cards, and — miracle of miracles
— he approved. He even encouraged Keith to invite Maori people to
school to teach their culture and language. Sylvia recalled, 'I fell ardently
in love with him.'

But on the next low tide he was gone and then who could Sylvia love?
Or more importantly, whom could she entice to love her?

It's true Keith loved her and she loved him, but marriage was such a dull,
predictable affair. Where was the euphoria of falling in love, the thrill of
the chase, the breathless wonder of togetherness, the sweet ache of parting?

At Horoera Sylvia wasn't an easy person to love. The relentless loneliness and inner turmoil was cracking her brittle mask. In Pakeha company
she overacted frantically to cover her vulnerability; the zany exciting
Sylvia of the previous decade became, at Horoera, a tiresome show-off.

Worse still, she could find no kindred souls among the other teachers
scattered around the district. They were conventional, down-to-earth
people; they knew right from wrong and they didn't believe in rocking the
boat. Collectively, they were part of that force for conformity and social
order known more recently as the 'great New Zealand clobbering
machine'. There was not a dreamer among them, no one who could see
past Sylvia's mask into her kaleidoscopic depths. So they never knew the
woman who was studying Keith's Correspondence School music textbooks and playing classics on the gramophone in search of the shape and
form of music; they never knew the woman who was reading poetry and
philosophy from the Country Library Service and studying the lives of the
great masters in search of the origin and nature of genius; they never knew
the woman who was preparing herself with face cream and exercise for the
wonderful future that awaited her in the world. They just thought Sylvia
Henderson was the strangest woman they had ever met.

> Sylvia was always, always ACTING! So if she was a loving mother she
> acted a loving mother. She had all the right phrases and all the right
> things to say. She always seemed to be putting on a show. She always
> seemed to be posing, no matter what she did. We used to joke about
> Sylvia — she's useless, she's a show-off, she's a fake, she's a this, that and
> the other. . . .[3]

Sylvia turned to the Maori. She was fascinated by their complacent unconcern for material possessions and money, by their simple homes with bare
earth floors and by the strange foods they ate: seaweed, puha and kanga
pirau. In her own Warner estimation — and in the estimation of main-
stream New Zealand — she was above them, and in their underdog status
she identified with them. From every standpoint, Sylvia felt comfortable
with the Maori.

John le Warner, from
Warner, A., *Sir Thomas Warner*.
L. HOOD

Handwritten history of the
Warner family.
L. HOOD

Henderson family (Keith, back left).

Sylvia and Keith (front right) with training college friends, 1929.

She followed Keith's example and enrolled in the Correspondence School Maori course. She joined the Women's Institute, where she insisted that the otherwise all-Maori membership continue to conduct meetings in their own language. If necessary one of the women translated, but Sylvia always tried to reply in Maori. The women of the local Ngati Porou tribe accepted and liked her, and they recalled that she enjoyed institute meetings. In between meetings, Sylvia practised the language and learnt about Maori folklore from her pregnant Maori housekeeper; she also assiduously practised her housekeeper's stately swaying walk and adopted it as her own for the rest of her life.

The teachers from nearby schools confirm that Sylvia related well to the Maori, but they had some reservations:

> Sylvia got on very, very well indeed with Maoris, but I think perhaps she was a bit patronising. It always seemed to us that she acted the part; she may have been warmly appreciative and friendly and liked them, but the way she did it made it seem like she was acting the Queen.[4]

Keith kept the Henderson home and school running smoothly. The Horoera people loved him, he was kind and fair, so unlike the previous headmaster, who had brutally thrashed their children. They gave him fish, kumara, watercress, puha and corn. Whenever the farmers killed they gave him meat. And when the big boys dragged up wood from the beach on sleds behind their horses, it was Keith who handed out the fresh scones.

Despite the community support and the employment of a housekeeper, life wasn't easy for Keith. Some days when the teacher from East Cape called for a game of chess on his way home from Te Araroa, he found Keith starting to buckle under the strain:

> Sylvia was always demanding attention from Keith. She'd say; Oh K get me a drink of water, K do this, K do that — when we were trying to play chess. Keith was the most amiable and gentle and mild mannered person, of course he'd do what she asked — but there were times when he'd be shaking so much with the strain that he couldn't move the chess piece.[5]

As the months passed, Sylvia began spending more time in bed and less time at school. For a while she taught the primers in her own home, then she stopped teaching altogether.

Keith sent her to the Blacks at Te Araroa for a break. While she was there Mrs Black consulted Nurse Banks.

'Mrs Henderson can't sleep.'

'Can't sleep!' snorted Nurse Banks down the telephone, 'Can't sleep! I'll make her sleep!'[6]

The next day she took Sylvia on her rounds. They tramped hills and forded rivers visiting the sick and injured. Sylvia slept that night, but she returned to Horoera essentially unchanged.

By the middle of 1939 she had become Keith's fourth child. He sat up with her at night, he abandoned his Correspondence School studies, he devoted himself to her care:

> Keith believed it was a matter of rest and he saw to it that I got it and my word, those beautiful breakfasts with omelette on toast, and the tasty dinners at night with flawless brown gravies, but although I ate everything I still got thinner. . . .[7]

Nurse Banks suggested she overcome her weakness by starting a programme of sitting up, a little longer each day.

> 'I can't.'
> 'Why not?'
> 'My dreams are too heavy.'
> As I lay in the darkness at night hearing the thud of the breaking waves my dreams had a chance to surface, trying to surge over my mind, but at least I had the sense to counter them, for I was coming to fear them, as I feared almost everything. During the long days I learnt poem after poem from an English anthology I happened to have in order to recite them in mind at night. . . .[8]

One day, when the rivers were low enough to allow a truck to take supplies to the lighthouse, Nurse Banks sent Sylvia to Te Araroa on the truck's return journey. She was cared for by the Anglican Mission Sisters at Te Araroa, while Mrs White at the East Cape lighthouse looked after Ashton and the Blacks at Te Araroa took in Jasmine and Elliot. Sylvia found herself in the compassionate care of five dedicated spinsters; she had probably never been so indulged in her life. Nurse Banks recalled:

> We had her in bed there for weeks and weeks and weeks. She was so pretty. And she looked so lovely when we tidied her up and did her hair and put on a fresh jacket. We tried to build her up, to give her some good food, but she was very poorly. She seemed to need something that we didn't have.[9]

Sylvia's weeping and histrionics tried the patience of the mission ladies; though the teachers in the district thought it was just another of Sylvia's acts, neither Nurse Banks, nor Dr Grant from Te Puia Springs, could do anything to halt the decline.

She was in fact suffering from a severe nervous breakdown, and after more than three months' illness she lost so much weight that her life was in danger. Dr Grant did not refer her to a psychiatrist; there were few such specialists in New Zealand in 1939, and anyway, Sylvia's problem was considered to be a nervous disorder. He sent her to a dour Wellington neurologist and disciple of Freud, Dr Donald Allen.

Lou Flavell, wife of the teacher at East Cape School, was appointed relieving teacher at Horoera while Keith took Sylvia to Wellington. As the passing weeks became months, Keith took a temporary job at the Correspondence School in order to stay with his wife. His colleagues on the Coast anxiously awaited his return. When a whole term had passed, Harry

Black wrote to Keith — what about the children? With both himself and Bernice working, and their own young family to care for, they were starting to feel the strain. Keith, normally the most thoughtful and conscientious of men, must have been under considerable strain himself; Harry Black wrote several times, but Keith never replied.

In Wellington the Hendersons stayed with Sylvia's brother Lionel:

> My chief memory is that she cried day and night; all the time just quietly crying to herself. She couldn't do anything — she wouldn't eat — Keith couldn't do anything with her. I thought she'd never get over it. I'd stand by the bed and try and talk to her — she'd just cry.[10]

Sylvia visited Dr Allen two or three times a week, usually wearing her new Royal Stewart tartan skirt and red beret. With her collapse at Horoera her preference in clothing colour had changed from blue to red; Nurse Banks thought red was bad for nervy people and Dr Allen also disapproved, but Sylvia wore red anyway: 'I can do anything in red, but cry and do what I'm told in blue.'

In his gruff way Dr Allen taught her about two great biological drives, one for the survival of the individual, the other for the survival of the species. The drive for individual survival, he explained, was essentially selfish; it compelled people to fight back or run when threatened, and to engage in a diversity of struggles to meet their personal needs. The drive for survival of the species, by contrast, was essentially selfless; it was concerned with love, caring and thoughtfulness, with procreation and parenting, and with personal sacrifices made for one's family and community. He likened the two drives to a pair of horses pulling a wagon. If they pulled in unison the wagon would move forward, if they pulled in opposite directions the wagon would be torn apart and the driver tipped out.

Sylvia heard this lesson through a haze of bromide. The message she received may not have been the one Dr Allen delivered, but it served her purpose admirably. She thought of the pair of horses as 'the two heavyweight instincts' and gave each of them a one-word caption. She called the instinct for personal survival 'fear', and the instinct for survival of the species 'sex'. This interpretation not only helped Sylvia to piece together the fragments of her disintegrated mind, it became one of the cornerstones of her later creative work with children.

After the paralysing anxieties of Horoera the label 'fear' would have sprung readily from Sylvia's undermind, but Dr Allen's Freudian exploration of the label 'sex' came as a shock. She wrote in her diary:

> My specialist asks me the most enthralling questions. And blushes — you should see them shooting all over me. . . . Doctor wants to know about our sexual adjustment next time but I won't have a word to say about that. . . .[11]

Her turbulent feelings were complicated by the fact that she had fallen in love with Dr Allen. Patients falling in love with their analysts is a common phenomenon, but according to his colleagues, it was an issue with which

Dr Allen seemed unwilling or unable to deal effectively, or indeed even to recognise.

While Dr Allen joined Floyd Duckmanton and a variety of others in Sylvia's fantasies, in reality both she and Keith struggled with a wealth of new information and possibilities. Their new knowledge of contraception meant that the sex life they had virtually abandoned at Horoera could now resume, and while the goal of orgasm helped to lure Sylvia into reality, she was inclined to blame Keith, and to retreat into fantasy, if she was left unsatisfied. In an unposted letter to Dr Allen she wrote:

> The sexual adjustment that you are supervising is nearer. There were some minutes very close to the door of heaven this morning, although the hot expectation of ecstasy last night was blotted out coldly by the preparation. This big force of Sex is yet to be made to pull in the right direction, in the same direction as the horses Right and Wrong. He's nearly the strongest of the lot, only exceeded in strength by Fear. I thought he would break away and I'd have to break and throw, or demand satisfaction from another male but the minutes this morning seemed to show me that one has to be looking in the eyes of a man loved to learn fulfilment. You know how I want fulfilment, Doctor.[12]

During her treatment Sylvia concealed from Dr Allen, and possibly from herself, memory of the childhood experience that had twisted sex and guilt into a painful knot in her undermind. Although she later wrote about the episode in an unposted letter to Dr Allen, the pain was never fully released. It served instead to feed and magnify her fascination with Dr Allen's teaching, and to make sex a major source of powerful imagery throughout her life and work.

Dr Allen also explored Sylvia's feelings toward her mother. Her awareness of her 'search for a mother' dates from this period, as she wrote three years later:

> It is a matter of note that after the years on the Coast the friendships I make harbour heartache. It seems I cannot love moderately or even singly, and I look for a mother in men and women the moment they reveal a regard.[13]

Dr Allen may even have given Sylvia permission to hate her mother; Freudian analysts of that period made hating one's mother almost obligatory, and Sylvia's son Elliot recalled: 'She hated her mother with a blind natural force.'

Dr Allen's most positive contribution was to encourage Sylvia to write. Her enthusiasm for writing could be seen as the result of Dr Allen's failure to recognise and resolve her love for him, for Sylvia nearly always wrote under the inspiration of love, and all her early writing was addressed to him. Undoubtedly his failure was literature's gain.

She made an immediate start in urgent pencil:

> I'm mad. I'm allowed to say what I like. I'm allowed to say yes no yes no when asked if I'd like a cup of tea because mental patients have

privileges and I have the darlingest mental specialist. . . . It seems that
. . . I live more in a world of phantasy than this one right here and the
thing to is to allow it right of my chest with a book. . . .[14]

Her writing gradually evolved into the series of never-ending, never-
posted letters, addressed to Dr Allen. In one such letter, written after she
had returned to Horoera, she relived a portentous therapy session:

> 'Blow it off your chest,' you advised one morning when the sun was
> coming between the blue curtains. 'Write something.' I had just told of
> my slavery to phantasy.
> 'But I haven't the talent,' I lied eagerly.
> 'You can write a sentence in English, can't you? You can put together
> a reasonably correct sentence. Short stories if you like. A lot of my
> patients write. One of my patients completed a book recently. I read the
> manuscript myself. . . . It was just an outpouring of himself. It's on its
> way to England now, it may pay its way.' You leaned your elbows on
> the desk and cupped your chin in your hands and gazed out beyond me
> across the harbour . . . bored.
> I thought — He doesn't really care if I write a book, he doesn't even
> think I can. He classifies me as short story material. I couldn't bear to
> think of any book of mine that it may pay its way. I would never put
> any manuscript of mine in his hands for that damnation. I would put only
> a best seller at his mercy. . . . I swore secretly and pitifully that I would
> write a best seller. . . .[15]

During her treatment in Wellington she wrote stream-of-consciousness
observations on herself and her life:

> I just smoke and gaze and feed from my treasure house, my treasure house
> where I keep my delicatest makebelieves and loveliest memories. . . . I want
> to live in my dream world alone but my specialist tries to drag me out
> and keep me out. That's why they say I'm mad. . . . I'm terribly in love
> with my specialist and in two minds about staying sane for him. . . .
> Doctor said this morning: 'Your fear is the fear of reality. You take
> refuge in the phantasy world.'
> Me: 'You don't judge me do you doctor?'
> Doctor: 'No, go on.'
> Me: 'Doctor if it was not for my babies and husband and the ones that
> love me I'd *like* to go mad and just lie and dream somewhere with
> someone to make me eat and keep me clean.'
> Doctor: 'Live like a guinea pig?'
> Me: 'Do guinea pigs dream?'[16]

After lengthy analysis Dr Allen announced — over Sylvia's protests that
she was not ready — that it was time to start rebuilding her life. 'I've got
to break some more before you build me doctor. . . . I've got to break, or
love, or go mad.' And she returned to Horoera with some old mental
wounds still unrecognised and unhealed.

Sylvia was consoled by the thought that her return to the feared wilder-
ness was a temporary one, for in Wellington her dreams of escape to creative
freedom had taken on a finite time-frame:

In a year's time if I've not been put away we will come to town. Keith can get to varsity, the children to school, and I'll have my studio that I've dreamt of for years; some easels, a couch in the corner, a baby grand in another, pots of paint and brushes on a bench, and at least three pictures on the go — dream pictures with lots of blue and shadowy things in them. Plenty of cigarettes, somewhere central in town, and lovely smocks covered in paint. Keith and I could lead our own lives then, both love our children, and meet at tea time.[17]

Back at Horoera Sylvia abandoned her fitful attempts to behave like a normal grown-up; instead, she adopted the child-Sylvia as her true identity. She was five years old — for five years felt like the cut-off point, the time when she started school, when her days with Papa were replaced by days with Mama, and Mama herself was transformed from a distant busy mother to a harsh school teacher. Sylvia the five-year-old hid from adults but revealed herself to children: a spontaneous, imaginative, demanding, questioning, petulant, talented, sensitive and insecure child. One day she was going to be famous; it was just a matter of getting on with her wonderful work and in time the whole world would hail her greatness.

After the breakdown she was uncompromising in her determination to pursue a self-defined career as an artist. She drew strength from her reading; from Freud's claim that inspiration was sexual energy, and from Havelock Ellis: 'The creative force which gives us no rest until we have finally given it representation.' The roles of wife, mother and teacher took second place to her artistic career. It wasn't a matter of selfishness, though that's how it looked to outsiders. For Sylvia, the need to keep the powerful forces of the undermind flowing freely through her creative vent was a matter of sheer emotional survival.

She began to develop her talents. She made Christmas cards that were sold in the store at Te Araroa (despite her ambition to be a great artist this appears to be the only time Sylvia actually marketed her artwork) and, as an eruption of long-suppressed emotions again began to overwhelm her, she wrote endless unposted letters to Dr Allen.

Through writing Sylvia brought to the surface the buried pain that had been left untouched by Dr Allen: the disturbing encounter with sex in her childhood; her love for Papa that was betrayed by his death; and her distress at the discord between her parents. And through writing she named her fears and refined the raw emotional power of her life into a grand, dramatic art form:

> . . . I am afraid, doctor, I am afraid: there is an ogre, doctor, an ogre: it stalks in the no-man's-land between waking and sleeping: an ogre, doctor, unseen yet felt, unshaped yet present . . . as my thoughts beat in baffled inquiry; 'What is it? What frightens me?' I hear through the taughtness of the night, and across the trying and despair of the months between, your voice of a year ago. I see you gazing concentratedly at me

across your desk: 'Your fear is the fear of reality.' The ogre, doctor: reality.

This immediate reality of the river Awatere who runs between us and the village, who has washed three men out to sea in the spring flood: of the threat to my babies of being left without a mother: of the possibility of their breaking a limb or swallowing some poison with medical attention halting at Awatere: the reality of K crossing Awatere for stores twice each Saturday: of the possibility of his being left to live alone: of every kind of circumstance and responsibility standing between him and his ambition: the reality of my lying here in this inaccessibility weakening day by day: of being left at the mercy of an indifferent native and the demanding children while K is away — the persistent sentence that lays me bare to the attrition of domestic urgencies: the reality of the answering blackness when we look outwards for care: of the intellectual and human isolation: of the snarl of sea's deep water: of the tree army of the forest: of the long fort of the ranges. And all the stored fears of the past: of falling: of anger: of the dark: of madness: of choking: of flooded rivers: of deep waters. And of all the vague bewildering fears that have crowded in on me since you drove me sharply from the haven of phantasy — my skulking place where relationship and circumstance, space and time, were my servants.

These crowding fears of my one-time servants; the littleness of me, doctor, when faced with reality. I can't stay Awatere's brawl! I can't prevent my babies' motherlessness! I can't stop K breasting Awatere for stores! I can't recover without care! I can't comprehend sea's fathoms! I can't disperse the forest army! I can't level the range! I can't insure myself against falling or darkness or anger or madness or choking or flooded rivers or deep waters! I can't measure the incomprehensible vastness of space! I can't halt the tread of time!

Yet all these things I could do in phantasy. The littleness of me now! Oh doctor the infinitesimalness of me! Why did you drive me out from the strength of phantasy into this reality that I fear? 'Your fear is the fear of reality.'[18]

The ogre struck with ferocity towards the middle of 1940, when there was a terrible accident. There are at least three versions of what happened. In her diary Sylvia accused a little Maori girl of pulling the rope while Jasmine was skipping; Keith told a close friend that Jasmine had been struck on the head by a swing; and the third version, told by Sylvia to a woman friend a few years later, places the blame on Sylvia heself: she was carrying Jasmine on her back when she lost her grip and the little girl fell heavily. Whatever the truth, the last version indicates that the accident inflamed Sylvia's profound sense of guilt.

At first Jasmine seemed unhurt but then she slid into unconsciousness. Dr Grant drove the eighty miles from Te Puia Springs to Te Araroa and was delivered by horse and cart to Horoera on the midnight low tide. He diagnosed a fractured skull and for four days Jasmine's life was in the balance. She eventually recovered fully; but the crisis, the guilt and the fear that Jasmine could be brain-damaged, left Sylvia again prostrated.

Despite her illness, when Mr Connor came to inspect the school in August 1940, Sylvia was ready for him. She may not have taught her pupils to read, write, or count, but she was determined to make an impression. She covered the blackboard with beautiful chalk drawings, she taught her class some charming concert items, then she went to bed. With Mr Connor as audience, Sylvia, reclining among the pillows and draped over with a black satin bedspread, conducted the concert in her own bedroom. At one point, when the item was not exactly to her liking, she leapt dramatically from the bed, revealing the most glamorous of negligees.

All the inspectors during the Henderson's stay at Horoera wrote encouraging reports. They admired Sylvia's art and noted that her workbook and scheme were presentable. But her illness had adversely affected her classroom work; for 1939 and 1940 Keith obtained excellent gradings, but Sylvia's were unremarkably average.

Nothing the inspectors or Keith or Nurse Banks or Dr Grant said or did lifted Sylvia's continuing malaise.

Keith applied for a transfer — not to Sylvia's longed-for city, but to another remote Maori school. Why? Here was a man dominated by Sylvia and apparently willing to do anything to make her happy, so why didn't he take her to the city?

There may have been a touch of desperation in Keith's continuation within the Native Service. In the country he would be insulated from the advice and criticism of friends and relatives about his wife, and in the country the worrying interest Sylvia displayed in men, and perhaps also in alcohol, would be more controllable. And anyway, Keith enjoyed Maori teaching; he enjoyed his pastoral role in the community, and he enjoyed being his own headmaster. The submission of job applications was one of the few areas of life over which he had complete control. Applying for Pipiriki may have been the act of self-assertion by which he countered the eroding helplessness of his Syliva-dominated existence.

EIGHT

Pipiriki

The valley is a cauldron of steaming passions irregularly stirred by Fate; a place where quite orderly, usually routine people, tourists included, drop their guards like clothes on a riverbank before entering turbulent waters; to act themselves out for once in a lifetime with no accounting to God, man, past or future, babbling in tongues of the red rata worn in the hair of the forest, of the yellow of the kowhai in spring and of the profligate roadside flowers, to the point of inebriation which honest souls seldom dry out from.[1]

PIPIRIKI WAS A MAORI VILLAGE FIFTY MILES UPRIVER FROM THE coastal town of Wanganui. The setting was beautiful . . . exhilarating . . . threatening . . . and Sylvia, struggling to recover from a shattering nervous breakdown, was vulnerable to all it had to offer.

Again there were Maori; adults relaxed and dignified in faded clothes and unlaced hobnail boots, babies snug in blankets on their mothers' backs, children semi-naked and exuberant.

There were Pakeha; the people managing the store and the guest house, and the farmer upriver. They dressed in city-bought clothes and their children wore shoes. And just across the road from Sylvia lived none other than a holy spinster: the Pakeha district nurse.

There was a road, narrow, winding, muddy, but a road nonetheless. Each day, slips and washouts permitting, a bus made the tortuous return journey from Pipiriki to Wanganui.

There was the river; placidly reflecting towering trees when calm; devouring incautious mortals in angry flood. The local Ngati Kura people swam in it, eeled in it, broke in their horses in it, and canoed up and down and across it. It dominated their lives.

There were spellbinding village dramas; illicit love affairs and even lovers' suicides.

To thirty-two-year-old Sylvia, Pipiriki was the nearest place to Paradise inside or beyond the romantic vistas of her imagination.

On her way to Pipiriki, more than a year after her treatment in Wellington, Sylvia revisited Dr Allen. He had by then become, in her fantasy world, the greatest love object of her life: an understanding, patient, insightful

man, and 'the most famous mental consultant in the country'. The real Dr
Allen fell far short of this ideal, and before her appointment with him
ended, Sylvia fled. But in her inner life he remained wonderful, and she
took to heart his major lessons: she could no longer ignore the old wounds
festering in her psyche for to do so would invite another breakdown, and
if she were to live more fully in the real world she had to keep her posing
and dreaming in check.

The first lesson was etched on her soul. Sylvia spent the rest of her life
obsessively examining, picking at and airing the old wounds. Under Dr
Allen she had tried to open them directly to the light, and for a while at
Pipiriki, in endless unposted letters to Dr Allen, she continued to do so;
but it was all too painful. As time passed she aired the old wounds under
the more comfortable cover of fiction and found counterfeit relief in
denying the wounds in herself but discovering them in others. Such
measures kept at bay the ever-present risk of emotional collapse, but the
wounds never healed.

The second lesson — about keeping her posing and dreaming in check
— was just too difficult. Face to face with reality, Sylvia felt ugly, worth-
less and vulnerable. She coped by posing, and she escaped by dreaming;
dreaming of '. . . a glamorous mysterious vivid life in the capitals of the
world with those of my own kind — artists, musicians and writers'. Posing
and dreaming to avoid reality could destroy her, Sylvia knew that; but how
could she live without dreaming? She tackled the problem with reckless
bravado: she threw all her talent and strength and desperation into one
glorious plan: her dreams would no longer remain mere dreams: she would
turn her dreams into reality.

First she added becoming a better teacher to her list of goals, then she
wove all her ambitions into a central design — to become a worthwhile
person.

A worthwhile person. At a superficial level this meant many roles competed for her time and energy — artist, writer, musician, scholar, teacher,
wife, mother — and in every direction her creative talents blossomed and
bore fruit. At a deeper level it meant embarking on a journey of self-
discovery; Sylvia desperately needed to understand who she was and what,
deep down, she truly believed. It was this search, and her commitment to
the intuitive understanding she thus discovered, that laid the groundwork
for her later contributions to both education and literature.

Her struggle to become a better teacher was a struggle to free herself
from Mama's influence: Mama's rigid methods, Mama's coldness, Mama's
anger. The anger was terrifying. By day, in the large airy infant room of
the two-room school overlooking the river, Sylvia thrashed the children
with her tongue. In nightmares she thrashed them uncontrollably with
sticks.

Despite the lessons of Dr Allen and the works of Freud she was reading,
Sylvia retained a curious tunnel vision concerning the connections between
childhood trauma and adult behaviour. She confidently diagnosed emo-

tional deprivation in the homes of her Pakeha pupils and in the early lives of her women friends, she hinted at it in her fiction, but when she considered her own behaviour and that of her Maori pupils, she never looked to the past. Although she was deeply ashamed and anxious about the violence she vented on her pupils, she simply accepted it as a fundamental part of herself.

At a personal level this acceptance seems like an evasion, a way of stepping past land mines of buried pain, but at a professional level, when she applied this acceptance to Maori children, it was a magnificent breakthrough. While her colleagues worried about the Maori 'problem' and tried to pinpoint a cause, Sylvia accepted Maori children as they were, without question or reservation. Whether the issue was head lice, violence, or poor reading ability, Sylvia never asked why, she just concentrated on how best to deal with it.

As she studied — not education but the Bible, novels, poetry, psychology, philosophy and Maoritanga — and as she pondered over the five-year-olds in her care, the forces that had been moving in her spirit since she first considered Maori teaching began to grow together and fuse: her problems, her talents, her joys, her needs, and those of the little Maori children, now seemed one and the same.

'I'm white on the outside and brown on the inside,' she explained to the district nurse. And later in her teaching career one of her favourite claims was: 'We're all mad! Artists, the Great Masters, Maori children, and me!'

The essence of their shared problem was communication. Faltering lessons on subjects like reading and number evoked boredom and frustration, and they were always being distracted by more compelling personal concerns. Sylvia complained to Keith:

> There's no communication . . . you see they're not thinking about what they're writing about or what I'm teaching. I'm teaching about 'bed' and 'can' but they were thinking about canoes and grandfathers and drowned men and eels. It seems to me . . . I seem to be *rude* to *intrude*. . . .[2]

Sylvia poured hours of preparation into set curriculum work, but the results were discouraging. In March she wrote:

> At school the number and reading are worse and the children's behaviour too, and at home the pace is tenser, making my own behaviour at school no better than the children's. . . . They're idle, naughty and frightened of me. . . .[3]

She tried orthodox methods for teaching reading, but few children learned to read; she tried unorthodox methods for teaching arithmetic — elaborate blackboard murals in which each colour represented a different number — but few children learnt to count. Yet those same unruly pupils became cheerful and co-operative when faced with activities more peripheral to her professional grading:

> The only time they show any sign of interest is when I let them draw,

when it seems that furtively they let escape the pictures rampant in the
mind — these pictures in the mind that offend so, that disorganise real
teaching. If only their black little heads had nothing whatever in them,
then all I would have to do is fill them up. It's what's in their minds that
makes them revolt. Empty children couldn't be naughty.

Or when I tell them a story. They attend to me then and sit wonderfully still. It seems then that their minds and my mind become one thing,
two friends arm in arm.[4]

For Sylvia, as for the children, it was what was in her mind that made her
revolt. Four months later she noted:

. . . rages remain. With dreams crashing in on reality and reality crashing
in on dreaming during the hours before school, I'm in an exclusive rage
when I get there. . . .[5]

But subtle changes were taking place:

. . . they've receded lately, the nightmares, when hidden in sleep I beat
the children . . . tentatively, reluctantly, I'm becoming interested in no
less than my infant room. From the reading I do in the early hours before
the household wakes, how could I not become interested? Freud, Adler,
Lipmann, Scheiner, Jung and Bertrand Russell explaining life and
children, and all the poetry at night.[6]

It wasn't a passion for intellectual understanding that drove Sylvia, but a
fascination with the vivid inner lives of her pupils. When the planned
lessons veered off course the occasion became less a cause for alarm, and
more a wonderful opportunity for Sylvia to record the whole event.

Consider the time Bernard tripped over Pearly's feet and the whole well-
planned spelling lesson fell apart:

'Look,' I suggest, 'the other children all have their feet tucked in.'
. . . 'Please,' says Tiny of the fairy feet, 'Pearly she haven got a shoes.
Please her feets too wide. Please her mother she take Pearly to town for
a shoes an please the man he carn make a shoes to get on Pearly her feets.'

There follows an animated discussion of the relative sizes of Pearly's and
Tiny's feet. Sylvia frets over the abandoned spelling lesson, but continues
to record the conversation:

'Please M's Hen'son,' from Olga . . . 'my father he said that Pearly her
father his feets theys big enough for a dance hall.'
Andrew joins in with pride. 'Please my mother she was at the dance
hall on Saturday and my mother she was drunk. Please she thrash my
uncle. . . .'[7]

Sylvia rose at four-thirty each day to study, and then spent from six until
eight with her family. After breakfast she gave the children elocution
lessons. She had learnt from her parents that New Zealand English, and
especially Maori English, was very second rate. But her own ideas on
correct speech, and her unique accent — self-conscious posh with an idio-
syncratic emphasis on the last syllable of every word — may not have been

a legacy from her parents. Her brother recalled, 'My father spoke beautifully, my mother spoke correctly, but Sylvia spoke like no one else on earth.'*

After the elocution lesson Sylvia practised the piano for an hour before beginning teaching at nine. Her diary entry about the arrival of the school piano shows that to Sylvia music was a source of both salvation and sin:

> The next morning, walking over to school, I tried to be strong enough not to give in to the allurement of the new piano . . . not to sink my hungry fingers into the luxurious keys . . . but at the sight of it I collapsed and lifted the lid. . . .Even if this is the sin of dreaming in the morning of reality, the sin of lifting myself from the ground to the forbidden heaven when I should be preparing my work . . . this sin is worth it.[8]

After school and in the evening she prepared school work and added a few lines to her writing projects: a diary of her present life, and the letters to Dr Allen, which were gradually turning into a novel based on her childhood. Then last thing at night, before falling asleep, she read poetry.

Keith's mothering role, a stop-gap measure at Horoera, had become a way of life at Pipiriki, for in Sylvia's self-defined reality the children occupied a very peripheral place, and in her inner world they barely existed at all. The Henderson's eldest son, Elliot, who was four when they moved to Pipiriki and seven when they left, recalled: 'Dad was the one who looked after us. I remember the security of him being there, milking the cow, chopping the wood, and so on, while Mum flitted in and out. . . .'

Keith received help from a Maori housekeeper and from the senior schoolgirls who came in once a week to bake, wash, iron, tidy and clean as part of their domestic science course.

Although her days were over-full, Sylvia couldn't live without love, so she made time for that too.

Love to Sylvia was the same emotional roller-coaster that has, since the dawn of time, swept up unwary mortals, spun them around, and dumped them back into hard reality. But in Sylvia's case, as with all her experiences in life, her loves were so much bigger and brighter that they appeared almost, but not quite, detached from the common human experience. There was hardly a time in her life when she wasn't falling in or out of love; indeed, she was often falling in both directions with several different people simultaneously. Despite the numbers involved, practical complications were few, for Sylvia preferred to love at a distance. There were a few notable exceptions, but usually the focus of her passion was oblivious to the intensity of her feelings.

Despite their ephemeral nature, her love affairs were, to Sylvia, profoundly deep and reciprocal. They had to be; she desperately needed to be

---

*In her old age Sylvia claimed to have modelled her delivery, not on the Queen's English, but on the style of English spoken by the Archbishop of Canterbury.

loved. As her alter ego Germaine expressed it in *Incense To Idols*:

> I might have been a good girl had I had a Mummie to love me; or even
> a Daddy to love me. But I've got to get other men to love me. I can't
> get women to love me; goodness knows why. . . . Illustration of a girl
> in search of parents. Pathetic, n'est-ce pas?

Her need to be loved was matched only by her need to love. Again, it
was a matter of emotional survival. The euphoria of falling in love pushed
back the depression that licked around the edges of her consciousness.
Compared to the bromide she continued to take regularly, and the beer
she drank on Saturday nights, love was a far superior antidepressant.
And the upheaval of falling in love provided the psychological shake-up
Sylvia needed to regroup the energies of her fragmented self. Whenever she
was in love her learning, and her creative output, were immeasurably
enhanced.

Having her love reciprocated while hiding her own feelings was a
problem. Direct acknowledgement by either party was out; it had to be
something more subtle. A gesture, a glance, a touch, an interest in her
work, a kind comment about her music, anything would do to prove that
she was loved and to inflame her own passion.

From all the men and women she loved, Sylvia sought attention and
admiration, but she was particularly anxious to be admired by men; they
controlled the status heap. If she could make men worship at her feet, then
everyone would see that she belonged at the top. So partly for this reason,
and partly because she just couldn't help it, Sylvia flirted compulsively
with men all her life. The poet Louis Johnson recalled his meetings with
her in the 1960s:

> She was a person who could make you — as a lone male talking to her
> — feel uncomfortable, in that you felt that there was a sexual connotation
> to everything that went on. . . . Yet what she really seemed to want
> wasn't love, but a tribute.[9]

In her love affairs with women Sylvia had a powerful need to be mothered,
but that was only the beginning. Buried hurts from the past, her present
weaknesses, her ideal self, every trait that she could not face directly in herself was projected onto her loved one. Falling in love with a woman meant
for Sylvia the explosive recognition of both the painfully unacceptable and
the impossibly idealised parts of herself in the other, and a desperate
craving to possess the other in order to make herself whole.

Dr Allen's deposing of Mama from the ideal-mother role she had played
in Sylvia's imagination since Papa's death had allowed Sylvia's old infatuation with spinsters to bloom again. It was almost inevitable that she should
fall in love with the district nurse.

By a curious quirk of fate the nurse turned out to be one of the two
sisters Sylvia had shunned as pariahs at Wairarapa High; the girl she
called 'Marie' in her autobiography, and 'Jean Humphries' in *Myself* — a
published diary of her Pipiriki years. After six months Jean was transferred

to Ekatahuna.* Nonetheless their short relationship made a lasting impact on Sylvia.

At first Sylvia was aloof and distant. Jean thought she recognised her — those beautiful ice-blue eyes — but it was several weeks before Sylvia admitted her true identity. As Jean remembers it, they became good friends and saw quite a lot of each other. 'She was very fond of poetry. She used to come over to my place a lot and we'd read poetry to each other. And I often went over to Sylvia's to attend to the children.' What Jean didn't know was that Sylvia had fallen in love. Sylvia wrote a series of unposted letters to Dr Allen about her feelings, and about how she made her eyes 'steady and welcoming' and applied 'the knowledge of listening that I had learnt from you' in order to win Jean's affection and admiration.

One evening, when Sylvia dropped in unannounced, Jean was on her way to visit the Templetons at the store. "Would you like to come too?' she suggested. But the friendly gesture failed to excuse what to Sylvia was outright rejection. She spent the evening weeping bitterly and plotting revenge. She'd do something absolutely vicious to Jean, she'd really hurt her. . . . She arranged to accompany Jean on her next trip to Wanganui; when the day came she changed her mind and didn't go. (Oh sweet revenge! That'll fix Jean Humphries! The bewilderment she must feel! The crushing disappointment!) The awful part was that Jean hardly seemed to notice. She returned as poised as ever the next day, with flowers. Sylvia noted in her diary:

> August. . . . Jean sent, but did not bring, some Iceland poppies from town. Had she brought them herself I would have forgotten everything of the disharmony between us, but they still looked lovely. . . . They pull the wild eye outward from the tumult within to softly revive the vision.[10]

By 10 August it was all over for Sylvia:

> I put Jean Humphries' Iceland poppies which were wilting . . . I put them in the fire — the flowers she had not brought up herself, that had come by a strange hand, that had carried no written message — and tipped out the used water. Through the quiet kitchen it diffused a smell of death . . . the death of love and friendship.[11]

The possibility of handling her friendships differently does not seem to have occurred to Sylvia; her decision was to avoid such relationships completely in future.

Jean first encountered Sylvia's version of these events in her old age. She was more than a little puzzled:

> Disharmony between us? I didn't notice it. . . . Sometimes I couldn't understand her but that didn't worry me. . . . I knew she was highly strung. . . . She seemed to take things seriously that went right over my head. . . .[12]

---

*In *Myself* Sylvia said that Jean enlisted in the army and went to war — a much better story.

The intensity of Sylvia's needs ensured that avoiding love outside the
family was not a realistic option. She fell next for young Mr Steele, the district officer of health from Wanganui, who came in early October, 1941,
to study tuberculosis among the Maori. He stayed only briefly, but when,
twenty-six years later, he read in *Myself* of Sylvia's three-year affair with
a young doctor he recognised himself and wrote her one very circumspect
letter.

The next district nurse was Joy Alley. It was she, not Mr Steele, who
stayed three years and became a key person in Sylvia's life.

Joy was the youngest of seven children. In many ways her family was
the antithesis of the Warners; the Alleys were outward-looking achievers
who believed in the Protestant work ethic, in service to others and in the
worth of the common people. Pipiriki was Joy's first district nursing post
and, after living most of her life in Christchurch, it was her first significant
contact with Maori. She was thirty-three years old and full of missionary
zeal. The successful Alley family and their egalitarian philosophy was both
a threat and a challenge to Sylvia. She admired Joy's wide knowledge of
philosophy, politics and the arts, and Joy in turn was fascinated by Sylvia's
creativity, passion, introspection and reckless unconformity.

Sylvia's impressions of the relationship were recorded in a diary she kept
at the time. When she revised it for publication in 1967 as *Myself*, she
changed Joy to the fictional 'Dr Saul Mada', and she presented the same
relationship in her autobiography as a stormy friendship with a nurse
named 'Opal Owen'. Joy's impressions were recorded in poetry and discussion notes at the time, and in recollections forty years later.

They first met when Joy made a professional visit to Sylvia, who was
ill with jaundice.

> November 12. . . . He [She] nursed me through the 'yellow peril' with
> a thoroughness and gentleness that equalled Jean's when I had grown-up
> mumps and that . . . stirred in me the old desirous secrets on the theme
> of mothering that has been imbedded in me ever since the Coast.[13]

Sylvia made a predictably doomed effort not to fall in love, and the emotional intimacy that grew between them was unprecedented in both their
lives. It created the conditions whereby the powerful forces of Sylvia's
undermind could break out and run wild. Her multiple selves whirled
through Joy's life like a tornado: she was a young child — demanding and
possessive, staging spectacular tantrums when thwarted; she was an
unloved older child — accusing, bitter, vindictive and withdrawn; she was
a self-appointed psychotherapist, confidently identifying flaws in Joy's
character and setting out to correct them; she was a dedicated student,
reading widely and puzzling over philosophy, psychology and literature;
she was an inspired artist of words, paint and music; she was a committed
teacher who spent most of every Sunday preparing lessons; she was a
loving friend.

With her passion for Joy engulfing her, Sylvia more than ever needed time and space to herself. During the summer holidays at the end of 1941 she discovered a deserted whare in a clearing, a short distance up the road to Raetihi:

> On the instant I went mad on the place. I saw it for what it was: a place of silence and peace for me — no voices, no banging doors, no pace, no rivalling passions face to face and no war either. 'I could have this place,' to the children, 'to study in and learn to write.'[14]

About a year earlier, two young lovers had committed suicide there. No Maori would go near the place for fear of evil spirits; to Sylvia that meant welcome privacy, and some thrilling raw imagery for her romantic imagination. The farmer who leased the whare used the main room for storing farm equipment, but early in 1942 he allowed Sylvia to use the kitchen and bedroom. Sylvia, Keith, Joy and Sylvia's sister Evadne, who was staying at the time, cleaned out the rooms and turned them into a studio. In the bedroom they scrubbed the lovers' blood off the walls; Joy fumigated to kill the fleas; Keith repaired the window and chimney and built a table and bed; and Sylvia wrote on the door in charcoal and lipstick: Selah. Selah was a Hebrew word from the old Testament Psalms which Sylvia understood to mean a pause or rest. In later years she referred to the whare as Selah Two, having retrospectively named her first study, at the back of Mama's Featherston home, Selah One.

Selah was often cold and draughty and, until Keith replaced the fireplace with a little stove, the chimney smoked. In winter Sylvia stayed away for weeks on end, finding peace simply in the knowledge of Selah's existence, but in fine weather she retreated there most days after school and for the whole of at least one day each weekend. She always walked there barefoot, symbolically shedding the trappings of civilisation to become closer to nature, and to herself.

> Rounding these corners, pausing at the waterfalls gazing at them enraptured, following the lazy-morning movements of the birds and heading for my haunted paradise, my personality changes. Off fall the wife, the mother, the lover, the teacher, and the violent artist takes over. I am I alone. I belong to no one but myself.[15]

At Selah she paused to admire new shoots on the cuttings she had planted, collected wood, lit the fire, cleaned up the rat droppings and dreamed of:

> . . . the bedroom done in chintz with pretty curtains blowing the dead away, the kitchen equipped as a study and the big front room as a place of music with floor rugs, wine and piano. Elegant people will come with their hair quietly parted. Terrific conversations plunging through till morning. . . .[16]

The bottle of sherry she kept there, and the few carefully chosen visitors, were symbols of the dream.

When the tidying-up was complete she wrapped herself in an oversized orange cardigan, folded back the sleeves, and settled down to work. Over the early months of 1942 she papered and painted the walls and drew two bright chalk murals: an Egyptian water-carrier captioned 'Moon of My Delight' and:

> . . . a great bird with wide-stretched wings and iridescent feathers, the whole of the colours in its eyes, and caption it 'My soul, there is a country far beyond the stars. . . .' . . . this bird is my hidden spirit.[17]

Then, as a counter to the eroding stress in her life, she printed above the fireplace in charcoal: Nothing Matters.

And when all that was done, she wrote. At first, inspired by Dr Allen, she wrote in a mood of openness and self-scrutiny, but gradually her efforts to relate to the outer world evoked again a compulsion to cover up and pose, and her absorption with her beloved turned the spotlight of self-analysis onto that much more comfortable target, Joy.

During her first summer at Pipiriki, Sylvia also accomplished a major art project at school: she drew a bright chalk mural of the Pied Piper of Hamelin high on the back wall of her classroom. Here again is the artist repeating herself, for she drew the same picture at Horoera, and she would draw it again at Waiomatatini and at Fernhill. For the Pied Piper was more than just a story: the colourful musician, the loner, the rejected artist, his revenge, his enchantment of children, the cripple, love as a destructive force — to Sylvia, the Pied Piper was a potent metaphor for everything that mattered in her life.

The mural formed a backdrop to class enactments of the Pied Piper story, just one of many European-based cultural activities Sylvia taught at school. And either in spite of, or because of, the foreign culture, such activities were unforgettable. Listen to Rosita Te Hore, who was in Sylvia's infant room:

> I don't remember her telling us stories, but I do remember her dressing us up with coloured gauze wings and teaching us to dance like fairies while she played the piano. And she taught us to use clay — sometimes we made all the characters for nursery rhymes out of modelling clay.[18]

Rosina Ropata, who was in Keith's class, has these memories:

> Mrs Henderson was the most fantastic person I've ever met. Whenever I hear the music from Sleeping Beauty it reminds me of the time she produced Sleeping Beauty at school. All the costumes for the maids and the princess were made of lace-bark; we had to go out and strip off enough bark for all the skirts.[19]

And these are the recollections of Bob Gray, a boy in Keith's class:

> Mrs Henderson taught us choral speaking . . . [He demonstrates an intense dramatic Sylvia, mouthing the words of the Pied Piper and marking the rhythm with eloquent sweeps of her arms.] . . . and that's how she would conduct us, as if she were in front of the symphony

orchestra. We did the Pied Piper so often I can remember it right through to this day.

I played the part of Brer Rabbit in one of her school productions. I had to bunny hop around the playground saying, 'You can roast me, Mr Fox, you can hang me. . . . But DON'T fling me into the briar patch!'

For the fancy-dress ball she made simple Chinese costumes for my brother and me; a piece of cloth draped around, and a flat hat made of cardboard with a bit of wool hanging down the back for a pigtail.

I can't remember doing any Maori stories though, or anything to do with Maori at all. The education we got was strictly Pakeha; very grand, very cultured Pakeha education. Maori education — nothing. I can't even remember singing Maori songs at school.[20]

It was as if in her school drama Sylvia had transcended art, music and writing, and had found in Maori children a brilliant new multimedia form of self-expression. The fact that she deplored the use of material from the European culture in the Education Department's reading books, while promoting it in her own teaching, would have been no contradiction to Sylvia in this context; after all, she was using working material from the native imagery of the child — it's just that in this case the child was herself.

But what about the stories Sylvia told the pupils in *Myself*? The wide-eyed times when her intuitive understanding of children moved outwards from her own child-self to the other five-year-olds in her care, when she took themes from her pupils' lives — the river, the taniwha, grandparents and canoes — and wove them into stories that held her audience spell-bound; why don't the children remember them? Perhaps the stories blended so seamlessly into their lives that they were forgotten. It's also possible that Sylvia did not tell such stories very often; indeed, the evidence from Pipiriki suggests that the classroom activities she highlighted in her writing were not the activities she emphasised in class, but the rare furtive activities that challenged her imagination and defied the Inspector. (This omnipotent being was not a real person but a monster from Sylvia's under-mind; welded from the most fearsome qualities of Mama, God, and the inspectors of her childhood, he clung to her shoulders and tightened the grip of guilt around her throat whenever she defied him.) So monocultural was Sylvia's understanding of what was respectable that the time she spent on Pakeha dramatic productions, at the expense of the curriculum basics, appears to have caused the Inspector no disquiet at all, while using Maori material for stories angered him, and evoked in Sylvia a thrilling sense of defiance — an emotion that at this time in her life sustained her writing, but inhibited her teaching.

The Inspector was also angered by her drive for creative self-expression, by the way she often impulsively ran away from school, leaving Keith in charge, while she wrote and painted in Selah, or simply wandered the riverbanks in search of a perfect autumn leaf. But even the running away led back to her Maori pupils and she began to take them, and guilt, with her when she escaped. They roamed the hills together and while Sylvia sat and read, the children played with frogs. In the classroom she worked on her clay creations and they worked on theirs:

> We slither into free occupation from plasticene and clay down to dreaming. . . . In my more offbeat thinking I suspect that with the dreaming ingredients of the mind worked off first, the labouring intellect would be clearer for practical application. . . . A teacher could be dismissed for such outlawry. . . . Get thee, Oh get thee behind me, Satan.[21]

Overriding Sylvia's guilt-tinged excitement was a fascination with the absorbing peacefulness of the room when she and the children were free to create: 'What happened to our common violence threatening from the undermind? Perhaps it was escaping by some other route.'

When Sylvia explored, through her writing in Selah, her classroom use of Maori children's creativity and of their own life experiences in her stories, she found more than just the thrill of defiance; here was the sizzling fuse on a charge of personal and educational dynamite: rapport with others on their own terms and in their own inner territory. For once in her life she could forget herself and in doing so, experience true communication with others. In an explosion of understanding Sylvia both lost and found herself in the inner lives of Maori children. But the Inspector disapproved, and his human manifestations were now much closer, a mere car journey away. Worse still, the enlightened Mr Ball had joined the army and most of the remaining inspectors were rigid, petty and unimaginative.

Fear of an unexpected inspector's visit not only inhibited Sylvia's classroom art and Maori story-telling. It drove her to abandon her Horoera innovation of reading cards with local English and Maori words, and it prompted Keith, who had tolerated the use of Maori in the playground at Horoera, to punish children for speaking Maori at school. The offending child had to stand in the corner, or go without a cup of cocoa at morning playtime. The strap was kept for more serious misdemeanors.

Inevitably inspections occurred. Mr Woodley came in 1941 and 1942, and issued favourable reports. Mr Fletcher and Mr Parsonage came in 1943 and 1944. They approved of Keith's work with the senior pupils, but were unimpressed with Sylvia's efforts:

> In the Primer division no schemes or workbook were presented. These must be prepared and presented next year. The timetable is also inadequate, and there should be a proper planning of the week's activities. Reading certainly needs a greater allocation of time.[22]

Each year at Pipiriki, as had been the case at Horoera, the inspectors gave Keith excellent gradings, while Sylvia's were never better than average.

Outside school hours Sylvia immersed herself in Maori culture. The local people held her in considerable awe; she was always beautifully groomed and lived life in a grand and dramatic way. She became a fluent Maori speaker and enjoyed animated conversations with old people who spoke no

English at all. She addressed gatherings of school parents in Maori and even defied Ati Hau Nui, a Paparangi tribal etiquette — which allowed only male speakers on formal occasions — by speaking on the marae. She also studied Maori art and crafts: she soaked flax in mud and made her own piupiu; she kept an outside fire going for days under a big iron pot to make Maori peanuts from karaka berries; she ate lamprey eels and pork bones with puha; she learnt to dry whitebait in summer and to preserve meat in fat; she even drank Mai's home-brew. And all the while she pondered on the relevance of the school curriculum to the Maori way of life.

One of the truths underlying the problem crystallised the day Ihaka started school. Dear little Ihaka, who sang so enthusiastically, lost inside his brand-new oversized clothes; at reading time Sylvia introduced him to the picture of a train and the word itself, and invited him to write it on the blackboard:

> . . . 'I can write train,' and the next thing he has written quite a good word except that it is not 'train'. What is this word? I look closer. It is 'canoe'. Then he forgets all about me and draws a canoe with the family sitting in it. . . . On account of Ihaka I got nearer to something this morning, a stubborn secret, about the inside and the outside of a child related or unrelated in his reading. But I don't know the secret and it's not in a book.[23]

Years later the secret revealed itself a little more and Sylvia threw herself into making hundreds of hand-printed, hand-illustrated Maori infant reading books, many of them featuring adventures in the life of a little boy named Ihaka. Nearly three decades later, on the eve of her departure overseas after twenty years of battles and crushing disappointments because her little books had not been published, Sylvia returned in secret to Pipiriki. One of the men from the village noticed a stranger at the old school and went to investigate. He found an elderly lady standing at the top of the school steps, stroking the door jamb and weeping quietly. He didn't know who she was, but she recognised him immediately: her little Ihaka.

There were many weekends when Keith insisted that Sylvia spend not one, but two whole days at Selah. She suspected that despite this apparent generosity, he resented her absences. The possibility that frequent breaks from his emotional and unpredictable wife may have been necessary for Keith's mental survival does not seem to have occurred to her, though this Saturday morning scene from her diary suggests that may have been the case:

> As I set off along the path from home, the children weeping behind, I too cried, but too pathetically I think, far too audibly, hoping to unmask K, but got the wrong result. Almost in tears himself he hurried after me, 'I send you off and you start this crying.'
> 'It's just that I love you all.'
> 'This won't do. You go to your work.'

'I haven't been sleeping lately.'

'It isn't fair for you to go on like this. Every Saturday. After all I do to help you and to get you off, even to offering you the whole weekend. Now you go and do your work.'

He turned on a furious heel.[24]

Forty years later Elliot recalled the pressure his father was under:

My mother wasn't home much, but when she was there she was a cosmic force that dominated in a way that no one dared to question: the importance of her feelings, of her emotional life, was paramount; if she was happy or angry or whatever, that was all that mattered at that particular moment. It was impossible to combat. My father tried for a while but it was exhausting — if Mum was ever thwarted there was a noble outrage. Dad gave up eventually and let it all flow over him, but I can remember great rows at Pipiriki and for several years after that. . . .[25]

The war in the Pacific raged during the Hendersons' four years at Pipiriki. At one stage Keith was faced with conscription into the army, but a national shortage of school teachers kept him at home. He served instead with the Pipiriki Home Guard, and attended home guard camp every summer.

The search for refuge from the threat of Japanese invasion brought a succession of Warners to Pipiriki: Daphne and her son; Lionel, his wife and two sons; Evadne and her baby; and Mama. There was also a Henderson visitor, Keith's mother. The guests were invariably shocked by Sylvia's neglect of her husband and children, and by the load of family care Keith was left to carry. But apart from some skirmishes with Keith's rigidly puritanical mother, whom Sylvia referred to as 'the She-Christian', Sylvia was too engrossed in her own life to notice their reactions. She also ignored Dr Allen's lessons on this subject ('The man must dominate . . . put your husband first. . . .'), and Joy was the only one who could reach her:

. . . she speaks words that upset me about her days being quite as full as mine and that other people besides me have a right to their lives, and I reply that art claims prior right before everything, before everyone, that it *is* everything, the speech of life. . . .[26]

Joy also had guests: visiting dental nurses, her sister Gwen, and Sophie Rhodes. Sylvia not only fell in love with the vivacious Sophie, she saw in Sophie's husband, Winston Rhodes, Professor of English at Canterbury University College and editor of the *New Zealand Monthly Review*, a potential sponsor for her great literary career. Thereafter Sylvia wrote regularly to Sophie and sent her manuscripts, and was thrilled beyond measure when a few years later she handed Sylvia's fledgling novel *Rangitira* to Winston to read.

Sylvia shared with Joy her programme of study, and her search for an underlying design for her life. They both read widely and, at Sylvia's suggestion, shared passages of personal significance on the topics of truth, religion, liberty, art, music, sex, happiness, sublimation, the Bible, music, sin, fear, work, beauty, time, death, genius, knowledge, education, faith, and sensuality.

It is 12 June, 1943. As they have on almost every Saturday night for the past eighteen months, Sylvia and Joy are spending the evening alone at the nurse's cottage. Sylvia, beautifully groomed and wearing her favourite red blouse, lies in sensuous repose on the mat in front of the wood fire. Joy winds up the gramophone, and as Beethoven crashes in the background they settle down to drinking beer and debating the meaning of life. Tonight they've brought questions to ask each other. Joy, her stately features softened in the firelight, diligently records the questions and answers.

Listen.

Joy: 'In your world of phantasy what role do you take?'
Sylvia: 'Repertory . . . when I'm in it now it's not to play a role but to call on and use the collection there for work. I don't use phantasy for escape now, I harness it.'

There is more here than the good news that Sylvia is bringing her undisciplined dreaming under control; leaping from the pages of Joy's 1943 notebook is a powerful technique for personal survival born of Sylvia's artistic insight. In time she will apply it to other five-year-olds, and years later it will crystallise into her basic teaching formula: *Release the native imagery of our child and use it for working material.*

But listen, the questions continue.

Joy: 'Do you ever feel insincere?'
Sylvia: 'Never to myself, often to others.'
Joy: 'What are your fears?'
Sylvia: . . .

The only time Sylvia faced her fears was in an unposted letter to Dr Allen from Horoera, when she was too weak and frightened to rise from her bed. But life is different now, she is up and about, and with her acting skills covering her nervousness, she is more or less coping. The ogre in her undermind is sleeping off his Horoera rampage and she doesn't want to wake him; her fears remain unnamed.

For the rest of her life Sylvia found her fears both too terrible to face directly and too terrible to ignore. She expressed them in metaphor, through music, art and fiction; during the following decade, as her own psyche began to resonate more powerfully with the inner lives of her Maori pupils, she learnt to caption and defuse her own fears through, and along with, the personal and intimate fears of Maori children.

Back on that Saturday night at Pipiriki, Sylvia's fears, though unspeakable, were never far from her consciousness.

Joy: 'Could you define happiness concisely?'
Sylvia: 'Freedom from fear.'

Now it's Sylvia's turn. Her questions are the sort that an artist and dreamer would ask herself, or in this case the version of herself she has projected onto Joy. Joy is intrigued and puzzled.

Sylvia: 'Do you feel yourself to be an isolated individual whose day will
    soon be over, or do you feel yourself to be part of the stream of life
    flowing from the first germ to the remote and unknown future?'
Joy: 'Up till now I have felt quite an individual.'
Sylvia: 'Does the world that shall come after you concern you?'
Joy: 'No.'
Sylvia: 'To what class do your affections belong — the reciprocally life-
    giving, or the blood-sucking type, which sucks the vitality of the other?'
Joy: 'I think . . . but I don't know.'
Sylvia: 'Can you escape from the prison of the ego sufficiently to enjoy the
    world to the full?'
Joy: . . .
Sylvia: 'The power to produce great art is very often, though not always,
    associated with a temperamental unhappiness so great that but for the
    joy an artist derives from his work he would be driven to suicide. Com-
    ment on this in relation to yourself.'
Joy: 'I can't see any connection here at all. You know I don't belong there.'

Joy was not, and could not be, Sylvia's ideal woman but Sylvia cast her
into the role regardless. At first Joy was thrilled by the attention and admiration, and by the gifts — books, sheet music for the piano, a ring,
paintings — that Sylvia bestowed on her, and she tried very hard to play
the part. For both of them life became a euphoric dream. All that mattered
was that they loved and needed each other. They spent their waking hours
either being together or wishing they were, and on some Saturday nights
they slept together. Both women were convinced of their own heterosex-
uality and they regarded sharing a bed as an innocent giving and receiving
of comfort and reassurance.

Sylvia's creative work flourished. Joy was the inspiration behind the
Pied Piper mural, the clay bust Sylvia did of Joy herself, and the great
stream of sketches and water-colour paintings she produced. Her desire to
live up to what she saw as Joy's high standard of musical appreciation
drove Sylvia to take music lessons in Wanganui, and to practise the piano
assiduously each day; during her Pipiriki years she reached what was probably the peak of her musical accomplishment in mastering the difficult and
showy third movement of Beethoven's 'Moonlight Sonata'. In her diary
entries she began to address Joy rather than Dr Allen. And it was to win
Joy's admiration that she settled down not just to write but also to plan
carefully the characters and development of *Rangitira*, a novel that blended
her newly surfaced childhood with all the passion and posing of her years
on the river.

Gradually the dream turned sour. Joy could not be Sylvia's ideal-
woman/ideal-mother/ideal-self. Nor could she live up to Sylvia's other
contradictory and confusing role expectation, for in the process of dis-
tancing herself from the ogres in her own undermind Sylvia had projected
them onto Joy. She began to see Joy not only as her inadequate self, but
as her most unworthy despised-self as well.

Sylvia's main complaint was that Joy did not love her enough. She tried to win her attention with tantrums. She changed the wording of one of Joy's heartfelt love poems to claim Joy's pain as her own. She set out to itemise Joy's failings, and in doing so to punish and hurt her. And all in the same evening she told Joy:

> . . . you're intellectually lazy and emotionally immature. . . . You're hard, unsympathetic and have limited understanding. . . . You're selfish and inconsiderate. . . . I'm disappointed in you. . . . You don't know what love is, or pain.[27]

By the end of 1943, in the process of tearing herself free from her dependence on Joy, Sylvia was becoming more clearly and defiantly herself:

> I must preserve my individuality and not be influenced by what others do. . . . I must set and maintain my own standard . . . whatever of heart pain the price. . . .
>
> And right now from this moment on this page, I promote myself to first class living whether possible or not, once and for all. Best hotels when I'm away, best trains to get away, no clothes but good ones fashioned for me *and*! . . . no more time than necessary among second class people. . . .
>
> I must be true to myself. Strong enough to be true to myself. Brave enough to be strong enough to be true to myself. Wise enough, to be brave enough, to be strong enough, to be true enough to shape myself from what I actually am. . . . That's how it must be for me to walk steadily in my own ways, as graceful as I feel, as upright as I feel, with a ridiculous flower on the top of my head . . . a sentimental daisy. For therein lies my individuality, my authentic signature, the source of others' love for me.[28]

But in Pipiriki, as always, love was her Achilles heel. By 1944, though she was not prepared to give up Joy, she had resumed her quest for the ideal lover. A passing flirtation with Wingo, the Don Juan of the Wanganui River, was of no significance to either party, though it did cause a flurry of gossip in the village and more than passing anxiety for Keith. Then, at a teachers' refresher course at Ohakune in February 1944, she met Walter Harris, the forty-year-old supervisor of teaching aids for the Education Department and close friend of Dr C. E. Beeby, who had in 1940 become Director of Education. Walter was charming, fey and widely travelled, with a passionate interest in music, drama, art and the opposite sex. As usual Sylvia flirted, and when Walter responded with interest she fell madly in love.

Over their two-and-a-half-year friendship he did no more than kiss her five times; four times in greeting or farewell, and once, after the Hendersons had left Pipiriki, on the beach at Port Awarua. Sylvia treasured every kiss, but forty years later Walter recalled only the one on the beach:

> . . . I do remember the feeling of elation as Sylvia and I who had gone for a walk (I think we began it on horseback) then scampered over the

sandy deserted river flats, sometimes hand in hand. We kissed once, for
the joy of living, for the sunshine, and for the freedom that was ours for
that brief outing. It was quite spontaneous and for me, at any rate, had
no sexual or permanent significance.[29]

From their first meeting Walter became to Sylvia 'the other man' in her life.
Since her dreams required that she fall in love with tall men, she thought
of Walter — as she also thought of Dr Allen — as tall, though in fact both
were short.

At the end of the Ohakune refresher course, and probably prompted by
Sylvia, Keith invited Walter to stay the weekend with them at Pipiriki.
There Sylvia bestowed on him the name Pan.

'I was not sure,' Walter recalled, 'whether she meant Peter Pan, the boy
who never grew up, or the Pan of mythology with his rather mischievous
love of life and music. In either case I simply accepted the compliment.'

Sylvia took him to Selah, and showed him her Pied Piper mural at
school:

It showed talent and imagination and was meaningful to the children:
each was there following the Pied Piper. I offered her a commission to
do a series of pictures of uniform size with captions, for a filmstrip, but
she refused. I got the impression she felt that there was too much discipline in her life already and that a filmstrip for the Department would
be an extra shackle.[30]

It is also possible that the idea of being officially approved of did not sit
comfortably with the secret delight she felt in being an outlaw of a teacher.

That Saturday evening was not a particularly memorable one for Walter
— he recalled gramophone music and light piano playing — but for Sylvia
it was unforgettable; she played 'Night and Day' and Walter sang 'Who is
Sylvia?'

. . . I feel there is a great deal of hot feeling banking up in the evening,
cross currents of emotion discreetly unspoken, most of it flooding love,
and the hot juices of passion interflowing that lubricate the works,
inspire ideas and fertilise blind action; fuel for great things. Here is the
stranger from afar, the right-hand man of the director general of education cohabiting in our home, with the strength to see me as I am, the
molten inside me, approving of and loving what he sees, almost adoring
me for it, from no performance on my part; which is surcease from trying
to win it from my sole audience Opal [Joy].[31]

By the next morning Sylvia's old anxieties over whether Joy loved her, or
loved her enough, resurfaced. She cast Walter aside and spent the day
quarrelling with Joy.

On Sunday, rather to my surprise I was paired off with the comely young
dental nurse and sent swimming, while Sylvia with, I think, Joy went for
a walk up the river. I'd rather have spent the afternoon with the more
interesting Sylvia, though the girl and I enjoyed plastering each other
with the fine papa mud and posing as statues.[32]

Walter left by bus the next morning:

> . . . he takes his leave of the others first then comes to me last, and kisses me in front of the Templetons, the tourists, the Maoris, the fowls, dogs and children, and on the mouth for all to see; his big blue eyes steady behind the large glasses and his full gentle lips on mine telling me how wasteful that paired walk had indeed been in the twilight of the noon forest.[33]

A few weeks after that visit Sylvia lost her precious Selah when the landowner reclaimed it for his own use. Her next Selah was in a clay bank among trees down the back of the nurse's cottage. Keith dug a cave, added outer walls of ponga logs, and topped the whole structure with an iron roof. Sylvia, Joy and Keith cut a fireplace into the clay, and while Keith and Joy dug a chimney down from the surface, Sylvia carved the clay into an imitation brick fire-surround complete with mantelpiece and bookshelves. When furnished with an armchair and small table, and sacks on the clay floor, her new Selah was complete.

While Sylvia found peace in Selah, Joy's needs were left unmet. Late in the winter of 1944, and under the cumulative effects of stress, exhaustion, and the toxic drug she was taking for a severe throat infection, Joy collapsed. At first she was hospitalised in Wanganui but Sylvia found the separation unbearable; after two weeks she went to Wanganui and brought Joy back to the Henderson home at Pipiriki. The doctor from Raetihi then stepped in and took Joy into his own home, but he was no match for the determined Sylvia; within days the whole Henderson family arrived on his doorstep and took Joy back with them to Pipiriki.

For two months Joy lay convalescing on the Hendersons' porch. Towards the end of 1944 both Joy and the Hendersons applied for transfers. As Sylvia observed in her autobiography, 'You never want to stay too long in a place, even Pipiriki. You use up the people.'

NINE

Waiomatatini

A flat riverbed of stones only lightly soiled over so that the grass was dried to whiteness. A scattering of black tree-manuka on the bleached grass gave the scene the blenched face of a nightmare when the artery of love is severed.[1]

WAIOMATATINI WAS THE MARAE OF THE GREAT NGATI POROU scholar and politician Sir Apirana Ngata. At the fine new school there were over a hundred Maori pupils, two Maori teachers and a junior assistant to help the infant mistress. But Sylvia was too unhappy to care.

Losing Joy was the worst part. Without Joy, anywhere they lived was the setting for a nightmare, but thanks to Keith's dedication to the Native Service, they were still among Maori and back in the area of her break-down — on the East Coast, only forty miles from Horoera.

Sylvia's distress was eased by a brief visit from Walter Harris soon after she arrived in Waiomatatini, and a short stay with the Harrises in Wellington towards the end of the year, but for the rest of 1945 she was overwhelmed with grief:

> The loss of Opal [Joy] I couldn't stand, even though we intervisited and tried to write letters; all the ideal girls since childhood embodied in one, the woman I'd sought and had found at last and her face was turned from me. It was no longer wonderful to her, or first with her since she'd fallen in love on VJ Day with a romantic young man. All she wanted from me now was ordinary dry friendship, not inspiration or love or anything vital. The agony of the ousted child was beyond definition.[2]

In her diary Sylvia reproached Joy with the story of Naomi and Ruth ('whither thou goest, I will go'), and wrote of her black night of the soul:

> My love. Now the tear dogs are up again. I didn't go to school today. I told Keith I wanted to be excused for another week. I haven't been to school at all since that letter I burnt — I haven't sorted myself out.[3]

When she finally dragged herself to school she set about disciplining the sixty children in the infant room. She taught them, as she had done at Pipiriki, a set of musical commands from the piano; the first eight notes of Beethoven's *Fifth Symphony* told them to stop what they were doing and look at her, and there were other phrases from the classics meaning 'sit on the mat', 'tidy up', 'dance', 'line up', 'march out' and so on. The children's obedience avoided the need for Sylvia to raise her voice, and provided an impressive theatrical performance for visitors.

Her means of obtaining obedience was less impressive; in her unhappiness she had fallen back on Mama's approach to discipline. She had a stick — the thickness of a blackboard duster and the length of two rulers — and any child who failed to respond immediately to the piano was whacked around the thighs and buttocks. Eventually, under pressure from angry parents, Sylvia replaced her stick with a ruler, or occasionally with a strap, and was more restrained in the use of both.

She was careful to hide her violence from Linda, her junior assistant. She noted in *Myself* that discipline was meted out:

> . . . with Hiki [Linda] out of the room of course, training her as I am that neither hand nor voice may be raised in this infant room, certainly not in rage, whenever working with children. There's no need for her to know that I'm not a real teacher but rather a lunatic with wings.

In a pattern Sylvia was to follow with all her junior assistants she familiarised Linda with her role not by giving directions but by instructing her to observe the classroom at work. Then, after one day's demonstration during which she often spoke so quietly that Linda couldn't hear what she was saying, she told Linda to take over.

Linda soon became more a substitute than an assistant. She taught the core subjects while Sylvia concentrated on art, music, drama, story-telling, nature walks and dance. She covered when Sylvia arrived late or left early, and taught all day when Sylvia didn't appear at all.

Most unnerving were the occasions when Sylvia, absorbed in her own misery, would drift in while Linda was teaching and either whisk the class off for a walk or strike up the tune that signalled 'jump and dance'. The room would erupt with excited, whirling children. When the point of maximum pandemonium was reached, Sylvia would simply drift out again — her Beethoven chords, which could have restored order in seconds, conveniently overlooked.

The one session Sylvia rarely missed was morning-talk time, when the children shared their personal news with the class. She always listened intently and not only tolerated, but to Linda's astonishment even encouraged, the revelation of intimate home secrets.

Sometimes Sylvia was both there and not there, physically present but away in a world of her own — reading, or more often, writing:

> She was always writing things. She'd give the children something to do, or just let them run riot around the room, and she'd have her pad out and be writing while the racket just flowed over her head.[4]

Later in the year when Linda was given a class of her own to teach, Sylvia continued to call on her:

> I'd be teaching and some little child would come along with a message from Mrs Henderson: 'Would you come and teach my class arithmetic?'

So I'd set my class some work and away I'd go to take the infants while she tooted off to her sod hut or wherever.[5]

The iron-roofed sod hut was Sylvia's Waiomatatini Selah, a vital resting place as she walked in unsteady grief along the borderline between sanity and madness. This Selah, built by Keith, Sylvia and the older schoolboys a short distance from the school residence and in full view of the whole community, became a focus of observation and speculation in the village. The Ngati Porou called it 'whare porangi' — the mad house.

Early in 1946 a miracle occurred. The *New Zealand Listener* published a short story with a Biblical title that spoke of alienation and longing: *How Shall We Sing the Lord's Song*. From that irresistible beginning flowed a tale of spiritual union; a union that after a decade of separation was triumphantly mended. The author was Barbara Dent.

> Waiomatatini
> Ruatoria
> East Coast
> 22 January
>
> Dear Barbara Dent,
> Here is my first fan letter. Not the first I wanted to write . . . but the first I have been bold enough to write . . . because I recognised your mind at once . . .
>   Your story in the Listener Barbara Dent was *lovely*. (Not that I haven't got more spectacular tributes than 'lovely' — but I'm not writing a clever letter . . .) I was shocked. It was *good*. It was more than good. I wanted to write to the author at once. I got my pad out and had the first page written before I found my pen . . .
>   I have put in my small mental list headed 'my own kind', Barbara Dent. And I don't know one thing about her other than that she wrote a story for the Listener and that she understands about singing the Lord's song in a strange land and that she realises, and *must* have experienced from the temper of her story, spiritual union . . .
>
> Please write to me.
> Sylvia Henderson

An intimate correspondence quickly developed. For Sylvia it meant '. . . a *tremendous* door suddenly swung open. It meant I only had to pick up a pen to touch my own kind.' They were both searching for meaning, truth and wholeness, and finding a companion on that lonely journey was a heady discovery. Even in the private terrors of their separate lives they found common ground:

> The waking in horror is what I often have — I even have a name for it, 'Hell-time'. It must be constitutional? No! The payment for being in a world made for the insensitive. The feeling of not belonging — cut off

from the herd. Basically speaking. I've often tried to get to the bottom
of this. Psychiatrists would say 'anxiety — sex etc' but I don't think so.
It's something deeper. For instance I don't think you would wake like
that if you lived in Montmartre in Paris. There'd be the *natural comfort* of
being with others like you.[6]

Sylvia's personal journey travelled through an examination of her life and
past. As she had explained to Dr Allen:

> I am writing to you between the covers of a book . . . [in order to] lay
> bare the idiosyncrasies and strange frustrated brilliancies of my family,
> protected though they will be by fictitious names and my own
> anonymity, for in no other way it seems can I carry out my endeavour
> to illustrate the influence of environment on my personal destiny. I shall
> try to write the exact truth about myself and others since this letter
> would be valueless otherwise. . . .[7]

Sylvia was shocked to discover that Barbara was travelling on a different
path; she was only twenty-six years old and the decade of separation in her
Listener story was more a product of imagination than of experience.

Sylvia soon began to capitalise on the eleven-year age gap. She was not
only older, her letters implied, but wiser, more experienced and more
learned than the youthful Barbara.

She paraded the authors, poets and composers she had studied: Olive
Shreiner, Virginia Woolf, Bertrand Russell, Walter Lipmann, Katherine
Mansfield, Gerard Manley Hopkins, Mary Coleridge, Beethoven, Mozart.
She also affected the pose of a sexually experienced and uninhibited
woman:

> . . . I hope you don't hope that we shall meet some day — I couldn't —
> having written these things to you that I have heretofore only whispered
> in the back of someone's neck at dawn — gasped with the weight of a
> heavy body upon me. I couldn't meet now — you see. There was an
> afternoon six or seven weeks ago that was raining heavily and found the
> other saying to me, This is rapture. Are you with me. I said yes. I said,
> Now I know all the answers, now I know why I am here. I'll never ask
> again why I am here. The other said, You can kill me now. I said, Now
> I'm pregnant. So you can see that it will be just letters with us — because
> I am *using* you (does that hurt too much?) to say these things to. I want
> to tell you. I want to say them — see them written. . . .[8]

As her later letters would indicate, these confessions must have been a blend
of her experience with Keith, Joy, and the men in her fantasies. No wonder
they couldn't meet; through letters Sylvia could hide her insecure self and
avoid the sort of relationship that at Pipiriki had brought fantasy and
reality into painful head-on collision. To further protect herself she stated
from the outset that the relationship would last only a short time; her
response to the loss of Joy had been to make impermanence part of her
great design of life:

You say, why a *short* time? Because being an artist at core I see things as

a whole and most deliberately look for an end where I see a beginning,
being what I call perspective. And being a musician also at core I live on
a wave of rhythm — off on, up down, birth and death, the latter being
the grand rhythm of life.[9]

As the correspondence progressed, Sylvia came to see Barbara not only as
an understanding fellow artist, but also as a projection of herself in whom
she could confront the unfinished business in her own psyche. She
demanded that Barbara confide in her, and urged her to write about her
childhood. Then she airily proceeded to analyse her character. She con-
cluced that Barbara was emotionally immature, sexually unfulfilled and
afflicted with a multitude of unresolved neuroses.

As well as analysing herself in Barbara, Sylvia wrote of her philosophy,
and brought into focus her explorations of who she was and what she truly
believed:

> Yes I believe in spiritual union, in a union not necessarily everlasting —
> but one long enough to conceive. . . . I have experienced [spiritual union]
> in varying degrees of rapture and agony and have conceived many times.
> But then I am polygamous at heart and at spirit.[10]

A polygamous nature was suggested to Sylvia by Dr Allen as an explanation for her craving for many men. It was a concept that appealed to Sylvia
enormously and she used it to account for her longing for union not only
with men, but with women and children too. As she explained to Barbara,
the physical component, the sex act itself, was not necessary for the
spiritual development that arose from the fusion of two people.

The union she sought was not an end in itself but an essential precondition
for her art:

> . . . my inspiration to live and do comes through them [other people] to
> me. I don't over-rate them . . . by saying that my inspiration comes *from*
> them! It doesn't. It comes *through them* [from the] unknowable places
> where real things come from. The core place where Schnabel says music
> comes from to the composer, where Mozart lifted his music neat and
> ready-made from . . . . I don't seem to be able to get it from there myself
> — but when I belong to someone in a significant way I feel it leap-
> ing. . . . I couldn't *do* anything unless it is because of somebody or for
> somebody. Less and less *for* somebody — as I grow older — more and
> more *because* of somebody.[11]

Her ephemeral relationships were full of uncertainty, but in a philosophy
born of bitter experience she embraced insecurity as the fuel of inspiration:

> I don't practise honesty strictly. It's so secure. And security is such an
> enemy — it clogs. Security in a friend, security in love — It clogs. It's
> the insecurity of questionable honesty, of love, that prods, spurs to
> action, stimulates.[12]

Sylvia wrote to Barbara two or three times a week, sometimes two or three
times a day, but she never forgot Joy. In an early letter she made a frantic
bid to draw Joy back into her orbit:

Candlelight. Selah. Monday. Barbara. I'm sending you an envelope addressed to a personality I know. I have a favour to ask . . . to write to Joy. Never mind these superficial why's who's what–shall–I–say — just write to Joy. . . . I want you to write to Joy — *now* — tonight. . . .

Friday. I have opened the letter up again to get you to write to Joy straight away. It's the one thing I ask of you. . . . Please wire me when you have written. This means much to me . . . you will do this for me won't you.[13]

Barbara and Joy did eventually meet but, though Sylvia's relationship with Joy dragged on through letters and occasional visits for almost another decade, Sylvia's goal of winning back Joy's devotion was never realised.

Sylvia was happier for having found Barbara, but she continued to spend most of her time in Selah and her teaching showed little improvement.

Her irregular school attendance was no longer just an issue between Sylvia and Keith; now there were other teachers to consider. The school was overcrowded and understaffed, and there was Sylvia drawing a full salary and hardly even turning up. Worse still, when she did appear — usually in the middle of a teaching period — she was likely to do something infuriating like ordering one of the teachers to bring her a fresh cup of tea. Yet so great was the staff's respect and affection for Keith, and so great was his capacity for repairing the damage Sylvia left in her wake, that the school continued to run smoothly. On the few occasions the other teachers complained, Keith simply counselled them to be tolerant and understanding; no one can remember him ever apologising for his wife, or reprimanding her or trying to persuade her to change her ways.

The issue of Sylvia's erratic attendance eventually came before the school committee and there was talk of seeking her dismissal. Keith was desperately worried. He delegated to Des, a close friend who was teaching in nearby Ruatoria, the task of warning Sylvia and urging her to reform her behaviour. Sylvia listened solemnly. Rather than responding with the anger Des had expected, she affected an air of sudden inspiration. 'You're so right!' she exclaimed delightedly, 'I shall turn over a new leaf!'

It was also to Des that Keith confided his belief that Sylvia was a genius, and that his role in life was to take care of her and allow her to develop. Much as he liked his other colleagues on the Coast, Keith knew better than to share such confidences with them; when it came to talking about Sylvia, their astonishment, their outrage and their grudging admiration totally overshadowed any sense of loyalty or discretion. They had never known anyone like her, and as she began to emerge from her grief she regularly accompanied Keith to the monthly teachers' meetings held at different schools around the district.

The meetings brought Sylvia face to face with her paralysing fear of strangers. She explained to Barbara:

I do suffer from the proximity of people. I suffer unendurably and get

out the pig iron to batter away the pain of it . . . my instrument [is] a pair
of heavy boots, iron shod, that stumble and smash with the feet of a
person — a lunatic I mean — who is blind with the pain of proximity.
Barbara I do suffer, suffer from the proximity of people. I can only stand
the touch of God and a lover [and — she inserted as an after thought —
children and husband] and the sound of them. The sound of other people
is worse I think than their presence. Sounds hit me on the body. Sometimes they are rough blows but mostly they are tearing claws down the
middle of my body. . . . Soundlessness — my peace is made in hours by
it. At Selah this morning there is just the wind round the walls that I
made, and the lark. It's a loving tender sound. Tender loving. I wish I
could live all by myself for the rest of my life. I've never told anyone my
endless suffering from sound and proximity. Only someone as raw edged
as yourself would know what I am talking about.[14]

Acquaintances confirm that unwanted social encounters literally petrified
Sylvia. She sat through such ordeals in trance-like rigidity, totally unrespon-
sive to the conversation and activity around her. But pulling against her need
for solitude was her need for love, admiration and intellectual stimulation.
She noted in her diary:

> I used up all my friends last year, and the year before that, on account
> of talking about my soul too much. But now that I've surfaced somewhat
> I could do with a friend or two. . . . Not that my using some of them
> up was not a very good thing. Some people are scrap material. However
> no-one writes, comes, or rings.[15]

The main attraction at teachers' meetings was the company of John and
Lesley Shaw, a couple remembered by the Henderson children as being
'vaguely bohemian' — which meant that unlike most of their colleagues
they were interesting, widely read and open-minded. After Saturday
meetings the Hendersons often stayed with the Shaws for the weekend.

Particularly memorable was the weekend John Shaw laid new concrete
steps. At the end of a Saturday night of philosophy, beer and music, he
reminded his guests to keep off the fresh concrete. Then, because the house
was overflowing with visitors, he went to bed on the porch. When he
woke at sunrise to see Sylvia flouncing nonchalantly down his newly laid
steps, his bellowed protest would have made a lesser mortal cower. Sylvia
simply stopped, turned slowly, and paused for dramatic effect before
delivering her verdict. 'John,' she declared regally, 'your steps are of no
cosmic importance.'

Such grand gestures became one of Sylvia's hallmarks. She needed to act
to conceal her fear of people; not being one for half-measures, she produced
some of the most astonishing performances her colleagues had ever seen.
One teacher recalled:

> I found her fascinating and often infuriating as a seemingly blatant poseur,
> which she undoubtedly would have revelled in had she known. Now I
> think she did know, and *loved* it!

How much of the outward image she so cleverly created was really the expression of a simple and sincere poetic self, and how much a deliberate tongue-in-cheek challenge to the smug and limited values of her teaching colleagues? I dare say we shall never know.

One such challenge I well remember and have often chuckled over with friends. The occasion was a gathering of East Coast primary teachers on a Saturday at my school. While the families played in the school grounds and large billies for tea boiled on an outside fire, inside we were deep in debate on some aspect of teacher grading for our Educational Institute remits.

Suddenly our eyes were riveted on the doorway. There appeared Sylvia: wide-brim-hatted, and wearing a pencil-slim skirt accentuated by a bright yellow cumberbund. She held aloft a huge bunch of buttercups just wrenched muddy and dripping from the stream bed and declaimed, 'I am filled with the pregnancy of Spring!'

For a moment there was utter dumbfounded silence — then she disappeared. You can imagine the ensuing laughter and some of the salty comments, but they were quickly hushed out of respect for Keith who was present with us.[16]

A yellow cumberbund to match the yellow buttercups — at a time in her life when Sylvia dressed almost exclusively in black, white and red, this colour choice reveals the planning that must have preceded this apparently spontaneous drama.

Colour played a central part in many of her performances, like the time she invited a teaching couple from Ruatoria in for a cup of tea. She brought out a beautiful turquoise tea set and a sponge cake with matching turquoise icing. 'Don't eat any of that,' she warned her guests. 'It's coloured with tempera!'

At least they were expecting no more than tea. For the unsuspecting visitors who arrived at the Henderson home in response to a dinner invitation, but were never fed, the shock was much greater.

Tales of Sylvia's eccentricity were repeated up and down the Coast in tones of delight and outrage. Conventional people were deeply offended — not only was Sylvia shocking and pretentious, the role reversal in the Henderson household was a terrible threat to the status quo; in post-war New Zealand, men were expected to be absorbed in their work, while child care and housework was left to their self-effacing wives. Inevitably hostility to Sylvia was coupled with sympathy for Keith, and endless admiration of his tolerance.

But not all Sylvia's colleagues were rigidly conventional: some took a vicarious delight in her reckless unconformity and her determination be true to herself; some glimpsed an attractive incandescence behind her outrageous mask; and when some heard her penetrating analysis of Herbert Read's *Education Through Art* at an informal book study group, they were driven to wonder whether behind the posing and pretence was an authentic Sylvia as genuinely gifted as the actress Sylvia pretended to be.

★

At school, despite the reprimand from Des, her attendance showed only
temporary improvement. Before long a pattern developed whereby the
new junior assistant, Pare, did the day-to-day teaching while Sylvia made
star appearances two or three times a week to take her favourite activities,
and to introduce the class to the reading books she had begun making in
Selah.

Many teachers on the Coast made their own infant reading books and
these were often discussed at monthly meetings, but at first Sylvia used
only the set texts. She took the opportunity of Inspector Golding's visit to
complain about their irrelevance.

'Why don't you make your own?' he asked. It was departmental policy
to encourage such innovations.

Sylvia saw the suggestion as an attack, and responded with vehemence.
'What are you short of in the department — brains or paper?'

'We've got brains all right. . . .'

'Sterile!' she declared, 'Totally sterile!'

From their previous contact the inspectors had concluded that Mrs Henderson was a poor teacher, a shocking wife and an embarrassing flirt. To
that impression was now added the concepts of 'hostile' and 'belligerent'.
There was even talk of insobriety. At Pipiriki Sylvia had rediscovered the
uninhibiting and pain-killing properties of alcohol, and in the solitude of
Selah she made full use of them. She wrote to Barbara:

> Have you ever drunk many bottles of beer and some wine — on your
> own — at Selah — taken off all your clothes and put on Beethoven's 7th
> symphony and danced it right through — on your own? It all makes
> significant living.

This is one of the few indications that Sylvia drank heavily in secret during
the 1940s. Her acquaintances knew that she enjoyed a social drink and
could, on a Saturday night, become a little intoxicated. But excesses of any
sort were so typical of Sylvia that no one was surprised or concerned.

By 1950 her drinking was becoming more obvious. On 14 August of
that year Charles Panckhurst, a relieving teacher at Fernhill School,
brought, on Sylvia's instructions, two bottles of sherry to celebrate the
opening of the new prefabricated classroom. By lunchtime Keith had
drunk one glass, Charles had drunk two, and Sylvia had polished off the
rest. The medical reality is that to reach a tolerance for alcohol of that
magnitude Sylvia must have been drinking frequently and heavily
throughout her five years at Waiomatatini, and probably for most of her
four years at Pipiriki as well.

Because women who drink heavily are notoriously secretive, and
because Sylvia's normally irrational, moody and self-absorbed behaviour,
and her neglect of her family, would not have changed radically under the
influence of liquor but would have simply become more pronounced, it
may have been years before even Keith realised what was happening.
When he did find out he probably felt ashamed, protective and over-

whelmed. Unsure of whether she was wilful, sick, or the frustrated genius she claimed to be, he appears to have done everything in his power to deny and disguise the problem. He took responsibility for their home and family, fended off the puzzlement of friends and colleagues, appeased Sylvia's rages and responded to her whims, and covered for her at school. Despite an official directive that staff absences of any duration be noted in the school log, he recorded only Sylvia's official sick-leave — usually a week or two a year — and turned a blind eye to her many other failures to attend.

Alcohol's ability to reduce inhibitions, allowing the solitary and fearful to become gregarious and foolhardy, must have been highly attractive to Sylvia. Her flamboyant social behaviour suggests that on such occasions she nipped regularly enough to maintain a mild high without becoming obviously tipsy. And in addition to social reasons for drinking Sylvia had deeply personal ones. She lived on an emotional cliff-edge and drew her artistry from the perilous frontier. Her insights into the primitive levels of her own inner life, into the aggression and sexuality, were glimpsed only by crawling to the extremity and peering into the void. Alcohol gave her the courage she needed to make the journey.

But she knew that artistic insight alone was not enough. Whether drunk or sober, Sylvia put hours of disciplined craftsmanship into defining in words, music and paint the raw truths she had gained from dark and drunken introspection.

After the inspector's visit, and his challenge 'Why don't you make your own?', she turned her insight and talent to the production of infant readers: a graduated set of four girl's books about houses, mothers and babies, and a similar boy's set about men and trucks. When a crippled boy named Koro started school, everthing changed. Koro was a CRIPPLE, a Cripple, a cripple. Koro was a cripple. His affliction resonated so powerfully with the child in Sylvia, with poor Papa's daughter, that from his first day at school nearly all the reading books she made were about Koro. Around themes such as birds, butterflies, eating and growing up, Sylvia prepared small reading books for children to take home, and chart-sized books to spread on the floor for groups to read. She also wrote songs, poems and stories; and once a week she introduced her latest work to the children. So great was her emotional involvement that when telling sad stories Sylvia herself would start to weep.

She divided the class into four reading groups — red, yellow, blue, green — each with its own place marked by a coloured circle painted on the floor, and each with its own piano chords that signalled 'Come to me'.

Towards the end of her Waiomatatini stay Sylvia brought mothers into the classroom to help with hearing each child read aloud, a move that soon evolved into a relaxed open-door policy towards the community.*

---

*At that time parental participation in New Zealand schools was usually limited to gathering firewood, emptying the latrine cans and attending concerts and displays of work.

Sylvia wrote little about this experiment and abandoned it at her next school. It would hardly be worth mentioning were it not for the powerful impression it made on Iri Tawhiwhirangi, a student teacher who spent one term in Sylvia's classroom and went on to become an influential figure in New Zealand education, and one of the architects of Te Kohanga Reo, Maori-language preschools:

> I remember her often. That speaks for itself — that a woman I spent a term with, who most of the time wasn't in the classroom, made this tremendous impact. A lot of things that have happened since in my own career I source back to the one term I spent with Sylvia Henderson. She believed in whanau learning — parents, elders, everybody could come in and share. There was never any question in her mind that they were untrained, or non-professionals.
>
> My input into Kohanga Reo was designed very much on her method of teaching — it was concerned with the creation of a learning environment, and not just a teaching environment. . . .[17]

As her approach became more pupil-oriented, Sylvia realised that the children were more interested in their own stories than they were in hers. During her last years in Waiomatatini she used both the children's morning talks, and their casual conversations, as a basis for her reading and writing lessons; an innovation consistent with the child-centred teaching advocated in Education Department publications of the period.

For the children, her infrequent visits were a great event: she awed them, she frightened them, she excited them, she enchanted them. She never touched them, but they always ran to touch and hold her, to trace their fingers around the kowhaiwhai border stencilled onto her white artist's smock and untie the laces on her red home-made clogs so that she could walk barefoot in the classroom. She never raised her voice but when the piano gave the order for silence the room became eerily quiet.

Sometimes her lessons centred on the children's fears. When injections were imminent she provided syringes to play with and apples to plunge the needles into, and she encouraged the children to express their feelings verbally and through art. The preparation was effective; when injections were given no one pulled away.

Every afternoon, whether she was present or not, Sylvia insisted that the children spend an hour working with clay or paint. Inspired by *Education Through Art*, and encouraged by the new primary school art syllabus, she abandoned her earlier emphasis on imitation and became committed to free and vigorous self-expression: '. . . I learnt for the first time to respect the schematic drawing of young children for what it was, captions of the imagery, and how to interpret its meaning.'

At the end of each school day the junior assistant and the older children folded back the wide outside doors on the infant room, hosed out the splattering of clay and paint, and scrubbed the room clean.

The children's paintings were never pinned to the classroom wall, that was reserved for Sylvia's own masterpieces: a strangely beautiful mural of the Pied Piper of Hamelin, and a changing selection of sketches and paintings on subjects like horses, Father Christmas, or the seasons of the year. She illustrated spring with a painting of snowdrops pushing up through snow — a substance even more remote from the lives of Ngati Porou children than were the mysterious trains in the Education Department reading books.

During 1946, with Sylvia preparing the work and Pare teaching it, progress was being made in the core subjects, but it would be later in the year before the inspectors returned to view the innovations. In the meantime Sylvia incurred their disfavour yet again.

The crisis was precipitated by Lili Kraus, the vivacious Hungarian concert pianist who, after her release from three years in a Japanese prisoner-of-war camp in Java, came to New Zealand to recuperate. She was beautiful and charming and the whole country fell in love with her. The Prime Minister gave her honorary New Zealand citizenship, and out of love and gratitude she returned in 1946 and 1947 to give concerts and masterclasses up and down the country. Wherever she went, from the smallest country meeting room to the biggest city hall, hundreds came to hear her play. In the isolation of Waiomatatini, Sylvia listened entranced to her broadcast recitals.

When Lili Kraus came to Gisborne the Hendersons and the Shaws drove eighty miles to attend her concert, and returned home again the same night. It was worth every pot-hole and ford along the way; the theatrical way that lady swept onto the stage and skipped delightedly around the piano, the way she slipped glinting rings off her fingers and placed them delicately at the end of the keyboard before beginning, and above all the way she created '. . . spiritual communion between the audience, myself, the music, and the Lord.'

Sylvia had to have more. She wrote to the Education Department requesting leave for a week at the end of July 1946 to attend two concerts in Wellington. Inspired by Lili Kraus, she dreamed her dreams and saw them coming true. She decided that she would present herself to that mortal equivalent of God Almighty — the Director of Education. She would take samples of the children's art . . . she would thrill him with her work . . . she would charm him . . . he would fall in love with her. . . .

In her excitement she forgot about not wanting to meet Barbara Dent, and suggested that she come to Wellington too. With her imagination in full flight nothing could stop Sylvia, not even a letter from the department declining to grant her leave.

Walter Harris, at his base in the Education Department, heard from the executive clerical officer for Native Schools, Alec Lake, about Sylvia's request for leave. 'He said of course he'd have to refuse, otherwise all

Native School teachers might want similar privileges.'*

The thrill of going to hear Lili Kraus seemed to loosen Sylvia's already tenuous links with reality. She went on to spend her days in Wellington in a world of fantasy. She claimed in *I Passed This Way*: 'I had no intention of seeing Hilton Morris [Walter Harris], called Pan, as I'd never pursued a man in my life, and left insolubles like love to Fate.' But according to Walter, she wrote and asked him to meet her at the railway station. He did so, and then escorted her to her sister Evadne's flat on the Terrace. He also accompanied Sylvia to the Thursday evening recital, a private fundraiser for war refugees, at which Lili Kraus wore trousers and played Schubert with her shiny black hair trailing in two long plaits down her back.

During the days between concerts Sylvia sat in on Lili Kraus's rehearsals, and went to call on Dr Beeby. At that time, after spending his first six years restructuring the primary service, the director had turned his attention to the secondary school system; a Cerberus at his door protected him from interruption. When Sylvia arrived unnanounced she was taken aside for an official scolding by taciturn Alec Lake and a man with a reputation for harassing teachers he disliked — the new senior inspector of Native Schools, Tom Fletcher.

The certificate Sylvia produced from the East Coast physician granting her sick leave was greeted by Lake and Fletcher with suspicion. Hadn't she applied for leave on cultural, rather than health, grounds? They arranged for her to see a Wellington doctor, Dr J. Bradbury, for a second opinion.

Sylvia left in a panic. 'Pan should be looking after me, he and his wife Meg [June]. Did he, a close friend and colleague of the director, know what was happening?'

To Walter — who did know what was happening — Sylvia's unauthorised leave was a Native Schools issue; he had no desire, authority or obligation to interfere. But to Sylvia his five kisses had sealed a love contract she waited in vain for him to honour:

> His offices were only on the Terrace, a block or two from Government Buildings, and at night he'd be at his home on the hill. One twilight I stood in the shadows across the street for a cold while, not to accost him but merely to see him leave at five for home. Waiting in the Wellington winter I thought of him and pondered on the meaning of the kisses of men. I didn't see him but when I reached home at Evadne's place I wrote him a note, every word of which I remember: 'Dear Hilton [Walter]: I'm in Wellington at my sister Evadne's place. Will you come and get me and take me home to Meg [June]? Sylvia.' To which I had no reply for thirty years.[18]

In the letter he wrote thirty years later Walter reintroduced himself and commented briefly on her fame. He then outlined his own life during the

---

*In later years Sylvia remembered the fateful letter as a telegram that read 'Do not leave your post. Beeby.' But in reality the director did not deal with requests for leave, and official telegrams were always signed 'Schools'.

intervening years, sent his regards to Keith, and closed with the formal subscription: 'Yours sincerely, Walter Harris.'

Only Sylvia could find undying passion in such a letter. As the mist rose from her inner eye she saw, bathed in the glow of love, an explanation for his neglect of her in Wellington:

> I supposed Pan had been faced with a choice of loyalties, his career and his director versus me, and he'd stood by his boss and his job. It would not be fair to say that his kisses had been invalid or that his love had failed the test. It had lasted all this time. Holding his long, impassioned letter I could at last see in hindsight that the whole long-drawn-out shady drama had not been a matter of Maori reading or of seeing Lili Kraus at all, but of a rather juicy jealousy in the rare air at the top. . . . Pan must have praised me to the director as a teacher and innovator, let slip his feeling for me, and the higher man hadn't liked it. That letter from Pan . . . still exists and I haven't answered it yet. As our Maori housekeeper on the River, Ruth, would say, 'All over a love, Sylv; all over a love.'[19]

A romantic explanation was the only explanation possible; in Sylvia's world there was no room for men as colleagues or friends, they had to be lovers.

And to Sylvia love meant betrayal. From babyhood she had been hurt by the people she loved; she grew up expecting, even demanding, that her lovers betray her. But the betrayal in Wellington was really no betrayal at all. The sad truth is that Walter never received her note (possibly because of Sylvia's practice of leaving her more emotional letters unposted), and Dr Beeby did not know of her existence until many years later.

Whether Sylvia's failure to contact Walter was by oversight or deliberate choice, it enabled her to experience the betrayal she had come to expect. It was as if her need for love was being over-ridden by an even more powerful need for rejection. Sylvia never recognised that need, but it recurred again and again as a unspoken driving force in her life. In the 1960s poet Louis Johnson's friendship with her ended amid similar accusations of betrayal:

> I became impatient with her over her remarks because I felt I had been a good friend and had given her a lot of support when she needed it. The truth of the matter probably is that Sylvia needed rejection more than she needed support — because that's what she fed on.[20]

Although Sylvia never stopped loving Walter, the Lili Kraus episode marked the end of their friendship and the beginning of a conviction that she had been personally singled out for persecution by the Director of Education.

After the official scolding Sylvia's more immediate concern was that she would be dismissed from teaching. But when she visited Dr Bradbury at the department's behest he was sympathetic and reassuring. She was less anxious about her future by Friday evening, when Barbara Dent came to meet her at Evadne's flat. Again, for Sylvia, fantasy and reality clashed head-on. Barbara recalled:

I was so looking forward to it — I had expected us to keep flowing together as we had done in letters — but Sylvia seemed utterly taken aback from the first moment she set eyes on me. She turned me around like a specimen in a case. I felt the shutters go up straight away. The only reason I could give myself for her behaviour was that I looked so young — in my pinafore dress and cyclamen blouse I looked like a schoolgirl in a gym frock — I think she was overwhelmed with chagrin that she had opened her heart and life to this kid.

The thing that completely put me off — she came and took my shoes off and put her slippers on me, kneeling in front of me. I thought this was an utterly absurd and inauthentic gesture, a parody of Christ washing the feet of the disciples. Evadne tactfully left the room — but the conversation was stilted.[21]

The next evening Sylvia, Barbara, Evadne and Joy (towards whom Sylvia was distant) attended Lili Kraus's concert in the Wellington Town Hall. Madame, wearing a flowing white satin gown and with her hair piled on top of her head, played the classics with a winning gypsy freedom. Sylvia returned to Waiomatatini more absorbed in music than ever. She spent five hours a day at the piano during the week, and seven hours a day at weekends. In the estimation of the few experienced musicians who heard her play, she never was an accomplished pianist, but she felt the music deeply and played with flamboyance and individuality. Her unsophisticated rural audience observed her closed-eyed ecstasy, her extravagant glissandos and theatrical hand-crossing, and concluded that she was absolutely brilliant.

Inspired by Lili Kraus, Sylvia focused even more determinedly on developing her talent. When Inspectors Goodwin and Golding visited Waiomatatini on 30 September 1946, they found Sylvia teaching art and drama to every class in the school, and the infant work suffering as a result. Their report read:

> Weak oral expression and practically no number activity are disturbing features of the infant division. Reading ranges from weak to fair, with even the simplest of words not recognised. The scheme should contain more detail, and the work book could be more logically arranged. The art scheme was quite full and seemed to be progressing satisfactorily. . . .
>
> In view of the unsatisfactory state of work in the infant room it is suggested that the special timetable be suspended, and the art, speech training, and dramatic work be taken by the individual class teachers.

Sylvia took particular exception to Mr Golding's comments on infant reading, especially since he had ignored her lovingly prepared books and had used only the Education Department texts to test the children. To Sylvia-the-persecuted he seemed to be saying, 'Not one child in the room recognised one word.' In response to her written protest he replied, 'I am prepared, in order to avoid any ambiguity, to amend the extract to read "with even some of the simplest words not always correctly recognised".'

The amendment did nothing to change Sylvia's grading increase for

1946/47: a rock-bottom zero. One of the Waiomatatini teachers recalled her reaction:

> She said, 'Well it really does surprise me that they couldn't see fit to give me any grading marks.' The rest of us were sitting there thinking — well heavens, you haven't done anything! At school she just wanted to do her own thing and she did it. By the time she arrived, and had her cup of tea and settled down, it was lunch time. And sometimes she wouldn't come back after lunch. There was one occasion when she didn't come to school for four or five weeks. . . .[22]

Sylvia's humiliation was magnified by the Education Department practice of publishing the grading of every teacher in the *Teachers' Register*. The shame of it. Her critics would laugh, and her contemporaries would see her falling behind in her professional advancement. Over several days of high drama Sylvia threatened to resign but Keith persuaded her to stay.

In a perverse way, that grading was the proof she needed. Now Sylvia knew, beyond a shadow of doubt, that she was being picked on by the department, indeed by the man at the top, the Director of Education himself. It was like living through her high school pariahdom all over again.

Sylvia's conviction was reinforced by the belief that every working teacher was entitled to an increase of one grading mark per year, regardless. But a perusal of the *Teachers' Register* reveals nothing unique or sinister in her zero increase. Of the 25,000 working teachers in New Zealand in 1946, Sylvia was one of more than 2000 who received zero grading increases that year.

The official disfavour, far from persuading Sylvia to change her ways, actually deepened her conviction that she was right and the department was wrong, and inspired her to pursue her unconventional life with even more vigour. At home, when Keith tried to persuade her to conform to the expectations of inspectors, teachers and school parents, the tension was never greater. Arguments went on far into the night and frequently ended with Sylvia's wailing exit to Selah. In the course of a stormy exchange over the need to do playground duty, Sylvia tore her latest creative writing into tiny pieces, threw a volume of Beethoven's sonatas out the window, and ran screaming down the road in her nightgown. The outcome was inevitable: Keith retrieved Sylvia and the music, and she still did not do playground duty.

In the school cultural programme the Maori teachers taught Maori crafts and music, and Sylvia taught European music, art and drama. She developed children's concerts into a high art form. Sometimes they were performed on impulse — like the time she provided an impromptu entertainment for a group of passing telephone linesmen — but the main regular excuse was the nationwide post-war relief effort. 'Food for Britain' concerts were held weekly. Admission: one penny. Every pupil took part and the whole district was invited to watch and participate.

The Click Clack Orchestra — a group of children dressed in white shirts and black bow ties who plucked, thumped, strummed, banged, blew and rattled a colourful assortment of home-made instruments — was a concert highlight. Many items were costumed enactments of poems or songs in which each verse was presented by a different group of children: The Wedding of the Painted Doll, The Pirate, Lochinvar, Hiawatha, The Pied Piper. Occasionally a Maori flavour was added, with masked actors playing the parts of birds or taniwha.

Sylvia reached her dramatic peak at the annual Fancy Dress Ball. There was European folk dancing, traditional ballroom dancing, dramatic and choral items, and the climax of the evening: the Grand Parade. As the children performed a precision-marching display, she played the piano so wonderfully that it sounded to her audience like a full orchestra. Responding to variations in volume and tempo, the brightly costumed children divided from columns of four abreast to two abreast, crossed over, interwove and rejoined.

To add to the excitement, Sylvia once dressed as Old Mother Hubbard, and on other occasions as a witch. The latter may well have symbolised her private struggle to understand her relationship with the Almighty. Sylvia's God was a demanding, temperamental, unforgiving Old Testament deity. Sometimes she called him 'Fate'. He was as powerful as Mama had been to the child-Sylvia, and just as frightening. A desperate ache for Mama's and God's approval burned in Sylvia's undermind all her life.

Although he lured her to Selah like a jealous phantom lover and there possessed her, she was not sure that he loved her. How could he, when he knew her ugliness, her sins and her guilt; when he tortured her mind as he had once tortured Papa's body? Or — a terrifying thought — was this force that possessed her perhaps more demonic than divine?

> . . . . a monster . . . inhabiting the mind, a ruthless invader, demanding, fierce, bumping round knocking things over, jealous of school and not prepared to accommodate either the wife or the teacher. The monster was the other man in the home . . . I'd . . . lock him up in some Selah . . . where I could go to him like a secret paramour and let him have his way with me, then return home again as a wife.[23]

In the grip of such a monster Sylvia may have felt, like the wicked Germaine in *Incense to Idols*, an intimate not of God, but Baal:

> Baal holds me with glittering golden hands adjuring me
> from clouds of incense to
> 'Let him that glorieth glory in this
> that he understandeth and knoweth me, for
> I AM BAAL!
> Which exercise hate, injustice and selfishness in the earth:
> For in these things I delight!'

Whatever the deity's identity, Sylvia feared and hated him; she hated his lovelessness and she hated his power. But she coped. She used the same approach that she used with all the people and organisations in her life whose authority she feared, whose approval she craved, and whose love was never enough.

In dealing directly with any such power she was extravagantly ingratiating, presenting herself as a delightful, interesting, sincere, loving and intimate friend. The hatred she hid was expressed only indirectly — in her writing, and in letters and conversations with confidants.

Although she claimed to Barbara that she was one of God's fast favourites, there was a period at Waiomatatini when her study of the writings of Gerard Manley Hopkins emboldened her to drop the pretence of contented familiarity, and confront the Lord directly with her complaints:

'Why have you apportioned me gifts when you won't let me use them?'
'Because I like my tools sharp.'
'But I'm no tool of yours.'
'It's not for you mortals to say. It's I who choose the steel I want, and I who temper it in the furnace.'
'But I spend half my time in the furnace, God. What for?'
'Because you're such substandard metal.'
'Then why bother with me?'
'There's work to be done, of course.'
'Well, can't you pick on somebody else?'
'Many are called but few are chosen.'[24]

Even an all-powerful deity could not give Sylvia the human interchange she needed. After a silence of many weeks she resumed writing to Barbara:

3.30 p.m. Selah. There's no way that I know of to begin but never mind. I'm begging letters from you again. *NOT* because I need them . . . I no longer need them. I merely *want* them. Please let us rise above all the incompatibilities. . . . I met Lili Kraus on the Sunday evening that you left — and heard her play several times during the week — with the result that Beethoven has been seriously challenged and I am enwrapped in some of her lovely Schubert encores. . . . I hope you are not too long in replying. . . .

Barbara told of her disappointment and confusion at their meeting in Wellington, and Sylvia replied stiffly:

Selah. Sunday. Thank you for your letter. . . . There can never be any established relationship between you and me on account of the stuff of which our minds are made. . . . I do not feel constrained to defend or explain myself. . . . However, that the things I say and do should not be understood, and are therefore claimed to be insincere is treatment I am accustomed to. . . .

For the rest of 1946 they exchanged brief, infrequent letters. But there was too much at stake to sever the ties completely. Towards the end of the year Sylvia confided to Barbara:

I have begun a novel too. . . . As soon as I get some of it typed what fun to send it to you. Would you let me read what you have done of yours. What an exciting business. *Strictly* confidential. I'm feeling better from

my ghastly experience of the last 18 months. Coming out of the night
and looking round for my friends.[25]

Barbara had sent manuscripts to Sylvia since the beginning of their correspondence, but several months passed before Sylvia felt able to share her
novel with Barbara. In the meantime Sylvia looked around for her friends.

She joined the Women's Institute but was more distant towards the local
community than she had been at Pipiriki. Although the speaking of Maori
was tolerated at school, Sylvia concealed her knowledge of the language.
Pare, who was her junior assistant for three and a half years, never suspected that Sylvia could speak Maori. Whenever Maori was spoken in
Sylvia's presence she'd say in tones of great irritation: 'What are you
talking about? What are you talking about?'

But Sylvia did fall in love with a Maori woman, an unmarried junior
assistant who was nearer Sylvia's age than the teenage Pare. Monika often
stayed for the weekend and Sylvia was heartbroken when, in 1949, she
went to Teachers' Training College in Auckland. For several years after
that Sylvia addressed her diary alternately to her two current sources of
inspiration: Barbara and Monika.

Although she fell deeply in love with women, it was in the company of
men that Sylvia really came alive. As she explained to Barbara, the sole aim
of her flirtations was to get herself kissed:

> . . . I'll tell you the secret of my love affairs. You wonder that I can bear
> the non-consummation. There's no non-consummation. At a kiss or two
> — if I'm in love — all is over with me. Unknown to the other. He goes
> aching. No one knows this.[26]

The Maori men on the school staff were among her targets: she wrote a
blow-by-blow account of her efforts to induce Rameka to kiss her; she
taught Bob to play the piano and, though she was usually vehemently dis-
paraging of rugby, gave rapt attention to his discourse on the game; she
even persuaded Willi that he was the only person who could print neatly
enough to do the blackboard captions she needed.

Sylvia was particularly attracted to the visiting Pakeha nature study
specialist, Mr Middleweek. She later lost interest when he seemed more
drawn to a Maori woman in the district, but for a while she flirted out-
rageously; at a party in his honour she wore a see-through blouse with
nothing on underneath. When he supervised the planting of trees around
the perimeter of the school grounds she accompanied him. Each time they
stopped he lifted her onto a fence strainer-post, where she sat coyly until,
when it was time to move on, he lifted her down. It is said that she stood
so close to the holes he was digging that he could see up her skirt, and
when she staged an unconvincing twisted ankle it was Mr Middleweek
who carried her home. The staff raised their eyebrows, the children giggled,
but Keith affected calm unconcern.

Through her flirting Sylvia may have been denying the lesbian implications of her passions for women. She may also have been denying that at

the age of forty she was growing visibly old; her maternal grandmother had possessed the most fearsome wrinkles her grandchildren had ever seen, and Sylvia was, with alarming rapidity, developing a resemblance to Grandma Maxwell. She had always believed she was ugly and now, despite heavy make-up, she saw in the mirror hard proof.

To counter her ageing appearance, and to enhance her sense of style, Sylvia dressed well. Her determination to wear nothing but the best must have strained the family budget; while Keith and the children wore old clothes, Sylvia dressed in smart hand-made artists' smocks and tube skirts. She also bought a fur coat, at least one expensive silk dress, and a beautiful pair of kid gloves. But despite the superficial glamour, she had to face the truth: she was growing old. Time was running out. Her sister Grace had died in South Africa, her brother Ashton had died in Wellington. Her own 'terrible thirties' had come to an end. She needed to firm up the philosophy and direction of her life, and press on urgently with her work.

In Selah, with the wind whistling between the drying sods, she found the peace she needed:

> No one knows the ecstasies I have had here and no one knows how much I have wept here. And no one will. I become myself here. And the inside of Selah is what I am like inside — no drapings or paper on the walls, a scrubbed table, books of poetry, a bed and a fire. I'm glad Selah is crumbling. It decays with me.[27]

She surveyed her talents. She found that her art was purely functional and her music lacked discipline. She resolved to focus on one major goal: to become a writer. She began to see this as an alternative career through which she could escape from her love-hate relationship with teaching.

She reworked incidents from her diary into short stories and submitted them to the *New Zealand Listener*. Initially her efforts were rejected, but in October 1948 she saw her first publication, a Pipiriki story, 'No Longer Blinded By Our Eyes'. She continued to work on *Rangitira*. In an indexed exercise book she made notes for each chapter and character, and had separate sections on seasonal changes in plant life, Maori history, and verbatim records of conversations. And all the while the manuscript grew longer:

> I've written seven or eight hundred pages of Rangitira and K says it's time I stopped. But I've barely begun to say what I want to. Why should I stop when I'd be lonely without it? I don't see why I should stop.[28]

In the Pipiriki version of *Rangitira*, crippled Papa was a former artist, in the Waiomatatini version he changed to a former concert pianist, and later, when she was a published author, her fictional Papa became a disillusioned writer whose books had been burned. Mama in *Rangitira* was at first banished to England, but she was too powerful to be suppressed; at Waiomatatini she resurfaced as a dominant character in the novel. Sylvia's alter ego initially appeared as Kaa, the Maori daughter of Papa and a Maori

noblewoman, and in a later version as the princess Huia, the daughter of
Kaa and one of Papa's sons.

Ironically there was in her real-life infant room a genuinely highborn
Maori girl, who was treated with special deference by the whole community. She was probably the only Maori pupil that Sylvia consistently
disliked; in Sylvia's world there was room for only one Maori princess and
she was that person.

With all her preoccupations at school and Selah, Sylvia had little time or
energy for home pursuits.

Her main domestic contribution was to decorate the house with the same
soft furnishing material she had used at Pipiriki: natural hessian. The cur-
tains, the bedspreads, the floor rugs and the covers for the lounge (or, as
Sylvia called it, 'the music room') furniture, were made from what looked
like old sugarbags decorated with stencilled Maori motifs.

Her maternal activity revolved around teaching the Henderson children
elocution and music, and watching them play sport. As they grew older
she became even less inclined to mother them and more inclined to
manipulate them into mothering her. His work commitments left Keith
little time to spend with the children, but at least by cooking and serving
the meals prepared by a Maori housekeeper, he ensured that they were
fed.

In their second year at Waiomatatini, Sylvia and Keith borrowed money
and cashed in their insurance policies to send Jasmine to boarding school
in Gisborne. Sylvia was convinced that her daughter yearned to be with
Pakeha city girls, ('her own kind'), and was severely shaken when the first
new friend she brought home was not white but brown. Elliot and Ashton
lived at home and attended Waiomatatini School. Outside school hours
they roamed the hills and river flats. For about a year they spent almost
every weekend with a family in Ruatoria, arriving by bicycle on Friday
after school — 'Mum told us to clear out' — and leaving after breakfast
on Monday morning.

During school holidays Keith usually took the children to his parents,
now retired to New Plymouth, or to his married sister's farm near Te
Aroha, while Sylvia stayed home alone.

Over the extended summer holidays of 1947/48, when schools were
closed by a polio epidemic, Keith found work as caretaker at the isolated
and beautiful Lake Waikaremoana camping ground. During their stay,
Sylvia, under the name of Lotus, lived out her Lili Kraus fantasies by
playing the piano in the hotel lounge in the evenings, while by day she
tolerated for a short time the job assigned to the caretaker's wife: hotel
laundress. The experience provided a fund of imagery for the stories she
continued to write.

After five years at Waiomatatini, Elliot reached high school age, Ashton
was only a year behind, and there was no money left for boarding school.

Keith and Sylvia applied for the positions of headmaster and infant mistress at Fernhill School, near Hastings, so that the boys could attend the local secondary school. Fernhill wasn't a Native School but it had a predominantly Maori roll, and the Hawke's Bay Education Board was keen to employ teachers with Native School experience. It was to be at Fernhill School that Sylvia's teaching career would reach its climax.

TEN

Fernhill

AFTER SEVENTEEN YEARS IN THE BACKBLOCKS, SYLVIA'S DREAM of living in the city seemed about to come true . . . except that Fernhill School wasn't actually in Hastings but ten miles away at Omahu, a Maori community comprising a pa, a church, a school, a store and a hotel. And Hastings itself, with a population of 17,000 and an economy dependent on the orchards, farms and market gardens of the surrounding Hawke's Bay plain, wasn't actually a city but a mundane, low-key town.

Despite her hunger for the arts, Sylvia's involvement in the cultural life of Hastings was limited to visiting the cinema and attending occasional classical music concerts. Although she initially joined a range of cultural organisations, she was too superior, too fearful and too busy writing to become actively involved.

She didn't miss much. The cutting edge of cultural life in Hastings in 1949, or anywhere else in New Zealand for that matter, was becoming blunt. The general election in November, two months after the Hendersons arrived at Fernhill, brought in a National Government whose traditional views reflected a growing conservatism throughout the country: artists, writers, intellectuals and advocates of what critics called 'playway' education, while not quite as unacceptable as socialists, communists and trade unionists, were highly suspect.

Sylvia found in the climate of conformity much to confirm her sense of alienation and her belief that New Zealand was an uncultured colonial backwater. She studied expatriate New Zealand writers like Katherine Mansfield and Robin Hyde, and her dreams of overseas escape began to bloom again. Early in 1950 she wrote to Barbara Dent:

> I'm not surprised that you have fallen out with everybody. It's a ghastly thing, New Zealand society. You're far better off without them. . . . We're going to LIVE in America as soon as Jasmine has finished boarding school. I've had enough of this dungeon.

But while reality kept her in Hastings, Sylvia reacted by declaring herself anti-royalty and pro-communist. Her interest in communism was probably motivated by a desire to impress Joy Alley, whose brother was pioneering industrial reform in China, and Winston and Sophie Rhodes, who were drawing fire for their left-wing political views. Sylvia's studies of Soviet life and history inspired the creation of a Russian-born heroine for her first published novel *Spinster*, and convinced her that warfare was a manifestation of her own great concern: individual violence. Her opinions were sufficiently radical to alarm her sister Evadne, to whom Sylvia wrote after a visit:

> From your letter it is apparent that I left somewhere in your high 'helicopter' flat an impression that I was pro-Russian, pro-Communist, and pro-enemy. I distinctly remember leaving it. If it's not on the piano in the drawing room then it's on the couch beneath the Mona Lisa, or did I drop it in the coat cupboard in the hall?

At Fernhill she expressed her convictions in a limited and typically theatrical way: she refused to stand for the playing of 'God Save The Queen' at public gatherings.

In her élitist Warner heart, Sylvia probably never took communism seriously. Her disdain for the masses erupted in a letter to Barbara later that year:

> Thursday night selah cold wet tired I do praise you for being mad. I've had a terrible hell for a fortnight with the house full of the PHILISTINE. I've been a ghastly exile in my own home, an outcast. The conversation rises no higher than the level of a flea and a dirty one. It centres round the time, the price of cornflour, the corns between your toes, and how far it is to Hastings this way compared with that way. I played the E Flat concerto with the orchestra tonight on the records and they talked me down about seeds. . . . O how lonely we can be among these monstrosities of drooling sanity. . . . NEVER AGAIN WILL I ENTERTAIN THE PHILISTINE. THEY CAME. I DIDN'T ASK THEM. I'VE WAITED ON SERVANT BLOOD. . . .

In the privacy of Selah — a sturdy shed behind the teachers' residence — Sylvia forgot about politics and the philistine, and settled down with a newly acquired typewriter to press on with her writing.

For most of 1950 she wrote not from the inspiration of love but to escape from the pain of her ongoing relationships with Joy, Monika and Sophie Rhodes. She longed for them constantly and enticed them to her with outpourings of affection and charm.

She wrote to Sophie:

> I'm going to Wellington next week to stay with Daphne. It would be lovely if you were there too. . . . There would be violets in the shops on the windy corners and the sea would be hitting the wharf with that glamorous smell. The bulbs would be all in neat beds in the Botanical gardens. . . .

Sophie had stayed with the Hendersons at Waiomatatini but her marriage and family kept her beyond Sylvia's emotional grasp. In their spinsterhood Joy and Monika were much more vulnerable. Joy recalled: 'She made me feel like someone who really meant something to somebody.' But whenever they met, Sylvia faced again the terrible truth that she could not possess her loved woman completely, and drove her away in bitterness and rage.

Joy's stay with Sylvia in January 1950 had a particularly acrimonious ending. Sylvia wrote to Mama after the visit:

> ... last Friday another ... letter went though the post ... to Miss Alley ... After seven years of kindness and patience that, looking back on, I can only call demented on my part, the WORM TURNED. ... It concentrated on two paragraphs of resentment. ... It referred to her as just 'another paltry, clock ticking, official' and 'an accomplished sadist'. It finished by telling her to take her forked tongue and her familiarity to someone else. . . and reminded her that she would find most luscious meat for her sadism in creative people. . . . after posting it I felt so wonderful that I walked about the house easily three feet off the ground ... wrote pally intimate letters to all my worst enemies and sang for the rest of the afternoon on exceedingly high top notes. . . .

But within days she was writing pally, intimate letters to Joy again, trying to win her back.

At that time Monika lived in Hawke's Bay and visited Sylvia at weekends, but Sylvia's unposted letters indicated that seeing Monika was just as painful as seeing Joy. She turned from women and buried herself in writing.

She was uncomfortably aware that Barbara Dent's stories and poems were appearing regularly, while her own 1948 story in the *Listener* was still her only publication. She resolved to finish *Rangitira* before the year was out.

Early in 1950 she discovered a fellow writer nearby. The Hastings paper reported that Dulcie Carman, a local author of romantic fiction, had had another book accepted for publication in Britain. '. . . I went to congratulate her and know her. . . . She was fluent and easy to talk to and I got so excited to think that someone else could mention a chapter. . . .'

Dulcie enlightened Sylvia about the need for double spacing and wide margins, but she was not one of Sylvia's own kind. The relationship foundered over Dulcie's suggestions for turning Sylvia's impressionistic fragments into a book, which Sylvia took as criticism of her style.

In October 1950, as soon as she had finished typing *Rangitira*, Sylvia posted, apparently on impulse, the first 450 pages to the Macmillan Publishing Company in New York. There were two pages missing from one section, five from another, and . . .

> I forgot to enclose return postage, forgot to enclose a covering letter, didn't register it and forgot to ask them to acknowledge it when they received it. However since then there has been a stream of notes adding all these things. . . .[1]

When Macmillans advised Sylvia that they published only biography and history she sent the manuscript to a London publisher and then, on discovering a series of typing and other mistakes in the carbon copy, recalled it. Discouraged by the thought of having to correct so many errors, she temporarily abandoned the idea of ever publishing anything. But she continued to write, keeping a diary of her work at school, reworking her old diaries into short stories and revising *Rangitira*. She gained the satisfaction of an audience by circulating instalments of her work to her 'private public': Barbara, Joy, Monika, Sophie, and her sisters Daphne and Evadne.

In addition to her own writing, Sylvia continued to provide detailed, thoughtful and patronising critiques of Barbara's work. She had always seen herself in Barbara, but was able to bring to Barbara's writing a detachment she could not achieve when examining her own efforts:

> It is a better book this time dear. The main faults are padding. . . . Pick the skeleton cleaner. . . . I believe you have genius but it is so layered in dross that only I, who am very like you but not a genius*, can see it . . . your most recent critic was a New Zealander was he not? Surely you would not expect a N.Z. mind to penetrate to any important depths? How can a N.Z. penetrate the dross when it is dross itself? . . . Your strength is in your knowledge of the fact that the main thing in life is WHAT PASSES BETWEEN JUST ONE PERSON AND ANOTHER. Communication. That IS life.[2]

In her letters to Barbara, Sylvia also deplored the use of clichés, mixed metaphors, explanations, and unnecessary adjectives and adverbs:

> Page 44, paragr. 2: 'she thought bitterly'. . . . to date you have *indicated* the bitterness per wind, sea, appearance. . . . To at last *say* that she 'thought bitterly' is superfluous. . . . Just give them another little action, a look or posture to *indicate* bitter thoughts. Let *me* the *reader* deduce that she thought bitterly. . . .

She applauded clarity, simplicity, integration in the line of thought, and 'organic design':

> The abstract design of this work of course pleases me vastly. . . . It requires COURAGE to break from the conscious order and stagger about in your buried life as you do here. A courage that betrays to me the ecstasy of your desperation.

And she expounded on her newly developed style of writing in the first-person present:

> The purpose is . . . to bring the content more vividly closer . . . I suggest this is the correct way of narration. We report what we see in imagery when we narrate. It is like talking at the pictures. 'Now this man he takes this girl by the throat etc.' Describing an image of the past, watching it, that is in the present.

---

*Her comment about not being a genius was probably not a reflection Sylvia's true belief, but an example of the way she often belittled herself in order to elicit praise from others. On another occasion, by protesting to the Hawke's Bay District Senior Inspector, 'I'm not even a teacher,' she provoked the response, 'You're a wonderful teacher'; a comment that she later used as proof of betrayal when he failed to give her the grading she was expecting.

Throughout 1950 Sylvia felt her creative output to be handicapped by a lack of love affairs. There was a young relieving teacher whom she flirted with and tried to mother, but for a long time he made little impression on her inner life. There was a fat farmer, but she couldn't induce him to kiss her; and there was a woman whom Sylvia found violently stimulating at first but later concluded, '. . . she's so far below what I want that I've lost interest . . .'.

The man who really attracted her was Rowland Lewis, Senior Inspector for the Hawke's Bay Education Board, who made three routine visits to the school in 1950. In appearance he was an archetypal school inspector: tall, with grey hair and a grey suit. He was also handsome, personable, courteous and efficient.

During 1951 his visits increased dramatically: one in the first term, two in the second term, and five in the third term; a remarkable level of attention to one teacher when the resources of the board were overburdened by the post-war baby boom. Sylvia fell in love with him and he inspired her teaching, but she couldn't get him to kiss her. So why did he keep coming back?

Sylvia's flirting probably didn't go unnoticed, but what really drew him was her classroom work. His approach to education was basically conventional and he knew most people thought Mrs Henderson was crazy, but he recognised beneath the craziness an infant mistress with a remarkable teaching method.

In many ways her approach was consistent with the times. Most infant teachers began the day with a period of free play followed by reading activities. Home-made books and wall newspapers were produced, dictated by younger children and written by teachers, or written by older children themselves. There was music and dance, and freedom of expression in a range of art media.

The difference was that while other teachers were committed to education, Sylvia was committed to creativity. Her emotional survival depended on it. So while most teachers felt that keeping the lid on their pupils' more explosive emotions was essential to effective teaching, Sylvia was determined to rip the lid right off:

> I see the mind of a five-year-old as a volcano with two vents; destructiveness and creativeness. And I see that to the extent that we widen the creative channel, we atrophy the destructive one.[3]

In many areas of self-expression — drama, music, art and dance — it was Sylvia's own creativity, rather than the children's, that reigned supreme. Consider her 1951 school concert, which didn't quite come off:

> The rain made all my little ones in the ballet wear their coats to the hall so that their tulle skirts were crushed flat. The feathery lightness of them over which I had spent such loving care might have been any unexciting material. And the rain rat-tailed their hair . . . so that the glow and the swing of it, which had been a feature of the conception in my mind was

absent in reality . . . and what with the rum I had taken before coming
. . . Beethoven and Chopin payed the cost. In the end this lovely dream
of mine, so much the true voice of feeling, so much the exercise of the
sympathies, so much the thrilling breath of organic activity coursing
through me, dragged its way through reality . . . and once again reality
proved itself no match for the idea.[4]

Dawn Percy, the Hawke's Bay art specialist who visited Sylvia's classroom
between 1953 and 1955, confirmed that in art, music and dance, Sylvia's
own needs, and her own inner life, were paramount:

> When I took the class for something like finger-painting I'd be
> encouraging the kids to explore, to push the paint around and play with
> making marks, and Sylvia would say, 'Come on Mohi, do a ghost, do
> a skellington' (and literally 'skellington' — it was some sort of 'in' joke).
> I felt she was interfering with the spontaneity of their art and I did discuss
> it with her, but to no great effect.
>
> Another issue was interpretive dance. I had seen quite a lot done in
> England and Sylvia was keen that I should see what she was doing with
> the senior girls. She played some marvellous chords of classical music and
> the girls all danced around doing this wonderful emotive dance. I said,
> 'But Sylvia, they're all doing it exactly the same!' She said, 'Well of
> course I had to teach them first. . . .'[5]

The gold and brown school uniform, introduced to Fernhill by the Hendersons and highlighted in *Teacher*, was another example of Sylvia's use of
the children to express her own inner vision. How else can you explain the
delight such a seasoned non-conformist took in seeing children all dressed
the same?

But when it came to the language arts — talking, writing and reading
— it was the children who taught Sylvia. Talking was what they did best.
In hearing their morning talks and casual chatter, Sylvia found such a fascinating reflection of her own inner life, that almost without realising it,
she developed a powerful new skill: she learnt to listen.

Those kids were talking about the most important things in the world:
birth, death, love, hate, sex, pain, happiness, fear. Being captioned and
defused effortlessly around her every day were all the unnameable, crippling fears of her childhood — dead Sylvia's ghost, Papa's lifeless corpse
and Mama's terrible thrashings — and the dream that fuelled her endless
flirting — her longing to be kissed.

To Sylvia, this identification with her pupils was a form of procreation:

> There is quietly occurring in my infant room a grand espousal. . . . They
> become part of me, like a lover. . . . The askance observation first, the
> gradual acceptance next, then the gradual or quick coming, until in the
> complete procuration, there glows the harmony, the peace.
>
> And what is the birth? . . . from the infant room it is work. A long per-
> petuating, never-ending, transmuting birth, beginning its labour every
> morning and a rest between pains every evening.[6]

The sense of espousal dissolved the aversion to touching Maori children that had marked Sylvia's earlier teaching career. Now, though she rarely touched or showed affection for her Pakeha pupils, she embraced her Maori infants with enthusiasm. Anna Vorontosov described the sensation in *Spinster*:

> He is heavy to lift but I can't resist the physical impact of him on me, on a person that has never been touched by a man since I left Eugene. . . . although I feel his paint brush wet through my smock I also feel that big something, . . . like a great instinct, unidentifiable and uncontrollable, take over.

From such espousal the 'key vocabulary' was born, for in listening to their stories, Sylvia came to realise that some words — different words for each child — were more meaningful and memorable than others:

> . . . these words of the key vocabulary are no less than the captions of the dynamic life itself, they course out through the creative channel, making their contribution to the drying up of the destructive vent.[7]

Her pupils learnt to read from their personal key vocabularies. Nearly every day, from their experiences at home or at school, Sylvia helped each child select a new key word. She wrote the word with heavy crayon on a stout piece of cardboard and gave it to the child. The word cards became as personal and precious to the children as the imagery they represented. Children who had laboured for months over 'See Spot run' in the new *Janet and John* readers took one look at 'corpse', 'beer', or 'hiding' and suddenly — they could read.

> Pleasant words won't do. Respectable words won't do. They must be words organically tied up, organically born from the dynamic life itself. They must be words that are already part of the child's being.[8]

Her classification of the key words under two major headings, Fear and Sex, reveals more about the explosive forces in Sylvia's undermind than it does about the children. Under Fear, which she considered to be the strongest instinct, she listed 'Mummy', 'Daddy', 'ghost' and 'frightened', while words associated with love and happiness — 'kiss', 'love', 'haka', 'dance', 'darling', 'together', 'me-and-you', 'sing' — were seen by Sylvia as Sex words.

To her pupils the key vocabulary was exciting, important, and fun. Pere Hanara recalled:

> One day Gilbert Nuku threw a ball inside and broke the window. He was sent to get the strap and when he came back Mrs Henderson gave him the words 'ball', 'window' and 'glass', and made him write them down. He learnt them. Gilbert was a bit of a dunce but when it came to the word 'window', he knew it. After school when we went home and played marbles in the dirt we used to talk about our words. 'I know a bigger word than you — what's your word?'
> 'My word is jalopy.'
> And Gilbert used to say, 'My word is window.'

I thought — Gee, Gilbert got a big word. I wonder what word I could learn next?[9]

The stories from which the key words were born were told in colourful Maori-English. Sylvia recorded them faithfully onto big sheets of paper and pinned them around the walls:

'I caught Uncle Monty pissing behind the tree. He got wild when I laughed at him.'
'My Dad gave my Mum a black eye.'

It wasn't exactly what the Education Department had in mind when it advocated the use of children's experiences in the teaching of reading, but it certainly worked. The excitement and the sense of release created an unprecedented enthusiasm for reading:

Our personal lives were exposed all round the walls. She encouraged it. She said it really makes you feel good. When she got a few with their stories revealed there was peer pressure on the others to do the same. We really caught the reading bug from wanting to read those stories.[10]

Sylvia didn't see the children's stories as an alternative to the departmental texts, but as the beginning of a process that would lead through *Janet and John* to their integration into the dominant culture. 'The issue is simply the transition of a Maori at a tender and vulnerable age from one culture to another, from the pa to European education.'

Janet and John, a British modification of the American *Alice and Jerry* books, were introduced to New Zealand schools in 1950. At the time the School Publications Branch of the Education Department lacked the expertise to produce local readers, and the Government Printer had no suitable colour-printing equipment. With their colourful illustrations and simple storyline (*Come, John. Come and look. See the boats. Look, John. See the boats*), *Janet and John* were an improvement on earlier readers, but compared to the home-grown reading taking place throughout the country, they were dull indeed.

To supplement *Janet and John*, teachers were encouraged to make books based on the children's own lives. So Sylvia made a graduated series of 'Maori Transitional Readers', each one about ten pages long, with a picture and a word or short sentence on each page. The central characters were Ihaka and Mere.

Ihaka was probably named after the little boy who had won her heart at Pipiriki, while Mere may have been the motherless girl mentioned in *Spinster* and *Teacher*. Motherlessness appealed greatly to Sylvia; nearly all her novels feature a woman who had grown up without a mother. Also, the word Mere had powerful associations: Maori for a skull-splitting weapon, and also for Mary, with its Biblical overtones; and French for mother.

Her experiments with illustrations and text varied in their effectiveness. Books that the children enjoyed were quickly worn out; books that failed to interest were burnt. Few, if any, of her classroom readers survived.

Her maxim was: 'First books must be made of the stuff of the child him-self, whatever and wherever the child.'

She based word recurrence and sentence length on *Janet and John*, but the drama, the vocabulary and the illustrations were very different. While other teachers were making books written in standard English about happy events like going to the beach, Sylvia's major theme was Daddy going away and either leaving the child or taking him or her along. She saw this as one of the most powerful and poignant dramas affecting her pupils; as it had been, and indeed still was, a powerful and poignant drama to the child-Sylvia deep inside her — the child-Sylvia who still wept over Papa's departures to hospital, rejoiced over his returns, and was devastated by his death. Around the basic theme, Sylvia wove stories of fears, crises, hatreds, drunkenness and beatings. In one book Daddy came home drunk from the pub and gave Ihaka a hiding, in another the beating was administered by Ihaka's Nanny.

The words she used were the children's own, and she put them together in the children's own way. Like his Fernhill counterparts, Ihaka asked 'Where's him?', and demanded 'Give it for me!' The shock value of the local vernacular would have appealed to Sylvia, but her acceptance and use of it probably went deeper; in identifying with Maori five-year-olds she would have felt again and responded to an elemental childhood need for unqualified approval — a need of which language is an integral part.*

Allowing Maori-English into her classroom made Sylvia a more relaxed teacher; at Waiomatatini she made children say, 'Please may I go to the toilet, Mrs Henderson,' or wet themselves in the attempt. At Fernhill, 'I want to go for a piss,' was cheerfully accepted. Incorporating Maori-English into her reading books followed from her acceptance of its verbal use, and making the illustrations schematic, rather than representational, followed from her observations of children's art:

> I feel that when I come down to their level in text it's a matter of har-mony to come back to their level in drawing too. . . . I should be ashamed to fall so far out of step with my five-year-olds as to see a tree as green or a sky as blue. In the Maori infant room over the years I have been brought up amid black roofs, orange houses, green ears, yellow faces, purple trucks and turquoise rain, so if I am charged with riot in colour it's the company I keep. How they draw I draw and what they write I write.[11]

---

*Eighteen years passed before the truth that Sylvia had grasped intuitively was estab-lished with academic precision. In 1968 William Labov, an American linguist, demon-strated that ghetto children did not, as was commonly supposed, speak a degenerate form of standard English, but a sophisticated dialect of their own with which they fluently expressed logical thoughts and abstract ideas, and focused on long-range goals. He argued that speakers of non-standard English do poorly at school not because they are socially, culturally or verbally deprived but because teachers consistently misunderstand and belittle their native vernacular.

It was a great idea in theory, but according to Pere Hanara, the kids weren't impressed:

> We thought she was a terrible artist because most of her figures were stick figures. One picture looked like a concrete path with a ball stuck in it; you couldn't tell it was Ihaka swimming until she read us the story. We thought her colours were funny too. We wanted real pictures. Janet and John had a real dog, with hair. John had shoes with laces. We wanted that sort of detail. Also John was an easier word to read than Ihaka. I liked *Janet and John* better, but what we really learnt to read on were those stories around the walls.[12]

Inspector Lewis was both fascinated and worried by Sylvia's innovations. He encouraged her to put her methods and theories into a coherent teaching scheme, he arranged for the appointment of a junior assistant to the infant room (an unusual step outside the Maori School Service), he lent her a large-print typewriter to aid the production of her transitional readers, and in July 1951 he brought Mr Lopdell, Senior Inspector of Primary Schools, to see her work.

Shortly after that he took a set of Sylvia's little books to the head office of the Education Department. They were seen by Mr Ball, the inspector Sylvia had fallen in love with at Horoera and who in 1950 had become Assistant Director of Education. He showed them to one of his associates, Mr Ewing, and then they lay on his desk until they caught the eye of the Director. Dr Beeby had never heard of Sylvia Henderson until then, but he was delighted with her books:

> They were lively, and I thought quite effective, though there was language in them that some parents may have objected to. I liked her idea of basing reading material on the children's own experiences.[13]

The problem was — what to do with them. Publication by the department was ruled out; a large sum had just been spent on the imported readers, and the feedback from teachers was that they were boring. It seemed that a reading text developed for one country, or even one classroom, was of limited applicability to other classrooms in other places. But Dr Beeby wanted to see something come of Sylvia's work:

> I said, 'I think the only thing we can do is send them back to Rowland Lewis and see if he can think of some way of using them in the surrounding district.' I saw no chance of universalising her little books, but I wanted to keep the work alive.[14]

Two months after Mr Lopdell's visit another head office inspector, Mr Pinder, visited Sylvia's classroom.

> Rowland Lewis told me that she'd come to Fernhill from the Maori Service where she'd had indifferent treatment. He said, 'I'm looking after her myself.' I spent the whole day in her classroom and came back bubbling over. She was *alive*. And marvellous with kids. It was exciting. The kids had piles of cards with words on and they sorted through and found

their own words. They were emotionally attached to the cards because they gave expression to an idea that really meant something. I saw her little books in use; there was no doubt that the kids were very keen on reading, and read very well.[15]

Sylvia asked Mr Pinder whether the Education Department would publish her readers but he was not keen on the idea. He was impressed by the lively vocabulary but he didn't like the illustrations, and like Beeby and Ball, he did not see publication by the department as a viable option.

But he too was keen to encourage her. He suggested that she send her books to the New Zealand publisher A. H. and A. W. Reed. When he returned to Wellington he sent Rowland Lewis one of the big-print typewriters purchased by the department for the use of sight-impaired children, which Mr Lewis used to replace the first one he had lent Sylvia.

Sylvia then recalled her original books from the department — who in turn recalled them from the New Zealand publisher Whitcombe and Tombs, where Mr Ball had sent them for comment — and threw herself into making a new set: she wanted to fascinate her pupils, she wanted to impress the department, and she wanted to delight Mr Lewis. But nine days after Mr Pinder's visit, when she was finishing the last of her set of four readers, she fell suddenly, totally, cataclysmically . . . in love.

The man Sylvia fell for was Charles Panckhurst, the young teacher who after relieving at Fernhill in 1950 was now on the staff of Hastings Central School. Charles still saw the Hendersons occasionally; he and his wife had a couple of meals at their home, he sometimes saw Sylvia in town on Friday nights, and at the end of September 1951 he attended the Fernhill School fancy dress ball. His wife either didn't go or left early, Charles can't remember. Indeed, the whole evening was singularly unmemorable as far as Charles was concerned.

For Sylvia the night throbbed with meaning. Charles went home with the Hendersons after the ball and sat and talked with Sylvia after everyone had gone to bed. He was the most attractive man she'd had to herself in a long time. And as she tried desperately, but unsuccessfully, to make him kiss her, the excitement lit the fuse on the longed-for explosion. She poured her exhilaration into a letter to Barbara:

Here is my flesh thrilling. Here is the meaning all over again. The pink sweet peas outside Selah glow, the blue delphiniums from my window glow, and the geraniums beneath the tank. Flowers are the barometer of my soul. . . .

I'm not drunk at the moment. Not from liquor. But I am inebriated with the meaning. . . .

My flesh thrills to the image of a man. A young man. A pathetic man. A good-looking man and almost a mad man. A man devastated from his lot of life. His body is slight but his thoughts are deep-sourced. His words old-fashioned but stately. His ways unpardonable but not boring.

I'm forty-two and he's twenty-four but on some essential plane we meet. . . . Over in the infant room time flies by, pushing away thought of him, until I am aware of an inner glow and stop to identify it. And there I find within the picture of Charles pushing his way through the crowd on shopping nights to me or facing me across my Selah table.

Apart from the fact that he was willing to spend time talking with her, while most of his contemporaries regarded Sylvia as decidedly odd and therefore to be avoided, Charles was a typical young man of his era — stable, friendly and unpretentious. In 1949, after four years away from home, he had returned to the Hastings area, where his parents still lived, and married a local girl he had known since high school. Despite his dark good looks, he wasn't the glamorous knight of Sylvia's dreams, but she was too ravenous to care. She dragged the unsuspecting Charles into her fantasies and there remade him in her own image. He became an alcoholic English loner — orphaned, disturbed and unloved.

After school and at weekends he haunted her life. At its height the obsession probably lasted no more than five days, since the events in Sylvia's diary marking the beginning (the fancy dress ball) and the end (the handing over of her new books and scheme to Mr Lewis) of the phantom affair were in real life only five days apart. But in committing it to paper — in her diary and letters to Barbara — Sylvia made it seem to last for weeks.

In her undermind she stirred the late-night talk after the ball, the occasional cup of coffee with Charles in town on Friday night, and their after-school discussions during the previous year into an intoxicating fantasy that totally possessed her:

Friday. Selah . . . I'm 42 Barbara and I can't stay up till 4am every time this young man wishes to. . . . This boy is killing me Barbara . . . on Friday night coffee, after choir practice Tuesday, on my right Keith, on my left Charles. At the Rank film Wednesday — on my right Keith, on my left Charles. Ballet Thursday — on my right Keith, on my left Charles. Friday shopping tonight presumably — on my right Keith, on my left Charles. Tomorrow Saturday at the vineyards — on my right Keith, on my left — Stop. Enough. Stop. Stop. . . .[16]

While the obsession lasted, the phantom Charles was always there, in Selah or at home, talking with her, singing with her, getting drunk with her. They drank brandy, rum, sherry, wine and lager: '. . . every time Charlie comes to the house I at once start drinking. It's the strain. I don't know why. I've drunk bottles.'

Years later Charles recalled drinking with Sylvia on two occasions when he was teaching at Fernhill in 1950: once when she invited him to Selah and gave him a glass of sherry, and again when Sylvia celebrated the opening of the prefab classroom by polishing off two bottles of sherry. During the following year, the year of the infatuation, when Charles in reality was no longer at Fernhill, he had no more than an occasional glass of beer at the Hendersons' home when he and his wife went there for a meal.

The undercurrents beneath Sylvia's obsession were revealed when she began turning her diary into a novel. As fantasy became fiction, the festering guilt of her long-ago abortion at Mangahume burst to the surface: Charles was her son — the abandoned child who stalked her dreams. In an early draft of the book that later became *Spinster*, the central character was a widowed Frenchwoman, haunted by the dead baby in her past:

> That night when her house was at its emptiest and at its stillest Madame woke. The image that had lain in waiting for this moment was close at hand. It was Charles vanishing into the darkness. Suddenly without a chance of defence coldness clutched her body as other images jostled forward before the inner eye. The dust deep in a long ago grave in England stirred and a form rose from it. It was a woman with a face like Charles. 'That was my son,' she told Madame. 'Could you not have brought him into the comfort of your home for one small hour?'
>
> The dust in another grave in France stirred. It was a ridiculously small grave, and a coffin no longer than an expensive chocolate box. At first the form that took shape was no more than two hands' length but it grew until it was the size of Charles. The face had no definable features and the voice was a not unrecognisable one. 'Mother,' it complained, 'That was me. Didn't you know that was me trying to get to you? I grew up in Charles. He was a spare. You turned me away and didn't bring me home . . . Mother,' spoke the voice in the night. 'You rejected me.'

In letters that to Barbara, and also perhaps to Sylvia, were totally convincing, she wrote of repeatedly drawing Charles to her with caring and seductiveness, and then cruelly driving him away. But when she finally dismissed Charles from her inner life, her reasons were practical rather than emotional. He was seducing her away from her work:

> Friday morning before school. . . . Such a short measure of time back, with Rowland Lewis written right across my mind there was nothing else I could do but wholly lose myself in Ihaka Book Four. But now, with not half the illustrations completed . . . all I can consider is learning Ravel's Bolero for Charles. . . .[17]

After a struggle her dedication to her work won the day. Although in real life Charles remained teaching in Hastings throughout the Henderson's eight years at Fernhill, in her diary Sylvia dispatched him to England late in 1951, leaving her heartbroken but relieved.

The anticipation of Mr Lewis's unannounced visits kept her at school nearly all day, every day, and in the early mornings, the evenings and after school she worked on her scheme and reading books. The new readers were for Mr Lewis alone; she designed and painted each one with care, and instead of stitching the pages together on her treadle sewing machine, she had them bound by a printer.

Two weeks after Mr Pinder's visit she presented the books and scheme to Rowland Lewis, and wrote to Joy that she had finished her work:

The book that is in me has reached the lap of the one it was written for. Not via the publisher. Bad or good, by academic, philosophical or literary standards, it is the best I can do and pockets what I have to say. It's on that lap and that's the full stop of the cycle of impulse.

Mr Lewis has my Maori Infant Reading Scheme, and my Maori primers. They were levered out from the inner, packed storehouses for him alone. He *has* these things. . . . He has held them in his hands, turned the pages, and read them before me, and taken them away to his masculine haunts. That's all I want. I'm fulfilled. I've finished.

To Rowland Lewis, Sylvia's work had just begun. He saw her as a talented teacher but because her scheme was disorganised and her little books lacked consistency he wanted her to develop them further. A few days after receiving the work he took Professor Bailey and Dr Fieldhouse from Victoria University of Wellington to see her classroom. She responded by cowering in a corner, but they were so captivated by the atmosphere of the room they hardly noticed. Professor Bailey recalled:

It was the intensity of life in the classroom that appealed to us. It was a noisy room, but vital and full of learning. The children were friendly and uninhibited. They kept bringing up their little books to read to us. Those little Maoris could read like mad. Their stories were full of violence and four-letter words, which seemed to be what Rowland Lewis was concerned about — he was probably worried that *Truth* would hear about them when the Education Department was already under fire for being too liberal. But it seemed to us that the colourful words were part of the youngsters' natural expressiveness which she was anxious to nourish.

We told Rowland Lewis that the basic principles of her work were sound, that she was tapping the most dynamic source of real teaching — the child's own life — and that it was worth taking the risk to encourage her.

He gave us to understand that she was working on a reading series of her own, which she wanted the Education Department to take up. We didn't see them but I have no doubt that compared to *Janet and John* her work would've been livelier and more closely related to the experiences and interests of the children. But during our visit I recall stating quite strongly that no reading books published in advance, and lacking the immediacy of the children's freshly remembered experiences and feelings, could take the place of her own method.[18]

Rowland Lewis set about supporting her with renewed enthusiasm, and Sylvia was greatly excited by his interest. She read into it the chance of publication (she wanted to be published so badly that the official caution did not deter her); she read into it the promise of a good grading; and she read into it — love:

I can't go through all the incident and counter-incident of that wonderful visit when he displayed me to the university — my teaching, my talking and myself — but I've left nothing unthought and I think he loves me or is near to it. Professor Bailey and Dr Fieldhouse must have seen it too, they must have. I'm breathlessly happy . . . I think I love him.[19]

Then she thought some more, and reached what for Sylvia was an inescapable conclusion: love meant betrayal. She wrote of her discussion on the subject with Keith:

> 'It's lovely being Mr Lewis's pet discovery, dear.'
> 'Yes, it must be.'
> 'But it will all be over in time, everything has its life.'
> 'Yes, he won't last long here.'
> We are drinking tea on the front step where Keith is doing the Saturday lawns.
> 'I don't mean chronologically, I mean that sooner or later he'll prove that he is only human. He'll hurt me or let me down, but I'll be ready. I'll expect it and accept it. He's given me the moment that I treasure.'[20]

After writing about the Bailey and Fieldhouse visit Sylvia drew her school diary to a close; with her scheme and readers finished the creative thrill was over, she was ready to move on.

She returned to the diary occasionally over the following years and would later submit it for publication, but for now teaching as raw material for art was exhausted. Also, that primal force that had driven her into teaching — her fear of Mama — had become subdued. Not only had she taken Mama's fearful power for herself, through the key vocabulary she had turned that source of conflict and violence into a wellspring of peace. Creative teaching wasn't easy and it didn't always work, but she had glimpsed its possibilities and was satisfied.

After 1951 there was only one incentive to continue teaching: the dream of a brilliant grading. Being graded, a stressful experience for any teacher, was for Sylvia profoundly disturbing. It wasn't just the memory of the zero grading, though that still rankled, it was the whole principle of the exercise: how dare they, those philistines, have the temerity to grade her, the great Sylvia Ashton-Warner Henderson? How dare they rank her in print alongside common teachers, when she was in a class all her own?

Since the Waiomatatini zero, Sylvia's grading increases had been insultingly average. But after Mr Lewis's recognition of her work she dreamed of something grand, a grading that would evoke eternal admiration and respect from teachers, from the department and from the country as a whole. Like Anna Vorontosov in *Spinster*, she believed:

> I'm the coming infant mistress in New Zealand. I am that now, in my own view. It's only a matter of time . . . I'll be recognised for what I am. I might even be invited to lecture at the Teachers' Training College on Maori Infant Method. And then I will be part of the world again, part of the country again and among my own kind.

Within the constraints of the grading system it was impossible for Rowland Lewis to give Sylvia the recognition she expected. In evaluating her coverage of the curriculum he had to consider her neglect of

The wedding of Sylvia Warner and
Keith Henderson, 1932.
SA-W PAPERS

Henderson family, Mangahume,
c. 1937.
SA-W PAPERS

Keith Henderson, Whareorino, 1932.
SA-W PAPERS

Henderson family, Horoera, 1939.
G. ROWLANDS

Sylvia carrying Ashton Maori-style, 1938.
J. HUGHSON

Awatere River mouth, Te Araroa in background, 1985.
L. HOOD

Old Pipiriki School, 1985.
L. HOOD

Walter Harris. *c.* 1945.
W. HARRIS

Joy Alley, *c.* 1945.
SA-W PAPERS

Henderson family, Waiomatatini, 1947.
SA-W PAPERS

Rowland Lewis, *c.* 1960.
R. LEWIS

Typical 1940s infant room, Ruatoria Native School, 1948.
NZ DEPT. OF EDUCATION, SCHOOL PUBLICATIONS

Fernhill concert group, *c.* 1951.
SA-W PAPERS

Expressive dancing, Sylvia's classroom, *c.* 1951.
SA-W PAPERS

Come on Kuri.

I want Daddy.
Come on Daddy.
Come home.
Come in the truck.

Pages from early Ihaka book *c.* 1948.
SA-W PAPERS

Banner made by Sylvia in 1950 for the
Fernhill School basketball team.
L. HOOD

Sylvia taking the key vocabulary, *c.* 1951.
SA-W PAPERS

Bethlehem School residence (Selah at right end of verandah), 1986.
L. HOOD

Bethlehem School, *c.* 1965.
SA-W PAPERS

Sylvia with Sir Herbert Read,
1963.
N. HILLIARD

Sylvia and Keith, off to dine
with the Queen, 1963.
K. HARDY

mathematics; in rating her efficiency he could not ignore her lack of a workbook, her failure to record pupil attendance, or the chaos in her room; and in considering her suitability for promotion he could not ignore the smell of alcohol on her breath or the times he had called during school hours and found her in Selah. After all his interest in her work and all the visitors he had brought to see her, the grading increase Rowland Lewis gave her was no better than average.

It was the betrayal she had been expecting. She withdrew her love for him and concentrated on her remaining hope for fame: becoming a published writer. After rewriting *Rangitira* she sent it to Whitcombe and Tombs, who returned it with the opinion that publication would not be an economic proposition. Her next move was to more vigorously cultivate a friendship with Winston Rhodes; surely a professor of English would launch her wonderful career?

Her stay with the Rhodes at Governors Bay at the beginning of 1952 was for her hosts a memorably bizarre two weeks: Sylvia was visited by a man she had picked up on the inter-island ferry; Sylvia went for a walk and, unable find her way back, knocked on the door of a nearby house and lisped, 'Here's a little girl who's lost her way'; Sylvia told Winston she was going to be a famous writer; Sylvia waded fully clothed into the sea and arranged herself elegantly on a rock with her red dress floating in the tide; Sylvia took a taxi to a last-ever meeting with Joy Alley, who was staying with her mother several miles away, and made Joy pay the fare; and one evening at around midnight Sylvia drank a bottle of sherry and spent the rest of the night pacing the floor and wailing, 'I want Walter! I want Walter!'

When Barbara invited her to stay the following year, Sylvia replied:

> You might as well know that I am a terrible guest and when I was down at Sophie's a year or so ago I didn't do a thing in the house for weeks. . . . I do nothing, but drink tea. I'm fastidious irritable lazy difficult and unreasonable and embarrassing and have love affairs that people don't like.

On her return home she sent *Rangitira* to Sophie.

> Sophie . . . said she wished to read it again but couldn't face all those 'flopping flapping pages'. . . . She said it was wearing to read *partly* on account of the paper. A broad hint to publish possibly. . . . Winston took it from her as she was packing it up to return. This is the height of my wish. That Winston Rhodes could read my *Rangitira*. I'm happy.[22]

She never told Barbara of Winston's reaction, but years later he recalled thinking, 'Oh dear, Sylvia. You'll have to do better than this.'

Despite Winston's doubts, Sylvia's determination to be published remained undimmed. Recalling Mr Pinder's suggestion, she made a new set of reading books, tied them up with ribbons and bows, and sent them to A. H. and A. W. Reed.

The managing director, Mr A. W. Reed, was a puritanical Methodist and teetotaller who routinely rejected manuscripts that failed to show a reverent attitude to life. But his interest in children's books, in education, and in things Maori, and the fact that he was an a enterprising publisher, worked in her favour. A. W. Reed was totally captivated by Sylvia's work. Sylvia wrote to Barbara:

> Reeds are *jumping* about Ihaka and my new Reading Scheme. . . . they say they are 'immensely taken' 'very enthusiastic' 'greatly appreciative' of my work and hope to spread it further afield. . . . However the publication of Ihaka depends apparently on the Ed. Department acknowledging them as textbooks in the Maori Schools which is a thing I never intended. And can't see it happening. They are to be done in *full colour* which brings deep breathing to my mind. *Everything*. At fantastic cost, they tell me. I feel I've met my publisher for all time. I'm trying to keep sex out of it — but you know me. It all may come to nothing anyway — but I did enjoy the afternoon tea with A. W. All this is *skite*.

The following month Reed wrote:

> We had a talk with Mr Ball and have found him very sympathetic and enthusiastic about your work. . . . He said that he knows that a certain number of copies will sell if it remains in its present form, but if it is 'vetted' by departmental officers and amended according to their own ideas it will be officially recommended which will make a very considerable difference to sales.
>
> As you will anticipate this will be an important matter to us, but at the same time I realise that the integrity of your purpose must not be interfered with in any way.

The key departmental officer was Mr Parsonage, Chief Inspector of Maori Schools (1948–1955), who signed the order forms for Maori school textbooks.

The head office of the Maori Schools Division had by 1952 moved to Auckland; 400 miles away from Wellington and, with the conservative Mr Parsonage at the helm, 400 miles away in spirit from the liberal policies of Dr Beeby. Mr Parsonage, like all his colleagues in the Maori Schools Inspectorate, considered Sylvia to be an unbalanced and inadequate teacher, and he could see no virtue in her work. Reed was disappointed but not deterred, and planned a special trip to Auckland to meet with Parsonage. But in October Parsonage was too sick, in November he was too busy, and in December he was too tied up with the pre-Christmas rush.

The two men finally met early in 1953 and Parsonage made his objections clear: the vocabulary was coarse, the grammar was shocking, the illustrations were incomprehensible, there was no coherent theme to the set, and the stories would frighten the children. As always, Sylvia was determined to be true to herself, but this time she faced a terrible choice: if she didn't compromise her principles she could lose what seemed like a once-in-lifetime chance to become a famous published author.

At first she protested to Reed:

It's not that I don't know the formula for a successful New Zealand book or that I can't do it. . . . It's just that I can't organise my heart. . . .

I can't copy anything or anybody, Mr Reed. I can't qualify my Infant Room reading work by the work already in the country. . . .[23]

But from time to time over more than two years of negotiations she offered to make a new series with a consistently developing theme, a dignified vocabulary, representational illustrations, and 'emotional and spiritual qualities that I can't see should be ignored in young children's reading'. Sometimes her offer was wholehearted, sometimes it was reluctant, and usually she changed her mind. She began at least four new series, but, after the first set, never sent a full series to either Reed or Parsonage. They kept asking for a complete set, or even a simplified outline of a complete set, but what they got were meticulously painted samples of book two, or book three, of a series she had in mind but failed to describe.

Her unpredictable swings between co-operation and defiance must have tested Reed's patience to the limit:

Poor old A. W. Reed is having a job handling Mr Parsonage and me. And he's cunning and persuasive and firm and hopeful and disinterested and sometimes he bluffs and turns his back but you don't know the whole story. . . . I haven't been able to get him to kiss me yet. His first letters used to be *Kindest* regards but now they're not. But you've no idea how I've played up. At one stage because I was angry with the Ed. Dept I took my books away from Reeds and sent them overseas. Or *wrote* overseas, then changed my mind and returned them to Reeds. He took all this. The whole lot.[24]

In his letters to Sylvia, Reed was unfailingly courteous and encouraging, and despite setbacks his interest remained high, but in a staff memo many years later he recalled: '. . . what an infuriating author I found her to deal with. Her eccentricity drove me up the wall.'

While Reed was persistent and enthusiastic, Parsonage was not. He never invited Sylvia to discuss her work with him in Auckland, or found time during his routine visits to Hawke's Bay to call on her, and he often put off replying to her letters for months. This was the sort of treatment Sylvia had come to expect from the Education Department, but so determined was she to see herself as the victim of Dr Beeby that the thought of Parsonage being responsible for her difficulties seems never to have crossed her mind.

Contrary to what she chose to believe, support for the books from the department in Wellington was strong; so strong that after two years of stonewalling from the Maori Schools Division, Reed was prepared to begin publishing without Parsonage's consent:

We have been conferring with the Education Department on a number of matters recently and were delighted to discover that in the Department there was a great admiration for you work and an anxiety to have some of your reading books, which has apparently not been shared by the branch of the Department dealing especially with Maori schools. . . .

I should imagine that there is no better way of fostering that enthusiasm and promulgating some of your ideas than to produce a first Ihaka book and I am wondering if you have finally worked out the details and have the material available. In whatever form you have it now, I wonder if you would be good enough to let us have a copy of the first book and we would be glad to look into the possibilities of its production as a Reader to start the series off as early as possible.[25]

Reed calculated that the maximum economical page size would be ten inches by seven and a half, but Sylvia insisted that book one needed to be bigger. Then Parsonage re-entered the debate and suggested that Sylvia produce a complete set for testing in other infant rooms. Sylvia argued with both men and co-operated with neither. Within a month the newly generated momentum was lost.

The transitional readers were not Sylvia's only literary preoccupation between 1952 and 1954. She also worked on and submitted several short stories, her teaching scheme, her *Diary of a Maori School*, and her new novel, *Spinster*. Her four stories, including one called 'The Key Vocabulary', appeared in the New Zealand journal *Here and Now* between 1952 and 1955 under the name 'Sylvia' and alerted the local literary community to a vigorous new writer in its midst.

Early in 1953 she sent her reading scheme to Sir Herbert Read. He replied warmly, but said it contained insufficient material to make a book. She considered adding her *Diary of a Maori School* and publishing the two works in one volume, but first she sent the diary to Whitcombe and Tombs, who replied: 'The material for a successful book is there, but it needs a certain amount of selective pruning and then rewriting in a more definite consecutive shape.'

In the course of rewriting, the power of fiction electrified Sylvia as never before. She wove in her passion for Charles, that had become blended in her undermind with her confused feelings toward her son Elliot — the real-life replacement for her lost baby, now grown to a handsome young man with eyes the colour of delphinium petals. And she closed the fictional relationship with her favourite romantic ending, a lover's suicide.

She turned the central character into a spinster. Sylvia had admired, longed for and loved a multitude of spinsters in her life, but Anna Vorontosov had a quality that all the others lacked: Anna Vorontosov could be controlled. Everything she did, said or thought was at Sylvia's command; compared to the torture of relating to Joy or Monika, relating to Anna was sheer bliss. And not only could she control Anna, Sylvia could become Anna. In her fantasy life as Anna Vorontosov she could enjoy the freedom of spinsterhood without the inconvenience of having no Keith to look after her.

As the world of the imagination become increasingly appealing, Sylvia turned away more often, and for longer periods, from unyielding reality. She took three months' sick-leave at the beginning of 1953 and spent her days in Selah. When she returned to school her interest in working with children and her involvement in extracurricular activities declined sharply, and continued to do so until her retirement from teaching in 1955.

During her peak teaching years (1950 to 1952), in addition to developing the key vocabulary she formed a school orchestra, which performed at concerts and flower shows around the district and was featured in a broadcast by the local radio station. She organised dazzling school concerts and fancy dress balls and, in an unlikely departure for the unsporty Sylvia, coached the prizewinning school basketball team.

But the school log records that in 1953 school concerts and outside entertainments by the orchestra ceased and the 'A' basketball team no longer won all its matches. After Keith was hospitalised for eight weeks with gallstones at the end of 1953 his extracurricular activities, like the film evenings he held for school parents, also ceased. After 1954 the highlight of the school year, the fancy dress ball, was no longer held. In 1956 the annual gala day joined the list of casualties.

Sylvia's letters to Barbara illuminate the shadow behind her withdrawal from school: her need for alcohol was becoming uncontrollable. By 1953, in letters written to Barbara Dent in an exaggerated Maori-English, she was indicating that her drunkenness was no longer confined to the privacy of Selah.

> Dear lunatic, I'm drunk and am typing very slowly. . . . Ah the indulgences between man an man! One of my loves Rev Carr who shake those hand wit me after dose church he come to see me dis afternoon. My hubban he bringed him back see? I am bare feet and I bring da bottle of beer an ONE glass nito the drawing rooms and discusses. we refers to god an them, and spiritual tings. Now this man he fqlls down in the mddle of a ssntence when I bappears wit dose beer. This man whose bread and butter is his sentence, the conceptii of it and the deliverance of it he fals down in the middle of his sentence whoxe life is the deliverance of stutnce pon sentens, he scrambles like a worm cut in half for the other half of his sentence. Ah rich rich rich rich rich. But he found the other half of his sentence and I drank glassafter gladd after glassa and gave him a line on how to preach. rich rich rich rich rich rich rich rich r

Her public behaviour, which at Waiomatatini had been outrageous, was now becoming embarrassing: a Maori parent invited in for a cup of tea sat opposite Sylvia across the dining table, but when she put her feet on the table so that he could see up her skirt and asked him what he thought of legalised prostitution, he fled. The acting headmaster when Keith was in hospital recalls Sylvia inviting him and the Reverend Tom Carr to her home and embarrassing them both by introducing every expletive she knew into the conversation; and a teacher from a school beyond Fernhill, when driving home one Saturday night, was astonished to see Sylvia dancing naked in the moonlight.

Early in 1954 she admitted to Barbara that she was drinking in school (though her colleagues suspected that she had been doing so furtively since her arrival at Fernhill):

> Sherry this time . . . Brandy is too harsh and dry sherry makes things jump. So it's sweet sherry. A glass full before school in the morning and one at lunch. . . . Somehow the woman must keep going, whatever the cost in alcohol. 3 p.m. Now I must lie down. Don't reply.[26]

The need to escape grew urgent. She booked and cancelled berths on overseas passenger liners so often that (according to Sylvia) the clerk at the travel office hid under the counter when he saw her coming; she put a request in the Australian teachers' journal asking for a summer holiday job; and she wrote, but did not post, a letter to UNESCO asking for work. But instead of travelling abroad she took three weeks' sick-leave in the middle of 1954, and again stayed in Selah.

The break didn't help. She blamed the circumstances of her life and the people round her for her continuing need to drink, and claimed repeatedly that she had stopped. Nearly a year after Keith's hospitalisation she wrote to Barbara:

> The brandy was the result of Keith being in hospital last year with a new head in his place. The only way I could get there was to drink myself there. At the time I was reading a book called 'The infirmities of genius' in which all these geniuses despised a trifle like brandy and lived on opium and hashish. The idea looked alright to me, since it got me to school anyway, except for the headaches and the real damage to my work. But it's all over now. . . . But brandy is handy on occasion. It doesn't inebriate: it only brings me from a condition of immobilising nervousness, or even crippling hysteria over fright over something, up to what I should normally be. It brings me UP to normality. To me it's a necessary social medicine. But I hate sherry, which does inebriate me, but like Lager. Very much. But the weeks go by and I never drink anything. Except last week at the inspector's visit, an inspection, I began to die in the prefab, and knew that I could never get through. I've tried before, so came home and began on the sherry because there was no brandy. I drank all day. They MUST have smelled my breath. . . .

Surprisingly, her grading that year was no worse than usual. But by then it must have been clear to Keith — and perhaps also to the inspectors and to Sylvia herself — that she could not continue teaching much longer.

For Sylvia the following year was even worse. Her heart was broken yet again — this time over the Reverend Tom Carr, minister of the Methodist church Keith attended in Hastings. He was a likeable, unsophisticated man, and a powerful preacher. She had first noticed him in 1951:

> Now a minister has always been a desired mate for me. Such inaccessibility, and such spirituality. Now this Reverend Carr shook my bare hand coming out of church the other night then followed us out and found occasion to shake our hands again, from which I have taken some encouragement. . . .[27]

By 1954 her interest had grown to an obsession. Her dramatic late entries into Carr's evening services used to unnerve the other worshippers: instead of slipping discreetly into a back pew, she would sweep down the aisle past the congregation at the back and the empty seats in front to sit immediately before the pulpit and gaze enraptured at the preacher throughout the sermon. Straight after the sermon she would stand up and make an equally dramatic exit.

But in February 1955 Carr was transferred to Christchurch, and in the early months of that unhappy year her letters to Barbara deteriorated into disjointed pencil scrawls:

> 20 to 10. that's the last of the 37% alcohol. I took it all at 9 a.m. . . . .
> 10.15: . . . I go into deep hells. I am full of alcohol — of desire for T.C., and spiritual agony, and married person for Keith. . . . Deep deep in the hell of hells the unconscious yours is the only face I recognise The Rev. T.C.
> 2.20. I'm heavily drunk in school. When I shut my eyes I swim.

The end came in June 1955: 'I have been ill since February and have had to resign.'

That same year Mr Parsonage left the Maori Service and withdrew from negotiations with Reeds, and Sylvia temporarily abandoned her ambition to publish her little books.

Two years later, when she and Keith had moved to Bethlehem School near Tauranga, she wrote to the Hawke's Bay inspectors requesting the return of the reading books she had given Mr Lewis at the time she left teaching. The cupboards, files, desks and shelves of the Education Board offices were searched and searched again. Mr Lewis, who had retired the previous year, came in to join the hunt. Then he and the inspectors searched at home. They found nothing.

Everyone could remember seeing some of her books. But when? And where? And what had happened to them? They worried about the annual clean-ups, and especially about the big clean-up when Rowland Lewis retired. Lewis had had less contact with Sylvia once her negotiations with Reeds were underway, but he did recall some torn and finger-marked books and was concerned that his secretary had mistaken them for rubbish.

Lewis's former colleagues suspected that if anyone had lost them it would have been another inspector, Harry Campbell. Campbell was a divergent thinker and collector of bright educational trivia. He had never been known to lose anything important, but the disorder in his office led everyone to suspect the worst. Campbell wrote to Sylvia explaining that the books could not be found. She insisted that they search again. And again. Finally Campbell, who like everyone else had no idea what had happened to them, told her they must have been burnt in the clean-up following Mr Lewis's retirement.

For Sylvia his explanation had a horrifying allure: from childhood, fires, with their exhilarating sorcery, had been her favourite form of destruction. In an early draft of her autobiography she wrote of two youthful episodes of arson (at Umutaoroa and Te Whiti), but later eliminated the incriminating sections, and in adulthood she made regular bonfires of her past writing. So while Campbell thought his story would bring the whole matter to a close, what he did was create a legend: the legend of the burning of the books.

What really happened to the books? One problem is . . . which books? In her negotiations with Reeds she produced at least four sets, either in draft or completed form. It is unclear whether it was a set of these, or an earlier set made for classroom use or for Mr Lewis, that was lost. In her response to Campbell's 'burning of the books' letter Sylvia wrote:

> . . . I would prefer to believe it was accidental, but when I gave them to Mr Lewis, the most precious things I could give to anyone, he neither acknowledged the receipt of them nor thanked me. There are languages other than words. It would have been more humane to have given them away. At least they would be still alive. I am afraid that my own religion and faith in another creature no longer operates. I will never forget the man who could burn them.[28]

This letter illustrates Sylvia's belief that Mr Lewis deliberately burnt her books, but also raises the question of whether in reality he ever received them. Aside from her claim that he betrayed her by not giving her a high grading, the evidence that he supported and encouraged her is strong. Add to that his reputation for being thorough, businesslike and courteous and one is bound to conclude that if he had received the books he would have acknowledged them. He certainly acknowledged something (stories or a new edition of her scheme perhaps?) that she sent him in May 1953: 'Thank you for this contribution. You must write a book some day.'

Perhaps, like the note over which Pan had seemed to betray her a decade earlier, the books were never sent. Or if they were sent they never arrived.

If they weren't sent, what happened to them? Did Sylvia, like Anna Vorontosov, bury them in the garden? Probably not, since the headmaster who succeeded the Hendersons at Fernhill rotary-hoed the entire grounds of the school residence and found nothing. Perhaps she lost or disposed of them herself, or took them with her when she left Fernhill.

Whatever their fate, their meaning for Sylvia lived on in *Spinster*, just one of the writing projects she pursued throughout the crises and drunkenness of her last years of teaching. Self-faith kept her going, as she explained to Barbara:

> The worst influence on your thinking is the forced humility. . . . That I think is the acutest test of an artist. To keep self-faith against the — to keep *hold* of self-faith against and beneath the currents of misunderstanding, derating and contempt. You have to hold so hard. To hold on so hard. Now and again we go under. Then we are washed away. Until we see another branch to snatch at: someone has recognised something

good in us. Something we have done is honoured, or we see an ephemeral light of recognition of us for what we are, in an appraising eye. . . .

The first lesson you must learn is this self-faith. . . . you are gifted, sensitive and clever. Above the average. You are to do more than look the average in the eye as your tentative equals. You are to *rightfully* look down on them. If you can't find your own near by, go *without*. From your choice, not theirs.[29]

During long hours in Selah, Sylvia watched Anna Vorontosov flower into a sensitive, unappreciated, brandy-swigging rebel, while a range of education officials from the director down degenerated into backward, small-minded cogs. Rowland Lewis became 'the inspector — ogre of the past again with its cloudy height, its red eyes and its black mouth.' She wrote about all these characters with a flair and conviction born of years of disciplined attention to her craft, and years of living her vivid inner life to the full.

When she submitted *Spinster* to Whitcombe and Tombs early in 1954, the small population of New Zealand (just over two million) made the publication of fiction economically risky:

There is merit in the work and the writing is vivid and compelling. Our market in New Zealand however is too small to make publication of this type of novel a practical proposition and we suggest that you submit the work to an overseas publisher.[30]

Her attempt to have her teaching scheme published in New Zealand was more successful. Around the time of her retirement she sent one version to A. W. Reed and another to Russell Bond, editor of *National Education* — journal of the primary school teachers' organisation. Reed, no doubt feeling that her little books were enough to cope with, declined to publish, but Bond was definitely interested. It arrived as a 'semi-coherent manuscript of jumbled text and drawings', but he was impressed by the vitality of the writing and the importance of the message. He reorganised the bundle into five instalments and published them from December 1955 to May 1956, under the general heading: 'The Maori Infant Room — Organic Reading and the Key Vocabulary.'

In her later writing Sylvia never acknowledged those articles. They were probably more than she wanted (because they undermined her claim to having been rejected in her own land), and less than she expected (because they failed to satisfy her appetite for universal admiration and fame).

The prospect of real fame came soon after. At the end of a newsy letter to Barbara on Christmas Eve 1955, she added casually: 'And don't let me forget the cable I had from London yesterday saying that Secker and Warburg want 'Spinster'.'

Within a week the implications of the cable began to sink in. She sent Barbara a brief clipping from the Hastings paper saying that Mrs Henderson of Fernhill had had a book accepted for publication, and wrote:

> Fame is a disappointment. Twelve hours was enough for me. Twenty-
> four settled me for ever. No more newspapers for me ever. I went to bed
> for two days over it. It's *ghastly.* . . .

But at least now the whole unhappy struggle of her life made sense. She
really was as unique and wonderful and famous as she'd always claimed.
The realisation released an eruption of bitterness. Triumph and vindication
turned to resentment and contempt. Those philistines who had failed to
honour her genius, who had conspired to persecute and humiliate her, she
hated them all: the loves who had betrayed her; the inspectors who had
graded her zero (or worse still, average), who had forced her out of
teaching and burnt her books; the publishers who had rejected her — all
of them, all of them. . . . And above all that unloving mother-country:
New Zealand. Her letter to Barbara continued:

> Do you want me to say 'Yah!' to anyone for you? Ah how I'm going to
> cut certain people in the street! People who could not see me as I am. You
> are about the only one I don't want to get out my knife to. At last I've
> got them all where I want them and *Inspectors* head the list.[31]

Rowland Lewis, cheerfully unaware of his role as villain, sent her a friendly
note:

> I was very pleased to see in the local paper that your novel has been
> accepted for publication. Permit me to offer you my heartiest congratula-
> tions and best wishes for future successes.

Success did not bring happiness. The adjustments to stopping teaching,
becoming a full-time writer, and being accepted into the literary world,
induced in Sylvia a bout of dangerously high blood pressure. Her need for
alcohol continued, but she learnt to control it for weeks on end by turning
to tranquillisers, cigarettes, very strong tea and work.

During 1956 she revised *Spinster*, prepared another set of infant reading
books and worked on a selection of short stories. She continued to keep
a diary, but wrote less often and less intimately to Barbara. The acceptance
of *Spinster* seemed to mark the end of her need for a confidante; during
1956 their correspondence dwindled and during 1957 it ceased altogether.

Sylvia's relationship with A. W. Reed also went into decline. In January
1956 she told him that a novel of hers had been accepted in London, and
that she had begun a new infant reading set, which she invited him to come
and see, since she felt it was too big to post. Reed, no doubt aggrieved that
she had not offered him *Spinster*, congratulated her on the book's acceptance,
expressed disappointment that he had not seen it, and stated firmly that he
could see no opportunity to call on her in the forseeable future.

She tried Whitcombe and Tombs with her scheme and some teaching-
related stories, but they felt that publishing solely for an audience of
teachers was not an economic proposition. She sent the same collection to
the Director of Education and, after hearing nothing for two months,
wrote a scathing letter:

Would you kindly send to me by return registered mail two pieces of work, 'Organic Teaching' and 'The New Race' which you have held since early August without acknowledgement. It is a routine, elementary courtesy to acknowledge receipt of an only copy; however trivial the content.

Dr Beeby was overseas at the time and the reply, on behalf of the Acting Director of Education, explained that the work had arrived without a covering letter, or any indication of her name and address, but had been read with great interest. Sylvia protested that a covering letter, seeking endorsement for the use of her scheme in teachers' colleges, had in fact been sent; and added that since Sir Herbert Read was interested in the scheme, and her London publishing house was interested in her stories, she would now send the work overseas: 'This is not the first time my work had been ignored in my own country and appeared subsequently abroad.'* The man at the department insisted that a covering letter had not been received, and went on to suggest that the New Zealand Council for Educational Research (NZCER) may be interested in publishing her work, adding:

I would think that teachers' training colleges, especially in the North Island, might be glad to make some use of it if it were to be published. You will understand that the Department does not prescribe books for the teachers' colleges, but we are always willing to draw their attention to material that we think would be particularly helpful in their work with students.[32]

Sylvia did not approach the NZCER — an innovative group that published for teachers and academics — but turned her attention to revising *Spinster*.

Her editor at Secker and Warburg, John Pattisson, suggested that although the elusive details of Miss Vorontosov's private life were part of the book's appeal, a little clarification would be helpful. Sylvia responded by pouring everything into *Spinster II*. The original book about a teacher and her infant class became submerged in a lengthy saga on the many emotional problems of Anna Vorontosov. Pattisson wrote to Sylvia, tore up his letter, went on holiday, and wrote again when he returned: 'Now though much — indeed most — of the new material is fascinating and excellent, it is too much . . . one can only stand her highly strung intensity for so long. . . .' He persuaded Sylvia to tone down or eliminate Miss Vorontosov's personal entanglements with the Reverend, the inspector, and 'the old Maori whose name I forget', and to confine her treatment of relationships to Paul (Charles/Elliot). By the middle of 1957 the revisions had been agreed upon and *Spinster* was ready to go to press.

But Sylvia was lonely. Apart from her fictional characters, she had only

---

*At that time — although *Spinster* had been accepted — none of her work had appeared abroad, but several pieces, including the instalments of her scheme, had been published in New Zealand.)

her family for company, and by 1957 her children were leading independent lives: Jasmine was living in Hastings with her husband and first child,
and Ashton was training as a motor mechanic in Wellington, where Elliot
was attending university. Sylvia didn't even have a lover to address in her
diary; in her despair she wrote to God:

> April 26: I'm a figure of ridicule and contempt. How do you live in a
> world where you are despised, no one even to talk to in my own language,
> and when I'm fool enough to utter one sentence of importance to myself
> — silence, embarrassed silence . . . I'll be glad when I'm dead. . . . What
> grounds have I left for still supposing that you have a use for me, living
> in a foreign land, uprooted. . . .
> April 29: . . . But I am not alone. You are my lover, God, I've had prac-
> tice in love affairs and am not unacquainted with the rhythm of love. The
> Hells and Heavens of it inspire me for the day, God. . . .'

But even God was not company enough:

> April 30: I told Keith that I want to go back teaching with him last night,
> but he does not allow himself the luxury of believing it, thinking that I
> will probably change my mind. I don't think so.

Sylvia kept insisting and in June 1957 Keith applied for the position of
headmaster, and Sylvia for infant mistress, at the largest and most presti-
gious Maori school in the country, Bethlehem Maori School, near
Tauranga, in the Bay of Plenty. Keith's application was successful and
Sylvia was offered the job of relieving teacher to a senior class for one term.
They took up their appointments in September 1957.

ELEVEN

Bethlehem

THE BETHLEHEM RESIDENCE SAT SQUARE IN THE SCHOOL GROUNDS surrounded by trees, classrooms and children. At the front, a short flight of stairs rose to a verandah with a small room at one end; this room became Sylvia's new Selah. When she wasn't teaching a class of eight-year-olds, or tending her beloved flower garden, she spent most of her time in Selah — reworking *Rangitira* into a trilogy, seeking publishers for her teaching scheme, short stories and latest set of infant readers, and writing a new novel, *Bachelor*.

The teaching was a disaster, '. . . completely out of my teaching context in a class I didn't understand and couldn't teach successfully . . .'.* But why worry about teaching when she was about to become a real published author: rich and famous and loved?

Secker and Warburg had taken a gamble with *Spinster* — an unpromising title by an unknown, fifty-year-old schoolteacher from an obscure country half a world away. The gamble paid off: the reviews were wonderful and the first printing sold out within a fortnight of its February 1958 launching. The second printing sold out within a month; by the time the book reached New Zealand — in late July — the third printing was selling well and Sylvia had signed a contract with Simon and Schuster for publication in America.

Spinster's arrival in New Zealand could not have been better timed. For decades the nation's fiction had been dominated first by Katherine Mansfield and then by Frank Sargeson. In 1957 and early 1958 came three stunning novels: Janet Frame's *Owls Do Cry*, Ian Cross's *The God Boy* and M. K. Joseph's *I'll Soldier No More*. The critics were agog with excitement; like wise men from the east they saw a wondrous event on the horizon: the birth of The Great New Zealand Novel. Then a literary star shone over Bethlehem . . . and lo! *Spinster* was born. The book was hailed as the best ever written in New Zealand, and was more discussed and praised in the media than any previous New Zealand novel.

Discussion ranged over questions such as: is it a work of fiction, or a thinly disguised treatise on educational theory and racial understanding? Is the weepy, theatrical, brandy-swigging, flower-communing Anna

---

*Sylvia claimed that after that experience she was graded too low ever to teach in New Zealand again, though in fact, as was routine for relieving teachers, she was not graded at all for her one term's work.

Vorontosov a possible person? Was teaching ever like this? And who is Sylvia Ashton-Warner, and how autobiographical is her book? It seemed that the only people who kept quiet were Education Department officials and folk who had known Sylvia in earlier days.

The acclaim from her despised New Zealand rained like hammer-blows on Sylvia's delicate psyche. She ignored the telephone, answered no fan mail, wrote no articles, accepted no speaking engagements and granted only one interview (which she later complained that she had been tricked into giving by her sister Daphne). Instead, from her Selah bunker she wrote long, passionate, unposted letters to reviewers of *Spinster*, revealing, among other things, why she could not, and would not, accept the approval of her country. 'I've hated New Zealand so much,' she confessed, '. . . I still hate it and I suppose I always will. . . .'

This hatred, one of the great driving forces of her life, depended on rejection for its survival. Sylvia dedicated herself to avoiding the approbation being showered upon her, and in time her efforts bore fruit. Her refusal to accept even the most undemanding of honours, such as membership of the writer's organisation PEN or an entry in *Who's Who in New Zealand*, ensured that before long the invitations dried to a trickle and she was able to settle back into her favourite role of neglected genius.

To reporters she justified her isolation by asserting that she was too modest and too busy; in private she claimed that those who sought to honour her really wanted to exploit her, and that appearing in public would invite attack from 'The Permanent Solid Block of Male Educational Hostility'; and in unposted letters she admitted that she was simply terrified and could not cope.

She may have coped better with the negative opinions people from her past were voicing in private — people such as Keith's friend from Whareorino, who, remembering Sylvia as a helpless new bride, insisted, 'Keith wrote that book. I'm pretty sure he must've done because Sylvia didn't have sufficient brains to write a book like that.'

Some people in the Maori School Service shared his opinion. Others conceded that Sylvia could have written *Spinster* and a few even loved it, but they all scoffed at her autobiographical-heroine-as-inspired-teacher.

Then there were the hurt and angry education officials associated with Sylvia's work at Fernhill. Hadn't they bent over backwards to encourage her? Anyone less sympathetic would have fired her many times over for her drinking, her absenteeism and her disregard for the curriculum. And what about the way she portrayed the Education Department, from the Director down? It was as if she was the only person in the country with new ideas. How could she do this in the midst of the most exciting educational reform of the century? And how could she, how *could* she, suggest that they would suppress an innovation so much in tune with the times?

Nonetheless they kept their reservations to themselves, no doubt realising that anyone from Sylvia's past who spoke out risked being labelled as one of the small-minded persecutors in her novel.

Under these circumstances the evidence of rejection that filtered back to Sylvia was slight, but whatever there was she collected assiduously. She picked up a few crumbs from the new Senior Inspector of Maori Schools, who paid a ten-minute visit to Bethlehem in March 1958. Mr Robertson didn't call on her at the residence (now what should she read into that?), but he did tell Keith he had read a proof copy of *Spinster*, and made no further comment (that surely was significant). In her agitation, Sylvia overlooked the fact that during the previous year Mr Robertson had approved her reading books for use in Maori schools and had encouraged the Hamilton publisher Paul's Book Arcade to publish them. Blackwood Paul was negotiating with the department about use of the books in regular state schools. (Because of an ongoing Maori migration to cities, most Maori children now attended state schools and publication solely for Maori schools could no longer be justified.) He was also negotiating with Sylvia about the illustrations: her latest set included fairies, which seemed inappropriate, and her riotous use of colour presented considerable technical difficulties.

During his visit to Bethlehem Mr Robertson enquired from Keith about progress on the Maori books and reiterated his interest in seeing them published. But to Sylvia that didn't count; what mattered was that he hadn't come to see her and he hadn't commented on *Spinster* — and that added up to one thing: rejection.

She expressed convictions of that sort in the few letters that escaped from Selah to her small circle of confidants, among them Blackwood Paul, John Pattisson of Secker and Warburg, and two enthusiastic New Zealand fans, literary critic Arnold Wall and poet and journalist Louis Johnson. Arnold Wall had chaired a radio discussion on *Spinster* among writer Ngaio Marsh, psychiatrist Harold Bourne and the literary-minded Anglican Dean of Christchurch, Martin Sullivan; he had also, for the first and only time in his twelve years producing the national radio network book review programme, broadcast two reviews of the same book. (One reviewer discussed *Spinster* as a novel and the other commented on its contribution to education.) For his part, Louis Johnson, secretary of the New Zealand branch of PEN, editor of the Parent Teacher Association journal *Parent and Child*, and publisher of the *New Zealand Poetry Yearbook* and the literary journal *Numbers*, had promoted *Spinster* widely and enthusiastically as a unique and valuable contribution to New Zealand literature.

Blackwood Paul, Arnold Wall and Louis Johnson were part of a vigorous cultural minority committed to stripping the post-colonial passivity from New Zealand society. As creative and sensitive men they knew what it meant to be artists among the uncomprehending philistines. Sylvia felt she had at last found her 'own kind'. But in time their warm letters became tempered with a niggling concern; wasn't she being a little ungracious, a tiny bit insular and juvenile, in her response to the tumultuous reception of *Spinster*? Sylvia saw their criticism as proof that she was the victim of a conspiracy, and promptly evicted them from the ranks of her own kind.

Arnold Wall let the correspondence lapse; Blackwood Paul confined himself to business letters; Louis Johnson was was more tenacious. He concluded that Sylvia needed a conspiracy to give her something to fight against in a society largely indifferent to the life of the spirit, and his commitment to New Zealand literature made him determined to support and encourage her, conspiracy need and all. Late in 1958 a chance meeting gave him the opportunity to placate Sylvia and regain his place among her favoured few:

> I was talking to Beeby . . . in a Wellington bookshop. . . . I pointed out your book to him and asked if he'd read it. He nearly clawed his way up the wall when I said I thought it was the best thing done here. He couldn't stand it![1]

Nearly thirty years later Louis Johnson recalled the incident:

> It was the physical reaction that impressed me, the way his hands leapt in the air when I mentioned the book. It was nothing to do with the author, or being anti her ideas or anything else, he just felt it was terribly unfair to him and his department.[2]

The tone of Johnson's letter was probably influenced by his own disenchantment with the Education Department — a job he wanted there had just gone to someone 'with more influence and less savvy' — but his main purpose was to impress Sylvia. She certainly was impressed. Here at last was solid proof that the Director of Education was orchestrating a campaign of unrelenting persecution against her. She indicated to Johnson that in this hostile world he was her only true friend; it was a highly successful formula for evoking loyalty from people she anointed as her own kind, and she used it repeatedly, and to great effect, all her life.

Towards the end of 1958, although Bill Moore of William Heinemann Ltd — the New Zealand distributor of *Spinster* — had become one of her confidants, she restrained herself from posting the letter she wrote him in a blind rage at the news that Janet Frame and James K. Baxter had been awarded State Literary Fund grants. There was no comfort in the fact that she herself had been awarded the Fund's ultimate accolade, the prestigious Scholarship in Letters. How dare they mention her on the same page as those two lesser mortals? She felt insulted, belittled, persecuted. She wanted nothing to do with their scholarship.

She suggested to the Fund that not only was she unworthy of the scholarship, but as she had finished her second novel, for which the assistance was offered, she didn't need it and wished to withdraw her application. The Fund stood firm and nearly three months after the scholarship was first offered, and long after the award had been announced in the press, Sylvia reluctantly accepted it.

Her second novel, built on discarded sections of *Spinster*, was inspired by her love and longing for the Rev. Tom Carr of Hastings, and her jealousy of his intimacy with the Almighty. John Pattisson found the first draft 'brilliant', stimulating, and evocative', but worried about its obscurity, its implausibility, its God-passages and its sob-passages, and the fact that the central character, Germaine de Beauvais, was too much like Anna. That wasn't what Sylvia wanted to hear. She immediately sent the manuscript to Bob Gottlieb, the dynamic young editor who had introduced *Spinster* to America. She had good reason to trust him: *Spinster* had reached bestseller lists in the United States and a breathtaking twenty thousand copies had been sold; it had been ranked by *Time* as one of the ten best books published that year; and Metro Goldwyn Meyer had bought the film rights.

In addition to being enthusiastic, supportive and competent, Bob Gottlieb had a talent for spontaneously tuning in to whatever wavelength brought out the best in his authors. His relationship with Sylvia elicited all that was charming and clever, witty and whimsical, fey and funny, and above all, extravagantly affectionate in his nature. When he responded positively to her manuscript she anointed him her only true friend. 'She made it clear to me,' he recalled, 'that she was clinging to somebody at the end of a lifeline from nowhere to somewhere.'

Which end of the lifeline represented 'somewhere' was a matter of dispute: 'The life of the Provincial,' mused Bob, '(definition: someone who doesn't live in New York, London, Rome or Paris) is all mysterious to me, Manhattan born and bred. To be so *away*. It must be nerve-racking.'

'I always thought wherever I was was the hub of the universe,' retorted Sylvia. 'That's what it feels like, you know. I'm always so sorry for you poor things way out on the fringe in the cold.'

Without telling him about her negotiations with John Pattisson, Sylvia at first said flatly of *Bachelor*: 'I can't do anything more about it or to it. I know there are some things to be done but I can't look at those pages again.'

But she soon found herself working with Bob to make Germaine more authentically French and the biblical passages less overwhelming. The resulting book, renamed *Incense to Idols*, confronted through fiction Sylvia's love-hate relationship with God.

According to her unposted letters, God had already played an important role in the lives of Anna Vorontosov and her creator. To a reviewer who wondered whether Eugene in *Spinster* was God, and who felt that the ending of the book was a mistake, Sylvia wrote of God as a powerful but benign confidant:

> God actually was my mate when I was working. But I . . . baulked at the risk incurred by mentioning too much God in a first novel. But God, like the poetic vision, very much likes things his own way and since he could not get into the book legitimately he squeezed through incognito in Eugene; the permanent love in the background, rejected so often yet in the end needed and used. . . . I conferred easily and habitually with God in making Anna and took his advice most of the time. He hated the happy ending and advised me against it.

But all that chumminess was sheer bravado. In a letter to the Dean of Christchurch, Sylvia was more frank about God's harshness:

> The discomfort of working close to God is that he keeps on putting you in the furnace to temper the steel of you. Sometimes you think you've been put in for the last time and that you'll never come out again. And when you do come out you are so sharp a tool and so sensitive that you can't bear anything else. You feel you must wrap yourself in velvet in a vellum case as they do treasured weapons. [That's] one of the reasons why Anna was so hysterical. . . . Anna was my attempt to portray a genius and they have to be like that. . . .

To all these perceptions, God as confident, God as lover, God as persecutor, God as bestower of genius, Sylvia added her sense of sin and guilt — and created Germaine de Beauvais.

Where Anna Vorontosov reflected the light side of Sylvia, Germaine de Beauvais — a cold, amoral, vain, selfish, clothes-obsessed, heavy-drinking, sexually predatory concert pianist who worshipped Baal, despised God, lusted after a clergyman, and was coldly indifferent to her aborted child — reflected the dark side. Just when Germaine had been brought to full, flamboyant life, Bob Gottlieb discovered a major flaw:

> A serious problem: still nervous about the baby-in-the-wine-glass incident; three of us here have checked with *five* doctors, gynecologists etc. They are all in agreement — that the incident as you tell it is biologically impossible. Apparently, at two months . . . the whole thing looks more like a wounded shrimp or a tadpole than like a tiny human being. . . . If you don't believe our backwoods medicos here, would you yourself inquire from a leading gynecologist or biologist in N.Z.? Unless the woolen curtain makes a big difference biologically, someone is being misinformed, and we have to clear it up soon.[3]

To which Sylvia replied grandly:

> Of course we are different behind the woollen curtain. We develop much more quickly in the embryo. We can talk before we emerge from the womb. Can't you? Aren't you barbarians completely formed at eight weeks in the womb? Here in the centre of the universe we spend only three months in the womb. Tell your earnest gynecologists that. . . .[4]

But she generously agreed to modify the text to accommodate Manhattan biology.

When John Pattisson and Bob Gottlieb had reconciled the different versions Sylvia sent them, *Incense to Idols* was published in Britain and America in September 1960 and released in New Zealand a short while later. There were a few laudatory reviews but overall, both in New Zealand and overseas, the reception was muted. Fans of the classroom scenes in *Spinster* who had been disturbed by Anna Vorontosov's passion and introspection were totally unhinged by Germaine de Beauvais; critics who felt that *Spinster* was overrated were quick to dismiss the new novel; puritanical reviewers hated it; patriotic New Zealanders were upset by its anti-New Zealand tirades; and ordinary readers found so little to like in Germaine that the book gave them no pleasure at all.

The first review to appear in New Zealand, penned by J. C. Reid of the English Department at Auckland University, was unqualified in its condemnation. Louis Johnson told Sylvia that Reid was a narrow-minded Catholic and dust-dry academic; but Sylvia did not want to be placated:

```
                                        Woollen Curtain
                                        March I5 60


My dear Mr. Gottlieb

        I would like to follow your lead and say Mr G. but I find
myself highly unwilling to forfeit those two excellent and extravagant
t's in the middle of Gottlieb which took me two clear seasons to learn.

        About the foetus. Of course we are different behind the
woollen curtain. We develop much more quickly in embryo. We can talk
before we emerge from the womb. Can't you? Aren't you barbarians com-
pletely formed at eight weeks in the womb? Here in the centre of the
universe we spend only three months in the womb. Tell your earnest
gynecologists that. Tell them we are easily three centuries before our
time.

        However I have with pleasure adapted this chapter to accomodate
Manhattan biology. With regards to the sex determination. . I think you
will find that no where in this chapter are assumptions made of definite
sex; it is all supposition. Although in N Z we are easily able to determ-
ine what sex we want before we even conceive. If any Manhattan biologist
or gynecologist has the inclination to study us I'll be glad to put
them up in Bethlehem. There are any amount of unoccupied mangers here and
I would gather for them fresh straw. . (Stop me if I've said this before.)

        I was impressed that an eminent New York publisher still has
the capacity to be 'nervous and dislocated) about a foetus in a wine
glass. I thought only authors were allowed to be that.

        I've had a lot of rain lately and I've been kept indoors for
weeks. I take it hard, beating off a rising fever to start again. If ever
I got on a Comet it wouldbe to escape this most disastrous, exhausting
, abnormal and inexorable temptation.

        With many kind thoughts

                S. Henderson
```

eight weeks in N.Z.

Letter from Sylvia to Bob Gottlieb, 1960.
R. GOTTLIEB

a fantasy she had cherished — that her book, like *Lolita*, would be banned in New Zealand — had not been realised; but in its place here was real, tangible rejection — rejection you could cut out of the newspaper and savour over and over again. While expressing hurt and outrage to her confidants, she made a point of writing, and posting, a grateful letter to J. C. Reid:

> . . . I take your criticism as seriously as you prepared it and believe it without reservation. . . .
> Thank you again for the time you gave, and the skill. It was indeed gracious of you.

Reid was thunderstruck:

> May I take this opportunity of congratulating you on the noble spirit in which you have received my review. I write sincerely when I say that, in some 25 years of book reviewing I have never come across such a balanced and tranquil response to a damning review. . . . May I wish you the utmost good-will and future placidity. . . .[5]

Sylvia showed no such placidity when she sent the review to John Pattisson. 'Is this a review or an attack?' she raged, and added:

> I'll sketch in some background to this for you. When I was teaching, my inspector told me to my face that I was a wonderful teacher, but when it came to grading he brought me down with a sledge-hammer. In loyalty I think to the Director, Dr Beeby. Dr Beeby hated me because his greatest friend fell in love with me one time, and he never forgave me for it. And never let me rise in my profession. . . .
> When *Spinster* came out the whole upper educational world led by Dr Beeby crystallised into hostility which reached me as deadly radiation. They remain that way to this day. . . . Now that *Incense* has come out with my attack on New Zealand the pattern is the same but the guns in this round are bigger. Dr Reid . . . is a big name in New Zealand letters . . . he belongs on the Beeby side. . . .[6]

After that review none of the others mattered, even though some were favourable.

The most perceptive review came from James K. Baxter, a gifted, bawdy, religious, heavy-drinking, social misfit of a poet, who saw Germaine as the-woman-who-tried-to-seduce-God. He delighted in her rejection of the Reality Principle and her devotion to her Mask-Self, and wrote with respect of the obscure creative anguish behind 'this strange, makeshift, crude, showy, sophisticated, magnificent book'.

When a caustic *Listener* reviewer described Germaine as a dipsomaniac and a nymphomaniac, letters springing to her defence and to that of her creator poured in for more than three months. One correspondent described Sylvia Ashton-Warner as 'the one New Zealand novelist, to date, likely to be rated as a genius'; another said she was 'the most important (and the most original) literary talent New Zealand has produced since Katherine Mansfield'; and James K. Baxter asserted that having liaisons with five men did not make a woman a nymphomaniac.

Despite all the discussion there was one aspect of *Incense to Idols* that everyone missed. The book was, Sylvia claimed both when she was writing it and after it was published, her drop in the bucket of public opinion against war. Against war? Was there a subtle global message behind the devastation caused by Germaine's Strontium 90 perfume, and the minister's pulpit prophecies of doom to the sinning city? Whatever the message, it totally eluded her readers. Sylvia was most disappointed. She had always been vigorously opposed to war, seeing it as a frightening expression of the violence in her own undermind. During the writing of *Incense to Idols* she was distressed by the presence of American military advisors in Vietnam. Later the deployment of combat troops drove her to send frantic, tearful letters to Bob Gottlieb; and when New Zealand soldiers joined them her desperation was so great she took a public stand, writing several letters to the newspaper and adding her name to a poster featuring prominent New Zealanders opposed to the war.

Throughout this period Sylvia assiduously cultivated both her friends and her isolation. She told Bob Gottlieb that since the release of *Incense to Idols* she had only one friend left in New Zealand, and when writer Maurice Shadbolt visited her early in 1961 he was moved by her loneliness: 'She was pathetically grateful for my having come to see her — her own words were that she had been ignored.'

Sylvia conveyed the same impression to all the other writers and musicians who came to see her, both before and after Shadbolt's visit — among them Frederick Page, Louis Johnson, Bruce Mason, Noel Hilliard, Barry Mitcalfe and Hone Tuwhare — and to anyone else she favoured with her attention. She told the few fans to whom she deigned to reply that his or her letter was the only expression of praise and thanks that she had received in New Zealand and that the reaction, otherwise, to both *Spinster* and *Incense to Idols*, had been one of spite and misunderstanding.

From time to time the burden of perceived rejection became so great that Sylvia revived her escape plans.

In July 1960 she made a solo trip to Sydney, Australia. Beforehand, knowing that she'd need someone to look after her, Sylvia asked the Australian distributor of *Spinster* for help. The publicity machine churned into action; when she arrived in Sydney reporters and photographers were waiting. Dazed by the heavy dose of codeine she had taken to steady her nerves for the flight, she agreed to an interview. When asked the purpose of her visit she said, 'I just came to buy a pair of gloves.' Then, though the visit was supposed to last a month, she came home after only a few days. Three weeks later a full-page article in the *Australian Woman's Weekly* carried the banner headline: 'From N.Z. — just to buy some gloves'.

Two years passed before Sylvia agreed to another interview, and again she used the glove story to divert the reporter. The occasion was a special screening of the film *Spinster* in aid of the Maori Education Foundation. In a rare public appearance, she launched the evening with a speech almost entirely in Maori. Her dramatic hand gestures were accentuated by sparkling diamantés sewn around the wrists of the long black gloves she had bought in Tauranga for the occasion: 'These are the gloves I bought in Sydney,' she told the reporter. At the conclusion of her speech she announced that she would not stay for the film, and walked grandly up the aisle and out of the theatre.

She knew that Hollywood had done its worst with *Spinster*. Problems with the film had set in early when Sylvia confessed that the inspector was based on an identifiable living person. With MGM demanding a signed release, the offended Mr Lewis refused to sign; with Sylvia's New York agent wondering whether he could be bought, the whole project was almost shelved. Eventually MGM accepted Sylvia's assurance that Lewis's threat of legal action was just bluff ('. . . what he's doing is shielding the Director . . .') and late in 1959 the search for a cast and location began.

The initial plan was to shoot the film in New Zealand. MGM approached the Education Department for assistance, and the request was referred to the November 1959 meeting of the Committee on Maori Education. The committee comprised representatives of teachers, education boards, the Education Department and the Maori people. Some Maori School teachers voiced a vigorous dislike of the book, and many committee members expressed reservations about co-operating with MGM, fearing that the New Zealand education system would be presented in a negative light. No decision was recorded and the matter was not discussed again by the committee.

The official departmental reply has not survived. Whatever it was, it did not deter MGM from sending three executives to New Zealand in mid-September 1960 to search, with assistance from the New Zealand National Film Studio, for a suitable location. They told a reporter that on 12 October forty exccecutives and technicians would be arriving, followed three days later by the stars Shirley Maclaine, Laurence Harvey and Jack Hawkins. They said that scores of local technicians and Maori extras would be hired and thousands of dollars would be poured into the local economy. And then it was all over. A disappointed nation was told that because of the stars' commitments to other films they had no time to travel to New Zealand. In late 1960 *Spinster* was filmed in Hollywood.

Sylvia refused to believe the MGM story. She told her latest confidant, playwright Bruce Mason:

> Now about that hold-up in the filming of *Spinster* — it is the Ed. Dept. digging in its toes. I enclose an extract from the Report of the 1959 meeting of the National Committee on Maori Education where it dealt with the filming of *Spinster*. What few know is . . . it was Dr Beeby who brought up the subject and it was all cver before it began. . . .[7]

Sylvia's conviction was unshaken by the fact that the minutes show no evidence of Dr Beeby's presence (and he had no reason to be there since he was not a member of the committee), nor was she swayed by the reality that MGM had come to New Zealand intent on proceeding with the film months after the meeting at which, she claimed, Dr Beeby had scuttled their plans.*

Shortly before the film was released, Sylvia discovered that among other travesties, MGM had replaced the 'brooding exotic Russian spinster in her forties by an American girl in her twenties from Pennsylvania'. She told Bob Gottlieb:

> My inner organs . . . jumped clean out of my body and whizzed outside. My heart was in the apple tree, my lungs among the carrots, my womb under the tank-stand and my pancreas in the tool-shed. I tried to get them back with a saucer of milk but they remain in absentum to this day.[8]

And she sent a less fanciful, but equally strong, letter to the newspaper:

> I have just seen the script and the stills from Metro-Goldwyn-Meyer's film of my novel *Spinster*. You may have feared that the worst might happen. I am telling you that very much worse that the worst has happened. . . . I hope one or two of your readers who were looking forward to the film of *Spinster* will fall ill to keep me company.

But, as in her dealings with the Literary Fund, J. C. Reid, Mama, God, and any other authority whose power she feared and whose approval she craved, in her direct response to the scriptwriter she sought only to ingratiate herself:

> I'm full of admiration for the way you have pulled the characters out of the book and stood them on their feet. . . . Congratulations on your elegant and respectful handling of *Spinster*. . . .[9]

Sylvia coped with the film as she coped with all her crises, by burying herself in writing. Her social life was correspondingly restricted; she never went to Rotary couples' nights with Keith, and rarely attended social functions connected with his other interests — which may have been just as well. When she did go to one teachers' social evening she offended just about everybody there, and probably embarrassed Keith too, though as always he carried on as if nothing untoward was happening. It was an occasion of high formality and the gold-trimmed invitations had gone out weeks before. The men wore dinner suits and the women wore evening gowns. Except for Sylvia. The famous author who had vowed at a younger age to wear nothing but the best was dressed in an old white blouse and an old black skirt, held together with safety pins.

---

*The possibility that Beeby intervened during MGM's 1960 visit to New Zealand is even more unlikely. Nine months before that visit he left both the Education Department and the country to become New Zealand ambassador to France.

During the same period she often disconcerted guests to her home by greeting them in garments ranging from a dragon-embroidered silk kimono to a dirty old dressing-gown, and sometimes further embarrassed them by ushering them in and then excusing herself, never to return.

Sylvia dressed relatively conventionally to attend occasional films, concerts and plays, but her social life effectively centred on her Tauranga friends and her grandchildren (Jasmine's family who lived nearby and, later in the sixties, Ashton's family who lived at Hastings). Unlike her confidants from further afield, her Tauranga friends were mostly women — interesting women who in Sylvia's eyes, though not always in reality, were spinsters. Among them was an artist, a public health nurse, a ballet teacher, a secondary school headmistress, a drama producer, a radio announcer and a journalist.

She rarely visited their homes — she was usually acutely uncomfortable in any setting but her own — but she often invited them to visit her. Occasionally they came for meals. If Keith cooked, the meal was presentable, but if Sylvia was the chef, anything could happen: sometimes she served a burnt roast, sometimes she served raw sausages, sometimes she served nothing at all.

Her special romantic dinners were something else again. For these the chosen woman came alone to find, amid candlelight, flowers, wine and music, a meal prepared by Sylvia's housekeeper and served by a pretty Maori girl decked out in a frilly white apron. If these dinners were supposed to light the flames of passion they were a dismal failure. For the most part her friends regarded Sylvia as an amusing, puzzling and demanding eccentric, with an enormous talent for writing and for school musical productions.

Sylvia nearly always produced the choral music for the Bethlehem School end-of-year ceremony. On the big night the hall was packed with children, parents, tribal and civic dignitaries, a guest speaker and Sylvia's friends. Ex-pupil Greg Tata recalls the excitement:

> Our white shirts were starched, our black pants pressed, and our black shoes shiny bright. Mrs Henderson always looked so beautiful in her fur wrap and her long sequined dress; every time she moved her dress cast twinkles all over the hall. It was the night of all nights. I used to say to myself — no other night in the world can match this. . . .[10]

In 1961 Louis Johnson was guest speaker and, like everyone else who witnessed these occasions, he was stunned:

> Before any of the speeches got underway Sylvia ran her hands up and down the piano and all these kids — they were perched on windowsills and in all sorts of positions around the hall — my God, they didn't give us Maori chants or anything like that — they launched straight into the first act of The Pirates of Penzance. I sat there in total disbelief! It was beautiful! But it had nothing to do with anything as far as I could see, other than the fact that they did it so bloody well. I looked at her and

I thought, 'How in the hell has she managed that?' It was the most unbelievable thing I have ever seen in a New Zealand school. It was really ornate music, and done in harmony and all sorts of ways and presented in a totally relaxed manner. A city choral society couldn't have done it better. . . . This is something I have to put against those other yarns you hear that Sylvia couldn't teach; by Christ, she got something into those kids. . . .[11]

It was as if during the weeks of practice she had cast a spell over the children or perhaps, as she claimed in *Teacher*, it was a matter of espousal. Greg Tata recalls the year she taught them the Hallelujah Chorus:

Every day Mr Henderson warmed up our voices and Mrs Henderson would come in as if she were making love to the air around her. She'd look up at her husband and flutter her eyelashes and say, 'How are you getting on dear? Are the children ready?' We'd stare at this flirting in amazement. Then as Mr Henderson left she'd turn to us and convey that what had been going on with him was about to continue with us. She had us absolutely mesmerised the whole time.

She started by telling a story;

'Do you know about George? Have you heard about George?'

'George who?'

'George — George — ' that's all she'd say. 'George — young boy he was — born a long time ago — would you like to know about George? Good — I'll tell you about George. George was born. . . .'

She'd get us really keyed up about George and then break off suddenly.

'Well let's get started, we'll carry on with the story tomorrow.'

She divided us into 'high boys', 'low boys', 'high girls', and 'low girls', and she used the height of her hands to indicate pitch. We didn't sing with the piano until we had learnt the whole Hallelujah Chorus 'a capella'.

When she finished teaching us the music she came to the end of the George story, and we found out that she'd been telling us about George Frederick Handel.[12]

Despite the energy she put into school music, and despite the dazzling results, Sylvia's primary concern was always writing — and getting published. Between 1959 and 1962 Louis Johnson published some of her teaching stories in *Parent and Child*, Winston Rhodes published a serialised version of the first part of *Rangitira* in *New Zealand Monthly Review*, and Bruce Mason published a new story in the journal of Maori issues, *Te Ao Hou*.

Undeterred by the disastrous film adaptation of *Spinster*, Sylvia sent the third part of *Rangitira* to MGM, and to Twentieth Century Fox, who had bought the film rights to *Incense to Idols*. When neither company was interested she offered it briefly to Bob Gottlieb, and then withdrew it for further revision.

After refusing to compromise with Blackwood Paul over her illustrations, she abandoned her efforts to publish her little reading books. Her decision came at a time when the purchase of colour equipment by the Government Printer ensured that the demand by teachers for home-grown infant reading material could at last be met. The Department of Education appointed a working party to prepare and test a series of readers suitable for use with the hundred thousand five-year-olds entering New Zealand schools each year. The resulting 'Ready to Read' books used a selected range of basic words and interest words to tell stories about New Zealand children in New Zealand settings. Whether anyone thought of including Sylvia in the working party is not known. After the impact of *Spinster* her name could hardly have been overlooked, but since education officials found her impossible to work with, any suggestion that Sylvia Ashton-Warner be involved would probably have been quickly rejected.

Word that the department was preparing its own books reached Sylvia through the press. She was furious. That their stated aim of making reading relevant to the interests of the child could be anyone's idea but her own was unthinkable. In angry posted letters, and enraged unposted ones, she expressed the conviction that the educational establishment, ever intent on persecuting her, had now out of sheer sadism stolen her ideas.

The department also distributed vocabulary lists to local publishers, asking them to consider producing books to support the official series. But when Blackwood and Janet Paul invited Sylvia to work with them again on the publication of her readers, she flatly refused.

The possibility of publishing her teaching scheme as a unit still remained. Since its serialised appearance in 1956, training college lecturers had been recommending it to students, and inspectors had been recommending it to teachers. And since the advent of *Spinster*, requests for more information on the key vocabulary had streamed in.

Despite her later claim that she was driven by misguided loyalty to restrict her search for a publisher to New Zealand, she did, after her earlier approaches to Whitcombe and Tombs and to A. H. and A. W. Reed, offer her scheme unsuccessfully to two British publishers, (Secker and Warburg, Routledge and Kegan Paul) before further exploring the local possibilities. In 1958 she sent her scheme to Blackwood Paul, but withdrew it a month later. In 1959 she asked the editor of *National Education* to publish it as a booklet entitled *Organic·Teaching*, but he had never undertaken a venture of that sort and was concerned about the cost. Next she again approached Whitcombe and Tombs:

> I want no more than to see my own work acknowledged in my own name [the original *National Education* articles had been signed 'Sylvia'] in my own country in my own lifetime.

But they felt that the market among New Zealand teachers would be too small.

In April 1960 she showed the scheme to Bill Moore, the New Zealand distributor of her novels. At that time his firm, William Heinemann, did not undertake local publishing, but Moore liked *Organic Teaching* so much he sought quotes for a print-run of three thousand copies. Despite a full work load, and without a contract to seal the agreement, he pursued the project with enthusiasm and tenacity. He made innumerable trips between Auckland and Tauranga to establish exactly what Sylvia wanted in the book. He cajoled typesetters who baulked at handling a manuscript in scrapbook form, and blockmakers who felt that Sylvia's snapshots could not be reproduced. By May 1961 the galleys had been printed, an order form announcing publication in June or July had been circulated to book-sellers, and Moore himself was cutting and pasting the final layouts.

For a few frantic weeks Sylvia faced the real possibility of seeing her dream realised — of having her work acknowledged in her own name in her own country in her own lifetime. Public interest was reaching alarming proportions: the prestigious Education Commission — appointed by the government at the beginning of 1960 to consider the entire publicly con-trolled system of primary, post-primary and technical education in relation to the present and future needs of the country — had heard much about her scheme in the course of taking evidence and sent two of its members to visit Sylvia in person. But . . . 'You've got to watch out for dreams,' she wrote in her autobiography, 'in case they come true.'

This was one dream she could never, never, allow to come true. It would mean, from her hated mother country, even more excruciating acclaim, even more terrifying acceptance. So while Bill Moore was putting the final touches to *Organic Teaching*, Sylvia sent her scheme to Bob Gottlieb in New York. The news, conveyed to Moore as a passing hint and a request for the return of the original typescript, came as a thunderbolt:

> Thinking back over what you said, it now occurs to me that you had in mind the possibility of sending the material to Bob Gottlieb for produc-tion in U.S.A.
>
> Of course I may be wrong in assuming that this is what you had in mind, but such an arrangement would not be acceptable to me. I would be happy to supply copies of our production to Bob at a special price for distribution in America. . . . Obviously after all the work and trouble and financial risk involved, it would be unacceptable to me to give away part of the market.
>
> The other matter which I should clear up with you when I come down next is the question of an author/publisher agreement. . . .[13]

Sylvia vented her rage in a letter to Elliot:

> Just now the two of us are deeply upset over the machinations of Bill Moore whom we have befriended and honoured in our home for years. He is bringing out my scheme in New Zealand but suddenly from private information in my drawing room he realises the demand for my scheme in America and means to send his wretched . . . edition to the U.S.A. dazzled by my dollars . . . and here is Bob Gottlieb of Simon and Schuster waiting to do it in all his American affluence advertising and skill with

all photographs and excellent paper. A base betrayal. . . . However all is
well as I have not yet signed any author–publisher contract with him. . . .
He is coming down next week to force me to sign this — which you can
well imagine I will not.

And so Sylvia saved her dream from souring into reality; she stopped the
New Zealand publication of her teaching scheme by refusing to sign the
contract.

She then wrote to the *New Zealand Monthly Review*, explaining that
because of the apathy and incompetence of local publishers and educationalists, despite Heinemann's announcement to the contrary, *Organic Teaching*
would not be appearing in New Zealand.

Bob Gottlieb was the delighted recipient of her scheme, and of almost
everything else related to her years of teaching:

> She told me — I've got all this material, boxes and boxes, I can never bear
> to look at it again . . . do anything you want — make a book, don't make
> a book, throw it out.
>
> In due course it arrived. Literally cartons of unsorted pages which ran
> from tearsheets from magazines, pictures of leaves she had shown
> children twenty years before, notebooks made by her Maori pupils,
> teaching plans, her journal that she wrote and rewrote and passed around
> among her friends. . . . Then she got out of her garage, where they had
> been leaked on, negatives of little snapshots of the school.
>
> I took it all home and spread it on the floor of our living room. For
> about two and a half months these papers were all over the floor while
> I tried to get them in order, and tried to figure out what was journals and
> what was letters, and what superseded what and what was a copy or
> another version of what. And slowly I got an idea of what this book
> might be. . . .[14]

'I love you. . . .' he wrote to Sylvia, 'I'm really very excited by it all —
let's make a book. . . .'

Moved by his enthusiasm, and unwilling to face the memory-laden
material herself, Sylvia handed the project over to Bob. *Teacher* was Bob
Gottlieb's work. Sylvia's only contribution was to eliminate or rewrite
references to punishing children with the strap. The original diary
recorded:

> Peta lost interest and picked up a book and began reading. 'Don't,' said
> Keith, 'read a book when Mrs Henderson is speaking.' He called her out
> and gave her a very bad strap. She took it all right though. Maoris have
> hard skin inside their hands, many of them, and in any case are
> accustomed to violence.

But in Sylvia's revised version Peta received no more than a 'growling at'.

At the end of 1962, Bob sent Sylvia the galley proofs and asked her to
expand on her introduction. Her reply, published at the front of the book,
was a real sizzler. She dramatised, reworked and reinvented her
experiences with New Zealand publishers into a harrowing account of the

crushing of her most cherished dream — to have her teaching scheme published in New Zealand. When it came to writing about the Education Department, she hinted at the unspeakable, and used rows of dots to provoke the reader's imagination:

> As for your question about how New Zealand Education received it ... how they treated me through the years of experiment . . . what happened when I began operating it . . . what they did to me then . . . my Gethsemene . . . and later when *Spinster* came out . . .[15]

She justified her reticence by claiming that New Zealand was her family and she was crippled by family loyalty. It was as if she was projecting onto her mother country the baleful image of her own unloving mother: the woman whose power she feared and whose love she craved; the woman she never forgave for her failure to love her; the woman she hated.

Between the writing of that introduction and the publication of *Teacher*, an event occurred that would have convinced anyone else that they held an honoured place in New Zealand society. It didn't convince Sylvia.

> The Master of the Household
> is commanded by Her Majesty to invite
> Mr and Mrs K. D. Henderson
> to a luncheon to be given by
> The Queen and The Duke of Edinburgh
> on board H.M.Y. *Britannia* at Napier
> on Sunday 10th February, 1963, at 1 p.m. for 1.15 o'clock

It was one of a series of dinners for distinguished New Zealanders held by the Queen at different ports around the country during her 1963 visit.

Sylvia persuaded herself that the invitation came personally from Her Majesty:

> I don't think I was on the official invitation list made at the Internal Affairs Department with whom I have been a persona non grata ever since I wrote *Spinster* [conveniently overlooking the fact that Internal Affairs, through its administration of the Literary Fund, had honoured her with the 1959 Scholarship in Letters]. . . . I think she must have scanned the list and noticed I was missing, and asked for me to be included. . . .[16]

Sylvia graciously agreed to make a rare journey out of Tauranga to meet the Queen, but she was not prepared to buy a new dress for the occasion. She wore a black nylon frock with white spots that she had bought three years earlier and had already worn to two school break-ups, Ashton's wedding and Elliot's departure for England. She painted an old handbag black, added a few spots with white shoe-polish, and made a hat from a black taffeta bow and some nylon snipped from inside the hem of her dress.

Dining with royalty cured Sylvia of any lingering antipathy she may have felt towards the monarchy; it was the Queen's eyes that won her over:

. . . beautiful, unwavering, yes, but also piercing, reading, examining, assessing, divining, charging, judging, and above all, inspiring. Eyes only to be found in a reigning monarch. Imperious eyes, ruling eyes; the same that executed Essex and Raleigh, sent Drake after the Spaniards and kept numbers of lovers at heel.[17]

Sylvia told Mama that the Queen spent more time talking to her and Keith than to anyone else; and that when the eyes of the two women met . . . worlds were spoken.

Another celebrity as special to Sylvia as the Queen came to New Zealand two months later. Since her discovery of *Education Through Art* at Waiomatatini, Sylvia had worshipped Sir Herbert Read from afar. Sir Herbert in turn had been impressed by Sylvia's teaching scheme and had just finished writing the introduction for *Teacher* when he was invited to come out from England to deliver the inaugural Chancellor's Lecture at Victoria University of Wellington in April 1963. As he told his university hosts, it was his desire to meet Sylvia Ashton-Warner that prompted him to accept.

As with everyone she felt drawn to, Sylvia had invited Sir Herbert to stay. His letter accepting her invitation was as thrilling as it was unexpected. On 21 April the Hendersons met Sir Herbert and Lady Reed at Auckland airport and brought them back to Tauranga. They left next day for a three-day drive to Wellington. To Sylvia's dismay, a personal relationship with Sir Herbert failed to develop:

a man of silence . . . he sees no occasion to speak at all. After dinner though — wines, whiskies, warmth and that — he'd talk. But then you couldn't hear him. . . . He liked me, I think, if that's important, and I liked him, enough to enjoy what passed for company in a man of silence.[18]

As soon as they parted, Sylvia felt driven to convey her deeper feelings. She wrote Sir Herbert a letter beginning 'My dear Master' and closing 'With affection and everlasting reverence', but she couldn't bring herself to post it.

Then she wrote to Lady Margaret:

Darling little Margaret: I want you to do something for me. I want you to go to Sir Herbert Read — preferably at the wrong moment when he's not in the mood — and put both arms right round him — kiss him on the left side of the neck — passionately — if you can reach it — If not the lapel of his coat will do — and say to him — I love you.

But she didn't post that one either.

The next highlight on Sylvia's 1963 calendar was the publication of *Teacher*. On 8 September the front page of the *New York Times Book Review* carried the banner headline: 'THE HOW IS MIGHTIER THAN THE WHAT — A Lesson for All the World to Study Is Taught in a New Zealand School.'

The claims Sylvia made in her introduction — that her treatment at the hands of the Education Department was unspeakable, that her lovingly made reading books were burnt, and that her cherished ambition to have her teaching scheme published in New Zealand was crushed by repeated rejections — caused an international scandal. And though she didn't claim that she was forced out of teaching by an abysmal grading, so much of *Spinster* was echoed in *Teacher* that her fans reached that conclusion too. Clearly Sylvia Ashton-Warner was a prophet without honour in her own land.

Her accusation that her books had been burnt evoked paroxysms of guilt in everyone who had handled them. They remembered seeing them . . . but they were damned if they could remember what happened to them. . . . All the evidence suggests that any books distributed by Sylvia were returned to her, but nobody knew that then. Educationalists and publishers up and down the country blamed themselves and each other. But before they could compare notes, the Education Department was called on to respond to Sylvia's accusations. The official statement read: 'We admit that Miss Ashton-Warner submitted three books ten years ago. They were not burnt but only mislaid.' To which Sylvia responsed: 'No amount of argument can bring life back into my four burnt books.'

The department reiterated that there was no question of the books being burnt, but as flowers, telegrams and mail poured into Bethlehem, and as *Teacher* shot up the *New York Times* bestseller list, it was clear that in this round of her war with the educational establishment, Sylvia had won a resounding victory.

The cool response from the Education Department and the unbridled enthusiasm of the public reinforced Sylvia's sense of her own uniqueness. She became more convinced than ever that she had not only invented the key vocabulary, as indeed she had, but that she was a lone voice — a committed and creative teacher who had pioneered child-centred education in the face of implacable hostility from the teaching colleagues and the educational establishment. She regarded the reality that many other New Zealand educators were using similar techniques as proof that the establishment had taken her ideas and was now claiming them as its own.

Her bitterness fed the enthusiasm for her work that spread around the world. It seemed as if every teacher who had ever felt unappreciated, every person who had ever felt a passing impatience with the establishment, became an instant fan. Along with a flood of mail, requests for interviews and for Sylvia to speak to interested groups poured in from throughout New Zealand and around the world. She either turned them down flat, or agreed and then changed her mind. On three occasions, after agreeing to a television interview, she sent the television crews back to Auckland with no more than a cup of coffee. To keep fans at bay she continued the practice, begun at the time of *Spinster*'s publication, of persuading friends to answer her mail. She also nailed a sign to a tree in her yard: STRANGERS GO AWAY.

Sympathetic New Zealanders reflected on her absence from her public arena. They couldn't recall Sylvia Ashton-Warner ever addressing a meeting or being interviewed. Her name didn't even appear in *Who's Who in New Zealand*. So it was true. She really had been ignored. Her fans were angry with the Education Department, effusively appreciative of Sylvia, and endlessly willing to champion her cause. Whatever it was.

So what exactly was her cause, what exactly did she convey in *Teacher* that lead to her being ranked, particularly in America, as one of the great educational innovators of the century?

Teacher, with its impressionistic fragments and emotive prose, was not a conventional teaching text. As the review in the Department of Education journal pointed out, the rationale behind her methods and the details of their application were not clearly spelled out, and her approach was not systematically tested or evaluated. but *Teacher* was as gripping to Sylvia's supporters as the key words had been to her five-year-olds: one read and they were hooked. So what if it's emotional? So what if it's unscientific? In these qualities lie its strength. To teachers and parents who longed for more humane and creative schooling, and for a more humane and creative world, Sylvia Ashton-Warner was a hero. For thousands of readers, *Teacher* affirmed the truths they held most dear and gave them the courage to translate those truths into action. Yet the uniqueness of each person's truth meant that the book revealed a different message to every reader.

For many teachers it was primarily a source of inspiration for the teaching of reading. This New Zealand teacher's letter is typical of hundreds Sylvia received:

> I began the key vocabulary method with two slow learners who both had a reading vocabulary of 5–7 words after more than a year at school. What a bomb! In a few weeks both knew 40–45 words including ghosts, giants, kiss, dead, buried, suffocated, axe, chop, fierce, scared. . . . The excitement spread. . . .

Teacher was also seen as a proclamation that any individual, however lowly, however unappreciated, was worthwhile and unique. Another New Zealand teacher wrote:

> . . . my early morning meditations and studies have been filled with the light from your book!! . . . Because of your book I will go to school today holding my head up a little higher knowing that I can only be me. . . .

Many teachers were excited by Sylvia's vision of communication; by the way she joyfully mingled words, music, drama and art to make facts, ideas and the life of the spirit leap across between teacher and pupil, between writer and reader.

Teachers struggling to stuff knowledge into unwilling learners found inspiration in her maxim: release the native imagery of our child and use it for working material.

Artistic teachers gained the courage to make creativity central to their classroom work. Teachers dissatisfied with the traditional approach to racial minorities embraced her message of respect for their culture and dialect. Unconventional teachers were delighted by her belief that instead of acting as agents of conformity, schools should dedicate themselves to releasing each child's individuality. Teachers who favoured spontaneity drew joy from the book's advocacy of liberating the emotions. Teachers who struggled to maintain a quiet classroom learnt to use, rather than suppress, the natural gregariousness of their pupils.

For readers concerned with mental health the book provided a formula for treating violence in children. And for those concerned with violence on a larger scale it was this book, not *Incense to Idols*, that addressed the fundamental issues of peace and war.

Poet Charles Brasch applauded the contribution of the key vocabulary to the understanding of style and personal identity:

> If poetry is naming, as Rilke and others have maintained, and if children start life by naming what means most to them, and from that go on to writing about what means most to them, we might have more poets — and fewer delinquents.[19]

Jeannette Veatch, an American professor of education, first became hooked on Sylvia's work through *Spinster*. As an unmarried woman resentful of popular fiction's stereotype of spinsters, she delighted in Anna Vorontosov's passion; as an educational tilter at windmills she identified with Anna's determination to challenge the establishment; and as a teacher of young children she recognised the key vocabulary as the key to reading.

The biggest windmill in Jeannette's life was the American textbook-publishing empire. In place of its rigidly programmed, mass-produced, basal readers, she advocated 'individualised reading': a method of self-selection and self-pacing using the varied and interesting children's books available in book stores. She saw individualised reading as the natural outcome of the 'language experience approach' in which children begin reading by dictating stories to their teachers and learning to read and write the words used.

For the many American teachers who shared Jeannette's philosophy there were two problems. Firstly, ranked against them were the publishers who printed basal readers, the professors who wrote them and the school administrators who bought them. And secondly, the language experience approach lacked an effective technique for easing very young children into reading instruction — a technique for unlocking the door between the images in the child's mind and the written word. Then Sylvia Ashton-Warner produced the key: the key vocabulary.

To Jeannette the conspiracy behind Anna Vorontosov's fall from grace was clear. The key vocabulary was such a threat to the basal-reader empire that no inspector or publisher dared to approve it. When she read *Teacher* in 1963 she was electrified by the discovery that the problems of Anna Vorontosov, and the triumph of the key vocabulary, were not fiction but reality. She fired off thirty-six postcards to spread the good news.

Thousands of American educators shared her enthusiasm. Almost over-

night Sylvia Ashton-Warner became a cult hero. If only they could bring
her to America! A lecture tour by Sylvia Ashton-Warner would set the
world on fire. She'd knock the stuffing out of the basal boys. She'd bring
the establishment to its knees. But she wouldn't come. They kept inviting
her, but she wouldn't come.

During 1965 Jeannette sent Sylvia information on her own key vocabulary work and expressed the wish that they could meet. At first her letters
were acknowledged by the Tauranga woman who answered Sylvia's mail.
Then in September 1966 an appreciative letter flew in from Sylvia herself.
She said, 'I hope your salary will support a trip to New Zealand.'

Jeannette didn't need to be asked twice. In July 1967 she and fellow educator Ardelle Llewellyn, weighed down with instructions from envious
friends to 'bring me back a lock of her hair', 'bring me back a photo', 'bring
me back *anything*', set off on the great pilgrimage. Prior to visiting
Tauranga they took part in a workshop for infant teachers in Auckland,
and discussed Sylvia Ashton-Warner with every educationalist in sight.
They were thrilled to find some who had known her personally, but the
feedback was alarming. Those terrible New Zealanders said that Sylvia
Ashton-Warner wasn't much of teacher, they said she was arrogant to
imply that she was the only one teaching that way, they said she was
irresponsible, they said she was unstable, they said she had been mentally
ill, they said she was an alcoholic. . . . But for all that some did admire her
work, and two training college lecturers provided a tape recorder on which
Jeannette and Ardelle were to preserve her words of wisdom.

They departed apprehensively for Tauranga, but after five days of Sylvia
at her most flamboyant and ingratiating they had no misgivings at all. The
day after they left they recorded their recollections on the machine Sylvia
had declined to use:

> The impression we were given of Sylvia was in retrospect really quite
> appalling. We think she has been dreadfully, grossly maligned. . . .
>   She told us that in the nine years since *Spinster* came out, not one person
> in this entire nation of three million people has ever made an overture to
> ask her to come and speak. . . . She is an embittered woman. . . . She is
> a tragically ignored person in her own home and this has hurt her deeply.

It was Sylvia's personality that won them over. Although Jeannette noted
that 'the word "charismatic" was invented for her', and that 'she will not
hesitate to spin a spell around you and make you listen', it did not occur to
either woman that there was a calculated technique behind her 'wonderfully
warm and receptive smile', her enthusiasm for their company ('she found
us so exhilarating . . . we enriched her'), and the way she listened intently
and heaped extravagant praise on their knowledge, their sophistication,
their cooking, and the gifts they brought:

> She's absolutely wonderful. . . . As healthy a personality as I've met in
> many moons . . . basically a very honest person . . . so modest, and
> genuinely so — this is not a false front. . . . She has this . . . serenity.[20]

They also found her to be 'utterly feminine', 'fantastically maternal' and 'totally sincere', and were gratified that she saw them as belonging to what she called 'the Real America', rather than to that offensive entity 'the Other America'. The latter included organisations like the National Council of Teachers of English, who had invited Sylvia to speak at a convention in Hawaii — they were nothing more than social climbers who wanted to enhance their own reputations by exploiting her; just like those Auckland lecturers who had sent down the tape recorder.

By the end of the visit the relationship between Sylvia and her awe-struck pilgrims had become, according to Jeannette and Ardelle, one of '. . . deep profound friendship. Genuine friendship. there wasn't a phony thing about it.' They concluded: 'She loved us and we loved her.'

Keeping up the charisma for five days non-stop wasn't easy for Sylvia. The loving face she presented to her visitors disguised a resentment she released in letters to Bob Gottlieb:

> Prof Veatch turned out to be what I call 'the Other America' rather than what I call 'the Real America'. . . . A clear-cut case of American aggression. . . . She arrived covered, dripping with my glory. . . .
> SHE WASN'T INTERESTED IN ME — OR ANYTHING ABOUT ME. She was interested only in Jeannette Veatch and how facts about me would adorn her.

Sylvia went on to complain about their conversation, the presents they brought, the food they prepared and the way they had to be praised and listened to all the time. All Americans who came to see her were like that, she told Bob, except for the Jewish ones; though in making that observation she was probably ingratiating herself to her Jewish editor, rather than expressing an honest opinion.

Jeannette and Ardelle weren't alone in being totally bewitched by Sylvia. Throughout her adult life hundreds of people — barefoot school entrants to sophisticated university professors — fell under her spell. The love and reverence with which she is remembered, even by people she had cruelly hurt, defies rational explanation. She seemed to radiate a magnetism more profound, more wonderful, and more irresistible, than can be explained by manipulative skills and superficial charm. But the skills and charm undoubtedly helped.

By the 1960s Sylvia's acting and writing abilities had developed to a point where she could convince almost anyone of her sincerity, even when the feelings and attitudes she presented were the exact opposite of those she held in private. Her fluent persuasiveness, and her growing charisma, suggests that no matter what role Sylvia played she believed in it totally at the time she was creating it, blissfully unhampered by any consideration of whether anything she said was actually true.

Among the Americans who made their way to Bethlehem were teachers, psychologists, psychiatrists, writers and publishing colleagues of Bob Gottlieb. Like Jeannette and Ardelle, they were impressed by Sylvia's charm and vitality, and distressed by her stories of how New Zealand had mistreated her. Helen Barrow from Simon and Schuster, who stayed with her in 1965, recalled:

> It was clear that any number of people from all over the world had found their way to see her, but never New Zealanders. She was very angry — she was *terribly* angry about that. They never recognised her educational programme, and they never recognised that they had a famous author in their midst.[21]

Sylvia's agenda for overseas guests included an interview with the media, a dinner or outing to meet her friends, a tour of Bethlehem School and a visit to the home she and Keith were building on a sunny ridge over-looking Tauranga Harbour. She indicated to her visitors that the purpose of the interviews, and the meetings with friends, was to impress the unappreciative public with her impact on the world scene. They took up the challenge with enthusiasm and praised Sylvia Ashton-Warner to the skies, unaware or too transfixed by her spell to realise that though she rejected invitations to appear in public on the grounds that those responsible wanted to use her to enhance their own reputations, she had no qualms about using her guests for precisely that purpose.

Many guests passed through Bethlehem during the building of the Hendersons' new home. Meeting Sylvia's demand for the open plan of a Maori meeting house blended with the memory-spinning ambience of a high-raftered, old-fashioned schoolhouse and the tranquillity of a cloister, and including her own semi-detached Selah, drove three successive architects to despair, but the design award the house received testified to its success. To the Hendersons the home they called Whenua was more than a place to live: it was the only house they ever owned, the only place where Sylvia could put down roots into the soil of her own country.

For visiting teachers, seeing Bethlehem School was far more important than seeing their hosts' new home. Many had visited other New Zealand schools before arriving in Tauranga, and had been impressed by the widespread use of language experience and individualised reading, with never a basal reader to be seen. But here was the genuine article: Sylvia Ashton-Warner's very own school. . . . The pupils greeted overseas visitors with a Maori welcome featuring dances, chants and speeches. That was the highlight. The next part, a tour of the classrooms, was for the educationalist a shattering disappointment.

Although Keith was loved and respected by Maori and Pakeha alike, Jeannette and Ardelle, as seasoned American school desegregation workers, were shocked by his, and Sylvia's, attitude towards the Maori:

> We were appalled to see that Keith and Sylvia had no insight whatsoever into their paternalism. . . . The whole thing was just noblesse oblige — the whole damn thing.

They were also shocked by the formality of the school — kids sitting in rows who stood up when they entered and droned, 'Goood mooorning . . .', kids spouting memorised speeches:

> 'On behalf of Form so-and-so we welcome you . . . blah blah blah.' . . . It was absolutely awful. . . . The kids were stiff and rigid and most unnatural. . . . all of the horrible things about formalised education that we hate so very very much.[22]

As Sylvia had predicted, when Jeannette returned to America she used Sylvia's name to advance her cause and her reputation:

> Because of these problems I had with basal readers I wanted to, in a sense, use Sylvia. She was so well known. Whenever I spoke at an international convention on Sylvia Ashton-Warner the room was packed. I held audiences spellbound just by talking about what her house was like and what sort of a person she was. . . . I was talking about this person they loved and I had met her and stayed with her — I had been anointed.[23]

But wherever she went Jeannette was careful not to reveal that most shocking of disappointments — that at Sylvia's husband's own school nothing creative or inspirational was happening at all.

Towards the end of Jeannette and Ardelle's stay, Sylvia confided to them an intimate concern: her distress over the dislocation in her relationship with her unofficial secretary, the woman she later fictionalised as 'Flo'.

Flo had first met Sylvia in 1958 when during a visit to Bethlehem School she mentioned her admiration of *Spinster* to Keith. He suggested that she call on Sylvia, and conveyed the impression that he would appreciate her help in looking after his wife. Perhaps he recognised in Flo — a pleasant, well-read, middle-aged spinster — the mother-figure Sylvia craved.

Predictably, Sylvia fell in love. But since she had learnt to keep her love affairs sealed in fantasy, their acquaintance of more than a decade was to Flo no more than a casual friendship.

Her passion for Flo drove Sylvia to reflect on her own nature. How could she reconcile the man-loving woman she wanted to be with the woman-loving artist who possessed her? How could she reconcile the overwhelming and contradictory needs that ravaged her soul — her need to make people love her, but, to protect her raw psyche from rebuff, her need to withhold her love from others? And how could she withhold her love when falling in love was the sacred fire-raising rite with which she lit the flames of her creative imagination?

Her long-held suspicion that she was two separate people crystallised into a firm conviction. She saw herself as a charming, compliant, sexy woman, and a rampaging male artist who lived life on his own unique terms. In a series of unpublished manuscripts she expounded on the nature of the artist. That he required 'attention, praise, service, sacrifice and unflawed devotion' was a normal and proper consequence of his temperament. What others called selfishness was his natural desire to be the only

one in his admirer's heart; his vanity was simply a manifestation of his need
to be thought wonderful; and if he seemed jealous that was just because an
artist was incapable of sharing those close to him in any important way.

But what made the artist really unique was his need for a complement.
A complement was a boring, untalented individual who drew joy, purpose
and inspiration from caring for an artist. Sylvia, who normally saw sex in
everything, persuaded herself that there was nothing sexual at all in the
artist–complement bond; it was a simple matter of parasite and host:

> The artist controls his complement as naturally as his own limbs and
> body, thoughtlessly, unconsciously, unwittingly arrogant, demanding
> and expecting from the other all he demands and expects from himself,
> until the parasite has to withdraw in self-preservation. Or, as has been
> known, the complement becomes interested in another artist and takes a
> change of union. Safe enough for the complement but for the forsaken
> artist it is a matter of impaired organs and severed arteries from which
> he all but bleeds to a finish.[24]

That was how, on reflection, Sylvia saw her relationship with Joy Alley;
and that was how she now saw her relationship with Flo — a relationship
threatened by Flo's friendship with Sylvia's fan, Karin.

In 1964 Karin, a talented young American teacher, poured her life, her
soul and her dreams into a long fan letter. Sylvia asked Flo to reply, and
to tell Karin that Sylvia would like to meet her, and wanted her to write
again. Before long, as an animated correspondence developed, Flo wrote
more about herself and less about Sylvia. The sparkling replies from Karin
and her housemate Genevieve brought welcome excitement and new
friends to Flo's otherwise predictable life. At the end of 1965 she spent a
wonderful holiday in America, from which evolved a plan for Karin and
Genevieve to come to New Zealand.

This was too much for Sylvia. Her jealousy towards Karin, long contained in her diary, spilled over into her relationship with Flo. After years
of reporting that Sylvia was 'delighted that the American dream was
working out so beautifully' and that 'Sylvia is entering into the spirit of
the plans with fun and happiness', Flo's letters began to indicate a puzzling
coolness: 'Sylvia is in one of her faraway remote moods . . .', 'Sylvia is
rather 'grand–dame' just now . . .'.

From the day Karin arrived in New Zealand, Sylvia refused to see Flo
or her American friends. And she poured her pain and rage into the novel
Barren Radiance.

The relationship that Flo, Karin and Genevieve saw as a straightforward
friendship in which Sylvia played a peripheral role was transformed by
Sylvia's tormented undermind into a frantic tale of women loving women,
with herself centre stage. The circular plot revolved around an artist, Pania,
who lived with a man called Alex. Her complement, Flo, had deserted her
for Pania's fan, the pseudo-artist Quella: Pania wanted Flo, Flo wanted
Quella, Quella wanted Pania, and Alex rated no more than a passing

mention. From Bob Gottlieb's reaction Sylvia wondered if he saw homosexuality in the book.

'Yes,' he replied. 'I definitely felt there was almost explicit lesbian sexuality in the pages I read. Not that they were all about to make love, but that only inhibition and self-delusion had prevented it to date.'

Sylvia was appalled:

> I did faintly allow the possibility but chose not to believe it. I'd been working on the maternal-filial impulses, deprived. . . . Is the artist-complement thing sex too? . . . Hell![25]

After a few more drafts she conceded:

> I've got to face it. There is homosexuality between Pania and Flo. . . . Unfortunately I am unacquainted with it or I would have seen it earlier or at least believed you in the first place. . . .[26]

But Sylvia found she couldn't cope with the idea of lesbianism. She abandoned the novel, and whenever necessary thereafter used the artist-complement concept to explain her relationships with the women she loved.

Barren Radiance was never published, and neither was Sylvia's favourite work, *Tenth Heaven* (the third part of *Rangitira*), but Bob Gottlieb brought out three Ashton-Warner novels during the late 1960s. *Bell Call*, published in 1965, was about the refusal of a young woman artist to send her seven-year-old son to school. The details were recognisably those of a family who lived near the Hendersons at Bethlehem. *Greenstone* (the second part of *Rangitira*), published in 1966, was a story based on Sylvia's childhood and set in Pipiriki. *Myself* (1966) was a diary of Sylvia's years in Pipiriki, in which her passion for Joy Alley was disguised as a passion for a young male doctor.

Sylvia resisted having any of her books after *Teacher* distributed to New Zealand, claiming that she could no longer face the venom of New Zealand reviewers. But that doesn't explain why she allowed *Teacher* into New Zealand, while insisting that J. C. Reid's review of her previous book was the one that 'drove my work from New Zealand forever'. Neither does it explain why she wanted to keep out her later books when *Teacher* was so well received. The truth probably lay with her hatred of New Zealand and with her inability to cope with the acclaim given to *Teacher*, but the reason she gave her publishers may also have had some validity: she feared that she would be sued. With *Bell Call* she feared legal action from the family involved, with *Myself* she feared retaliation from Joy Alley, and with *Greenstone* the problem was Mama.

Withholding her books from New Zealand meant withholding them from Secker and Warburg, as by international agreement books published in Britain could be automatically distributed to New Zealand, while books published in the United States could not. Her frequent changes of mind, her signing and cancelling of contracts, and her disloyalty to the firm that had brought out *Spinster* infuriated Fredric Warburg. The day after Mama died in 1967 Sylvia reinstated her cancelled Secker and Warburg contract for *Greenstone*, and after some indecision agreed to the British publication of *Myself* more than a year after it came out in America. But when Sylvia's London agent advised Fredric Warburg three years after *Bell Call*'s American debut that Sylvia was now willing to reinstate that contract, he replied tersely: '*Bell Call* — Ashton-Warner: I think not.'

It wasn't until Sylvia offered *Bell Call* to Robert Hale and Company, in 1971, that the book was published in the United Kingdom.

With the impending publication of each book, whether in America or Britain, Sylvia panicked. That she felt herself under siege was vividly illustrated by her habit, from the mid-1960s on, of referring to her favourite drink as 'laager' — the South African name for an armed encampment. She often retreated into her laager, and her alcohol consumption was heavy. People outside the family rarely saw her inebriated, but the smell on her breath, the sight of her purple nose and the fact that she could drink more than two litres of beer at a sitting was well known to her friends.

Her precarious mental stability was further eroded by the effects on her nervous system of nicotine from endless chain-smoking, caffeine from endless tea-drinking (beginning with seven cups before breakfast), much codeine (a non-prescription opiate she began taking for headache and continued taking because she couldn't do without it), occasional courses of a high-blood-pressure medication, which had severe depression as a common side effect, and a sedative prescribed to help her sleep (probably a barbiturate in the early 1960s — which compounds befuddlement when taken with alcohol — and librium in the late 1960s).

With every panic attack Sylvia wanted to run away and hide. Inevitably the overseas escape dream returned to haunt her.

But she was terrified: terrified of flying, of driving, of inoculations, of being interviewed, of being photographed, of being praised, of standing in queues, of being assaulted by music and conversations not of her choice. In short, she was terrified of losing control of her surroundings — of losing control of her mask — of losing control of her life. She told Bruce Mason that she was content to climb to the top of the woollen curtain and peer over ('I hang on with one hand and write with the other'). She answered many overseas invitations by saying that she was an ugly old grandmother who didn't want to travel at all, and suggesting that they charter a plane to New Zealand, where, from the patio of her new home, she would address the assembled multitude. She was dismayed that no overseas groups took up the suggestion.

Although some busloads of student teachers visited her at Whenua, Sylvia's general popularity within New Zealand during the late 1960s underwent a steady decline. The public was disappointed that her almost unprocurable later books failed to match the brilliance of *Spinster* and *Teacher*, the educational establishment was defensive about *Teacher*, and within the literary community there was envy of her income and fame. But more than anything else, there was widespread irritation with Sylvia herself. Most of her confidants and many of her fans lost patience with her over the way she persistently rejected attempts to honour her while continuing to complain that she was unappreciated. And in her unrelenting hostility to her country she had, in the opinion of many New Zealanders, gone too far.

Trying to keep her books out of the country was bad enough, but her decision to give her personal, literary, and educational papers to the Boston University library was the last straw. When the news broke, the National Librarian phoned and implored her to change her mind. She promised to do nothing final until she spoke with him again, and then dispatched an urgent telegram:

> THANK YOU FOR CALLING THIS MORNING BUT IT IS FAIR TO TELL YOU THAT NO LETTER OR VISIT OR ANYTHING ELSE WILL PERSUADE ME TO CHANGE MY MIND STOP I WOULD NOT LEAVE SO MUCH AS AN ASTERISK TO THIS COUNTRY

The equally urgent response read:

> THANK YOU FOR YOUR DISCONCERTINGLY QUICK DECISION WHICH IS YOURS ONLY TO MAKE AND MUST BE RESPECTED STOP CANNOT FORBEAR TO POINT OUT THAT YOU ARE LEAVING A LOT IN AND TO YOUR COUNTRY SO WHY NOT MAKE A JOB OF IT

But because of her hatred for New Zealand in general, and for the Alley family in particular (the National Librarian was Joy Alley's brother), Sylvia was unmoved.

A few weeks later she came across an article about 'The Great Manuscript Rush' in America, which made her doubt the wisdom of her earlier decision. But driven by anger towards New Zealand, and by the attractive exemptions her manuscript donations earned for her United States taxes, she kept sending material for another fifteen years. Then, towards the end of her life, she accused the Boston library of losing her little Maori reading books, and kept her remaining papers at home.

The New Zealand literary community responded to the general disillusionment with Sylvia by downplaying the significance of Sylvia Ashton-Warner's writing. The first serious critical appraisal of her work, by Dennis McEldowney in *Landfall* in 1969, drew a rebuke from poet Charles Brasch on the grounds that Ashton-Warner's work was unworthy of serious attention. With her supporters deserting her, Sylvia had only Keith to fall back on. Keith the rock. Keith the one stable influence in her life. It is true that his attitude to her work was one of indulgence rather than understanding, but he was always there when she needed him. Good old Keith.

Keith's health began to deteriorate in 1966. Two weeks in hospital followed by six weeks' sick leave brought no improvement. Further tests led to the removal of his cancerous bladder at Auckland Hospital in November 1967. Although the surgeon, Mr Gaudin, declared him cured, Keith's wound did not heal. By the time of his April 1968 follow-up visit he was losing weight and in constant pain. Mr Gaudin gave him a good report.

After his August follow-up Mr Gaudin cauterised the still-unhealed wound and again declared him cured. Keith continued to work nearly every day and attend meetings nearly every night, sustained by the hand-written note he kept on his wardrobe shelf and read each day:

> I am getting stronger every day. I am feeling better and know that my recovery is continuing and making sound progress. I want to be thought of as sound and fit. I am extremely well looked after and regard my return to health and strength as certain.

For once Sylvia was the more realistic partner in the marriage. When the wound had not healed by November, though Keith continued to insist that there was no problem, she asked a Tauranga surgeon to examine him. An X-ray showed sinuses down to the bone, with no healing at all. Keith wrote apologetically to Mr Gaudin, reporting the result and suggesting that if further surgery was needed he would like it done in Tauranga after the end of the school year. Mr Gaudin replied that complications were not infrequent and that further surgical exploration would be reasonable. He said there was no urgency.

Keith's condition deteriorated rapidly during the remainder of 1968 and Sylvia was frantic with worry. He made light of her forebodings, and of the concern expressed by the Tauranga surgeon, saying that his weakness, and the pain that racked him night and day, were caused by nothing more serious than an injured back.

He stayed on his feet for the end-of-year school functions and for an emotional farewell at the pa. In hospital next day his doctors broke the news that he had only months to live. Keith told Sylvia: 'They don't know what they're talking about.'

Less than three weeks later, on 7 January 1969, at the age of sixty, Keith died. And less than three months later, on 29 March 1969, at the age of sixty, Sylvia left New Zealand, vowing never to return.

TWELVE

Escape

25 February 1969

My dear Jacquemine: I have left Whenua for ever. Shortly I leave New Zealand forever. I am at Ashton and Margaret's place at the moment. Elliot brought me here last night. I have left Whenua to Jasmine and David. I have signed Ashton Power of Attorney over my entire estate.

I am sufficiently well off to build for myself in Mauritius a small modest compact habitation, not in order to lean on and draw on your people but only to be near my people — which your family are.

I will be self-sufficient. I need to retreat from the world. The world will not find me in Mauritius. I need to forget the past. I mean to — hope to come incognito — not famous: I wish to be nobody — and live as nobody . . . I'm now no longer able to wait for anything or anyone in my urgent need to forget the past and forget this country. I am bringing nothing from New Zealand with me — nothing from Whenua. Shortly I will go up town and buy new clothes . . . I'll never recover until I am in another country . . .

As well as everything else in New Zealand I wish to leave my tears behind me.

With love to you all

Sylvia Henderson.

JACQUEMINE LATHAM-KOENIG, ELLIOT'S WIFE, WAS THE ELDEST daughter of a noble French family whose ancestors had fled to Mauritius during the French Revolution. Like Sylvia's dream-self she was an aristocrat with a hyphenated name who had grown up surrounded by servants. Until she left home to attend the Sorbonne in 1963, at the age of nineteen, she had never used an iron or washed a plate in her life. Jacquemine and Elliot met in Paris in 1964 and married in 1967. They were living in London, where Elliot was teaching and Jacquemine was pregnant with their son Vincent, when Sylvia casually informed them, three months after the wedding, that the kowhai tree she had planted in their honour had died.

When Elliot was called to his dying father's bedside at the beginning of 1969, Jacquemine and Vincent went to Mauritius, where Elliot was to join them on his way back to London.

Elliot arrived home the day before Keith died and stayed with his mother during her first weeks of widowhood. As with everything else about Sylvia, her grief — her shock, anger, denial, yearning, depression, numbness and idealisation of Keith — was larger than life.

The Maori community honoured Keith with the only tangi ever held for a Pakeha without marriage ties to the Ngai Te Rangi tribe. The casket, draped with a kiwi feather cloak, was carried shoulder high onto the Judea marae and laid in front of the meeting house. The women keened and wept, the men expressed through oratory their love for Keith and their grief at his passing. The Maori mourners wore black. The Pakeha mourners, who didn't know any better, wore sombre colours. Sylvia, who did know better, wore bright green.

She later claimed she had worn the Bethlehem School colour in honour of Keith, but her startling attire may really have been a shell-shocked expression of anger towards Keith for abandoning her, envy of his centre-stage role, and jealousy at the love and respect being showered upon him.

After shocking the Maori, Sylvia went on to shock the Pakeha. She held the funeral for this Methodist son of a Methodist minister in a Presbyterian church. The officiating clergyman belonged to Keith's Rotary club, which suggests that at some level of her turbulent mind Sylvia was trying to punish Keith for a character trait that had disturbed her deeply throughout their marriage — his interest and concern for people other than his wife.

Without Keith, Sylvia was adrift in meaninglessness:

> Saturday morning. How shall I fill it up? Whom shall I kiss? Is my small washing worth doing? Where are my boundaries, where is the framework I lived in? Where are the 'musts', the routines, the everlasting adjustments to another personality so different from my own? Is my own personality allowed to be itself now on its own? What is my personality freed? Have I got one? If so, where is it?[1]

The urge to run away and hide overwhelmed her. She decided to become a recluse. But when Elliot left to visit Ashton she found one night alone was too much. Even with Jasmine's older children staying overnight, the echoing memories were unbearable. She decided to leave New Zealand forever.

But where could she go? America wanted her, but she was frightened of America. Israel wanted her (six weeks before Keith died she had been invited to help establish a Rotary-sponsored peace school there in 1970), but she was frightened of Israel. Elliot was going to Mauritius; she would go to Mauritius too. But just in case that didn't work out she wrote to Wellesley Aron, chairman of the Israeli peace project, and said she was on her way.

A terrible tear-filled month went by as Elliot left and her own passport, visa, inoculations and tickets were arranged. Then she was free; free to run forever from her pain, her past and her old self.

Finding a new self was even more difficult than finding a new country. Perhaps new clothes, in new colours, would help. She had worn blue during her childhood and courting days; red, and later red, black and white, during her teaching years; black and white during her life as a writer; and bright green for her husband's funeral. Now she needed something completely different. She bought a glamorous orange satin dress patterned with white flowers, a matching chiffon coat that floated about her as she walked, and orange shoes.

The new self turned out to be as panicky and fearful as the old. Yet she coped. This highly-strung woman who fell apart at the most trivial of crises not only coped with the funeral and with the daily necessities that had always been Keith's responsibility, she got herself packed, organised and onto the plane. It seems that despite nearly forty years of behaving as if she was helpless without her husband, Sylvia did have a level-headed, practical side to her nature. When Keith was around she projected it onto him; with his death she had no choice but to claim it back.

But she never enjoyed playing the sensible grown-up, and it was as dangerous as blocking the vent of a volcano for her to play it for too long. In the years that followed, Sylvia handed over the role, gift-wrapped, to every unsuspecting mother-substitute who fell into the eddying currents of her life.

She took a heavy dose of librium to steady her pre-departure nerves. After an overnight stop in Sydney she took another dose for the long flight to Mauritius, and yet another after a brief stop in Perth. By the time Elliot, Jacquemine and Vincent met her in Mauritius she was lethargic, incoherent and confused. But the beauty of Jacquemine's homeland, an emerald, palm-fringed, tropical hideaway in the turquoise Indian Ocean, struck like a sunbeam through Sylvia's mental haze. She declared herself in love with Mauritius.

As the librium wore off so did her enthusiasm. Within a week the heat, the cockroaches, the scorpions, the lizards, the hotel staff, the strains in Elliot's marriage and the knowledge that he had decided to leave Jacquemine and return to London alone, threw her into despair. Again she wanted to run away and hide. Undeterred by news of a fatal bomb blast at the Hebrew University of Jerusalem, where the peace school was to be established, Sylvia decided that living under the care of a Rotarian had to be better than living in Mauritius. Encouraged by a cable from Wellesley Aron saying that progress was being made on her arrangements, and that he would advise her when they were finalised, she set off for Israel.

Before leaving she made herself known to the local Rotary club and so impressed the president he sent a cable to his counterpart in Bombay, asking him to look after Mrs Henderson during her stopover in his city. On the strength of that cable Sylvia extended her planned one-night Indian stay. After earlier visiting a school in Mauritius, she spent most of her week in Bombay on Rotary-arranged visits to schools. For someone who claimed to hate teaching, and who had taken little interest in education since resigning from teaching thirteen years earlier, her enthusiasm for visiting schools seems surprising. Perhaps she was seeking comfort in familiar surroundings, and reassurance in the company of children. The reason she gave was that she was conducting research for the work she planned to do in Israel.

Wellesley Aron had invited her to write the peace school textbook. He asked her to name her salary, publisher, illustrator and photographer. There would be no deadlines, and the university would provide living quarters, staff and equipment. On her third day in Bombay a cable arrived from Wellesley protesting that he was not ready, to which Sylvia replied that she was coming anyway.

It wasn't that she didn't like India — the colours, the contrasts, the VIP treatment, the elegant air-conditioned hotel and the obsequious servants enchanted her; it wasn't that she couldn't cope — she had learnt to change currency, book in and out of hotels, send cables, arrange taxis and alter flights like a seasoned traveller; but the novelty of self-sufficiency was beginning to wear thin. She wrote to Wellesley: 'I know it is the wrong time for me to start work but I'm anxious to get near you and under your wing. . . .'

Wellesley met her at Tel Aviv airport. Although her early arrival was far from convenient, he made her welcome and assumed responsibility for her comfort and welfare. He was charming and authoritative, and under his attentive care Sylvia quickly reverted to her impractical, imperious, panicky self.

Her mental stability was not helped by the fact that the war she feared was no longer confined to her own psyche. On the drive from Tel Aviv to Jerusalem, overturned jeeps, grim reminders of the 1967 Six Day War, rusted by the roadside, while roadblocks and vehicle searches reminded her that the hostilities continued. When she went shopping she saw armed soldiers patrolling the streets and warplanes streaking overhead. At the bank and the supermarket her handbag was searched. She heard screams in the night.

After two nights in a Tel Aviv hotel she fled in panic to the accommodation Wellesley had arranged for her at a Christian hospice in Jerusalem. The Reverend Gardiner-Scott and his wife were not expecting her until the following week, but Wellesley had shown her the hospice and she couldn't wait. It was glorious, it was wonderful — it was the castle of her childhood dreams:

> . . . made up of a towering church joined to living quarters, with battlements and a tower that you can see for miles with the Scottish flag flying on the top. All in stone. Inside it is marble with stairs and arches and domes and foyers and a reception room larger than a hall. . . . A piano.
> . . . Shadows and reflected light on the white marble . . . trees . . . gardens . . . at the end of a no exit road with no traffic rushing by. . . . I couldn't imagine a more beautiful and seemly place for me to stay and work.[2]

In the valley below her balconied window, shepherds in flowing robes tended their flocks, while on a distant hill old Jerusalem lay like a fawn-pink dream in the soft spring air. At night she drew security from the

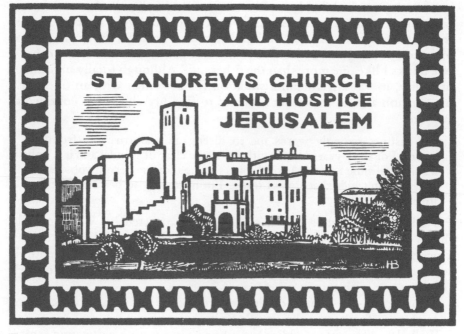

W. GARDINER-SCOTT

sound of her host methodically locking doors and windows, and turning off lights.

Her happiness with the hospice spilled over into her relationship with the Gardiner-Scotts:

> Our relationship with her was very close and happy. She had a rare sense of humour and one could see from her relationship with our daughter Tanya, aged about ten, that she had a gift in getting alongside children; the secret being that she treated them as equals and was never patronising as many teachers can be. . . . She could get down on her knees and play marbles with the children on the lounge floor and at the piano she charmed the children with her playing and singing.[3]

At the hospice Sylvia felt safe enough, and happy enough, to dispense with the sensible grown-up role completely.

Apart from breakfast, which was supplied by the hospice, guests were expected to provide their own meals. The Gardiner-Scotts familiarised Sylvia with the local supermarket and introduced her to the hospice kitchen, but she had no intention of shopping or cooking, so she didn't. When Wellesley brought her mail each day he asked solicitously, 'Are you eating, yes? You're not eating enough. I don't think you're cooking your food, no? I'll arrange something.' The greater his concern, the more helpless Sylvia became. Before long the Gardiner-Scotts found themselves doing Sylvia's shopping and cooking her meals, and Wellesley found himself becoming more and more puzzled by her behaviour.

Wellesley recalled that he and his wife treated Sylvia to the same hospitality they extended to all visitors from abroad, but Sylvia concluded from their attention that they had both fallen in love with her. She read passion into their every gesture: 'Both love me and get jealous one of the other if one thinks I like one more than the other. . . .' Although totally unfounded in reality, it was a frightening situation for a woman with an overactive imagination and no sheltering husband to find herself in. She confided to Ashton:

> My instinct strongly warns me to disengage unobtrusively from the Arons. For sixty years I lived with my name clear of scandal and it is only a matter of time before Major Aron's feelings for me become obvious to others. Can't hide that sort of thing. I'm not going to become involved in anything messy.[4]

For all her fears Sylvia couldn't help being attracted by Wellesley. She flirted with him at every opportunity, but declined to fall in love, convincing herself that though his love for her was great, it was not entirely selfless. 'I'm the goose that is to lay the golden egg,' she told Ashton. 'He cherishes me with this in mind.'

Also, he wasn't calm enough, understanding enough, self-sacrificing enough. . . . In short — he wasn't Keith.

Wellesley Aron was a soldier and a businessman with a dynamic centre-stage personality. Less forceful people became responsive, dedicated and malleable under his leadership. Sylvia soon realised to her horror that he expected her to do the same. When he arranged for her to address a Rotary conference, and go sightseeing with two famous visiting scholars, she resolved to do nothing of the sort; when he suggested that she plan model peace lessons for a television series to be screened around the world, she ignored him; and when he told her that the royalties from the textbook she was being employed to write — royalties Sylvia regarded as exclusively her own — were to be used to establish a Chair of Peace at the university, she resolved to withdraw from the project completely.

But because she was so charming towards him, and never argued or attempted to explain herself, Wellesley knew nothing of her thoughts. He was just bewildered by her failure to co-operate.

> One day when I went up to the hospice to see her she came out of her room and said, 'Now don't talk to me please.'
> I said, 'What do you think I've come for?'
> She said, 'I know what you've come for but I don't want to be disturbed. I am now five years old and I'm typing a story and trying to develop a theory about education for five-year-olds and I don't want to be disturbed.'[5]

During her second week Sylvia began her non-co-operation in earnest. She ignored the telephone, refused to meet with the Arons and told the Gardiner-Scotts that she was working and could not be interrupted. But the problem of extricating herself from the peace project remained.

Then an urgent cable arrived from Elliot's friend David Halley: PLEASE FLY LONDON IMMEDIATELY STOP ELLIOT VERY ILL STOP HOSPITAL TROPICAL DISEASES. Sylvia packed and left for London next day.

En route to London one of the brittle bands of self-control holding down the tension in her undermind snapped. At Heathrow a hostess escorted Sylvia from the plane and through Customs, and handed her over to David Halley. 'She was weeping,' he recalled. 'And very, very distraught.'

On the way to the hospital David explained that an amoebic infection of the gut had spread throughout Elliot's body; his life was in the balance.

When Sylvia saw her son — gaunt, jaundiced, hollow-eyed and gasping for breath; with drip and blood transfusion attached to his arms and a feeding tube through his nose — all the horror of Keith's final illness came back to her. Keith had died, now Elliot was dying too. She slept the first night at the hospital and for the next three days spent most of her time there. She appealed to the local Rotary club, to her London agent and to the Queen for help with accommodation. Both her agent and the Rotary people found sleeping quarters for her near the hospital, but a note from Buckingham Palace advised her that the Queen had nothing available.

On the third day Ashton arrived from New Zealand, and Jacquemine, having left Vincent with relatives, flew in from Mauritius. From then on, Sylvia, Jacquemine and Ashton stayed at Elliot's Clapham flat and Jacquemine took over the hospital vigil.

Elliot continued to deteriorate, rallying briefly when the surgeons drained a pint of pus from his abcessed liver, then fading again. 'All seems lost,' Sylvia wrote in her diary.

Jacquemine did not give up hope. She stayed by Elliot's side, checking and rechecking. Is he comfortable? Has he had his medication? Does the blood transfusion match his blood group? Is the blood running freely? Is the drip dripping? — and called for help whenever anything seemed wrong. When she had been in London a week Sylvia said to her, 'You are very tired. I'll take care of him in the morning. You sleep.' As she had earlier explained to David Halley, 'At a time like this a mother, rather than wife, should be at the side of a man.'

Ever since they met in Mauritius their relationship had been strained. Jacquemine was afraid of her formidable mother-in-law and anxious to be accepted; Sylvia was afraid and jealous of Jacquemine. Most of the time an exaggerated politeness between them was the only indication of tension.

Sylvia had neither the will nor the strength to fight for Elliot's life; she just wanted to be with him when he died. At eleven that morning Jacquemine received an urgent call from the hospital to come at once. Elliot was passing away. An hour earlier, with his mother at his bedside, Elliot's blood transfusion had run dry. It was Fate (which, as Sylvia confided to Bob Gottlieb, was another name for God). Fate had killed her husband. Fate had torn her from home and family. Fate had tossed her wildly around the world. Fate was killing her son. She told the distraught Jacquemine that she had been too frightened to call a nurse. 'Then,' Jacquemine recalled, 'I started to hate her.'

Despite setbacks, Elliot began to improve. After four weeks in hospital he took his first shaky steps. Ashton returned to New Zealand, Jacquemine took two part-time jobs, and Sylvia named her room at Clapham 'Selah', and settled down to write.

Mostly she wrote, but did not post, a tortured interior monologue addressed to Ashton and Jasmine; telling them how upset and lonely she was and how she wanted to run away and hide, telling them of Elliot's homecoming, of Jacquemine's lack of domesticity, and of the addition to the household of Elliot's unemployed actor friend, Graham Eaton. Before long she recognised in her pile of unposted letters the material for a new book. How would it end? She recorded the events and conversations around her and filtered their implications through her turbulent undermind in order to find out.

From the hours Sylvia spent at her typewriter it was clear to Elliot, Jacquemine and Graham that she was working on a book. When she wasn't working she was so often upset they were glad to see her occupied. They had no idea the book was about them. The first Elliot knew of it was after a blazing row between Sylvia and Jacquemine. It was the first open hostility between them and it occurred when, after a four-month separation, eighteen-month-old Vincent rejoined his mother.

Sylvia had been unable to relate to Vincent at Mauritius. He was so foreign, so like Jacquemine's father, and so unlike any Warner or Henderson she had ever known. She wrote in her diary that when Elliot asked her to help mind Vincent in London, 'I refused unequivocally.'

The child slept in the room opposite Sylvia. He often woke in the night and cried. Jacquemine noted that Sylvia's bedroom light shone through the high corridor window and onto Vincent's bed. Perhaps, she suggested, the light was disturbing him.

Sylvia, frozen with fury, made no reply. But she wrote later:

> . . . though we both smile as we part I'm aware of crumbling rumbles
> in the undermind as though some great wall was beginning to tumble,
> eroded at the base, hearing in myself, And now they won't let me work
> at night.[6]

Next day, after going shopping, she drew a piece of dark curtain material from her bag and threw it in Jacquemine's face. '*This*,' she said savagely, 'Is for *your* child.'

'You attacked my work,' she added bitterly, and went on to itemise everything about Jacquemine that had been upsetting her for months, concentrating on her neglect of her husband and mother-in-law, on the hours she kept, and on the standard of her housekeeping.

Jacquemine recalled:

> All day there was this huge, huge scene. And Elliot was sitting there

saying, 'I can't choose between my wife and my mother.' That was what she obviously wanted.

Elliot, too, recalled the outburst:

> She accused Jacquemine of having been responsible for my illness because of what she called her 'Asian kitchen'. Jacquemine said 'Are you accusing me of killing him?' Mum said, 'Yes.'

Sylvia blamed her loss of control on the sedative she took to calm herself after having her work attacked, and on her inability to distinguish between the fiction she was writing and the reality around her.

Shortly after the argument she confessed to Elliot that she had been writing a book about their lives at Clapham but had now resolved, as a gesture of goodwill, to destroy the manuscript.

> She said she had taken the manuscript down and burnt it. I was sceptical about that. When she was ready to leave London I looked in her suitcase. I saw the manuscript was still there.[7]

The resulting novel, *Three*, was published in 1970 by Bob Gottlieb, who had moved from Simon and Schuster to Knopf in 1969.

Years later Graham Eaton reflected on the use Sylvia made of him for her book:

> I realise now that she had her antennae out all the time for little things she could use. Lots of the conversations in *Three* were what I was saying at the breakfast table. I was talking about my mother and so on, and lo and behold there's the whole conversation in the book. Also I read odd bits from plays to her, not knowing it was all grist to the mill.[8]

Jacquemine, on looking back, suspected that Sylvia manipulated the events at Clapham in order to develop her plot:

> She wrote in the book about an incident when she went out and came back and Elliot and I were making love, she heard us from behind the door. I remember that day. She said very firmly that she would not be back for three hours. We began to make love. She came back after five minutes and tiptoed in and listened behind the door. When I came out and found her I said, 'What are you doing here?' She said, 'Oh I was too sad, I decided to come back.'
>
> Also she used to ask me about my job as if she was interested, but it was I think to pick up words and phrases for her book. She made a caricature of my accent and way of talking.[9]

After their efforts to befriend Sylvia and to accommodate her needs, the appearance of *Three* left Elliot, Jacquemine and Graham feeling used. And the ease with which the characters, events and conversations could be identified made the distortions of reality in the novel particularly galling. Graham was most irritated by the implication that he and Jacquemine were in love, and that he had attempted suicide:

> Sylvia was a woman of intense imagination and she naturally took the

writer's preogative to use what was happening around her to make a
novel. I don't know to this day whether she actually believed that what
she wrote in that book was really happening, because it was completely
untrue.[10]

Sylvia portrayed herself in the novel as a jealous, oversensitive, self-
pitying, insecure mother-in-law, but Graham's recollections do not support the suggestion in *Three* that her primary purpose in staying was to
care for her son:

> She was bashing away at her typewriter at all hours of the day and night.
> Her writing seemed more important to her at that point than her son. I
> think she just wanted to be there. The idea of her acting as a nurse just
> wasn't on.[11]

To Sylvia, the propriety of using the people around her for her work was
not the issue. The issue was her own emotional survival. Turning uncontrollable reality into controllable fiction was her only way of coping.

July passed, and then August. The book grew longer. But though
Graham left and Vincent returned, Elliot and Jacquemine showed no sign
of bringing the drama to an end. Sylvia's recurrent panic attacks became
more frequent, and more intense. She wrote to the German translator of
Spinster, and to Jeannette Veatch, Bob Gottlieb and several other
Americans, begging them to save her, to take her away. And her decisions
to leave or stay swung about as wildly as her moods.

Then, for the third time that year, Fate intervened. A letter arrived from
Ashton with the devastating news that Jasmine's husband had suddenly
died. He added that Jasmine was seven months pregnant with her sixth
child, and that both he and Jasmine wanted Sylvia to stay in London. He
said he would sell Whenua and buy a home for Jasmine near him in
Hastings.

Sylvia returned to New Zealand immediately, deeply concerned for Jasmine and fiercely intent on protecting her real estate. She arrived home
with her emotional resources in disarray to find Jasmine depressed,
exhausted and in poor health. Neither woman could provide the comfort
and support they both needed so badly. They lived from day to day,
drawing their will to survive from Mama's example of unquenchable
resistance in the face of adversity. The children were unhappy, defiant and
quarrelsome and they soon proved too much for Sylvia. She retreated to
Selah and spent most of her time writing to her dead husband about the
turmoil around her.

When Jasmine was hospitalised for a week prior to the birth, the tide of
responsibility began to rise over Sylvia's head. She employed a housekeeper and kept her mind steady by continuing to write. When she
emerged from Selah to find that her three-year-old grandson had smashed
her reading glasses and lost the case, dragged the clothes from the upstairs
bedroom and tipped them down the stairs, and then wandered onto the
road, she attacked the housekeeper for failing to supervise him.

'How can I watch him all the time and do my work?' she protested. 'I can't do my work!'

'That,' said Sylvia coldly. 'Is your problem.'[12]

The new baby was mercifully placid, but the inroads he made into Jasmine's sleep further raised the family stress level. Even in the depths of the self-absorption Sylvia recognised that Jasmine was badly in need of help. When the baby was two weeks old she took over his care at night, leaving Jasmine to cope with all the children during the day. Sylvia enjoyed the baby, and being free during the day gave her the time, and the detachment, to record the drama around her:

> J is falling apart. . . . The ship is sinking and I can do nothing to stop it. . . .
>
> My nerves deteriorate. I know J's sleep is a priority yet I wrecked it last night by upsetting her by losing my temper. . . . I'm no more than another child whining to J, demanding her attention. . . .[13]

Sylvia sent her running commentary on life at Whenua to Bob Gottlieb, but it failed to satisfy him:

> . . . what you've done gloriously in *Three*, which is to take recent life-material and transmute it into art, hasn't happened here; what I've read, anyway, is undigested lumps of life.[14]

Sylvia was desperate to publish; her income from royalties was dwindling and her bank balance was in overdraft. But she became so depressed she couldn't write at all: 'There's a hollow where my work should be that nothing I know can fill. A drafty place, a cavern, a chasm, a bottomless crevasse.' She decided to abandon writing and help with the children instead, freeing Jasmine to supplement the family income by making elegant cane baskets. But she couldn't cope with the children. She raged at them and thrashed them. She tipped out their meals when they quarrelled. Then she fled to Ashton's for a break.

She returned feeling no better, and with every passing week sank deeper into despair. Then, as grief and exhaustion threatened to swamp her, she reached for the lifeline that had brought her through her breakdown at Horoera and through Keith's final illness: she made a fresh start on the story of her life. But in the turmoil of Whenua writing couldn't keep her afloat forever. She had to escape. She had to find herself again. She had to rediscover, or re-invent, the person she used to be: that brilliant writer and educationalist, Sylvia Ashton-Warner.

Then at the end of July 1970 an invitation flew in from America, and Sylvia Ashton-Warner lived again. The letter came from a group of parents establishing an alternative elementary school in Aspen, Colorado: 'It would be of tremendous value to us if you could come and teach and "show us the way".'

At that time the counterculture, from which the alternative school movement was born, was beginning to flex its political muscle, and nowhere was this more evident than in the Rocky Mountain town of Aspen. During the 1950s and 1960s Aspen had developed into a ski resort and cultural centre. When Haight-Ashbury turned sour in the summer of 1967, Aspen seemed like a good place to go. The permanent Aspen population of around two thousand, comprising mainly businesspeople and old-timers from the town's silver-mining past, was suddenly swelled by several hundred alarmingly hairy and colourful hippies. And as the reputation of Aspen as a 'wayout' place spread, they were joined by student radicals, alternative lifestylers, left-wing liberals and bored dilettantes looking for excitement.

In 1969, in a moment of high-spirited lunacy, one of their number stood for mayor of Aspen on a 'Freak Power' ticket. When he lost by only six votes the newcomers knew their time had come. They were going to overthrow the old order. They were going to change the world.

Changing the school system, getting rid of the regimentation, the hierarchical structure and the dull curriculum, seemed a great place to start. And who better to lead the revolution than that inspirational rebel: Sylvia Ashton-Warner?

Since Keith's death, Sylvia's horizons had closed around her like a thick fog. She was only dimly aware of the emergence of the counterculture and had no idea that the Aspen school group was part of it; but she was thrilled that the unintimidating, handwritten invitation asked her to demonstrate rather than talk. And she was thrilled that the lettter came from a cousin of Elliot's former girlfriend. Sylvia knew her family and, though she didn't like them much, the letter made her feel she was not dealing with total strangers.

The idea of actually going to Aspen was really no more than a fantasy to sustain her in her grief. As a working teacher Sylvia had lacked the commitment, and the administrative and interpersonal skills, to run an established school in her own country. Her chances of successfully establishing a new one in a foreign country fourteen years after retiring from teaching, when she was sixty-one years old and her emotional resources were at their lowest-ever ebb, were virtually zero. But she needed a dream to follow, and this was it.

In her reply she outlined the recent crises in her life and added wistfully:

> I now have seven dependent relatives, Jasmine and six children, with no Keith to help me. I cannot *afford* to come to Aspen. I would have otherwise. . . . Had there been a return fare and salary attached I would have been able to come.[15]

The Community School parents were electrified. They had few funds, no teachers and no school building — but with Sylvia Ashton-Warner to lead them anything was possible. Within days they obtained a house, rent free, for Sylvia's use, and raised the money for her $15,000 salary and her return first-class airfare from New Zealand. The bulk of the money came from donations — though most school parents lived at a subsistence level, some were wealthy in their own right, and others had wealthy friends and relatives willing to help out.

After that the project snowballed. The Physics Institute building, used only in summer, was made available to the school rent free, and another distinguished teacher, Wanda Gray, whose innovative work with underachievers was well known in the United States, was employed to run the upper school. Scores of American teachers clamoured for the privilege of working with Sylvia Ashton-Warner; some were willing to work for token salaries and some were willing to work for nothing; the most promising were hired. Sixty local children were quickly enrolled, and a number of families moved to Aspen so that their offspring could attend the school.

In order to influence the state education system, and in the hope of obtaining state funding, the Community School wanted to operate as a pilot programme within the public school system. The state commissioner of education and the local superintendent of schools supported the project, but a vigorous conservative opposition voiced its disapproval in Aspen. The local Board of Education, caught in the middle, agreed that the Aspen Community School could become a public school, but would receive no public funds. The Community School parents were undeterred; they had heaps of determination, enough money to survive, and Sylvia Ashton-Warner was on her way.

In September 1970, in a blaze of optimism, the Aspen Community School began.

THIRTEEN

Aspen

THE ASPEN COMMUNITY SCHOOL OPENED ON 15 SEPTEMBER AND the infighting began at once. Sylvia arrived on 3 October and walked straight into the crossfire. She was so absorbed in her own problems she hardly noticed.

The school she came to was throbbing with the excitement of getting organised. Prior to her arrival, assistant teachers Judy Sheldon and Harriet Crosby had taken over the five- to eight-year-olds. Judy had been trained by an American Ashton-Warner enthusiast in the 'organic method'; Harriet was an untrained volunteer.

At the same time Wanda Gray, senior teacher to the older children, had drawn up a curriculum for the nine- to twelve-year-olds and, assisted by two other teachers, had begun translating that curriculum into action. The expectation among parents and staff was that Sylvia would do the same for the younger children. But that wasn't what happened. Wanda recalled:

> I don't think Sylvia understood that her job was to start the school for the younger children. I think she thought she was going to be a sort of visiting professor and just showcase her teaching method.[1]

The only prior indication of Sylvia's own expectations came in a letter to school parent Margaret Albouy:

> *What I'm looking forward to:* setting up a wide table by a wide window in a wide room. Equipping it again. . . . I'm looking forward to this very much. I can't say how much. . . .
> *What I I fear in Aspen:* the cold. . . . The sound of radio and TV assaulting through the wall over which I have no control. . . .

She didn't say anything about looking forward to teaching and the only question she asked about the school was whether it was centrally heated. She closed with: 'I'm a child again; my adulthood is bracketed in dream behind. I'm looking forward to the other children.'

At midday on 3 October Wanda Gray and the Albouys met Sylvia at Grand Junction airport. They were expecting not a child, but a dynamic educator. The woman they met was a frail old lady. By 1970 Sylvia's complexion had become so heavily wrinkled that on a good day she looked ten years older than her sixty-one years. This was not a good day. At seven in the evening of 1 October she had left Auckland. After fifteen hours of flying and five hours of stopovers, after crossing the International Date Line and passing through five time zones, she had arrived in San Francisco, according to local clock and calendar, one hour before she left New Zealand.

Jeannette Veatch and Ardelle Llewellyn looked after her in San Francisco. Jeannette had mixed feelings about Sylvia's American plans. During the years since her 1965 visit to Whenua she had generated a stream of glamorous invitations for Sylvia to speak in the United States. That Sylvia had refused every one was bad enough; that she had now accepted a job at some off-the-beaten-track school Jeannette had never heard of was even worse. She made the best of a disappointing situation by showing Sylvia off to her friends and colleagues; Sylvia was too jet-lagged to object.

On Sylvia's second evening in San Francisco, Jeannette arranged a large cocktail party in her honour, after which a group of Ashton-Warner fans, unmindful of Sylvia's need for rest before her early morning departure for Aspen, swept her off to a late-night dinner at Fisherman's Wharf. By the time Sylvia reached Grand Junction next day she could barely stand, and in the car on the way to Aspen she told Wanda: 'They tried to kill me last night.'

During her first weary evening in Aspen many school parents brought food to the gracious six-bedroom home loaned for Sylvia's use, and did their best to make their new teacher feel welcome. But Sylvia felt disoriented and vulnerable. Part of the problem was altitude. Aspen, a picturesque mountain village nestled among golden aspens, literally took her breath away. The low oxygen level at eight thousand feet made her gasp for breath, and the low humidity made her lungs dry and sore. At night, alone with her fears in a big empty house, the terror of not being able to breathe inflamed her panic and shattered her sleep.

But she put on a brave face and went to school. And it was not like any school she had ever known — or even dreamt about.

The Physics Institute was a long, low, narrow building divided into small rooms. The cramped space, the rowdy children, the crowds of visitors, preschoolers, babies and dogs, and Sylvia's own poor health made attending school a stressful experience, but the respect and consideration she was accorded there made it almost worthwhile. After two weeks she wrote to Jasmine:

> There is nothing that is not done for me. If I want letters posted someone from the office immediately gets in a car and drives to the Post Office. If I want shopping done Mary, my shadow [Mary Settergast, a Berkeley student writing a dissertation on Sylvia Ashton-Warner], has been detailed to approach me every morning and ask what I want. My social life is organised in a series of private dinners every Saturday night, according to my wishes; parents by the dozen are standing by in case I would like someone to drop in for a cup of tea. . . . If I'm sick Betty Benton [school parent] gets in touch with the doctor. . . . I let Bruce [Bruce Thomas, school administrator] know I wanted academic company while I was evolving the new application of my formula, and this he supplies himself in meetings at school, walks on the plain, and an

appointment for tea at my place. Any equipment I want for the infant room is made by some carpenter parent. I said I wanted tea mid-morning and an electric jug is bought, cups, and a little table (though no one understands teapots . . .). Margaret Albouy herself is I think the one to supply personal friendship . . . I live in an enchanted world.

It was Sylvia's charisma that won over her Aspen friends. Fellow teacher Mike Stranahan recalled:

> She was very sensitive to people's characters. She could talk with someone for a few minutes and divine, by some process I never under-stood, their real character, their real motives, their real likes and dislikes, their real urges and desires. She would talk to the inner person as if the outer mask was not important. I saw her do this lots of times, and she was very good at it. People responded to it very well. They always like that in her, and I did too.[2]

But when it came to the practicalities of classroom teaching the spell was broken. Sylvia's enchanted world became the setting for a nightmare.

As a woman who had always fought for educational and personal freedom, and who had turned unconventionality into an art form, Sylvia should have felt at home at the Aspen Community School, but she didn't. She felt overwhelmed and bewildered, and she couldn't cope. One of the most disturbing aspects of the school was the lack of hierarchy. There was no headmaster and, apart from the leadership expected from the senior teachers, no ranking order of staff. And on matters educational even the parents and pupils were not as unquestioningly respectful as Sylvia thought they should be.

In day-to-day classroom activities Sylvia was disturbed by the realisa-tion that Wanda Gray and Judy Sheldon were the only staff who seemed to know what they were doing. Mike Stranahan, the only other trained teacher, worked in Wanda's section of the school. He ran experiments using white mice. The mice kept escaping and adding to the general mayhem by hiding under carpets where they were, from time to time, trodden underfoot. During the winter he rewarded his students by letting them jump into snowdrifts from the back of his pick-up truck as he drove slowly along the road.

Mike Burns, who also worked in the senior school, was a student radical with no background in education. His classes were disorganised, but fun. Wanda and the two Mikes were later joined by Ed Bastion, a musician who lived in a teepee and studied Buddhism, and by another untrained teacher, Lewis Simon, who, as far as anyone can remember, never actually taught anything but just wandered around the school. Whenever a child gravi-tated towards him he would say, 'C'mon kid, let's go freak around town.' Then he and the child would amble off for an hour or two. Nobody seemed to mind.

In the junior section (now, at Sylvia's insistence, restricted to the twenty-five children aged seven and under), Judy was a capable teacher, but Harriet, whose background was similar to that of Mike Burns, taught, according to Sylvia, while lying on the floor with her hands in her pockets, chewing gum. Mary, the Berkeley research student, was also often recruited to help with teaching in the junior school.

The school was run by a parent board. The parents ranged in respectability from physicians and restaurateurs through mime artists, painters, leather clothes makers and palm readers to 'gonzo' journalist Hunter Thompson, author of *Fear and Loathing in Las Vegas* and other classics. Collectively they were among the best educated, most widely read and most opinionated activists in the nation. They were proud of their school and committed to the ideals of equality and freedom it represented, but the fundamental source of disagreement among them was — how were those ideals to be achieved?

At school meetings, philosophic exchanges were long and heated, and concrete actions were few. To the parents that was how it should be: the process was as important as the product and there was learning to be had in every situation. To Sylvia the meetings were a waste of time, and they confirmed her long-held conviction that Americans were undisciplined, garrulous and arrogant.

The question of what limits, if any, should be placed on the unfettered exuberance of the children was debated at length. Some parents believed that when freed from external restraints their children would grow rapidly and confidently into self-directed, constructive members of society. Others worried that their kids would learn little without direction. When Sylvia came down heavily in favour of structure and discipline, some upstarts had the temerity to disagree with her, to actually suggest that she, Sylvia Ashton-Warner, was not the final authority on matters educational. It was all very hard to take.

While debate raged, the teachers went ahead, as far as architectural limitations and parental interference allowed, to do pretty much what they liked. What Sylvia liked best was to turn her classroom into a refuge. When she realised there was no refuge to be found at this school, the effort of attending became a crushing burden.

She fortified herself for school each day with tea, codeine and librium, and later with increasing quantities of lager, brandy and whisky. On discovering that codeine and Bell tea couldn't be purchased in Aspen, she sent an urgent request to New Zealand for codeine tablets concealed inside packets of Bell tea. While she awaited their arrival her nightly distress was compounded by the nightmares and anxiety characteristic of codeine withdrawal.

Because her colleagues thought you made tea by dunking teabags into cups of hot tap-water, and never stopped for tea-breaks anyway, Sylvia had to pursue her passion for tea alone. She set up a tea-making centre in the furnace room of the school. Because of the low boiling point of water at high altitude, her kettle frequently boiled dry. All too often acrid smoke from the melting kettle handle was sucked into the furnace and belched out around the school, adding to the general discomfort of the working environment.

By far the most disturbing aspect of school for Sylvia was the work expected of her. Wanda recalled Sylvia's approach to school administration:

> I don't think she'd done any managerial work before. It was very confusing for her. She didn't know how to work with people, she didn't know how to direct people or how to motivate people. She treated her staff like they were servants and nobody liked that.[3]

Sylvia was also expected to teach and she hadn't taught for fifteen years. Back then her most successful work had come in short concentrated engagements with children she knew well. How could she repeat the performance now? The liveliness of the Aspen children was familiar enough, but they were white skinned, articulate, sophisticated strangers who treated her with disturbing familiarity. How could she apply her work to them?

She needed obedience and attentiveness for her method to succeed, and she had, in the past, used the strap, the stick, the ruler or her bare hand to ensure full co-operation. In American schools, hitting children was unacceptable. How could she successfully demonstrate her work here?

She needed a piano so that she and the children could break off and dance when the tension became too great, but the only piano at this school was in the foyer; there was no space in the tiny classrooms. How could she ever teach in this place? The conditions were overwhelmingly unfavourable — but she had to perform.

On her fourth day at school she gathered some children around her for a key vocabulary lesson. They had trouble understanding her accent and she had trouble understanding theirs. They were unsettled by her aloofness, her heavy make-up and by her insistence on being addressed as Mrs Henderson when all the other teachers were known by their first names. Some children wandered off while she was talking and only two offered her a word — the first casual, inconsequential word that entered their heads. Sylvia felt humiliated, and she blamed the children.

The theory she developed as a result of her Aspen experience had in fact taken root years earlier. During the 1960s she had written to Bob Gottlieb about what she thought was wrong with America. She said that Americans had lost contact with nature and their own feelings, and cared only for the two-dimensional worlds of technology and the dollar. She had also written in *Teacher* (before the advent of television in New Zealand) of her concern that the inner resources of children would atrophy from over-exposure to film, radio and shop-bought toys.

When her first days of teaching confirmed her worst expectations she wrote to Jasmine:

> . . . the young American mind has already engaged in mutation. . . . It is hit at so hard in childhood by the constant mass communications media

that it's gone different. It almost has no native imagery. I have found, and have said so, its vision fragmented, its attention span concertinaed. It can't interest or entertain itself but has to be entertained. . . .

When I try to release key words, captions of the inner imagery, I find no imagery. . . .

As the weeks went by, Sylvia's rapport with the children improved a little, but her relationship with her staff deteriorated steadily. Judy, Mary and Harriet were irritated at the way she treated them, and disillusioned with her approach to teaching. Mary recalled:

Wanda and Judy looked on kids as people and related to them very well indeed. Sylvia just marched in and said what we assumed she had said to Maori children, and then wondered why she wasn't getting the proper responses.

When she took a lesson she would call for attention in a very dramatic way, as if the whole thing was a stage setting. But you could see her heart wasn't in it, ever, with the kids.

Once we realised that she wasn't a growing person and wasn't open to new ideas we lost a lot of respect for her. There didn't seem to be anything we could learn from her that we couldn't read in her books.[4]

With no classroom joy to sustain her, Sylvia turned increasingly to alcohol, and her problems escalated. Mary continued:

One day she came in late smelling of brandy and screaming about the empty sandbox and how we had not lived up to our responsibilities. I remember thinking, 'How could you possibly accuse anyone else when you're behaving so irresponsibly yourself?'[5]

Despite the stress, Sylvia attended school regularly throughout October. Her greatest support came from Margaret Albouy, whom Sylvia came to regard as her complement, and from Bruce Thomas, a parent who had taken on the task of school administrator. In her inner eye Sylvia saw Bruce as her protector, her island of stability, the man she could depend on to keep her from harm. Then in early November an explosive argument at a Community School meeting blew her island of stability clean out of the water. Bruce Thomas left Aspen.

During November Sylvia's school attendance became irregular. She spent a lot of time at home preparing little readers for the children, transforming her school diary into a book, and interviewing parents about their children's key words. Parent Su Lum wrote to friends about her interview:

She put a great deal of emphasis on these words Hillery had chosen, and their meaningfulness to Hillery, while I felt that the words reflected Hillery's desire to fulfil the obligation of COMING UP WITH A WORD. That is, there were no Fear words, or Care words, or Love words, really. I am sure that if Hillery really felt free she would be saying things like, 'I wish I could see my Daddy', 'I am afraid to die' (a big subject), 'darkness', 'monster', 'vagina', etc. When she comes up with 'I like clay', 'she dropped it', and 'the flower pot' I can visualise her wildly Groping for Something to Say.

By December Sylvia had become so disillusioned with the school and its children she could think only of escape. But the difficulties in doing so were formidable: she needed somewhere to go, someone to organise the trip, someone to take her and, since she had resolved never to fly again, she needed to fight down her terror of the precipitous mountain road out of Aspen.

Then Jeannette Veatch invited her to Phoenix for Christmas, and offered her own car, with a reliable graduate student at the wheel, for the return journey. Sylvia struggled for weeks with the decision; one moment she was terrified of travelling, the next she was desperate to escape. When she eventually agreed to go, her fears began to focus on Jeannette. Would she respect Sylvia's wish for a peaceful holiday, or would she subject her guest to painful public exposure? Margaret Albouy wrote to Jeannette about the problem:

> Her stay in San Francisco . . . absolutely exhausted her. . . . I warn you to be very careful with your plans for her stay . . . it will be up to you to keep social engagements to a minimum. Here she goes out to dinner only on Saturday nights . . . she is obviously not in the best of health. . . .

Sylvia revealed none of this directly to Jeannette, but was instead so unfailingly ingratiating that Jeannette soon forgot all about Margaret's warning — Sylvia's ten days in Phoenix were spent in a continuous round of visitors, cocktail parties, dinners and education gatherings.

The two women also found time to discuss Sylvia's future. It was a topic in which they were both passionately interested. Since her pilgrimage to Whenua, Jeannette had been unflagging in her enthusiasm for linking her name with Sylvia's and, in the teeth of Sylvia's passive resistance, for managing Sylvia's American career. Following Sylvia's landfall in San Francisco, she had sent out a flood of letters informing the American educational world that Sylvia Ashton-Warner had arrived in the United States. As a result, a tide of invitations for Sylvia to speak at major conventions all over North America had poured into Aspen. To Jeannette's chagrin Sylvia immediately rejected most of them, and later backed out of the few she had initially accepted, usually after arrangements were finalised and programmes printed and, on at least one occasion, after the convention had actually begun. But Jeannette never gave up trying to launch Sylvia on a high-profile American career. Sylvia loved the flattery of the invitations and the occasional thrill of accepting; it was only the prospect of following through on her acceptance that frightened her.

When, during her stay in Phoenix, Sylvia expressed interest in staying in America after her one-year contract in Aspen ended, Jeannette went job-hunting on Sylvia's behalf. First she introduced Sylvia to her boss at the University of Arizona, but he was unimpressed. Next she fired a salvo of letters to friends in educational institutions all over the continent, suggesting they offer Sylvia a job. The invitations began to stream in as soon as Sylvia returned to Aspen, but she was in no condition to accept them.

Her health had been steadily eroded during her three months in Aspen. When she went to Phoenix her blood pressure was high, her chest was weak and she was constantly tired. The exhaustion of her stay with Jean-nette compounded her problems, and the gruelling return journey brought her to the point of collapse. The long days of fast driving had tired and frightened her, but that wasn't all. The worst part was that after success-fully giving up smoking before she left New Zealand, she had spent four stressful days with a driver who smoked. By the time she returned to Aspen Sylvia had resumed smoking. Her breathing difficulties, and with it her depression, panic and lassitude, immediately intensified. In early February she spent five days on oxygen in the Aspen hospital, emerging too weak and dispirited to continue at the Community School any longer.

She decided to devote all her remaining energy to writing her diary-based book about Aspen, but instead of finding peace of mind at home, she became so overwhelmed with guilt at her truancy that out of sheer panic she tried to cut her ties with the Community School completely. Wanda recalled:

> She stayed in her house with all the shades closed. After a few days I decided I'd better go and see her. She peeped out to see who it was and told me to come in. Then she closed the door and pulled the shade and said, 'They're putting in the knives.' She meant — they're after me, they're trying to get me, they're going to do something to me because I'm not going to school.[6]

'They' were, as always, the authorities; in this case the Aspen Community School Board. In discussions with parents and staff Sylvia had, from the time of her arrival, expressed fear of the board. As far as her Aspen friends were concerned that was silly. Apart from the disillusioned junior staff, everyone connected with the school adored her and basked in the glory of having her with them. But when she suddenly stopped going to school some parents did become upset. Until then they had willingly accommo-dated her eccentricities and forgiven her shortcomings, but this was too much. They had spent a fortune on her salary and return first-class airfare, they were seeing a negligible return on their investment, and the school was facing financial collapse.

The junior school staff were also upset, both by the extra work forced upon them by Sylvia's absence and by the fact that only she and Wanda were paid regularly (as part of the initial agreement with the Board of Education their salaries had been collected in advance and were kept in escrow exclusively for that purpose), while Judy, the only other paid staff member and the person now doing all Sylvia's work, received only token payments at irregular intervals. Despite constant fundraising, the Com-munity School could not afford to replace Sylvia, or even to pay Judy an adequate salary.

The parents were divided over what to do about their wayward celebrity. Some wanted to fire her, others wanted to retain her for the grant-attracting potential of her name, and a third group, who remained convinced that she was charming and wonderful, wanted only to protect and cherish her. Eventually it was agreed that both Sylvia and Wanda should present evaluations of their work to a school board meeting. Sylvia prepared a presentation based on the book she was writing, supplemented by samples of the children's work.

When the fateful day came Wanda went to collect Sylvia.

'Do you know why I'm here?' she asked.

'Oh yes,' said Sylvia stiffly. 'It's the sacking party, and I'm ready.'

Wanda's report was straightforward, but Sylvia's presentation gradually turned into a poetic and moving exposition on the needs of the artist. Like everyone else at the meeting, Wanda was stunned:

> She started walking around the room and talking about how difficult it was to be an artist, how nobody was protective and nobody gave any support, how she was a poor artist looking for a wing of protection. She walked to the window and looked out over the beautiful snow-covered meadow and it came to everyone that here's this little old lady all alone, far away from her homeland, just being an artist, and here are all these evil people trying to sack her. The head of the board couldn't stand it. He said plaintively, 'Mrs Henderson, is there anything we can do for you?' She said yes, that she had great difficulty finding good lager in Aspen. The outcome of the sacking party was that a case of beer was delivered to Sylvia every week.[7]

Although Sylvia felt her defection from school was a major issue, in the turmoil of Community School politics it was a just another diverting skirmish in their great battle for survival. The main external threat came from a vociferous conservative group, Save Our Schools (SOS), which had mounted a campaign to expel the Community School from the public school system. According to Mike Stranahan, their message was:

> . . . hippies should not be educating kids; hippy kids should have their hair cut and behave like so-called normal kids; and, because of the scarcity of public school funds, the Community School should not be allowed to get its hands into the public till.[8]

The main internal threat came from the complex and bitter 'irreconcilable differences' between members of the parent board that led, during January, to the formation of two rival groups, each claiming an exclusive right to run the school.

By mid-February the group led by Wanda's husband, Farnum Gray, triumphed over the smaller group of founder-members, which included Sylvia's complement Margaret Albouy. Sylvia was deeply disturbed by the split. From the time of her arrival she had turned to members of both groups for care and protection; the open hostility between them left her feeling ever more exposed, more vulnerable and more panicky. She would later react to the split by cutting herself off from Margaret Albouy, but her initial response was to impulsively accept at least three job offers for the coming academic year, and then to book a passage on a ship due to leave San Francisco for New Zealand long before the next academic year was scheduled to begin.

One of the job offers she accepted was in Aspen. It arose from Farnum and Wanda's bid to ease the Community School's financial woes by applying for inclusion in the federal Office of Education 'Teacher of Teacher-Trainers' (TTT) programme, a scheme designed to give academic educators first-hand experience of educational innovations taking place in the community. The Gray's hope was that a TTT salary and equipment grant would keep the Community School afloat.

In their proposal, Sylvia Ashton-Warner was the star attraction. Her title would be Professor of Education and she would conduct morning work-shops for groups of four teacher-trainers during three-week TTT sessions, and also serve in the undefined role of non-teaching consultant to the school.

Sylvia kept her other plans for the coming year secret and went along with the application. Although she was anxious to escape from Aspen, this opportunity for a less demanding high-status role on a familiar stage did attract her; she had dreamed of training teachers ever since her years at Fernhill, and she liked the idea of working with adults — they were so much more respectful than children.

In early March four high-ranking officials from the TTT administration in Washington spent four days inspecting the Community School. Mike Stranahan recalled the frenzied preparations:

> We swept the floor and cleaned the school from top to bottom. People laundered their clothes who hadn't laundered their clothes for a good long time. People got haircuts who hadn't got haircuts for a good long time. . . .[9]

And Sylvia, who hadn't been seen for a good long time, appeared full of graciousness and charm at the welcoming cocktail party, met with the visitors at school and was the dazzling hostess for a dinner held in their honour.

The Washington group was enormously impressed with both Sylvia and the school. Over local radio they expressed delight with its positive tone and high level of parent involvement; they spoke approvingly of the class-room use of child experience and of the high standard of work they observed; and they noted that as an experimental unit within the public system the school could make a major impact on education throughout the state. On the eve of their departure they offered the Aspen Board of Educa-tion a grant of $100,000 for the establishment of a TTT programme at the Community School, and an additional $25,000 to cover the board's administrative costs.

The board, mindful of SOS fears that Community School supporters were plotting to turn the Aspen public school system into hippy heaven, declined the grant and voted soon after to cut the Community School's ties with the public education system. At this blow Sylvia developed what seems like a death wish for the Community School, while the school parents, undaunted, continued the fight.

For the Board of Education elections in May they put up their own candidate, Connie Harvey. With two of the five board members already sympathetic, Connie's election would guarantee the school a secure future. Sylvia for her part took two major initiatives during the lead-up to the election. Firstly, after shunning the media for twenty years, she chose this critical time to go public. If in doing so she had thrown her weight behind the school she may well have won them the election, but she didn't. In press and radio interviews she declared herself firmly neutral in the SOS/Community School debate. Her other initiative was to begin spending an hour or two each day at local public schools while continuing to stay away from the Community School. She claimed in her autobiography that she was trying to reconcile the warring factions of Aspen, but to Community School supporters she seemed to be changing sides.

Resentment of her behaviour increased when word spread around Aspen that Sylvia Ashton-Warner had been shabbily treated at the Community School. Sylvia denied that she was the source of the rumour. When Connie Harvey's bid failed, Sylvia wrote: 'The ostracism is holy, like a cathedral.' But her diary went on to record that, far from ostracising her, to the end of her Aspen stay Community School staff and parents continued to visit her regularly and care for her needs: they brought her food, prepared her meals, took her out to dine, did her shopping, collected and posted her mail, and changed her library books and records. And in between chores they shared her late afternoon tea- and beer-drinking sessions.

And all the while the Community School's fight for survival went on. In late May hopes were revived with news that liberal Antioch College in Ohio was willing to oversee the school's TTT programme, and dashed soon after with word that the Washington grant had been slashed. The upheavals and uncertainty drove Sylvia to send frantic letters to everyone she could think of in United States, and to Elliot in London, begging them to come and save her. While she was waiting to be saved she brought her Aspen book *Spearpoint* to a close by writing about the collapse of the Community School.

The central image of that bitter, impressionistic book was that of a mutating spearhead-of-civilisation race, rocketing into the two-dimensional world of technology; an image that fitted her preconceived fantasies about Americans but was totally inappropriate for the real-life idealists of Aspen. *Spearpoint* included descriptions of her pupils' behaviour — their games, their stories, their interests, and their interactions with others — which showed that in the context of their unusual school they were for the most part normal happy children. But Sylvia closed her eyes to her own evidence and claimed repeatedly that they were shallow, unfeeling mutants. Indeed such was her determination to prove that they were without imagery she even presented their lack of pent-up hatred and violence as faults.

Bob Gottlieb was not entirely happy with *Spearpoint*, feeling that it was long on generalisations and short on specifics, but when Sylvia insisted she could do no more he accepted it anyway. The book was published by Knopf in 1972. Its impact was small compared to that of *Teacher*, but it contained enough Ashton-Warner vision and fire to ensure that its sweeping generalisations and wild inaccuracies were lost on all but the people she wrote about.*

A few days after she finished *Spearpoint* Sylvia's world was thrown into even greater confusion by the unexpected restoration of the Washington grant. She wrote to Jasmine: 'I'm not a bit pleased about it, as I wanted to come home, with a good excuse for coming home.'

She decided to go home in June regardless, but she also agreed to speak in Boulder in late June at the University of Colorado Third Annual Reading Conference.

During the intervening weeks school closed for the summer, the Grays finalised arrangements for the TTT program in October, and Sylvia pursued two conflicting courses of action: she tried to find someone to drive her to San Francisco in time to catch the 24 June sailing of the *Orsova*, and she made a new smock of blue-spotted white silk to wear at the Boulder Reading Conference on 28 June. When she failed to arrange her escape in time she sought other last-minute ways of avoiding the Boulder conference. But every time she notified organiser Don Carline of her with-drawal he phoned her, or travelled to Aspen, and persuaded her to recon-sider. When the time came, Wanda drove Sylvia the 220 miles to Boulder and gave a short introductory talk about the Community School prior to Sylvia's scheduled appearance. Then it was Sylvia's turn.

At the sight of a thousand excited reading specialists she turned desperat-edly to Don Carline: 'I can't go through with it! I can't go through with it!'

He took her arm firmly and steered her onto the stage, muttering through clenched teeth, 'I've invested a lot of time and energy in getting you here. You're not backing out now.'

After a hesitant beginning she organised a lively key vocabulary demon-stration with a group of teachers acting as five-year-olds, and talked in her ethereal and metaphoric way about the mind of our child and the meaning of his imagery, about her philosophies and feelings, and about the poetry and drama of her life. She was magnificent. When Don Carline tried to bring the seventy-five-minute session to a close, her spellbound audience insisted she continue. And later in the day, by popular demand, she took a second session.

---

*Not least among the inaccuracies was the fact that the school did not die but went on to become, in the 1980s, one of the most successful and lasting alternative schools in the nation.

'I behaved very nicely,' she commented to Don afterwards. But despite the triumph she never found the courage to speak before a large audience again.[10]

Back in Aspen Sylvia found the environment changing. The snow was thawing, the wild flowers were bursting into bloom and the aspens were spreading green shade throughout the valley. Sylvia liked nothing better than to wander at will, savouring the joy of being abroad and . . .

> . . . recalling some long-past picture which had arrested me when young, of a solitary cloaked wanderer. . . . The picture had taken form in romantic reality. . . . When walking alone I was full of good company and fondled my sorrow.[11]

Even in the sub-zero winter she had enjoyed walking. Those who remember little else about her stay in Aspen recall the sight of Sylvia Ashton-Warner patrolling the streets in snow boots, green balaclava and grey Siberian squirrel fur coat, using a cut-down ski pole for a walking stick. When spring came she put away the coat and wore a green cape instead, and wandered abroad sucking on a silver demitasse spoon in an effort to give up smoking. And through all seasons she measured her tread across snow, ice, slush, mud and dust-dry summer soil with the ski pole walking stick.

During her walks she observed the winter crowd leaving and the summer crowd moving in. She watched the big marquee going up in the meadow. She saw the summer festival burst into life. She attended a succession of poetry readings, concerts, art shows, seminars and plays. *The Crucible*, a story of witch hunt and persecution, made the deepest impact. 'You'll never know what Aspen is . . .' she wrote to Elliot, 'until you've seen Arthur Miller's *The Crucible* well done on the stage.'

Another feature of the summer was the number of American teachers and students who made their way to Aspen to meet and pay homage to Sylvia Ashton-Warner. Following her own inclinations, and the requests of visiting fans, she held a series of informal seminars at her home to demonstrate the key vocabulary. Again she cast a spell over her audience. One grateful participant wrote:

> . . . somehow I always knew and loved you and of course I'll go on loving and having known you. Carrying you on with me is completely natural. And so much goes with you, your smile, noise in the classroom, media for expressing, native imagery, your smock, your cane, the make-up on your feet. . . .*

---

*The smock referred to was probably Sylvia's brown velvet Aspen favourite, which she usually wore with loose-fitting black trousers. In contrast to the bright colours she had favoured in younger days, her Aspen wardrobe was dominated by sombre browns, greens and blacks.

But no matter what happened in Sylvia's outer world — no matter how loving the fans, no matter how supportive the new friends among Aspen's summer residents, and no matter how exciting the festival — in Sylvia's inner world the conviction that she was being exploited and persecuted continued to grow.

She booked cabins on cruise liners leaving San Francisco for New Zealand in July, August and September. But when October came she was still in Aspen, and the TTT programme began. She set up the living area of her home as a model infant room, with easel, paper, paints, crayons, sand and water tables, wooden blocks, blackboards, chalk and a piano, and welcomed the first intake of trainees: Selma Wasserman from Vancouver, Bill Cliett from Gainesville, Tom Turbyfill from New Mexico and Pat Spitzmiller from Denver. The unreal beauty of the valley in autumn — the clear blue days turned gold with sun and spinning leaves, the silver-frosted nights — was a fit setting for the enchantment they were to experience.

At workshops Sylvia introduced the group to her 'organic morning' and took their key vocabularies. Bill Cliett wrote of the experience:

> She asked me my name and talked with me as though I were the most important person in the world and my every word a revelation. . . .
>
> We talked about my loves and fears, my life, my friends. Soon I had my Key Vocabulary. . . .
>
> At the end of this first session she knew more about us than many we had known for years. Yet she never seemed to ask anything of us. We confided so freely in her friendly manner, and we left as a family rather than most recent of friends.[12]

During afternoons and evenings they met with Sylvia over drinks and meals, and all day she held them spellbound with the vitality of her being, the warmth of her manner, and the poetry, mystery and wisdom of her words.

They were so bewitched that even aspects of Sylvia's behaviour that would have concerned them in anyone else seemed no more than delightful eccentricities in such a wonderful woman: her claim that she was a five-year-old child entranced them, her talk of being on a 'lager and lettuce diet' (if she drank more than six bottles of lager a day, as she usually did, she ate only lettuce the next day) charmed them, and the vast collection of brandy bottles in her coat cupboard (she said they were presents from *Spinster* fans, and that she never drank the stuff) enchanted them further.

Sylvia seemed reluctant for them to visit the Community School, but on the Monday of the second week they went. The mess that met them at the door was unforgettable: '. . . children's clothes scattered hither and yon, books lying open and torn on the floor, bits of food scattered around. . . .'

They saw worthwhile work in the classes run by Wanda Gray and Angela Foster, the British-trained infant mistress who had replaced Judy Sheldon. But apart from that, during the rest of the morning, and for the braver members of the group during the rest of the week, everything they saw confirmed their first impression that the school was educationally and organisationally a disaster.

Their findings were similar to those of Jeannette Veatch, who had made a two-day visit to Aspen the previous May in response to a stream of panic letters from Sylvia:

> It was miserable, lousy laissez faire. The kids could do anything they wanted. There was dog stuff on the carpet. A guy was smoking — smoking while he was teaching children! I had no respect.[13]

Unlike the inspection team from Washington, Jeannette and the TTT group saw the school in its natural state. Their impressions may have been coloured by Sylvia's obvious unhappiness with the school and by her belief that it was on the point of collapse. And the gross inadequacy of the school's hit-and-miss voluntary cleaning system wouldn't have helped. The staff and parents at that time knew that the school was dirty, untidy and disorganised but they had no misgivings about the quality of education being offered; not only were their children happy at school, in statewide education tests that year they scored higher than children in the local public school system.

After the school visit the TTT group attended a staff meeting and found the teachers strangely uncommunicative and defensive. The staff for their part were in an invidious position. They knew something had gone terribly wrong in their relationship with Sylvia Ashton-Warner but they couldn't explain it to themselves, let alone to anyone else. Many felt too guilty to criticise her, knowing they had failed to give her the respect and devotion she so clearly expected. And even those without guilt kept quiet: criticising Sylvia Ashton-Warner in the 1970s in North America was as unthinkable as criticising Mother Theresa of Calcutta.

The TTT visitors, shattered by what they had seen, delegated to Tom the task of disclosing their impressions of the school to Sylvia. She responded by saying she would need a few days to think, and by cancelling TTT workshops for the rest of the week. At the end of the week she took the group out to dinner and told them with an air of sad resignation that she could not speak of the horrors of her year in Aspen, that it was too terrible even for her to think about. She said it had been worse than her husband's death.

Her companions were distressed by her appalling experience and awed by her unwillingness to speak out against those who had mistreated her. Such generosity she showed, such nobility of spirit. Sylvia then confided to them that she had booked passage for New Zealand from San Francisco in November. She asked Bill to enquire into hiring a driver to take her to the ship.

When Bill's search for a driver proved fruitless, and he returned to find Sylvia already packing, his great mission in life became crystal clear: he had to drive her to San Francisco himself. Although he had lived all his twenty-six years in tropical Florida and had never driven in snow or mountains before, he had to do it. He had to deliver that treasure, Sylvia Ashton-Warner, to safety.

Fourteen years later, with the benefit of hindsight, Bill conceded that there must have been other ways for Sylvia to get to San Francisco — taking a taxi to the nearest railway station being the most obvious — but at the time such possibilities never crossed his mind:

> Part of it was the charisma and part of it was the child — the feeling that here was this five-year-old child I had to protect. I had to take care of her. If I didn't nobody else would. She desperately needed me. I really had the feeling that if I didn't drive her out of there she would be stuck in a horrible situation with no way to get out.
>
> And there was the excitement and adventure of being of service to someone I thought very highly of. She had tremendous presence. I said to myself this person is not like anyone else I've ever met. This is someone special who is worth making sacrifices for. I ended up late back at work and out of pocket but none of that mattered.[14]

Selma suggested that instead of sailing for New Zealand, Sylvia could come with her to Simon Fraser University in Vancouver. She said that Sylvia would be welcomed with open arms, and truly appreciated, in Vancouver. Sylvia liked the idea, but since a university appointment couldn't be arranged overnight she decided to travel to San Francisco and wait there until either the ship sailed or word of the Simon Fraser appointment came through.

Then, as the dream of the Great Escape began turning into reality, Sylvia became transfixed by terrible fantasies about the consequences of her plans. 'They' would be beside themselves with fury. . . . 'They' would come after her with hideously sharp and gleaming knives. . . . 'They' would GET her. . . . Selma recalled:

> Suddenly she was in terror of her life. She prevailed upon us not to tell anyone in Aspen she was leaving. We had to leave in absolute and complete secrecy.
>
> We were totally caught up in this intrigue. She really believed her life was in jeopardy and it never occurred to us to doubt her.[15]

And so it came to pass that on the evening of 18 October 1971, four intelligent, well-educated normally rational people conspired, in the high unreality of Aspen, to save Sylvia Ashton-Warner by spiriting her away under cover of darkness. They resolved to leave the following night.

Next morning Bill hired the sort of large, heavy, low-slung car Sylvia felt safe in, Pat scoured the grocery stores for empty cardboard boxes, Tom suffered a moment of truth and returned to New Mexico, and Selma played 'Lara's Theme' on the piano to keep Sylvia calm.

During the afternoon and evening, assisted by Selma's husband Jack, they surreptitiously packed Sylvia's belongings into suitcases and cardboard boxes. Bill drove the car up close to the gate and after dark they loaded up the trunk, leaving the briefcase containing the manuscript of

Sylvia's autobiography, from which Sylvia refused to be separated, to be
loaded in the morning. The conspirators parted for a brief and fitful sleep,
then at half past four Pat tapped on Sylvia's window — it was time to
move.

They collected the remainder of Sylvia's belongings and drove to Bill's
apartment. From there Bill drove them to Selma and Jack's apartment,
where they ate a hearty breakfast of eggs, bacon and toast.

Then — crisis — Sylvia remembered she had to collect a prescription
before she could leave. While Sylvia and Bill waited for the drug store to
open, Pat set off on her return journey to Denver, and Selma and Jack, the
head of the convoy taking Sylvia to San Francisco, left in their two-seater
sports car for Salina, Utah, the first scheduled meeting point on the
journey. The realisation that they could be pulling off what seemed like the
greatest educational coup of the century made them anxious to get away.
Sylvia filled in the pre-dawn hours drinking tea and smoking, and Bill,
realising there was something wildly unethical about taking government
money to attend the first of a series of courses to which a tutor had been
contracted for a year, and then spiriting off that tutor after only two weeks,
wrote an apologetic note to Farnum Gray, explaining that it was something he just had to do.

The glistening frosty night was giving way to another golden day by the
time Bill took Sylvia's arm and guided her down the icy apartment steps
to the car. 'All that is gold does not glitter,' he observed, quoting Tolkien.
'Not all those who wander are lost.'

At the drug store he stood furtive guard while Sylvia collected her
prescriptions. Then they were off, winding slowly down the mountain,
glancing back all the way, fearing pursuit. As soon as they crossed the
Utah border Sylvia relaxed. She was safe, she was out of Colorado. Mid-
morning they stopped at a small roadside cafe. As Sylvia drank her tea she
studied the pattern of intersecting black lines in the white formica tabletop
before her. 'This is a perfect social map of Aspen,' she told Bill. 'The only
way out is to jump off the side of the table.'

They met Selma and Jack as planned at Salina, where, in the space of ten
minutes, the keys to Bill's hired car mysteriously disappeared. All he did
was pull up at the motel door, open the trunk, unload the overnight
luggage, and then — the keys were gone. They were in a one-horse town
in the middle of nowhere. Stuck. All that evening and for most of the next
day Bill, Selma and Jack searched frantically, enlisting the help of the local
garage, and finally calling the car hire firm for the code needed to have a
new set of keys made.

Sylvia, totally unconcerned by the fuss, passed the time strolling along
the unimposing main street of Salina. It was the opening of the deer-
hunting season and she wasn't the only stranger in town, but, in her ankle-
length fur coat with her wavy grey and auburn hair flowing around her
shoulders and sucking on a silver spoon, she was by far the strangest. Her
appearance was too much for one of the locals, who screeched his pick-up

truck to a halt beside her and leaned out of the cab.

'Are you a deer hunter?' he asked doubtfully.

Sylvia removed her teaspoon with a flourish and tossed back her hair. 'No,' she said grandly. 'I'm a *darling* hunter.'

After three more thrilling, slow-driving days, with Sylvia singing 'Beyond the Blue Horizon' on every one of them, the travellers reached San Francisco. Sylvia reimbursed Bill for her accommodation, and for the car hire and running costs, and he flew back to Florida: mission accomplished. Selma settled Sylvia in a downtown hotel and delegated to local Ashton-Warner fans the task of taking care of her while she and Jack rushed back to Vancouver to finalise Sylvia's appointment. Within a record five days it was all organised. Anton Vogt, a Norwegian-born New Zealander on the staff of Simon Fraser University, drove down with his wife Birgitte and brought Sylvia back to Vancouver. On 1 November 1971 she arrived at her new home.

It was weeks before anyone in Aspen heard where she had gone, or how. And they never managed to figure out why.

The first clue Jeannette Veatch received as to Sylvia's whereabouts came in November, in the form of an unsigned postcard from Canada:

> Three cheers for the red, white and blue! Britannia rules the waves! Hail the mighty maple leaf! I have a spare room. Silent night, Holy night! What price education? The Lord is my shepherd; I shall not want. Tooti's goodbye to the U.S.A. The Last Post. Good King Wenceslaus went out — I like ports on the Pacific Coast. Who is Sylvia — what is she? Who is Jan: what is —

FOURTEEN

Vancouver

SIMON FRASER UNIVERSITY, SWATHED IN CLOUD ATOP BURNABY
Mountain, was agog with excitement. Do you know who's coming?
Sylvia Ashton-Warner! THE Sylvia Ashton-Warner! Universities all over
North America have been clamouring for her — and she's coming to us.
She's coming to our campus!

Her astonishingly rapid appointment was somewhat irregular, even for
avant-garde Simon Fraser. Although Sylvia Ashton-Warner was a living
legend, she had no university degree and had never worked for a university
before. But her international reputation, augmented by Selma Wasserman's
enthusiastic recommendation, was enough to pitch Dan Birch, Dean of the
Faculty of Education, into a frantic round of string-pulling and red-tape
cutting that culminated, after only two weeks, in a six-month visiting
professorship for their distinguished guest.

On 3 November 1971, the day after her arrival in Vancouver, Sylvia
moved into the modern ground-floor apartment Selma and Jack had found
for her in the Montecito residential complex at the foot of Burnaby Mountain. She met two Australian families, the Kendalls and the Allens, who were
to be her neighbours, and set up her desk at a window overlooking the tree-
lined courtyard. Next day she bought a grand piano and a teapot. She felt
blissfully safe and happy.

Two weeks later she visited the campus, and wrote about it to her family:

> Simon Fraser is eight years old. A young university. It wants to hit out
> and do something. Magnificent modern architecture covering the whole
> of the top of Burnaby Mountain. About 10,000 students I think. Many
> cafeterias, libraries, bookshops, printing press, computer centre, quad-
> rangles, theatres, trees, steps, film centres, sports centres, hostel, child care
> centre, covered swimming pool, lecture halls, study rooms, bank, paths
> everywhere. Overlooking the inlets from the sea, the city on the plains
> beneath; and the towering surrounding mountains. . . . Everything up
> there. A miniature city. There's nothing else up the mountain, just the
> university. . . .

It was most impressive, but she wasn't going to teach there. That wasn't her
style. Not any more. No more working for people on their terms, in their
settings. 'Let the mountain come to Mohammed,' she told her neighbours,
while to Dan Birch she conveyed the simple message that she intended to
teach in her own home.

I didn't warm to that initially because I felt that the point of hiring some-body like Sylvia was to be a catalyst to encourage others to think in different ways, and the informal contact that would occur on campus was an important element of that.

But it became clear very fast that if we were going to have her con-tributing at all it was going to be on her terms, and if we wanted to get the best out of her we had to do our best to meet those terms; and it wasn't as if she could spell out all her terms up front. Her terms were how she felt.[1]

There was an awkward university policy, the legacy of a student strike in the turbulent early years of the institution, which prohibited lecturers from taking classes in their own homes. So in his letter recommending that Sylvia's appointment be confirmed Dan did not mention her intention to teach off-campus.

But he could not avoid the requirement to provide a complete résumé of Sylvia's life, and that created more problems:

I asked her for a full curriculum vitae and received a somewhat ideosyn-cratic response. She didn't include her age so I asked her for her date of birth. Her reply was that age is indeterminate and irrelevant and besides she wasn't sure what it was because her parents had had two daughters named Sylvia only one of whom had survived and she wasn't sure which one she was. That was very characteristic of the way in which she dealt with the bureaucracy — she didn't have an awful lot of patience with it.[2]

All faculty members were required to submit a revised résumé each year, so in 1972 Dan supplied Sylvia with the correct university form and instruc-tions for filling it in, but Sylvia refused to be diverted by such tactics. She furnished him with a strangely ethereal account of her life encased in a cover made from a supermarket bag and sewn along the spine with brightly coloured wool.

Sylvia's disregard for the administrative niceties of her role — her off-campus teaching, her refusal to attend faculty meetings and sit on com-mittees, and her prima donna memos to the dean (she even sent one saying that all her memos were copyright) — was a source of admiration to the students, school teachers and faculty members who made the pilgrimage to Montecito, and of outrage to her less sympathetic colleagues on the mountain who wondered how on earth she got away with it.

But her critics said little. The halo effect — the universal reverence for her name that had protected her from serious attack at Aspen — was even more evident in Vancouver. Simon Fraser, for all its flexibility and innova-tiveness, was a respectable institution. Its faculty members were more conventional and respectful than the irreverent rebels of Aspen, and its students came more to learn than to question. It was clear that Sylvia was rocking the boat, but because of the ever-present risk of losing their celebrity overboard, no one moved.

Everything she needed to transform her lounge into an infant room — sand table, clay table, water table, blackboards, paper, chalk, wooden blocks, crayons — was supplied by the university or built to her specifications by a university carpenter. Returning the room to a lounge between workshops was simple. Three was no furniture to move; after casting a critical eye over the lounge and dining suites Selma and Jack had rented, Sylvia had said, 'Dearest — it'll all have to go.' She kept only one easy-chair and a couple of kitchen stools. Having virtually no furniture not only made her home more convenient for workshops, it ensured that the respectful educators of every rank who flocked to see her had no choice but to sit at her feet.

Sylvia was ecstatically happy, and so keen to start teaching that she began twice-weekly informal workshops before the carpenters finished her equipment. The informal beginning gave her a chance to refine her workshop technique. It was like the dress-rehearsal for one of her school concerts, but this time the stakes were high: she was the most famous name at the university — she had to perform, and perform well.

Turning on the charisma was no trouble, creating a mood of excitement and vitality was easy, but the course also needed content. Throughout the 1960s she had largely ignored the relentless demand for details of her method that followed the publication of *Spinster* and *Teacher*. But her acceptance of the Aspen invitation brought with it the realisation that she had to produce not only theory, but guidelines on putting that theory into practice. At the Aspen Community School, at her informal Aspen workshops and at TTT sessions, she had expounded on the need to guide children on a reading and writing progression from key words to brief phrases, and then on to full sentences. In Vancouver those instructions became more specific. Her method drew nothing from current pedagogic theory (which she refused to read, claiming that it cluttered her own imagery) and bore only limited resemblance to the activities, real or imagined, that took place in her own classrooms in New Zealand. But it did give students who failed to grasp her deeper message something to take away with them from her workshops, and the following year it provided a framework for the application of her method to elementary schools throughout Vancouver.

Her workshops became formalised into twelve-session courses (two mornings a week for six weeks). They were known to the university as Education 402 and to Sylvia as 'Mornings With Young Children'. The need to travel off-campus disrupted student schedules, but there were always many more applicants than Sylvia's apartment could accommodate. For the lucky thirty who attended each series the experience was unforgettable:

> It was such a new experience — going to someone's house for a university course, and then entering and finding this person playing classical music on a grand piano. As more and more people came in you could feel the wonderment, the sense of — what's going to happen?[3]

There she is: Sylvia Ashton-Warner. A vital and astonishing presence. The loose brown slacks rolled up to her knees are relatively new, but her faded handmade smock, with its food and drink strains, cigarette burns and frayed seams, is more than twenty-five years old. Her long grey and auburn hair curls down her back from a child-like bow at the nape of her neck. Her skin is weathered and leathered; her face is wrinkled, her hands are wrinkled, her bare feet are wrinkled. She looks about eighty years old — which may be why she wears such a thick mask of pancake make-up, even on her legs and feet. Though why she wears flower decals on her toe-nails is anybody's guess.

The music stops. . . . There is an expectant hush. . . . The great lady speaks:

'My name is Mary,' she says. 'And I am five years old.'

She asks her students to become five-year-olds too and, swinging between the roles of teacher and child, leads them through her organic morning.

The first hour is output time: a time for talking and playing. A time for expressing through any creative medium, including the key vocabulary, the uniquely individual feelings and experiences of being five.

The rest of the morning is input time: a time for sharing key words and sentences, and a time for the teacher to offer new material to the now emptied and receptive minds of her pupils. Despite her professed abhorrence for imposing foreign cultural material on the native imagery of children, in New Zealand Sylvia used input time, or any other time that suited her, to teach European songs, dances and plays to her Maori pupils; and during Vancouver input time she taught Maori songs, dances and stick games to her Canadian students.

She also used input time to talk about her teaching formula: *Release the native imagery of our child and use it for working material*, and about her poetic formula: *Touch the true voice of feeling and it will create its own power, its own pace, its own style and its own vocabulary.* For students and teachers who came to Education 402 expecting to take away Sylvia's message in a few scribbled notes the experience was a waste of time. But for those open to new experiences, Sylvia's workshops changed the way they taught and the way they thought. Knowing and working with Sylvia Ashton-Warner changed their lives:

I thought she was quite odd, but wonderful. I very much fell under her spell. The workshops were very intimate and very dramatic. There was a lot of emotion — people hugged each other, there was a lot of singing and dancing. We all became very close.[4]

It wasn't just what she taught and shared with us. She gave us a way of being with children that was far more than technique. Her influence continues with me beyond the next book or the next method I read about — it's much deeper. It's about letting children be themselves; it's a way of looking at and evaluating what's really important in life and bringing that to kids.[5]

When I absorbed what the key vocabulary was about I could hardly believe it — here was someone talking about working with kids who was willing to wade right into the emotional content of their lives. It was such a powerful thing, not just for children but for anyone you wanted to get close to. She was the opposite of a conventional teacher in that her purpose was not to socialise people and make them fit in, but to open up the wellsprings of their own souls.[6]

Like all those attracted to Sylvia, these students glimpsed behind her outrageous mask an unquenchable incandescent core of spiritual truth. People were drawn to her like moths to a flame. Those who flew too close were dazzled and burnt, but for most it was enough to dance in her orbit, and marvel at the illumination of their own souls.

In addition to workshops, Sylvia held an open house most afternoons from four o'clock, and made it known that people who brought casseroles and lager were particularly welcome. Dan Rubin was one of many young folk greatly influenced by Sylvia and her soirées:

She had a salon scene going. Most afternoons this haphazard collection of people would stop by on their way home from the university. I guess some of them really took a shine to her. I certainly did, because she was such an iconoclast. She had an incredible way of cutting through social reality to get at something that was going on that you hadn't even admitted to yourself was happening. It was a really lively scene. It was so refreshing and interesting. She had a way of catching a glimmer of truth and pointing it out and questioning it.[7]

Another enthusiast was Helen Ryane:

She was pretty crazy in a way, but so brilliant and insightful. She really valued feelings. She valued the spiritual very much and would say things from that angle instead of from the logical rational point of view. Being around her made me question my whole value system.[8]

One of Sylvia's greatest strengths was her ability to listen. When conditions were right she could focus her intense undivided attention on almost anyone, and bestow on them the profoundly flattering and illuminating gift of her wisdom and understanding.

But like a powerful magnet she repelled some people as vigorously as she attracted others. To Dean of Education Dan Birch, her polarising impact seemed to arise from her effort to elicit the true key vocabulary of nearly everyone she met:

What people often saw in their dealings with Sylvia as something right off the wall, something not in the usual line of social or professional interaction, I saw as a kind of probe, designed possibly to jolt but primarily to either give her clues as to what was important to the individual, or to make the individual reflect on that for themselves. After any encounter with her you always found yourself thinking about it, and learning something.
    People reacted in one of two ways. Either there was confusion and resentment. A sense of: that isn't what I'm here for — where's this woman coming from anyway? Or there was a very reflective sense of

being drawn immediately into an intimate interaction that was totally out of keeping with the fact that you had met this person thirty seconds before.[9]

At Simon Fraser Sylvia soon found herself surrounded by legions of loving fans willing to fetch and carry and shop and cook and housekeep and do any odd job that needed doing. When she wanted passionfruit for a New Zealand fruit salad they scoured every specialty food shop in Vancouver; when she wanted a little elementary school chair to sit on somebody stole one for her. . . . But the adoring crowds were never enough; what she really wanted was the special intensity of a complement, and for this role it was the unattainable that lured. The woman Sylvia loved and wanted, the woman on whom she focused her insatiable need for mothering, was Selma Wasserman.

In Sylvia's status-conscious Warner-world Selma was an admirer, and therefore Sylvia's inferior, but she was also Dr Wasserman, Ph.D, an important person in an important job at an important university, and therefore Sylvia's superior. Sylvia worried a lot about her position in relation to Selma. In Sylvia's child-world Selma was the loving mother who had cared enough to save her from Aspen, and who would go on loving and caring for her for ever and ever.

Selma recognised the dangers right from the start:

> I'm a very giving person — the real Jewish mother thing, I was brought up on that — and here was this wonderful lady that I loved and adored who was all alone and vulnerable. She said to me once, 'Dearest, you are such a good lookerafterer, and I am the best lookerafteree.' It would have been very, very easy for me to fall into the trap of servicing her. I could have made a career out of it, and I knew that would be very detrimental to my health and my work. So I set up clear guidelines very early in the game.[10]

Though Selma continued to be a loving friend who visited or phoned most days, and sometimes took Sylvia out for meals or shopping, she did not commit herself totally to her care. Sylvia continued to love and respect Selma, but she never forgave Selma for failing to mother her completely.

In her search for a complement Sylvia turned to Molly Bradley, a former New Zealand infant mistress who had, in her earlier teaching years, been highly graded for the sensitive and effective reading scheme she had developed at an isolated Maori school; a scheme that had been picked up by the Education Department and used for demonstration purposes to other teachers. Molly recalled that when she read *Spinster*:

> It was a very moving experience. All her techniques were so close to those I had done myself. Though we never met until Vancouver, Sylvia Ashton-Warner was always very close to my heart.[11]

When Molly heard that Sylvia was at Simon Fraser she put aside an

invitation from the dean to apply for a job in the Faculty of Education so
that she could spend her time at Sylvia's workshops. She attended every
session for the first two series of 1972:

> It wasn't long before we became the best of friends. Sometimes she
> would ask me to take over the workshop, usually in the middle of the
> morning, while she went and had a rest. It was pretty intensive and
> thoroughly enjoyable and everyone who came responded well. We were
> really delighted with everything we were doing.[12]

Sylvia often invited Molly to stay for lunch and they spent many afternoons shopping or sightseeing together. To Molly, she and Sylvia were
good friends with independent lives and independent plans for the future,
but Sylvia's perception of the relationship was different. She never spoke
or wrote about it, but her tearful fury when Molly considered accepting
an attractive job offer while the workshops were in progress suggests that
in her inner world Sylvia saw Molly as her inseparable, adoring complement. That a complement would want to do anything but care for a child-
artist forever was to Sylvia unthinkable. When the workshops ended and
Molly did apply for a faculty position, green flames of jealousy licked
though Sylvia's tinder-dry sanity. She gave Molly such a damning reference that she didn't get the job.[13]

Sooner or later Sylvia found such betrayals at the heart of all her close
relationships, and with each perceived betrayal she became more suspicious
and withdrawn. By March 1972, even a flattering two-year appointment
to a full professorship did little to lift her spirits. She turned to her Australian neighbours for support and they responded willingly. But both the
Kendalls and the Allens worked at the university and had their own
children to care for. Although Sylvia leant on the women and flirted with
the men (she called Ian Allen 'my great big handsome Australian'), they
never came close to satisfying her needs.

Sylvia's sleep suffered and her health deteriorated. She continued to
produce her winning style twice weekly for the May–June workshops, but
in the days between she felt tired, lonely and unwell. To help her with her
two summer sessions, Dan Birch appointed a young American student
couple, Frank and Ann Olsen, as her teaching assistants. The fact that they
were married was very important to Sylvia; after hero-worshipping spinsters for most of her life she had changed, at the time of Keith's death, to
hero-worshipping married couples.

Frank and Ann had attended Sylvia's first course and were among her
most dedicated fans. They loved to sit at her feet when she held court and
were thrilled when she honoured them with requests for help with shopping or household chores, or in dealing with her social engagements. Their
formal appointment to Sylvia's service was the most exciting event of their
lives:

> She called us her family and we felt very close to her. She trusted us and
> confided in us, and it was our responsibility to take care of her. It was

Selah (left) and cloister, Whenua, 1984.
L. HOOD

Henderson extended family, Tauranga, *c.* 1965. Adults from left; back: Sylvia, Ashton's wife Margaret, Ashton, Keith, Jasmine's husband David; front: Jasmine.
SA-W PAPERS

Mauritius, 1969. From left: Mme. Latham-Koenig, Vincent, M. Latham-Koenig,
Elliot, Sylvia, Jacquemine's sister, Jacquemine.
E. HENDERSON

Wellesley Aron, *c*. 1970.
W. ARON

Sylvia in Jerusalem, 1969.
W. ARON

Clapham Mansions, 1985. Elliot's 1969 flat in first-floor bay window.
L. HOOD

Aspen Community School, 1970.
SA-W PAPERS

Sylvia with Anton Vogt and Selma
Wasserman, 1972.
D. BIRCH

Sylvia with Su Lum and Hillery, 1971
S. LUM

Selma's key words, 1971.
L. HOOD

Sylvia, Aspen, 1971.
S. LUM

Sylvia keeping her distance from the New Zealand establishment (personified by Allan Highet, Minister for the Arts) at the 1980 New Zealand Book Awards.
DOMINION

Mount Maunganui from Whenua, 1984.
L. HOOD

Sylvia, 1982.
SA-W PAPERS

Selah, 1984.
L. HOOD

a wonderful time of exhilaration and learning. She stretched the breadths and depths of our lives. We were emotionally, spiritually and educationally the richest people in the world.[14]

One óf the challenges of their role was to protect the artist in Sylvia, and to anticipate her needs:

We always answered the phone for her. We'd say, 'Just a moment please,' and then depending on her instructions we'd tell the caller she wasn't in, or whatever.

We protected her from insensitive students too — there was so much insensitivity, it was simply appalling. One time students passed notes while she was talking — after that we always tried to sensitise the group to the uniqueness of what was going on. Also we'd interrupt people's questions if we felt the question was out of line as far as Sylvia was concerned. There was one student who tried to pin Sylvia down and that was something Sylvia wouldn't stand for. This woman was most insistent about wanting to know which interpretation of Schubert's E-flat piano impromptu Sylvia approved of. I just stepped right up to her and put my arm around her and escorted her right out the front door. She never came back.[15]

Sylvia's helpless prima donna act was engaging to some and infuriating to others, but behind it was a very real need for protection. She once told Selma, 'I have to be very careful with what's happening around me because I feel and sense everything.' Such exquisite sensitivity made most experiences painful and every one intense. Which is why she went out rarely, and only on her own terms, and why she retreated so often into her laager. Her acute sensibilities, which enabled her to sense the hidden feeling of almost everyone she came in contact with, were also the basis of her otherwise baffling claim that she was 'pathologically compassionate'. She may not have responded to the feeling of others, but she certainly felt them.

The Olsens took care of Sylvia's day-to-day shopping, housework, appointments, workshop preparation and administrative chores. They even protected her from Bob Gottlieb, who tried to phone her several times over the publication of *Spearpoint*. When she and Bob had been in London in the summer of 1969 she had refused to meet him, and ever since she had been on the same continent she had even refused to speak with him on the telephone.

But Sylvia was not totally dependent on Frank and Ann when she went out. She had a local taxi driver schooled to arrived promptly, speak respectfully and drive slowly just for her. Usually he took her to the Lougheed Mall, where she would wander happily for hours, drawing elegantly on her long cigarette-holder, eating sausage rolls from the Lougheed Deli and watching the world go by. Sometimes he also took her to the garden centre to choose new plants for her much-loved patio garden, or to an empty church, where she would sit and meditate. But when she felt really lost and lonely he took her to those hated places where she felt most secure, to the places where she could find self-forgetfulness in the company of small children; he took her to visit the schools of Vancouver teachers who had attended her workshops. Although she was upset by the regimentation she found there, she responded cautiously to Selma's plan to introduce and evaluate her organic morning in nine classrooms at a range of Vancouver elementary schools.

The Vancouver Project began with the selection of nine primary teachers who took part in one of Sylvia's workshop series in the summer of 1972. They then took the organic work to their classrooms and the results were evaluated over a two-year period. Sylvia hated terms like 'project', 'evaluation' and 'method', and feared that her teaching style would wither and die under the spotlight of academic scrutiny:

> The only blight which I thought might halt its self-propagation would be for it to fall into the jaws of academic analysis in unintelligible multi-syllabic jargon by which so much living on this continent is programmed to die from verbose manhandling. . . .[16]

The word 'spearpoint' surfaced in Sylvia's mind when she contemplated the Vancouver Project, so she released it through her creative vent by naming the nine young women project teachers 'the Spears'. With her more destructive feelings towards the project thus defused, Sylvia was able to consider its advantages: it offered lasting recognition for her work and the chance for her to see more of both Selma and the pretty, awe-struck Spears. Overall, Sylvia came out cautiously in favour of the Vancouver Project.

That wonderful summer of 1972, with its two exciting workshops series, the launching of the Vancouver Project, and the constant loving attention of Frank and Ann, came to a shattering end: the Allens, the Kendalls and the Olsens all left Vancouver at once. When Frank and Ann told Sylvia in July that they were leaving the following month, she seemed not to believe it. She never referred to their departure and behaved in their presence, right to the end, as if they were staying forever. When they returned a year later to visit, full of warmth, love and hope for a happy reunion, Sylvia's painfully icy reception left them devastated. Only then did they realise how much their departure had hurt her.

Unbeknown to the Olsens, Sylvia had begun to turn against them as soon as they told her they were leaving. One day she came home and found that someone had searched through her papers. What did this mean? Sylvia stirred the evidence around in her undermind and confided to Selma her craziest, most paranoid and most improbable betrayal senario yet: those terrible unloving Olsens had done it. Those terrible unloving Olsens had been sent by the CIA to spy on her, and now they couldn't wait to get away. She went on behaving as though nothing was amiss, because she didn't want them to know that she had seen through their little game. But she couldn't wait to get rid of them. And she never wanted to see them again.

The curious and unlikely truth is that Sylvia's bizarre senario may have been partly true: her papers may well have been searched, and the CIA may well have been involved. The CIA connection was through Ann's radical sister, who, as a result of her involvement in a terrorist bombing incident in the United States in the 1960s, had gone underground. All Ann had seen or heard of her in years was her photo staring out from posters of the FBI's 'most wanted' list. Wherever Ann and Frank went in the early 1970s their apartments were searched and their friends were interviewed. When they came home one day in the spring of 1972 and found that their Vancouver flat had been searched, they knew that the hunt for the prodigal sister had been extended to Canada.*

Sylvia was lost without Ann and Frank. Who would love her now? Friends like Selma, Helen Ryane, Dan Rubin and Sylvia's niece Gwenda, who lived in Vancouver, continued to keep her company (Helen took her to the film *Jesus Christ Superstar*, about which Sylvia remarked, 'It failed to show the charisma and humour that made people leave their families and follow him . . .'), but worries over her lack of true love drove Sylvia to find strange ephemeral romances around every corner. She invited Selma's father, an unlettered glazier, to one of her soirées, and then accused Selma of trying to match-make. And she fell fleetingly in love with a mysterious man at Montecito. Selma recalled:

> She told me one day that she had a big secret.
> 'Oh God you've got to tell me!'
> 'You'll never pry this out of me!'
> 'Come on, you've got to tell me! You've got to tell me!'
> 'You'll never pry this out of me! But it's a wonderful secret!'
> She just drove me crazy. Then she told me she had seen this man in Montecito and he was so wonderful that she had fallen in love with him on the spot. She'd been walking and he'd asked her whether she'd like to take his arm. She said I wasn't to know his name because I would blab it all over. She said, 'I never thought I would fall in love again.'
> I said, 'Well — is something going to come of it?' She didn't respond. A few days later I asked her whether she had seen him again. She wasn't talking about him any more. Who knows what it was all about?[17]

In the real world there was no one to give Sylvia the endless love she needed, and the awareness of that void sent her life into a tailspin. Although in her inner life she continued to be a male artist, in her outer life her scattered personality fragments spun wildly and coalesced into two striking identities: Professor Ashton-Warner — very important person — and Mary — five-year-old-child. She wrote to Elliot:

---

*It was the police who searched their apartment — their neighbours saw three policemen climbing in the bathroom window and couldn't figure out why the first one didn't open the door for the other two.

I've dropped the name Henderson except on bank and legal documents. . . . I'm known round here by my own christened name: Professor Ashton-Warner. From now on, on anything I publish, I'll use just 'Ashton-Warner'. I'm steadily dropping the memory-laden name, Sylvia. Most people — always students and teachers and children and Montecito — know me as simply 'Mary'. Nothing else. . . .

You can leave the Sylvia out of my name now on the envelope. It's too long. I use just Ashton-Warner now.

Mary soon became the dominant persona. Even the letters she wrote to Bob Gottlieb began 'Dearest Grown-up' and were signed 'Mary'. Later Mary became the similarly pronounced Maori word Mere — a hand-held stone weapon, described by Sylvia as a 'skull splitter'.

For school visits she dressed in her fur coat and matching hat and sallied forth as Professor Ashton-Warner. Then suddenly, on reaching the school gates, she became Mary. She would sit at a little desk or on the floor with the children and do her lessons. And when recess came, instead of going to the staffroom as an honoured guest, she would head outside to play with the kids. Her behaviour disappointed the staff and provoked streams of anxious messages from playground attendants: 'There's a strange old lady playing with the children. . . . She says that her name's Mary. . . . She says that she's five years old. . . .' One principal, more status-conscious than most, insisted in the teeth of Sylvia's obvious reluctance that the famous visitor sign the school guest-book. Sylvia, frowning fiercely, took up the pen in her left hand and scrawled across the page in uneven five-year-old script: MERE.

All the while her unhappiness intensified. After taking the first workshop of the series scheduled for November and December 1972 she cancelled the rest, and wailed to anyone prepared to listen that the university was exploiting her, that she just wanted to be an artist, that nobody understood her, and that she could never teach again. At the same time she started a short-lived preschool for Montecito children at her home, and began repeatedly resigning from the university and booking passage to New Zealand, only to cancel both the next day. An end-of-year visit from Elliot, who had also spent the previous Christmas with her, failed to halt her disintegration.

Her relationship with the university authorities deteriorated steadily. Early in 1973, halfway through her two-year appointment, she demanded that the university subsidise her rent and electricity, and pay for the glass door broken by one of her students. In response Dr Wilson, the Academic Vice-President, ruled that she should conduct all future classes on campus. That was when Sylvia resigned for good. She claimed that the dean was devastated by her resignation but Dan Birch's letter to Dr Wilson suggests that it was received with relief:

Attached you will find a letter dated June 13th officially accepting Sylvia Ashton-Warner's resignation.

I have written this so that the acceptance will be clear and unequivocal even though it may be implicit in my letters to her of April 24th and June 4th, also attached.

During a late-night panic attack around this time Sylvia phoned Elliot and begged him to come and save her. 'Ring me in the morning,' he said. 'When you've calmed down.' She immediately phoned Jasmine and told her to send over her oldest grandchild, seventeen-year-old Corinne, and Robyn, the eighteen-year-old daughter of Jasmine's new husband, Bill Beveridge. Then she booked passage for all three to return to New Zealand aboard the *Arcadia* in September. Secure in the knowledge that family members were coming to care for her and take her home, Sylvia decided that despite earlier refusals, she would take one last summer workshop series — but in her own apartment, of course. When a New Zealand student couple, John and Cheryl Kirkland, wrote from the United States asking if they could work with her for the summer, they were promptly employed as her teaching assistants.

From that time on, in anticipation of the protection the newcomers would afford her, Sylvia began to disengage from her Vancouver friends. One of the first relationships she severed was with her colleague and countryman Anton Vogt, who had collected her from San Francisco and delivered her to Vancouver. As a New Zealander Anton had felt responsible for helping Sylvia to fit in at Simon Fraser, and had become increasingly embarrassed and irritated by her failure to do so. But despite the strain between them, they were still friends when the Vogts were about to go on leave in the spring of 1973. Anton invited Sylvia to the farewell party, but she refused to go. Selma heard about Anton's irate response from Sylvia later that day:

> He said, 'Look here you bitch, you can't go on being a prima donna all your life.' I don't know what the hell else he said but after he called her a bitch that was the end of it. Sylvia was just beside herself; she was furious. It was such a trivial thing, but she couldn't have anyone talk to her like that. She never mentioned his name again. She said, 'He is no longer in my consciousness.' She never spoke to him, or spoke of him, or saw him again.[18]

Around the same time Sylvia began to disengage from Selma. Selma didn't know at first, because the initial disengagement took place entirely in Sylvia's undermind. After spending most of her time in Vancouver working on her Canadian diary and on the story of her life, Sylvia began in the spring of 1973 a passionate exposition 'Essays on Artist', addressed to an unnamed 'dearest' who could only be Selma. Through writing she justified her increasingly imperious, irrational and withdrawn behaviour in terms of the artist's absorption with his work. Like so much else in her life at that time, her sexual imagery became totally egocentric:

> The mind is male; the raw material, female. . . .
> While the mind is fusing with its raw material, the mind ejecting its

sperm into the womb of its raw material . . . it's a matter of utter privacy;
of silence, stillness and forgetfulness of any damn thing in his life. He
hides himself to protect himself from the shock of interruption; there's
nothing more wrecking, wracking than the interrupted sex act. He hides
himself, rejects people, refuses to answer the door or the phone or a
loving remark from a friend, all of which the heathen call moods. . . .[19]

She attributed the artist's indecisiveness to the shock of being interrupted,
and his need for Heidelberg lager to the pain of returning to earth from
the heaven of his imagination. It all made perfect sense to Sylvia, but not
to Bob Gottlieb, who rejected every manuscript Sylvia sent him from
Vancouver.

Sylvia used the arrival of her granddaughters in May, and of the Kirklands in June, to complete her disengagement from Selma. She worked on
the Kirklands the same magic that she had worked on the Olsens:

> It was the clarity of an intense relationship that goes beyond words. . . . She
> opened up a whole world for us. She changed the direction of our lives
> and opened up the possibilities of thinking about things we'd never
> considered before.[20]

They were her family, and she was the treasure they had to protect. It was
like a repeat of her escape from Aspen, except that this time Selma was not
saviour, but persecutor.

In her unforgiving psyche Sylvia had turned Selma into that terrible
archetype: the woman who failed to love her enough. She conveyed to the
Kirklands that Selma had mistreated her in ways too painful to speak
about, and they dedicated themselves to protecting her from the source of
her torment. Selma for her part was shattered. After two wonderful years
of caring and sharing she found herself suddenly — inexplicably —
excluded:

> Sylvia used to pull the curtain across as a signal to people that she didn't
> want to be interrupted, but she told me I could interrupt her anytime,
> regardless.
>   When the Kirklands came and took her over they cut me off. If I called
> at Montecito on my way home, which I usually did, they would say,
> 'She's busy and she can't see you,' or 'She's resting and she can't see you,'
> or 'Come another time.' They would never say, 'I'll ask her.' I felt very,
> very hurt. I withdrew myself from coming.[21]

Throughout her last six months in Vancouver Sylvia's mental stability
deteriorated steadily. The combination of heavy drinking, valium, and a
blood pressure medication with drowsiness, depression and nightmares as
side effects, accelerated her decline. At the same time her heavy intake of
codeine tablets, nicotine (from cigarettes) and caffeine (from tea) continued
unabated.

She may also have suffered from nutritional deficiencies, because she
seemed to eat little, if anything, when alone. For parties she could turn on
roast lamb and vegetables, followed by rhubarb pie and cream, and she

enjoyed her food on the rare occasions she agreed to go to a restaurant (it had to be quiet, well lit, uncrowded, elegant), or to someone's home (she had to be the only guest), but though she often put lamb or pork chops on her weekly shopping list and didn't look undernourished, when her friends brought casseroles or food to prepare at her apartment they always found her refrigerator bafflingly empty. So what did she live on besides lager for most of the week? Lettuce leaves?

Throughout her deterioration Sylvia's incandescent core burnt on undimmed. Although even her most loyal admirers thought the painful and ineffective face-lift she subjected herself to at the end of May was a sad and bizarre move, Sylvia herself presented it in a humorous light in some sketches she did for Selma, and, by continuing to maintain her almost impenetrable public mask of charm and vitality, she concealed from all but her closest friends the severity of her inner turmoil.

Facelift — Sylvia's version, 1973.
S. WASSERMAN

Admirers kept coming, and her afternoon sessions grew larger and more frequent. On these occasions Sylvia often changed into a long, gaily coloured chiffonous gown and become Madam Heidelberg — an ethereal creature who responded to classical music by wafting around the room in an expressive, free-flowing dance. Her guests often stayed on for spontaneous or planned parties, from which Sylvia would retire to bed at about nine o'clock, tired from her pre-dawn writing session and laid out by lager.

Granddaughters Corinne and Robyn were too deeply enmeshed in Sylvia's life, and too buffeted by her moods, to save her from disintegration. And though she was visited by some old friends during this time — Bill Cliett from Florida, Roselle Linskie from Nevada (who had visited her in New Zealand and kept in touch ever since), and her former Tauranga complement, Flo — none stayed to care for her forever.

The presence of the Kirklands during July and August brought temporary stability. They held together both her workshops and her life. When they left the magnitude of Sylvia's deterioration became shockingly obvious. The Kendalls, back from leave, wasted no time in helping Corinne and Robyn pack Sylvia and deliver her to the *Arcadia* for its 10 September sailing.

Two days before they left, Sylvia, Corinne and Robyn moved into a hotel, where Sylvia held a great farewell party. Fans came in their hundreds and Selma came too:

> I wanted to be with her, I wanted to share with her, but I couldn't make any contact. She was just out of it, she was totally inaccessible. I was broken-hearted. It was like the mad scene from *Lucia di Lammermoor*; she was in the middle of this wild party, inviting everyone to come to the ship next day to see her off, and I was in the hall crying. . . .[22]

Selma didn't go to the ship, but everyone else did. There were drinks, flowers, kisses and tears. The band played; streamers fluttered, cries of farewell filled the air. Suddenly the crowded dock fell silent. Everyone was pointing and staring: there was Sylvia at a rail high above them, swaying rhythmically in an expressive Maori action-song of farewell. Then, amid rapturous applause, she waved once and was gone.

Later, as the *Acadia* ploughed out to sea, Sylvia sat at the bow and drank herself into a stupor. The dream of overseas escape lay in ruins at her feet.

FIFTEEN

Selah

And where am I staying now, you ask. In Selah. For the duration. The beauty alone is therapeutic: the trees and the harbour through the windows and the very same Mount. Utter stillness, utter quiet, utter privacy within sight of the faces I love. Utter security. The only conditions to recover and all of them here. The birds call me to work at dawn and you see, with no pollution, the stars. I work a little every day, a little. . . . I never go into Whenua. Live alone in Selah. Keep clear and keep my mouth shut. . . . I hear from North America, flowers too, but don't answer. Though many over there love me madly. But not here.[1]

DESPITE THE TRANQUILLITY OF SELAH, LOVINGLY FURNISHED with the chair, carpet, bed and bedcover she had brought home from Vancouver, the trauma of returning to the hated motherland soon proved too much for Sylvia. Of all the depressions in her life, that first year back in New Zealand was the deepest. She had dreamed of living out her days in her self-contained Tauranga Selah while Jasmine and her six children lived on in the adjacent family home; when Jasmine married Bill Beveridge in January 1972, he sold his own home and moved into Whenua with his three children to preserve that dream. To Sylvia in far-off Vancouver the arrangement looked perfect, but the reality turned out to be unbearable.

The shock of finding strangers under her roof and the indignity of having to compete with ten other people for Jasmine's attention was devastating enough, but on top of that Sylvia had to contend with the sudden loss of celebrity status and the awful realisation that, having lived her dreams of fame and escape, she had nowhere left to run to and no dream to lure. Consumed by bitterness, she withdrew into Selah with her tea, codeine, blood pressure pills, cigarettes, lager, valium and a new grand piano — and brooded. Her blood pressure rose to dangerous heights and her lager consumption spiralled out of control.*

She focused her resentment on her new son-in-law: so what if he was useful around the house and good to his wife and children, he had taken

---

*In retrospect she blamed her drinking problem in Vancouver on the eight per cent alcohol content of Canadian beer and claimed that she could drink unlimited quantities of the two per cent New Zealand product — though in fact both brews were similar, containing five and four per cent alcohol respectively.

over her daughter, her home and her grandchildren, and that was unforgivable. In recurring rages she accused the Beveridges of being 'parasites'
and 'imposters' and threatened to call the police to evict them, only to
weep later to Jasmine that she could not live alone. She began impulsively
changing her will to disinherit her children, and regularly summoned
Ashton to take her to Hastings, which he would do, only to have her
demanding tearfully next morning to be returned to Tauranga
immediately.

Throughout the crisis she continued to work: revising her Canadian
manuscripts, composing ghost stories, writing an angry tirade about the
'ostracism, persecution and ridicule' suffered by the artist in New Zealand,
and giving thought to the publication she had under way in Canada.

Before leaving Vancouver she had handed over her collection of children's songs and stories *O Children of the World* (which Bob Gottlieb and
the Simon Fraser Faculty of Education had declined to publish) to her
friend and admirer Dan Rubin. Dan had worked on the *British Columbia
Access Catalogue* (a local equivalent of the *Whole Earth Catalogue*) and was
happy to use his publishing experience to help Sylvia. By the time she
arrived back in New Zealand Dan's father had drawn the illustrations for
the book and Dan had spent many hours and several thousand dollars
preparing the manuscript for publication. The final production was under
way when he received a cable from Sylvia withdrawing permission to publish. He was devastated:

> Up to that point she'd been supportive. I felt really jerked around. How
> could she do this? Then I realised we had a contract that was all fair and
> square and she couldn't back out. I decided if she was going to screw me
> around I'd show her.[2]

He published a thousand copies of *O Children of the World* in March 1974.

Years later Dan weighed the distress of that experience against the
enrichment that knowing Sylvia had brought to his life. Like almost
everyone who came close to her and was hurt, he had absolutely no
regrets:

> It was a really awful scene for me at the end, but even so it was worth
> it. I wouldn't have traded that whole experience for the world, not for
> anything — the chance to get to know her and learn the things I learnt
> from her. . . .[3]

Dan had been lashed by the outer edge of a storm centred on Sylvia's
Tauranga home. For nine turbulent months Jasmine, Bill and Ashton made
Sylvia's peace of mind their top priority, but as far as Sylvia was concerned
everything they did was wrong. She wrote to Elliot:

> I'm fighting with my back to the wall as the most docile animal would,
> for his right to live, and to be a person and to be what he is: an artist
> however miserable.
>
> I don't want any sons. I don't want a daughter. . . . I live imprisoned
> in a small prison in solitary confinement for nine months, with hostility

all round me, not only from here but from this country. . . . The reasons? Because I'm a leading international thinker. . . .

By mid-1974 Sylvia's family had had enough. Jasmine and Bill bought a home of their own in Tauranga, and Ashton resigned from his informal role as Sylvia's business manager.

These moves seemed to Sylvia like further betrayals, but the peace of Selah and the faint light filtering in from the outside world was just enough to make her pause at edge of total disintegration and turn back. Although she continued to describe herself as living in 'solitary confinement in Siberia', she found pleasure and comfort in contact with her few remaining Tauranga friends and with other sympathetic New Zealanders.

Within a year of her return she had begun corresponding with writer Ian Cross, and had been visited by musician Frederick Page, educationalist Jack Shallcrass, and writers Ruth Gilbert, Barry Mitcalfe, Bruce Mason and Maurice Shadbolt. Their undisguised concern did not go unnoticed. She wrote shakily to Mason after his January 1974 visit, 'I saw your face as you sat there and looked at me. I knew you were reading everything. . . .' After that she made several unsuccessful attempts to stop drinking, including one at the time of Maurice Shadbolt's visit in July:

> She said to me, 'I've become an alcoholic. I drink all this Dominion Bitter.' And it was true; there were a fair few bottles around.
> She said, 'I've got to stop'.
> She offered me a drink but didn't have one herself. Then she asked me to take away all her beer. She said she was going to be teetotal from that point on. I had a Holden station wagon which was empty and honest to God I must have stacked ten or twelve crates into it — about half the bottles were full and half were empty. I rattled all the way back to Auckland and arrived home like a bottle merchant. I was drinking her beer for months afterwards.[4]

But when her friend Flo called next day, Sylvia told her indignantly, 'Maurice Shadbolt came to see me and do you know what he did? He brought some beer and he got me drunk!'

Sylvia was never able to stop drinking for long, but after Shadbolt's visit she did manage to keep her alcohol consumption under unsteady control.

In October, just as Jasmine and Bill were preparing to move into their new home, Sylvia developed another health problem. The pain in her hip, caused by pressure on the sciatic nerve, intensified to the point where she could neither sit nor walk. After five weeks in traction in Tauranga Hospital she came home in November and was able to accept the Beveridge family's departure relatively peaceably, for she was incubating a wonderful idea. Flo, her former complement, had cared for her aged mother for years but now the old lady had died, so wouldn't it be lovely if Flo moved into Whenua and cared for Sylvia instead? When Flo refused, Sylvia's unrestrained rage brought their relationship to a permanent end.

Although Whenua lay empty, Jasmine and Bill called in every day to deliver meals and check on Sylvia's wellbeing, and at the end of 1974

Elliot came out from London to spend Christmas with her. Slowly Sylvia regained strength and mobility. As her interests turned outward she began a lasting and intimate correspondence with Selma Wasserman, and agreed to take part in a New Zealand television documentary about her life and work.

Over the previous fifteen years Sylvia had either refused outright, or later backed out of, scores of invitations to appear on television. In Vancouver she did allow a videotape to be made of one of her workshops, but later insisted that the tape be wiped. She equivocated about this latest invitation too, but eventually the $1500 appearance fee, and the possibility of the film being distributed overseas, won her acceptance. 'I want to talk to the world,' she told the organisers. 'I want to talk to the world.' When she learned that the film was being made for United Nations Women's Year, and that one of the organisers had once worked for the BBC, she referred to the project as 'the BBC-UNESCO film'.

During rambling preliminary discussions, in an apparent reference to her present situation, Sylvia talked about the nature of the artist in his declining years:

> Now this artist would have put all the best of himself, all that is good and beautiful, into the interpretation of this piece of work, and all he has left is the residue which is ugly. This is why artists' lives are notorious, why they're terribly hard people to live with. This is why they can't integrate into society. . . .[5]

She refused to be interviewed on camera, but suggested that they bring a group of young teachers to Whenua and film her taking an organic teaching workshop.

On 18 January 1975 a dozen young men and women assembled in Whenua for two days of filming. As the minutes ticked by, the tension grew. Would she or wouldn't she turn up? Finally, nearly half an hour after the appointed time, Sylvia made her entrance. She wore baggy brown knickerbockers and a smock so ancient that its rotted seams were held together with safety-pins. She said not a word but sat down at the piano and began playing Schubert.

Later she took the group through her organic morning. The outcome was a disjointed disaster. Only brief snippets were usable for the final documentary. An in-depth interview could perhaps save the film — but would Sylvia co-operate? Perhaps, just perhaps, she might accept if Jack Shallcrass from Victoria University of Wellington was the interviewer?

Shallcrass was the only New Zealand educator of any standing that Sylvia had ever allowed near her. Long before they met she had been attracted by his outspoken opposition to the Vietnam War, and he had visited and corresponded with her regularly since the late 1960s. His friendship with his subject and his media experience made him the obvious choice for the job, but was friendship enough to induce the camera-shy Sylvia to agree to be interviewed? Fortunately for the film producer there was another factor: in the secret recesses of her heart Sylvia had fallen in love. She agreed to the interview, and later confessed to Selma that she began each day by greeting a photo of Shallcrass she had cut from the *Listener* and mounted on a piece of cardboard.

Oblivious to Sylvia's infatuation, Shallcrass conducted the interview with warmth and sensitivity. The result, despite Sylvia's obvious tension, was a success. One reviewer observed:

> It was like watching a nervous horse being gentled by an experienced trainer . . . drawing from so touchy and inflammable a personality the words that would help to reveal and define her distinctive talent, and the daimon that still drives her.[6]

Shallcrass began by asking Sylvia what in all the world was most important to her and she talked about her search for the origin of feeling, and of her need to isolate and harness the impulse to kill. The discussion then ranged over the conflict between the woman and the artist, Sylvia's teaching philosophy, her hostility toward New Zealand and her hatred of teaching, but it seemed that in the final analysis none of these things really mattered. When asked what she wanted to be remembered for Sylvia burst out:

> I felt my vocation was to be a concert pianist . . . it's my language Jack, this language comes from the great masters, the great geniuses . . . they speak in magic. . . .

'When we began,' he observed gently, 'I asked you what in all the world was most important to you — and I think you've answered it.'

Sylvia, her eyes welling with tears, fled behind her mask. 'Well you had to work for it, didn't you!' she snapped.

Because she had attacked New Zealand Sylvia expected a hostile backlash. But instead the screening of the documentary was followed by an avalanche of supportive phone calls, telegrams and letters. Almost in spite of herself she found her feeling for her motherland beginning to mellow.

But as her anger waned, and the ravages of age and alcohol began to overtake her (in the documentary the palms of her hands showed the plum-coloured shininess characteristic of liver damage), her inspiration also started to fade. She sent her revised Canadian manuscripts and some recent ghost stories to Bob Gottlieb and to A. H. and A. W. Reed (the New Zealand publisher at the centre of her long-ago Maori infant reading books drama). But Bob complained to Sylvia's New York agent about 'yards of goods which don't make a book that's publishable', and an internal memo at Reeds described the work as 'a porridge of complacent and turgid blah'.

There was only one manuscript left. The one that had sustained her through Keith's final illness, and through all the confusion and distress of her years abroad: the story of her life. In draft form it was finished, but it would undergo extensive rewriting and revision before it was complete. After months of tactfully declining her submissions Reeds were thrilled to receive what appeared to be the freshly written beginning of a new manuscript:

. . . a thirty-six-page fragment of a story about her own childhood, magic-
ally written, smooth and clean and beautiful autobiography. Vintage
Sylvia.[7]

Heartened by the positive response she received from Reed editor Dale
Williams, Sylvia applied for and received a grant from the New Zealand
Literary Fund to finish the book. For the next three years she dedicated
herself to writing with renewed purpose and vigour.

But while her inner world swelled with meaning, her outer world felt
empty. She still liked people to call her Mary or Mere and vigorously
avoided the name Sylvia (after signing a letter to the newspaper 'Ashton-
Warner' she added, 'Please don't use the "Sylvia" in my name. It's too long
and unwieldy and sounds pretentious'), but she was no longer a five-year-
old child. For once in her life the way she felt and the way the world
perceived her were as one: she was an unhappy and ailing old lady.

Although she complained constantly of being neglected, she did not lack
for company. In addition to regular visits from her remaining Tauranga
friends, and occasional visits from those further afield, she saw Jasmine,
Corinne (who had married in 1974) and Corinne's daughter Adele (who
was born in 1976) nearly every day. But always she wanted more. Above
all she wanted a loving, caring and truly devoted son or daughter living
permanently in Whenua.

In early 1975, with Jasmine settled in her own home a mile away, Elliot
back in London and Ashton about to move to an isolated fishing lodge in
Northland, Sylvia felt particularly abandoned and vulnerable. She wrote to
Elliot and begged him to come home, and when Ashton's business
arrangements suffered a last-minute hitch she telephoned and told him
solicitously: 'If you find yourself without a home and with no firm there's
always Whenua. . . .' He said nothing. Then when news came that Ashton
and his family had arrived safely at Kingfish Lodge, another possibility for
her future occurred to Sylvia. She wrote excitedly to Elliot:

I'm so awfully happy. . . . He said he would come and get me. Right.
I buy a small baby grand and plonk it in one of the cabins. . . . And it
won't be for two nights or so. . . I'm dying to get there, El, they've given
me photos of the whole show . . . by Christ I'm going to Kingfish Lodge.

But Kingfish Lodge turned out to be less than satisfactory. Ashton sold it
and moved back to Hastings before Sylvia was able to pay a visit.

Although no one lived permanently in Whenua, there was a steady
stream of short-term residents. Elliot returned to visit every year or two
and Ashton and his family often came to stay. New Zealand and overseas
visitors sometimes stopped overnight, and during university holidays
Jasmine's older children and their friends moved in. And on one occasion,
when Sylvia's sciatic nerve trouble flared up, Corinne, her husband and
their baby lived in for two weeks to care for her.

But most nights Sylvia was alone with the wild creatures of the dark:

. . . at night I'll hear the sniffing of hedgehogs and the sound of the birds nesting in the guttering above Selah. . . . The wild life knows me. At night about 10.30 or 11 p.m. wild young humans creep up the bank through the lilies and trees on the prowl and cavort silently but they're the only ones I ring the police about when they peep in my window and wake me. They don't take anything or break things, just drawn to the moonlit sanctuary like the other wild life. . . .[8]

She rose early each day and as the wild things melted into the dawn she wrote about her life. Each time she looked back the pattern became clearer: like all children she was born an artist, but whereas most children are steamrolled into conformity at the age of five, she enjoyed a childhood so beautiful and free that she stayed a five-year-old artist forever. That she emerged from childhood into a lifetime of unrelenting 'persecution, rejection and spiritual murder' was vivid proof of society's intolerance of the unconforming artist.

She rewrote and dramatised most of her earlier account to prove her point, turning a simple tale about a gifted misfit into a harrowing story of ostracism and persecution. Then she wove through it the romance and excitement of love. It was so thrilling and naughty that Sylvia was soon overcome by guilt. Surely the feared mother country would punish her most dreadfully for her sins? Her anxiety exploded into fury when Dale Williams, out of editorial thoroughness, compared her latest account of her Pipiriki years with *Myself*, and asked Sylvia about the discrepancies between them. Sylvia withdrew the book from Reeds without explanation and sent it to Bob Gottlieb at Knopf. Then she wrote to Selma:

> . . . this MS can't come to this bloody country, to have NZ's hands mauling over my unspeakables. There's a bloody house called Reed in Wgtn . . . hoping to co-publish with Knopf and break into the North American market, per this MS. No way . . . . The bloody woman editor . . . is unsophisticated and touches untouchables and says, 'But is this true? What about MYSELF? Your MS is supposed to be documentary', whereas Bob says, 'Art has priority. If art requires a certain composition then composition it is, must be. It's ART I'm after.' [Gottlieb was actually talking about her fiction when he wrote that, but Sylvia never did recognise the difference between fact and fiction] . . .
>
> I think the integrity of an MS depends on whom you are writing to. When I try to write for NZ I am cramped, furtive, timid, lying and limited. When I write to the US I want to throw up eveything regardless.

But even writing for the United States proved a struggle; there were many times when reliving the past became unbearable and Sylvia wanted to stop.

Added to the pain of the past was the pain of the present. The hip problem continued to worry her, and during 1977 and 1978 she had cataracts removed from her eyes and a malignant growth removed from one eyelid. There followed more than a year of eye infections and contact lens problems, through which she continued to work. As she explained to Elliot, '. . . my inner eye can see at least as well as Beethoven's inner ear could hear.'

Supported by steady encouragement from Bob Gottlieb, and using the large-print typewriter she had bought to make children's books in Aspen, Sylvia completed her autobiography in December 1978, just in time for her seventieth birthday. Ashton's and Jasmine's families gathered in Tauranga to help her celebrate, and flowers, presents and cards poured in from New Zealand and around the world. Bill Cliett marked the event by completing the Tolkien verse he had begun on that magic morning when he and Sylvia had run away together from Aspen. 'The old that is strong does not wither,' he wrote. 'Deep roots are not reached by the frost.' And the Kirklands, who to their eternal shame overlooked her birthday completely, received a stern telegram: WHERE'S MY PRESENT.

Bob Gottlieb completed the editing of *I Passed This Way* early in 1979, and after several changes of mind Sylvia finally allowed it to be co-published with Reeds. Contrary to her worst expectations, the book won both an American honour (the Delta Kappa Gamma Society International 1980 Educator's Award) and the non-fiction section of the 1980 New Zealand Book Awards. After years of refusing invitations of any sort because she was afraid to travel, Sylvia was so excited by the New Zealand award she flew to Wellington for the ceremony.

During her seven years of self-imposed 'solitary confinement in Siberia', her opportunities to charm and impress had been few, but at the book awards she demonstrated that neither age nor frailty, nor reclusiveness, had dimmed her powers to beguile. Reed publisher Paul Bradwell was enchanted, ('She was Queen of the May! She was vibrant! She was absolutely incredible!'), and editor Dale Williams was thrilled to learn that Sylvia thought she was simply wonderful:

> Sylvia sought me out and we met for the first time. She was jubilant and hugged me, thanked me, and, doing a little dance, said that it was all due to me that she had started writing again with her old strength. She explained that she had not known what she was writing at the time of the eccentric manuscripts, and said she had been ill and had had adverse reactions to some of her drugs: she had not been herself for a long time. (That cleared up *that* mystery; I had wondered whether she was a secret drinker.) Now she wanted to let me know how my encouragement had kept her going and restored her faith in herself and so forth.[9]

Apart from her trip to the book awards, Sylvia confined her spellbinding to the few friends and strangers she allowed to visit her at home. One visitor was television host Max Cryer, who left convinced that Sylvia was an avid rugby fan (she actually detested the game). She told him she would appear on his chat show only if she could share the set with a group of brawny footballers. He had it all arranged before she backed out.

Another regular visitor was film producer Michael Firth, who approached Sylvia in 1976 with a proposal to make a film based on *Teacher*. His first meeting with her was odd, to say the least:

> She opened the door and I said, 'Hello, I'm Michael Firth. I've come to

Whenua

9 Levers Road

Otumoetai

Tauranga

NEW ZEALAND

My cup runneth over

Sylvia's response to receiving the 1980 Book Award.

talk to you about the film. You must be Sylvia Ashton-Warner.'

She looked at me quite blankly and said, 'No'.

I thought this must be a friend of hers, so I said, 'Is Sylvia Ashton-Warner in?'

'No, dear, not here.'

I said, 'Is this 9 Levers Road?'

'Yes.'

My wife and I had just driven for three hours to get there and we'd been invited to stay for the weekend so I wasn't about to turn around and go home.

I said, 'Are you Mrs Henderson by any chance?'

'Yes, dear. Come on in.'

Next day she explained — 'I was just giving myself time, dear, to see if I was going to like you. I didn't want to spend the whole weekend with two people I wasn't going to like.'[10]

Sylvia had frequent changes of mind about the film, but she kept her reservations to herself and concentrated on weaving a spell around her guests. Firth recalled:

We got on very, very well. We became part of her family.[11]

She enjoyed her lager and we'd sit and talk for hours. She was a charismatic talker. When you left after a weekend it was like coming back into another world. She absorbed you completely.[12]

Firth's plans developed slowly; Sylvia died before the film was completed.

In 1979, just as she was finishing *I Passed This Way*, the symptoms of her final illness began to appear. After an investigation for a persistent bowel disturbance, a benign tumour was removed. The condition did not improve. Cancer was suspected but Sylvia deferred the recommended operation.

Throughout 1980 her health worries were diverted by the public acclaim accorded to *I Passed This Way*. In order to please Paul Bradwell, with whom she had developed a fey and affectionate relationship, she agreed for the first time in her life to personally publicise one of her books. She gave three interviews: two for radio and one for television. The radio interviews were relatively straightforward, but the television filming ran into problems. Sylvia was on the point of cancelling everything when the television team arrived, but at the last minute she decided to proceed. After much discussion with interviewer Angela D'Audney over what to wear and how to do her hair, the interview began.

A: Sylvia, you became a teacher it seems, because other options were closed to you. You had no alternative. Yet teaching became so important to you.

S: No, it never became important to me.

A: You talk about hating teaching and yet you were obviously a fine teacher.

S: Yes, dear, other people say that, I don't know, I didn't say that.

A: But you do profess opinions on teaching so it must have —

S: Oh you won't find me professing. . .

A: This enormous fun you were having with the pupils, you and the children, just how did you teach them that way?

S: Well you'd have to define 'teach'. The children learned a great deal more than normal, so you can't say it wasn't teaching, can you?

A: But can you describe the method for me?

S: I've written four books on it, dear. I won't bore you.

A: Any chance of doing it briefly — just right now?

S: No, I've resigned. I've written four books. I can't just do it all again so don't ask me, you or the public.[13]

After several more responses in the same vein the director called a halt and took Sylvia to task. As she told Paul Bradwell later: 'I talked with her like I used to talk to my naughty Aunt Kath when she was in one of her less endearing phases.'

Sylvia, who had probably never been spoken to like that in her life, was somewhat chastened; when the camera rolled again she was a little more co-operative. She discussed her childhood, her work and her feelings about New Zealand, but no matter what approach D'Audney took she would not discuss the formative influences in her life. 'Oh no, dear,' she insisted repeatedly. 'Artists don't get formed, they're born.'

By the time the excitement over her autobiography had faded away, Sylvia's bowel disturbance had become too serious to ignore. In 1981 inoperable cancer was diagnosed. The surgeon could do no more than remove some diseased tissue to ease her symptoms. The equanimity with which Sylvia received the diagnosis suggests that she didn't really believe it. In defiance of her declining health she toyed with the idea of running away again and won invitations to take short courses at Boston University, Simon Fraser University and Waikato University in nearby Hamilton. But after much indecision she concluded that they all wanted to exploit her, and decided to stay home.

For a year from September 1980, with Elliot living in Whenua during his sabbatical leave from London, Sylvia was not alone. But inevitably, particularly when Elliot's friends were involved, there were strains. Years later he reflected:

> I got the feeling that she would have been happy only if her children had locked themselves in the house and remained with her for the rest of her life. On the other hand if we had done that she would have said, these useless children, parasites — you couldn't win.
>
> She seemed to regard the fact that her children had relationships with other people as a gross betrayal — a sort of temporary aberration that we would eventually come to terms with and reject.[14]

On one occasion when Elliot had friends to stay he told Sylvia he wanted Whenua to himself. She said nothing but was obviously outraged. He questioned the validity of her reaction, but by then the belief that her family, her nation, the world and life itself were committed to persecuting her had driven and inspired Sylvia for more than seventy years. Elliot could not convince her otherwise, though he did try — as this verbatim account he wrote at the time shows:

E: If you feel any resentment or anger towards me for anything that I have said, or not said, or done, or not done, then you must tell me.
   Since you refuse to reply, would you like me to do the talking?
S: I know it all and have no need to talk about it.
E: I'd be interested to know what it is that you know.
S: I am not a troglodyte. I don't have to be banished to my cell just because you have some friends here. What will they say — is that horrible old woman hiding in her cave because she doesn't want to see anyone?
E: When I have my friends down here it is important to me that *I* be in control of my own territory. I am not banishing you to Selah. I am requesting permission to have the house to myself for the weekend.
S: But I don't like the way you said it. 'I *want* the house to myself.'
E: Of course I said I *wanted* the house to myself. I made a request to you.
S: You didn't make a request, you just demanded. It's because I'm old and ugly, that's why you just don't want anyone to see me.
E: But you are inventing that idea and then making *me* responsible for your fantasies. You have a perfect right to your fantasies, but don't visit them upon me.
S: I only come in here because I want to help. I have given you everything here. Everything is yours to use as you wish and I try not to interfere. But just because you have people here you want to lock me in a cave like an old witch so that no one can see me.
E: Look! That is a figment of your imagination. I repeat — I am not responsible for your imagination. You are casting *yourself* into the role of the rejected woman and then blaming me for the role *you* have adopted.
S: You have caused me great distress. What you have done is very, very hurtful.
E: I do not *cause* your feelings. you are the master of your own feelings. I simply, utterly and categorically reject the idea that I am the instrument of your unhappiness. Do you understand? You are the instrument of your own unhappiness.
S: You did cause me distress. 'I *want* the house,' you said. You offended me. You spoke as though I had no business here. You just wanted to get rid of me.
E: You are ignoring the spirit of the original request. There was no offence in it. No offence. Can you see what you are doing? Is it possible for you to deviate into self-awareness for a moment and understand what you are doing? *You* are making *my* request into an *offensive* demand. And you refuse to see what you are doing. You are casting yourself into the role of the offended, unwanted and rejected old lady. *You* are doing that, not *me*. And now you expect me to shoulder the blame and to show contrition and regret for an injury I never inflicted.
S: I will not have this inquisition. I get this all the time. I will not have you invading my privacy in this way.
E: What you see as an inquisition is an attempt by me to establish that

it is vital for me to be master of my own house when I receive my own friends. Since I have been in New Zealand I have constantly had to accommodate myself to other people's territory. Now I want to operate on my own territory. Is that too big a concept for your imagination to stretch to?

S: I know I am wrong. I know I am a monster.

E: Look, you don't understand — I do not want you doing the dishes either after the meal or early in the morning. Doing the dishes slices through the conversation. How can I lie around and get drunk and talk if everyone is crashing about in the kitchen? Neither do I want you asking people where they slept, as you did last time.

S: I know I did that last time. I know it was a gross and ugly intrusion. I am sorry for it. It is my home and my beds. I bought all the blankets, chose all the sheets. I am concerned for their comfort. What I said was taken the wrong way.

E: Well ask them *how* they slept, not *where* they slept.

S: I know I am a monster. I don't want to come in this weekend, anyway. I know I am a wretched ugly monster. I will stay out of it — *right* out of it.

E: If you persist in missing the point that is your business. But you will be invited in for coffee and meals and you will be very welcome. But it has to be on my terms.

S (wanders off slowly, pauses in the corridor, turns, comes back, knocks): I think I will just stay in Selah this weekend. I would prefer it that way.

When Elliot returned to London, Whenua lay empty, but not for long. A couple of years earlier, when it became clear to Sylvia that none of her children would ever live permanently in the house, she had begun to pin her hopes on the younger and more compliant Corinne. Early in 1982, partly in response to Sylvia's unrelenting pressure, partly out of concern for her grandmother's deteriorating health, and partly in reaction to a crisis in her own life, Corinne moved into Whenua with her six-year-old daughter.

Throughout 1982 and 1983 Sylvia grew steadily weaker and the gnawing pain in her gut intensified, but she continued to receive visitors, walk in her garden, visit Jasmine and send out her much-rejected manuscripts to every publisher she could think of. There was, however, one sign of deterioration she could not ignore: though she continued to rise in the dew-damp dawn and sit at her work table, she could no longer write — the imagery had gone.

Then in March 1982, during a bout of anger on learning that Michael Firth intended to base his film on *I Passed This Way*, as well as on *Teacher*, she found good reason to start writing again. No one else could be trusted to write the film script; she would write it herself. She enrolled in the International Correspondence School scriptwriting course to train for the task.

Concerned that she would not receive impartial treatment if her true identity were known, she worked steadily, happily and successfully through the first seven parts of the twelve-part course under the pseudonym of Lili Williami. She collected newspaper clippings to aid her scriptwriting inspiration, including this unsourced, undated item:

> One can of course treat the current push to canonise St John as belated, due recognition for his lonely labours. One could also see it as evidence of how fulsomely the establishment rewards its eccentrics once they have been safely defused.

Sylvia was heartened that year to receive, in recognition of her lonely labours, an M.B.E. in the Queen's Birthday Honours List. 'I am enchanted by this friendly gesture from my country,' she told a reporter. But she knew deep down that the gesture had really come from the sovereign herself, so she added, 'I was touched to hear from Her Majesty the Queen, whom I was fortunate to meet and lunch with aboard H.M.S. *Britannia*.'

Her local Member of Parliament, Keith Allan, performed the investiture at a small private gathering at Whenua. For a while the excitement of the occasion diverted Sylvia's anxiety over the inexorable progression of her disease. Then at her November check-up the blow fell. The cancer had spread to her liver; she had little more than a year to live. A few months later, after previously turning away at least three would-be biographers, she accepted the author for the task and met with her during the closing months of her life.

Although Sylvia was often tired and dispirited, she persisted with the scriptwriting course all through 1983 and gained consistently high marks. Since she had no imagery of her own to call on, she turned to an old Brazilian novel, *Epitaph of a Small Winner*, by Machado de Assis, and adapted it into a screenplay.

By the end of the year she was receiving morphia for pain and beginning to hallucinate at night. By January, knowing that death was near, she had Jasmine and Bill take her to visit the churches of Tauranga. She chose the Anglican Holy Trinity Church as the setting for her funeral.

By February she could barely walk. 'There's nothing much I can do now — except the occasional letter,' she wrote to Elliot. 'I lie down a lot and think.'

Sometimes her thoughts were about her motherland. Her feelings had mellowed since the 1975 documentary when Jack Shallcrass had begun a question with, 'As a New Zealander . . .', and Sylvia had cut in, 'I'm *not* a New Zealander! I'm a landed immigrant from Canada!'

By 1978, when she wrote the epilogue to *I Passed This Way*, she called herself a New Zealander and closed with, 'Whatever my disasters in this country . . . these islands turn out to be the one place where I would wish to be, and Whenua the one inn I desire.'

But in that last chapter she maintained the purity of her theme of 'persecution, rejection and spiritual murder' by insisting that she had never been asked to lecture in her homeland since her return from abroad. (In fact she had received invitations to speak at several national educational conferences.) She also claimed that she hadn't been asked to teach in New Zealand, which was true — the invitation to teach at Waikato University came after her autobiography was published. But that invitation made no difference to her convictions anyway; for the rest of her life Sylvia evoked sympathy and indignation from supporters by insisting that despite everything she had to offer, and the wonderful acknowledgement she had received abroad, she had never ever been asked to teach in the land of her birth.

In the epilogue to *I Passed This Way* she also failed to mention the New Zealand television documentary about her, but she did write of the time she declined a request from Jack Shallcrass for a radio interview with the stinging rebuke, 'You're too late, New Zealand. You've missed your chance.'

Sylvia affirmed that her sense of rejection was unshakable when, in 1982, A. H. and A. W. Reed decided to publish *I Passed This Way* in paperback. Paul Bradwell asked Sylvia for a new preface because the original one had included the declaration, 'I'm one who's been both rejected by and who has rejected my country', and had emphasised her wish to leave New Zealand forever. In the years since that was written, New Zealand had shown its appreciation in the form of the Book Award and the M.B.E. and Sylvia had made the country her home; surely a new preface would be appropriate? 'I'm unable to do it,' Sylvia replied. And she clung stubbornly to her bitterness for the rest of her life.

Her strength waned rapidly during February 1984. District nurses called daily to attend to her medication and to bathe her, but she remained mentally alert. By mid-February she needed almost constant nursing care, so Jasmine and Bill moved into Whenua. In March Ashton came home for a week from his new job in Malaysia, and later that month Elliot returned from London to stay until the end.

A crisis in early April pitched this complex, gifted, passionate, sensitive, imperious, isolated and frightened woman deep into the valley of the shadow. She emerged terrified that God would never forgive her, and flung every remaining spark of her formidable willpower into a last, desperate fight. Each night, as Death came through the darkness to claim her, she sat defiant and exhausted in her armchair, forcing herself to stay awake. Each day, safe in the benign reality of home and family, she lay in bed and slept.

Three times during the night of 27 April she struggled back from the engulfing darkness, then after a lifelong nightlong battle a new dawn broke and she relaxed.

At home in Selah, at seven thirty on the morning of Saturday 28 April 1984, with Jasmine and Elliot beside her, Sylvia Ashton-Warner passed away.

EPILOGUE

Although she lived and died with her outer life fragmented, at Sylvia Ashton-Warner's core there was a consistency uniquely her own. She explained it this way:

> . . . the human mind revolves kaleidoscopically and as it turns, its many separate facets reflect and respond to the changing circumferal circumstances and, since each facet is spoked to the central axis, to the central personality, therefore each and every separate response is legitimate, integrated and true.[1]

Her central personality was that of an artist — sensitive, imaginative, talented and unique. She expressed her artistic inspiration in ways that were both readable and poetic, and her insights came to the public at a time when the life spirit of the age was saying the same thing in many different ways. For all these reasons she will go down in history as one of the seminal voices of our time.

The potency of her ideas, and her astonishing power to polarise her audience, lives on beyond death. At the mention of her name, down-to-earth people turn misty-eyed with adoration, and mild-mannered individuals explode into rage.

What is the secret of her impact? What life-force enables her to move people so?

Perhaps the power of Sylvia Ashton-Warner to attract and repel lies not in her, but in ourselves. Perhaps it is the shock of recognising ourselves in the flashing mirrors of her soul that drives us to frenzied celebration or fevered denial.

It may be that in Sylvia Ashton-Warner we see our own suppressed irrationality, and the embodiment of our own dreams.

GLOSSARY OF MAORI WORDS

haka: posture dance, chant of welcome or defiance
hoiho: horse
kai: food
kanga pirau: corn that is fermented, usually in running water, and eaten with sugar and cream
karaka: spreading tree with orange fruit
kowhai: native tree with bright yellow flowers
kowhaiwhai: style of patterns normally used on meeting house rafters
kumara: sweet potato
Maoritanga: Maori culture
manuka: tea tree
marae: ceremonial area in front of a meeting house
pa: village
Pakeha: person of European descent
piupiu: flax skirt
ponga whare: house built of tree-fern logs
puha: green leafy vegetable
pukeko: hen-sized wading bird
puriri: large native hardwood
rata: large forest tree with bright red flowers
tangi: ceremony of mourning
taniwha: water monster
tui: songbird with tuft of white feathers at throat
whanau: extended family
whare: house
whenua: land

REFERENCES

To minimise superscripts in the text, numbered references have been provided only for major points requiring clarification and for long quotes where the source of the quote is not indicated in the surrounding text.

Publication and location details of the sources in the references can be found in the bibliography.

Abbreviations:

AS: Anonymous source (informant who did not wish to be identified).
ATTC: Auckland Teachers' Training College.
HBEB: Hawke's Bay Education Board Archives.
Int.: Interview with the author, 1983–87.
IPTW: I Passed This Way, Sylvia Ashton-Warner.
LA: Letter to the author, 1983–87.
LBDF: Letter to Barbara Dent from Fernhill, mostly undated, 1949–57.
LBDW: Letter to Barbara Dent from Waiomatatini, undated, 1946–49.
MSA: Maori School Archives.
Myself: Myself, Sylvia Ashton-Warner.
SA-W: Sylvia Ashton-Warner.
TA: Tape recording sent to the author, 1983–87.
Teacher: Teacher, Sylvia Ashton Warner.
ULDA: Unposted letter to Dr Allen undated, 1940–46 (Sylvia Ashton-Warner Archives).
V&L: Veatch and Llewellyn tape recordings, 1967.

Chapter 1: Beginnings

1. The three quotes in this paragraph are from *IPTW,* 64, 15 and 5.
2. *IPTW,* 124.
3. Cliett, W., 'SA-W's message for American Teachers'.

Chapter 2: Primary School

1. D. Mason, Int.
2. N. Linard (née Warner), Int.
3. L. Warner, Int.
4. SA-W, *Greenstone,* 118, and N. Lingard Int. Although *Greenstone* was presented as fiction, SA-W insisted that it was a true account of her childhood.
5. SA-W, *Greenstone,* 39.
6. *IPTW,* 13.
7. Inspector's report, March 1916, HBEB.
8. ULDA.
9. SA-W, letter to W. Rhodes, *c.* 1967.
10. Inspector's report, July 1918, HBEB.
11. ULDA.
12. *IPTW,* 29.
13. *IPTW,* 32.
14. *Ibid.*
15. *IPTW,* 36.
16. *Ibid.*
17. *IPTW,* 42.
18. *Ibid.*
19. ULDA.
20. *IPTW,* 46, 47.
21. *IPTW,* 43.
22. *IPTW,* 69.
23. N. Lingard, Int.
24. *Ibid*
25. *IPTW,* 58.

Chapter 3: Primary School

1. *IPTW,* 81.
2. *IPTW,* 98.
3. D. Edwards, Int.

4. *IPTW*, 100.
5. AS, Int.
6. *IPTW*, 100.
7. *IPTW*, 101.
8. *IPTW*, 90.
9. *IPTW*, 107.
10. *IPTW*, 127.
11. ULDA.
12. *IPTW*, 16.
13. *IPTW*, 127.
14. *IPTW*, 126.
15. Freud, A., *The Ego and Mechanisms of Defense.*
16. *IPTW*, 142.
17. *IPTW*, 147.

Chapter 4: Pupil Teacher

1. *IPTW*, 148.
2. *IPTW*, 172.
3. *IPTW*, 158.
4. *Ibid.*
5. *IPTW*, 154.
6. *IPTW*, 162.
7. *IPTW*, 166.
8. *IPTW*, 167.
9. *IPTW*, 171.
10. *IPTW*, 165.
11. *IPTW*, 159.
12. *IPTW*, 165.
13. *IPTW*, 176.
14. *IPTW*, 180.
15. *IPTW*, 182.

Chapter 5: Auckland Teachers' Training College

1. All the above comments from interviews with former ATTC students.
2. M. Pope (née Kyle), Int.
3. *Ibid.*
4. *IPTW*, 189.
5. *IPTW*, 194.
6. *IPTW*, 195.
7. *IPTW*, 196.
8. *IPTW*, 203.
9. *IPTW*, 204.
10. *IPTW*, 201.
11. *IPTW*, 204.
12. *Peka*, ATTC, 1929.
13. *IPTW*, 206.
14. *IPTW*, 207.
15. *IPTW*, 208.
16. *IPTW*, 210.
17. *Ibid.*
18. *IPTW*, 214.

19. AS, Int.
20. *IPTW*, 211.
21. *IPTW*, 215.
22. *IPTW*, 221.
23. *IPTW*, 220.
24. *IPTW*, 222.
25. *IPTW*, 223.
26. *IPTW*, 227.
27. *IPTW*, 230.
28. *IPTW*, 234.
29. *Ibid.*

Chapter 6: Wife and Mother

1. *IPTW*, 213.
2. *IPTW*, 239.
3. *IPTW*, 240.
4. *IPTW*, 242.
5. AS, Int.
6. *Ibid.*
7. J. Hughson, Int.
8. *Ibid.*
9. *Ibid.*
10. N. Lingard, Int.
11. *IPTW*, 245.
12. Barrington and Beaglehole, *Maori Schools in a Changing Society*, 244.
13. *IPTW*, 245.

Chapter 7: Horoera

1. *IPTW*, 264.
2. K. Dewes, Int.
3. C. Flavell, Int.
4. *Ibid.*
5. *Ibid.*
6. H. Black, Int.
7. *IPTW*, 276.
8. *Ibid.*
9. I. Banks, Int.
10. L. Warner, Int.
11. SA-W, Wellington diary/letter, 1939.
12. *Ibid.*
13. *Myself*, 72.
14. SA-W, op. cit.
15. ULDA.
16. SA-W, op. cit.
17. ULDA.
18. *Ibid.*

Chapter 8: Pipiriki

1. *IPTW*, 296.
2. *Myself*, 23.
3. *Ibid*, 34.
4. *Ibid*, 35.

5. *Ibid*, 41.
6. *Ibid*, 42.
7. *Ibid*, 44.
8. *Ibid*, 31.
9. L. Johnston, Int.
10. *Myself*, 41.
11. *Ibid*, 52.
12. AS, Int.
13. *Myself*, 54.
14. *Ibid*, 60.
15. *Ibid*, 148.
16. *Ibid*, 116.
17. *IPTW*, 298.
18. R. Te Hore, Int.
19. R. Ropata, Int.
20. R. Gray, Int.
21. *Myself*, 168.
22. Inspector's report, 14 Oct. 1944, MSA.
23. *Myself*, 86.
24. *Ibid*, 153.
25. E. Henderson, Int.
26. *IPTW*, 303.
27. J. Alley notes, and SA-W, diary, *c.* 1943.
28. *Myself*, 182.
29. W. Harris: LA.
30. *Ibid*.
31. *IPTW*, 306.
32. W. Harris, LA.
33. *IPTW*, 307.

Chapter 9: Waiomatatini

1. *IPTW*, 316.
2. *IPTW*, 324.
3. SA-W, unposted diary/letter to J. Alley *c.* 1945.
4. L. Goldsmith, Int.
5. *Ibid*.
6. LBDW.
7. ULDA.
8. LBDW.
9. LBDW.
10. LBDW.
11. LBDW.
12. LBDW.
13. LBDW.
14. LBDW.
15. SA-W, diary, *c.* 1947.
16. AS, LA.
17. I. Tawhiwhirangi, Int.
18. *IPTW*, 342.
19. *Ibid*.
20. L. Johnson, Int.
21. B. Dent, Int.

22. M. Penfold, Int.
23. *IPTW*, 360.
24. SA-W, diary, *c.* 1948.
25. LBDW.
26. LBDW.
27. LBDW.
28. SA-W, letter to S. Rhodes, *c.* 1949.

Chapter 10: Fernhill

1. LBDF.
2. LBDF.
3. *Teacher*, 33.
4. SA-W, diary, *c.* 1951.
5. D. Percy, Int.
6. *Teacher*, 210.
7. *Ibid*, 33.
8. *Ibid*.
9. P. Hanara, Int.
10. *Ibid*.
11. *Teacher*, 72.
12. P. Hanara, Int.
13. C. E. Beeby, Int.
14. *Ibid*.
15. B. Pinder, Int.
16. LBDF.
17. LBDF.
18. C. L. Bailey, Int and LA.
19. SA-W, diary/letter, *c.* 1951.
20. *Ibid*.
21. SA-W, *Spinster*, 242.
22. LBDF.
23. SA-W, letter to A. W. Reed, Nov. 1952.
24. LBDF.
25. A. W. Reed, letter to SA-W, 22 Sept. 1954.
26. LBDF.
27. LBDF.
28. SA-W, letter to H. Campbell, 16 Oct. 1957.
29. LBDF.
30. A. Iverach, letter to SA-W, 1 June 1954.
31. LBDF.
32. A. E. Campbell, letter to SA-W, 5 Nov. 1956.

Chapter 11: Bethlehem

1. L. Johnson, letter to SA-W, 24 March 1959.
2. L. Johnson, Int.
3. R. Gottlieb, letter to SA-W, 8 March 1960.

4. SA-W, letter to R. Gottlieb, 15 March 1960.
5. J. C. Reid, letter to SA-W, 11 Oct. 1960.
6. SA-W, letter to J. Pattisson, 6 Oct. 1960.
7. SA-W, letter to B. Mason, 11 Oct, 1960.
8. SA-W, letter to R. Gottlieb, 2 March 1961.
9. SA-W, letter to B. Maddow, 15 March 1961.
10. G. Tata, Int.
11. L. Johnson, Int.
12. G. Tata, Int.
13. W. Moore, letter to SA-W, 8 June 1961.
14. R. Gottlieb, Int.
15. *Teacher*, 23.
16. SA-W, diary/letter to Mama, *c.* 1963.
17. *Ibid.*
18. SA-W, letter to E. Henderson, May 1963.
19. C. Brasch, letter to SA-W, 7 March 1964.
20. V&L.
21. H. Barrow, Int.
22. V&L.
23. J. Veatch, Int.
24. SA-W, unpublished MS, 'Essays on Artist'. Although written five years later, this quote summarises the sentiments expressed all through SA-W's 1967 writing.
25. SA-W, letter to R. Gottlieb, 17 Oct. 1967.
26. *Ibid.*, 28 March 1968.

Chapter 12: Escape

1. SA-W, diary, 1 Feb. 1969.
2. SA-W, letter to E. Henderson, 30 April 1969.
3. W. Gardiner-Scott, LA.
4. SA-W, letter to A. Henderson, 3 May 1969.
5. W. Aron, TA.
6. SA-W, *Three*, 216.
7. E. Henderson, Int.
8. G. Eaton, Int.
9. J. Latham-Koenig, Int.
10. G. Eaton, Int.
11. *Ibid.*
12. SA-W, diary/MS, 1970.
13. *Ibid.*

14. R. Gottlieb, letter to SA-W, 23 Jan. 1970.
15. SA-W, letter to K. Doremus, Aspen, 7 July 1970.

Chapter 13: Aspen

1. W. Gray, Int.
2. M. Stranahan, TA.
3. W. Gray, Int.
4. M. Settergast, Int.
5. *Ibid.*
6. W. Gray, Int.
7. *Ibid.*
8. M. Stranahan, TA.
9. *Ibid.*
10. D. Carline, Int.
11. *IPTW*, 427.
12. Cliett, W., 'A Personal Account of Three Weeks with SA-W'.
13. J. Veatch, Int.
14. W. Cliett, Int.
15. S. Wasserman, Int.

Chapter 14: Vancouver

1. D. Birch, Int.
2. *Ibid.*
3. M. Cuming, Int.
4. J. McConcachie, Int.
5. M. Cuming, Int.
6. D. Rubin, Int.
7. *Ibid.*
8. H. Ryane, Int.
9. D. Birch, Int.
10. S. Wasserman, Int.
11. M. Bradley, Int.
12. *Ibid.*
13. D. Birch, Int.
14. A. & F. Olsen, Int.
15. *Ibid.*
16. *IPTW*, 471.
17. S. Wasserman, Int.
18. *Ibid.*
19. SA-W, 'Essays on Artist', unpublished MS, 1973.
20. C. & J. Kirkland, Int.
21. S. Wasserman, Int.
22. *Ibid.*

Chapter 15: Selah

1. SA-W, letter to E. Henderson, 20 Dec. 1973.
2. D. Rubin, Int.
3. *Ibid.*
4. M. Shadbolt, Int.

5. Transcript of tape recording made of preliminary discussions re documentary, M. Noonan, 1975.
6. J. Bertram, in *Comment*, Feb. 1978.
7. D. Williams, LA.
8. SA-W letter to E. Henderson, 20 Feb. 1977.
9. D. Williams, LA.
10. M. Firth, Int.
11. *Ibid.*

12. *NZ Woman's Weekly*, 23 Sept. 1985.
13. Transcript of unbroadcast section of *Kaleidoscope* interview, 24 March 1980.
14. E. Henderson, Int.

Epilogue

1. SA-W, 'Essays on Artist', unpublished MS, 1973.

BIBLIOGRAPHY

UNPUBLISHED

Note: The Sylvia Ashton-Warner, Bruce Mason, Charles Brasch and Secker & Warburg Archives, and the author's tape recordings, correspondence and interview notes are all held under restricted access. Access is also restricted to all the unpublished papers not held in public archives or libraries.

A. *The author's taped interviews/interview notes/correspondence (1983–87) with Sylvia Ashton-Warner and people who knew her, held in the Hocken Library, University of Otago, Dunedin, including data from:*

New Zealand: more than 170 informants (twenty relatives — including relatives of Keith Henderson, five people who knew her mother, six fellow high school students, three people who knew her as a pupil teacher, ten fellow Teachers' College students, five junior assistants, twenty-four friends and acquaintances, twenty-six teaching colleagues, seventeen education officials, eighteen pupils, seven publishers and thirty-three others).
Israel: two informants.
Britain: four informants.
USA: twenty-nine informants.
Canada: twenty-one informants.

B. *Private papers:*

New Zealand:
Sylvia Ashton-Warner Papers, held by her family.
Warner family heirlooms, Dominion Museum, Wellington.
Bruce Mason Papers, Library, Victoria University of Wellington.
Charles Brasch Papers, Hocken Library, University of Otago, Dunedin.
Lili Kraus file, Radio New Zealand Archives, Wellington.
Winston Rhodes Papers, Alexander Turnbull Library, Wellington.
Papers held by original owners: J. Alley, B. Dent, D. Edwards, N. Hilliard, J. Hughson, M. Noonan, B. Pinder, M. Shadbolt, L. Warner.
Israel:
W. Aron Papers, held by W. Aron.
Britain:
Papers held by original owners: E. Henderson, J. Latham-Koenig.
USA:
Sylvia Ashton-Warner Archives, Mugar Memorial Library, Boston University, Boston.
Papers held by original owners: M. Albouy, W. Cliett, K. Kosoc, E. Lieb, S. Lum, G. Rodriguez, J. Veatch.
Canada:
Papers held by original owners: J. and C. Kirkland, F. and A. Olsen, A. and B. Vogt, S. and J. Wasserman.

C: *Official papers:*

New Zealand:
A. H. & A. W. Reed Archives, Alexander Turnbull Library, Wellington.

Auckland Teachers' Training College Archives, Auckland College of Education, Auckland.
Education Department Archives, National Archives, Wellington.
Hawke's Bay Education Board Archives, Napier.
Maori Schools Archives, National Archives.
NZ Educational Institute Archives, NZEI, Wellington.
Reed Methuen papers, Reed Methuen, Auckland.
School logs/pupil registers/committee minutes from Bethlehem, Bideford, Eastern Hutt, Fernhill, Hastings Central, Pipiriki, Rangitumau, South Wellington, Te Pohue, Te Whiti, and Umutaoroa Schools, held at schools, education board offices and private homes.
Transcript of *Kaleidoscope* interview, TVNZ Auckland, 24 March, 1980.
Britain:
Secker & Warburg Archives, Reading University, Reading.
USA:
Aspen Community School Archives, Aspen Community School, Aspen.
R. Gottlieb Papers, Knopf, New York.
Canada:
Sylvia Ashton-Warner file, Simon Fraser University, Vancouver.

D. Theses, reports, research and teaching papers:

Cliett, W. 'A Personal Account of Three Weeks with Sylvia Ashton-Warner'. University of Florida, 1971.
Gunter, J., *et al.*, 'Ashton-Warner Literacy Method'. Ecuador Non-Formal Education Project, 1973.
Middelton, S. 'Releasing the Native Imagery'. Auckland College of Education, 1982.
Pearson, L., 'Challenging the Orthodox: Sylvia Ashton-Warner: Educational Innovator and Didactic Novelist'. MA thesis, Waikato University, 1984.
Wasserman S., 'The Vancouver Project, A Study of the Key Vocabulary Approach to Beginning Reading in an Organic Classroom Context'. Simon Fraser University, 1974.
'What I did on my Research Semester or The Abduction of Sylvia Ashton-Warner'. Simon Fraser University, 1971.

PUBLISHED

A. Books

Ashton-Warner, S., *Spinster*. Virago, London, 1980.
Incense to Idols, Secker & Warburg, London, 1960.
Teacher. Virago, London, 1980.
Bell Call. Hale, London, 1971.
Greenstone. Simon & Schuster, N.Y., 1966.
Myself. Secker & Warburg, London, 1968.
Three. Knopf, N.Y., 1970.
Spearpoint. Knopf, N.Y., 1972.
O Children of the World. first person press, Vancouver, 1974.
I Passed This Way. Knopf, N.Y., 1979.
Stories from the River. Hodder & Stoughton, Auckland, 1986.
Ball, D. G., *A Life in the Twentieth Century*. D. G. Ball, Eastbourne, 1982.
Barrington, J. M. & Beaglehole, T. H., *Maori Schools in a Changing Society*, NZCER, Wellington, 1974.
Bowlby, J., *Loss*. Penguin, London, 1980.
Burr, A., *Families and Alcoholics*. Constable, London, 1982.

Cumming, I. & Cumming A., *History of State Education in New Zealand*. Pitman, Wellington, 1978.
Ewing, J. L. & Shallcrass, J., ed., *Introduction to Maori Education*. NZUP, Wellington, 1970.
Faderman, L., *Surpassing the Love of Man*. Morrow, N.Y., 1981.
Fincher, J., *Sinister People*. Putnam, N.Y., 1977.
Freud, A., *The Ego and Mechanisms of Defense*. International Universities Press, N.Y., 1946.
Labov, W., 'The Logic of Nonstandard English' in Keddie, N., ed., *Tinker, Tailor . . . The Myth of Cultural Deprivation*. Penguin, 1973.
McKenzie, D., 'Teacher Education in New Zealand: an Appraisal' in Robinson, G. and O'Rourke, B., ed., *Schools in New Zealand Society*. Longman Paul, Auckland, 1980.
Mason, H. G. R., *Education Today and Tomorrow*. Government Printer, Wellington, 1944.
Rhodes, H. W., *New Zealand Fiction Since 1945*. McIndoe, Dunedin, 1968.
Stead, C. K., 'Sylvia Ashton-Warner: Living on the Grand' in *In the Glass Case, Essays on New Zealand Literature*. AUP, Auckland, 1981.
Stevens, J., *The New Zealand Novel 1860-1965*. Reed, Wellington, 1966.
Storr, A., *The Dynamics of Creation*. Atheneum, N.Y., 1985.
Thompson, H. S., 'Freak Power in the Rockies' in *The Great Shark Hunt*, Warner, 1982.
Veatch, J., *et al.*, *Key Words to Reading*. Merrill, Columbus, 1973.
Warner, A., *Sir Thomas Warner, Pioneer of the West Indies, A Chronicle of his Family*. West India Committee, London, 1933.

B. Booklets and pamphlets:

School jubilee booklets from Koru, Mangatahi, Te Pohue, Te Whiti, Bideford, Rangitumau, Waiomatatini and Wairarapa High.
King, M., *Kawe Korero, a Guide to Reporting Maori Activities*. New Zealand Journalists Training Board, Auckland, 1985.
Manuka. Auckland Teachers' Training College, 1929.
Peka. Auckland Teachers' Training College, 1929.
Reading books and teacher's manuals used in New Zealand schools 1911-69.
Wairarapa High School Yearbook, 1925.

C. Articles:

Ashton-Warner, S., (S. Henderson), 'No longer Blinded by our Eyes', *NZ Listener*, 8 Oct. 1948, 17.
(Sylvia) stories in *Here & Now*, 1952-55, and series of five articles in *National Education*, Dec. 1955-May 1956.
Stories in *NZ Monthly Review, Numbers, Te Ao Hou, NZ Parent and Child, NZ Woman's Weekly*, 1959-68.
Three articles *NZ Listener*, 1974, 1975, 1981.
Beeby, C. E., 'Centennial Address'. *National Education*, July 1983, 106.
'The Place of Myth in Educational Change'. *NZ Listener*, 8 Nov. 1986, 53.
Blakey, J., 'Ashton-Warner Reading Instruction Strategy & Piaget'. *Education & Society*, 1:95, 1983.
Bourne, S., & Lewis, E., 'Delayed Psychological Effects of Perinatal Deaths'. *British Medical Journal*, 289:147, 1984.
Cliett, W., 'Sylvia Ashton-Warner's Message for American Teachers'. *Childhood Education*. 61: 207, 1985.
Dent, B., 'How Shall We Sing the Lord's Song'. *NZ Listener*, 11 Jan. 1946, 22.

Fugard, A., 'How Inner Torment Feeds the Creative Spirit'. *N.Y. Times*,
    17 Nov., 1985, Section 2:1.
Kirkland, J., 'Creating & Recognising Communicative Metaphors'. *Early Childhood*
    Development and Care, in press, 1987.
McEldowney, D., 'Sylvia Ashton-Warner: a Problem of Grounding'. *Landfall*,
    23:230, 1969.
Mitchell, I., 'Sylvia Ashton-Warner in the Secondary School'. *Education*, 29:24,
    1980.
Warner, M., 'A Day at School — 70 Years Ago'. *NZ Woman's Weekly*,
    13 May 1957, 58.
Veatch, J., 'Individualised Reading: a Personal Memoir'. *Language Arts*, Oct. 1986.
Wasserman S., 'Aspen Mornings with Sylvia Ashton-Warner'. *Childhood Education*,
    48:348, 1972.
    'Key Vocabulary: Impact on Beginning Reading'. *Young Children*, 33:33, 1978.

D. Official papers:

Currie, G., *et al.*, *Report of the Commission on Education in New Zealand*.
    Government Printer, 1962.
NZ Education Gazette, 1930–60. Education Department, Wellington.

E. Newspapers:

Aspen Today, Aspen Times, Auckland Star, Bay of Plenty Times, Dominion, Evening Post,
    Hawke's Bay Herald Tribune, New Zealand Herald, Wairarapa Times-Age.

E. Tape recordings and films:

Endeavour TV, *Sylvia Ashton-Warner*. National Film Library, Wellington, 1977.
Radio NZ Interview with Sylvia Ashton-Warner by S. Crosbie, 14 April 1980.
Kirkland, J. 'Sylvia Ashton-Warner'. Teaching tape, Massey University,
    Palmerston North, 1984.
Veatch, J., and Llewellyn, A., 'Impressions of Sylvia Ashton-Warner' (four tapes).
    Auckland, 1967.

INDEX